MW00790057

AVID
READER
PRESS

ALSO BY TOVA MIRVIS

[illegible]TION

[illegible]le City

[illegible]utside World

The Ladies Auxiliary

MEMOIR

The Book of Separation

WE WOULD NEVER

A NOVEL

TOVA MIRVIS

AVID READER PRESS

NEW YORK AMSTERDAM/ANTWERP LONDON TORONTO SYDNEY NEW DELHI

Avid Reader Press
An Imprint of Simon & Schuster, LLC
1230 Avenue of the Americas
New York, NY 10020

This book is a work of fiction. Any references to historical events, real people, or real places are used fictitiously. Other names, characters, places, and events are products of the author's imagination, and any resemblance to actual events or places or persons, living or dead, is entirely coincidental.

First Avid Reader Press hardcover edition February 2025

AVID READER PRESS and colophon are trademarks of Simon & Schuster, LLC

Interior design by Ruth Lee-Mui

Manufactured in the United States of America

1 3 5 7 9 10 8 6 4 2

Library of Congress Control Number: 2024942824

ISBN 978-1-6680-6162-6
ISBN 978-1-6680-6164-0 (ebook)

For Bruce, always.

AUTHOR'S NOTE

This book was inspired by a true story I have followed over the years, one I could never quite stop thinking about. How, I wondered, could this tragic story, and so many others like it, happen? While the news supplied me with a seemingly endless array of facts, I always came away from my Google searches dissatisfied, my questions unanswered. As a novelist, I relish the way that fiction allows us to enter into the complexities of stories that we otherwise might hover above. And so, I felt compelled to use the true story as a springboard and imagine my way inside, in search of some form of understanding. It was in this spirit that this book was conceived and written. While the plot of this book is inspired by real events, this is a novel. The characters, action, and dialogue are invented by me and not intended to portray any real person or represent any real events.

WE
WOULD
NEVER

MAINE, 2019

I watch the video in the middle of the night, trying to understand. The ex-wife sits behind a gray table in a small police interrogation room. The walls are cinder block, the lighting is fluorescent, her hair is blond. On the video, her face appears grainy, the way you would see someone on a security camera.

"We called you here," says the police officer sitting across from her, "because there's been a shooting. I'm sorry to tell you this, but your ex-husband, Jonah Gelman, was shot inside his home this morning. He was taken to the hospital, but unfortunately he didn't make it."

"Oh my god," the woman cries, bringing her hands to her mouth and hunching forward.

"I know this is a shock," the officer says, his voice gentle, his words unhurried. "But I'm hoping you might be able to help us understand what happened."

The ex-wife begins to weep, with long gasping sobs that sound more animal than human. Frantically, she looks around the room, as if she can't believe where she finds herself.

Wide awake, I replay the news clips that I'd once tried to avoid but now watch compulsively, in the hope that one of them will yield something new. "Here's what we know so far," says a reporter standing in the front yard of a blue Victorian house, yellow police tape visible behind her. "Noted writer and popular professor Jonah Gelman was inside his home a block from the Binghamton University campus when he was shot once in the chest." There are interviews with friends and colleagues, all of whom describe Jonah as serious, brilliant, and ambitious. "He was the person to turn to if you wanted to hear the unvarnished truth," says a friend, who attended Yale with him. "He could be uncompromising, but it was out of a sense of deeply held conviction," says another friend. His literary agent reveals that a few days before Jonah was shot, he had emailed her to say that he was nearly done with his much anticipated second novel. Standing outside his Manhattan office, his editor, a gaunt man with black glasses, blinks back tears. "Jonah had incredible promise. He wasn't one to get distracted or let anything stand in his way."

In the days after the murder, thousands of calls were made to the police, some to report potential clues, others to offer theories that ranged from the credible to the preposterous. A jealous colleague. A deranged fan. A student irate about a bad grade. As always, there were a handful of confessions, which turned out to be false. I wonder if those people live in a world of delusion. Maybe they feel guilty about something else.

Lying next to me, in a double bed in a small room in a cabin twenty miles outside of Bangor, Maine, my daughter is asleep. My headphones are on, and my laptop screen is darkened so the light doesn't rouse her. Outside, dogs are barking, piercing the overwhelming quiet, but my daughter doesn't stir, a peaceful form under the flannel blankets, which do little to keep out the cold.

On the screen, the police officer interviewing the ex-wife has cottony white hair and ruddy cheeks, and he sits impassively as she cries.

"I don't understand. Who could have done such a terrible thing?" she is asking.

"Before I can tell you more, I need to find out where you were this morning," he says.

The ex-wife tells the officer that she was getting a massage, a gift from her brother. She had left the spa and was walking to her car when she got the call requesting that she come to the police station. She had been alarmed, of course, but had agreed.

In the interrogation video, the officer poses more questions: where was she last night (at home, with her daughter) and had she spoken to anyone on the phone or in person today (her mother, twice, and her brother a few times as well).

"I realize this is hard, but I need to ask," the police officer says patiently, almost disinterested. "Is there anyone you can think of who might have wanted to harm your ex-husband?"

She sobs into her hands, but when she regains control, her voice is steely. "When we first moved here, Jonah used to talk about someone in his department who hated him. They got into a fight and . . . Jonah could be stubborn. It made some people upset, but I don't think that—" she says and stops.

"And what about you? How did you and Jonah get along?" the police officer asks.

The ex-wife takes a deep breath. For a moment—I hit pause to capture it—she looks afraid.

"Our divorce hasn't exactly been amicable," she says. "It should have been over by now, but there's been so much fighting and it keeps dragging on. My family has been upset about everything that's happened and they've tried to help me, but . . ."

The police officer leans forward, and in what is surely an act of superhuman restraint, his tone remains casual. "Can you think of anyone in particular who might have wanted to help you by doing something like this?"

Her hand flies to her mouth and the thought occurs to her—you can see it alight in her head—that she shouldn't be speaking so freely.

"No. Of couse not. No one I know would ever do something so awful," she insists. She's looking not at the police officer but directly into the camera that has been recording her this whole time—standard protocol, she was informed at the start—as if aware that she's speaking to all of us.

On YouTube, where I watch the video, there have been 130,000 views and 2,527 comments so far.

"An Oscar-worthy performance," says one of the comments.

"Please. She is WAY too composed for someone who just found out the guy is DEAD," says another.

"No chance anyone could fake that reaction. She's crying because she still loved the guy."

An hour in, the ex-wife asks to check her phone, which she's allowed to do—she's there, after all, of her own volition. Not once does she ask for a lawyer or object that the interview has lasted for too long. As the questions continue, the feeling in the room shifts. She speaks less freely and crosses her arms, ceasing to see the officer as an ally. Perhaps she senses that she's shifting in his mind as well.

"WE ALL KNOW SHE'S GUILTY," writes a woman, who provides a link to a statistic claiming that, on average, most Americans tell one to two lies per day, and another to a study asserting that it's the hands that give us away: those who are lying are more likely to gesture with both hands than those who are telling the truth.

I replay the video to see if she'd used both hands or one. I shut the computer and close my eyes, but there is no reprieve. Outside, the dogs are still barking. The wind is howling. I google all the names again, but no matter how intently I search, nothing helps me understand.

"I know we've kept you for a long time, and I apologize for that," the officer is saying to the ex-wife.

I lean closer to the screen to study her face. Who is she, what has she done, what should she have known?

"It's okay. I understand why you brought me here," she says wearily, her attempt at bravado fading before she gets the words out. "It's always the ex-wife."

It's impossible to believe that the woman on the screen is me.

In the pool, in the West Palm Beach blistering July heat, Sherry Marcus was teaching her granddaughter to swim. The sun glinted off the blue water, and the palm trees in the garden flapped gently. Sherry had buttered sunscreen to both her own body and to Maya's, whom she was now instructing to put her face in the water, to blow bubbles, to cup her hands and make scooping motions.

"You can do it," Sherry cheered.

Maya swam a few strokes on her own, nearly making it halfway across the pool, but once she realized what she'd done, she startled in fear and reached for Sherry.

"Don't worry, I'm never going to let anything hurt you," Sherry promised. She held on to Maya, gazing into her blue eyes, which mirrored her own. Otherwise, Maya looked like her father. She had his dark, almost black hair and angular features that looked like they'd been sculpted with a knife.

"We are going to have such a fun week while you and your mommy are here," Sherry sang out and listed all the places she wanted to take her.

"Can we go everywhere?" Maya asked as Sherry spun her through the water. When Maya was born, Sherry entered the hospital room to see her daughter, Hailey, cradling a swaddled baby, a sight so beautiful that she wished she knew how to paint: a mother and daughter brushed in gold. With your own children, there were always things to regret. Holding Maya for the first time, she'd understood that this was a chance to begin anew.

"We can do whatever you want!" Sherry said. Ever since her kids had grown up, she felt dulled by the quiet of every day, so little required of her, so little to look forward to. She worked part-time in her husband Solomon's dermatology office. She swam every day. She had lunch with friends and did volunteer work and went to her book club and took tennis lessons. These activities secured her days, each a pin holding down the corners of herself, but nothing could keep her in place the way her children once had.

Six weeks earlier—had it already been that long?—Hailey called her from Binghamton, where she and Jonah lived. "He's leaving me. He said he's tired of being miserable," Hailey said, crying so hard that Sherry couldn't make out every word. There would be time later for the details, but in that moment all she wanted to do was hold Hailey and absorb some of the pain. "We are here for you. You won't have to do this alone," Sherry promised. It had been ages since one of her children called her in need. Hailey was thirty-four, the youngest of her three—Nate was almost forty now, Adam thirty-eight. Even though Hailey was an adult, Sherry's desire to protect her hadn't diminished. She had to stifle the urge to call Jonah and scream at him for doing this to Hailey, to Maya, to all of them. Every day since then, she had spoken with Hailey to see how she was holding up, asking what she could do to help, booking plane tickets for her and Maya to come to West Palm for the week while Jonah moved out of their house.

"And look, here comes your mommy!" Sherry said to Maya, who had asked twice where Hailey was. Even a child this young could tell when something was wrong. Hailey had gone inside an hour before at Sherry's urging, to start arranging consultations with potential lawyers. When she'd picked Hailey and Maya up at the West Palm airport, she was struck by how red Hailey's eyes were, ringed with dark circles, and her carefully applied makeup proved Sherry's long-standing belief that sadness was the only feature you couldn't hide. Hailey had been one of those people who smiled all the time, who never said a mean word about anyone, but for the past few years, she seemed dimmed, like someone had ever so slightly lowered her lights. Sherry had once believed that Hailey told her everything, but in the seven years that Hailey and Jonah had been married, she had become more reticent; the inner workings of her daughter's marriage lay beyond her reach. Even when Hailey claimed that everything was fine, Sherry could detect the hollowness in her voice. Often she had the feeling of being at a theatrical performance—once the audience was gone, the actors scrubbed the makeup from their faces, the set was broken down and put away.

"Can you believe how well Maya is swimming?" Sherry said to Hailey as Maya, with increasing confidence, doggy-paddled across the pool. Hailey perched at the edge, dangling her feet into the water, and cheered Maya on. People often commented on how much Sherry and Hailey looked alike, both of them petite, with wavy blond hair, though Sherry's was no longer natural, and even Hailey's now benefited from a few highlights. "My mini-me!" she liked to exclaim when people asked if she and Hailey were sisters.

"Did you call a lawyer?" Sherry asked Hailey in an undertone.

"I didn't think I could talk to anyone without crying," Hailey admitted. "Jonah wants to move at such a fast pace, but he's probably been planning the divorce for months. He just texted me that he's starting to move stuff over to his new place. I told him to take whatever he wants."

"You didn't come to an agreement about that before you left?" Sherry asked.

"I couldn't think clearly. I just wanted to come home."

"Don't worry. I'm sure that can all be worked out. I just hate to see you so sad," Sherry said.

"I still don't believe this is real," Hailey said. "I keep thinking that he's going to call and say he didn't mean it and somehow everything will be fine."

"Why didn't you tell me that you and Jonah were having a hard time?" Sherry asked.

"I didn't want you to be upset," Hailey admitted, and Sherry felt a stab of remorse. Of course she wanted to believe that her daughter was happy, but how could Hailey not have understood that what she desired most was to be close, to know the truth about her life?

Once Maya grew tired of swimming, they got out of the pool. The three of them were wrapped in blue-and-white-striped beach towels and stretched out on chaise lounges when Nate came through the lanai and into the backyard.

"Uncle Nate is here," Maya screamed. She ran toward him, and he picked her up and, to her delight, tossed her in the air. At the sight of Nate in his blue medical scrubs, Sherry felt a surge of pride. He had the same blond hair as she did, only his was curlier. He had bright blue eyes and a disarming smile.

"Please be careful. One of these days you're going to drop her," Sherry cautioned.

"What do you think, Maya? Should we listen to Grandma?" Nate asked.

"Again," Maya screamed. It was easy to see why Maya loved Nate. He played a series of games with her that involved pretending to walk into walls or smash one of her toys over his head—a world of falling down and breaking apart that made Maya shriek with joy.

When Nate put Maya down, he gave Hailey a hug. "Is this what it takes to get you to come visit?" he asked.

"I guess I should look on the bright side. Now I'm going to be here all the time," Hailey joked.

Around Nate, Hailey always lightened. As a child, Hailey had idolized

Nate. She was his best audience, laughing at every joke, and was often enlisted as a sidekick for whatever game he came up with. In turn, Nate was unusually protective of Hailey. He patiently taught her how to swim. He was willing to play whatever part she assigned him in the dances she performed in the living room, even when it involved her dressing him in a variety of costumes. With Hailey, Nate exhibited none of the rivalry he had with Adam. The boys were only eighteen months apart, but opposites—Nate exuberant and rambunctious, Adam serious and tentative. For Adam, she had to coax, cajole; for Nate, contain, control. With both, she needed to be vigilant. If she looked away for a moment, something would inevitably break or someone would get hurt. There were stretches of days in which she took care of everything at once. She tucked one boy under each arm and read to them on the couch, sure that she was in possession of all she could ever want. She had been an only child, born to older parents, and had always carried with her the longing for a sibling. It felt like a miraculous feat, that she could create the close, bustling family she didn't have when she was a child. But the good feeling never lasted. Inevitably Nate would grow restless and provoke Adam, who would get upset and cry, and the rest of the day would be ruined by fighting. She pleaded, in vain, with the boys to get along and reminded them that they were lucky to have each other. She explained that with a sibling, you always had someone you were close to—it lessened the chance that you would find yourself alone. Solomon inevitably came home when the eruption of tempers and tears was at its worst, and used up by a day of seeing patients, he had no energy left. He simply walked away, leaving her to deal with the scolding and the begging and the negotiating and the punishing.

In those years, before Hailey was born, they lived in Boston, where Solomon was newly hired as a physician at Beth Israel and an instructor of dermatology at Harvard Medical School. Their house was at the top of Summit Avenue, on the Brookline-Boston line, the second floor of a two-family in which everything was old, kindling her wish to someday have a home that was airy and bright. Though she was born in Boston, she hated the winter, when taking the boys out required the donning of snowsuits, the installing of feet into boots. Anyone who extolled the beauty of snow never had to carry a stroller down the icy stairs from their door to the street. When Sol took a job in Miami at her urging, she was so filled with hope. The house they bought—a small white stucco with a red Spanish roof and two palm trees in the front yard—was in Miami Beach. It was a world away from where she'd grown up, in Randolph on Boston's South Shore, on a street of mostly Jewish families, immigrants or the children of immigrants, in a tiny house that was freezing all winter. But the only remedy her mother ever offered was to put on a sweater: love and heat, in equally short supply. Florida, though, was unmarred by the past—in the salty air, the ocean breeze, she could begin anew. At first, Sherry was surprised by how scalding the Miami summers were—nothing prepared her for the blast of heat upon stepping outside, for the feeling that the air itself could scorch you. But she would rather be too hot than too cold—better to have too much of a good thing than not enough. As she walked down Collins Avenue, one boy on each side of her, she'd lift her face to the sun. The Atlantic Ocean was to her right, Biscayne Bay to her left. New high-rises were being erected, all glass and sandstone, white and light. They'd lived in Florida for a few months when Sherry discovered that she was pregnant. Of course all you wanted was a healthy baby and of course you would be happy with whatever you had, and of course you would love them all equally; yes, yes, yes, but nothing could quench her desire for a daughter.

Nate was ten, Adam was nine, and Hailey was almost five when they bought this house. When they first moved to Florida, West Palm was regarded as an alligator-infested swamp with nothing but a mall. But during the years they lived in Miami Beach, West Palm had started to boom. The house she fell in love with was three blocks from the beach. It had four bedrooms, an open floor plan, an atrium with a double-height ceiling, and a skylight that flooded the rooms with sunshine. There was a large backyard for the kids to run around in and, best of all, an oval pool tiled in iridescent blue and a delicate white statue of a swimming goddess with cascading hair, flanked by dolphins and starfish and seashells.

"We are going to live in this pool," Sherry declared to Solomon when she first convinced him to look at the house. He didn't love Florida as much as she did—sometimes they laughed at how out of place he looked, wearing long pants at the beach or socks with the sandals she bought him. But even he understood that the house was perfect. On their first night living there, the three kids ran through the rooms, the boys suddenly best friends leading the way, Hailey trying to keep up, all of them exclaiming that, compared to the old house, each room seemed as enormous as a movie theater. Sherry quietly basked in their excitement, not wanting to disrupt them when they were getting along. When they saw the pool, they begged to swim, and though it was late, she allowed it. The sight of the three of them splashing happily in the water confirmed her belief that this pool would bring them together.

Now all three of them were grown and gone. Now Adam, her own child, barely spoke to her.

"How was today? What did I miss?" Sherry asked Nate. Hailey and Maya had gone inside to get dressed, and Nate joined her by the grill, which he liked to claim was the altar upon which they offered their most heartfelt sacrifices. She laid out the skewers of vegetables and strips of steak, which was Hailey's favorite meal. When the kids were young, she was often exhausted by dinnertime, but now she longed for the flurry of children all needing something. Without them, the house felt too quiet. She understood why, once their children grew up, people sold their houses—these remnants of a lost civilization, monuments to what once was. It was one of the reasons she constantly made plans with friends. She switched on in the presence of others, a small filament inside beginning to glow.

"The schedule was packed, but it was mostly my patients," Nate said.

"I hope you didn't feel the need to point that out," Sherry said. With a fork, she pierced a piece of steak—it was still pink, but they all preferred it that way.

"I didn't, but Dad was annoyed at me anyway, and I have no idea why," Nate said and popped a piece of meat into his mouth.

"Are you sure you didn't do anything to upset him?" she asked.

"You know I'm always working on something," he said.

"Nate—" she began.

"It's nothing you need to worry about," Nate said and flashed an innocent smile that brought her back to when he was a child. He never intended to cause real harm, but he had a habit of joking around, then getting carried away. When Adam left the dinner table to go to the bathroom, for example, Nate would hide his plate under his chair. One time, Nate claimed that a jar of soapy liquid was lemonade and only told Adam the truth after he took a swig. When she reprimanded Nate for these infractions, he initially acted like he didn't care that she was angry, but eventually, he came running to her, wanting to be ensconced once again in her love. Sol wasn't as forgiving. He claimed that Nate needed to learn that there were consequences, that not everything could be so easily undone. She heard the accusation in Sol's voice: Nate only misbehaved because she was too easy on him, too willing to yield. Sol couldn't understand that when it came to her child, she was always going to yield.

Sol had tried to act nonchalant, but she knew that he was shocked, then quietly thrilled, when Nate chose to specialize in dermatology. After his residency, Nate got a job at a large hospital practice in Miami, but complained about too many rules, too much bureaucracy. And though Solomon didn't often share his worries with her, she knew that his practice's numbers were starting to decline. It didn't matter that he was widely considered to be an expert in melanoma, or that he was so dedicated that he saw anyone, regardless of their ability to pay. It was true in most fields, but in dermatology even more so: people wanted a younger doctor, they wanted to believe that something newer and better awaited them. She was the one who suggested to Sol that he hire Nate. Though Sol claimed that this kind of proximity would lead to conflict, she wasn't dissuaded. It had taken months, but eventually Sol saw the wisdom of her idea. And just as she anticipated, it was working out beautifully. There were occasional moments of tension, but as far as she could tell, Nate and Sol were closer than ever. The office was thriving. Not a week went by without someone telling her what a good job Nate was doing. Not a day passed when she didn't feel grateful that the three of them could work together.

"Just promise me that you're not going to do anything to upset Dad," Sherry said.

Before Nate could respond, Sol was coming outside to join them. He was seventy, older than her by seven years, and had a broad build and thick gray hair that could be unruly; it was always falling into his eyes, and she was always brushing it away.

"What happened?" she asked Sol, once Nate walked away.

"Nothing. It was a regular day," he said.

She surveyed Sol. "Are you okay?" she asked.

"I'm fine," Sol snapped.

Sherry felt a swell of unease, but pushed it away. Everything was going to be fine. She checked the grill. She finished setting the table. She went to the garden and snipped a handful of her favorite flowers, the birds-of-paradise that grew shoulder-high, like a flock that swooped down and stood watch. When they first moved in, the yard had little landscaping, just some begonias along the fence and a few bromeliads. She knew little about gardening, but she was determined to learn. She wanted to feel that, when she swam, she was in a pristine blue oasis in the middle of a lush paradise. There were always gardeners, but she worked alongside them, tending, uprooting, replanting. When she came inside, she was sweaty, dirty, and completely invigorated. She expanded the garden farther into the yard. She had palm trees planted and added dense beds of heliconia, dragon trees, and hibiscus around the pool. She had a stone path laid so that she could walk among the plants, and lights installed so that she could enjoy the green lushness even at night. Sol and the kids teased her that she was growing her own jungle, but she didn't care—it was a pride not unlike giving birth. Slowly, with the work of her hands, she brought her vision to life.

They were all seated around the table in the dining room, which, like most of the house, was decorated in shades of coastal blue, so that even when Sherry was inside, she felt part of the pool, the ocean, and the sky. At the center of the table, she had placed a glass vase with an arrangement of the birds-of-paradise.

"Here we are. All my favorite people under the same roof," Sherry said.

"I won't ask what that says about Adam," Nate said.

"Do you have to bring that up now?" Sherry asked.

She looked away from Nate, but her gaze landed on the oversized family picture that covered most of the dining room wall. The picture was taken at her sixtieth birthday celebration, which Adam refused to attend. She loved birthdays, and for her sixtieth, she planned a party for herself. She hired a photographer, and wanting everyone to match for the pictures, she and Hailey both wore light blue dresses, as did Maya who was a few months old. She asked Sol, Nate, and Jonah to wear white dress shirts, with light blue ties she bought for them. Jonah, however, showed up in a French-blue shirt and a red tie. "I didn't realize it was a mandatory dress code," Jonah said. "Well, you'll definitely stand out," Sherry quipped, trying to act like it didn't matter. From the start, she had liked Jonah and was determined to be close to him. She was proud of the fact that Jonah was a successful author. She read his novel, about a son trying to uncover why his mother mysteriously disappeared from the family a decade earlier, and even if it was a little dark for her taste, she told him how much she loved it. She invited him to speak at her book club, and once, when she came upon a stranger on an airplane reading it, she went up to her and bragged that the author was engaged to her daughter. There were moments when her unease rippled: when Jonah joked about how often she and Hailey spoke on the phone, or claimed that she was so involved in the wedding planning, she should be the one to stand beside Hailey under the chuppah. Because he said these things with a smile, Sherry tried to convince herself that he was just kidding, and she forced a laugh. Hailey was happy, and that was what mattered most. At the engagement party Sherry threw, she walked over to Jonah, surrounded by a group of her friends, and looped her arm through his. "You know what they say. You're not losing a daughter but gaining a son," she proclaimed.

Sherry had no idea that the tension would long outlast the wedding. She didn't realize that she would always be in the position of trying to entice them to come to Florida for a visit or to pick a weekend for her and Sol to come to New York City, where Jonah and Hailey lived when they first got married. All too often, the answer was no. Jonah rarely got on the phone when she called and though Hailey claimed he wasn't home, she sensed that he was beside her, monitoring every word. When Hailey and Jonah did visit West Palm, Sherry spent hours in the kitchen preparing a meal that she wanted to be perfect, yet Jonah sat silently at the table. His reticence was hard to abide, so Sherry flooded him with questions. She asked him what he was writing, but he didn't like to talk about it. Sometimes she asked about his childhood, but he said he preferred not to dredge up the past. When she ran out of questions, she was the one to talk—about her friends and her plans for the garden and the books she was reading, anything to fill the space.

About this uncomfortable dynamic, about every possibly snide comment, Sherry didn't say a word. She told herself that Jonah was just shy. He wasn't accustomed to so much family time. But she felt on edge around him. She noticed how, when he spoke to her, he made a funny little smile and surveyed her a moment too long, as if considering all possible responses before reluctantly choosing the least offensive. She began scrutinizing everything she said in his presence, worried he would find something to criticize. In her own house, with her own family, she felt chastened. She started calling Hailey when she knew Jonah wouldn't be around. Sometimes she couldn't help herself and would broach the subject with Hailey of why they saw her and Jonah so infrequently, why Jonah seemed so unhappy in their presence. Hailey always assured her that Jonah was just under a lot of pressure, that of course he loved them—he thought they were great! Sherry heard the tension in Hailey's voice, but she wouldn't tell her the truth.

When Maya was born, the pain of being kept at a distance sharpened. Her desire to cradle this baby felt like a physical need—she was overcome by the prospect of being able to touch a sliver of the future, of being in the presence of something both a part of herself and so much larger. If she had tried to put these feelings into words for Jonah, he probably would have laughed, so instead she told Jonah how, when her own kids were young, she'd had no family willing or able to help and how glad she was that he and Hailey would never have to feel so alone. If nothing else, she'd thought that an offer of unlimited free babysitting would sway him. But he acted like she'd said something amusing, and after that beat of silence and that funny smile, he responded, "You don't have to worry, I think Hailey and I can handle this." He balked when she tried to hold Maya and claimed it was time for her nap. He had Hailey offer reasons for why this weekend or next weekend or every weekend for the rest of their lives wasn't going to work. It sometimes seemed like Hailey and Maya lived in another country, under the rule of a ruthless dictator.

All through those years, she still hoped that, despite the tension, Hailey and Jonah would move to Florida. It wasn't something she would have dared suggest, not even privately to Hailey, but Jonah could write from anywhere and Hailey had often talked about her desire to move back home. And then, a little over three years ago, at the end of a phone conversation, Hailey casually mentioned that Jonah had applied for teaching jobs and received an offer at Binghamton University, of all places. "Is this what you want?" Sherry gingerly asked. "It's Jonah's only option. Please don't say anything to him, but he's having trouble finishing his book and needs to get a job until he does," Hailey explained. "We can help you out, if you need money," Sherry offered, hoping Sol wouldn't mind, but Hailey quickly said no. As disappointed as Sherry was, she didn't say a negative word. She coated her voice in false cheer when she congratulated Jonah on the new job. She offered to come watch Maya while they packed up their apartment. Only to Sol did she complain, but he held up his hand to stop her. "It's good that they want to be independent," he said. He refused to see, as she did, that they were being purposefully kept away.

At the dinner table now, Nate's phone buzzed and he quickly tapped out a text, then turned the phone over to hide the response. Hailey's phone was also beeping constantly, but she appeared intent on ignoring it.

"Who are you so busy texting?" Sherry asked Nate. The question slipped out before she could stop herself. When he was in his twenties and early thirties, he had girlfriends for brief periods of time and she made the mistake of getting her hopes up. Now that he was on the verge of turning forty, she'd stopped asking.

"No one important," he said.

"Nate doesn't tell us anything," Sherry said, smiling to mitigate any sense of complaint. "I see him every day and I know nothing."

"Why are you so sure that I have anything to tell?" Nate asked.

"Hailey would know. Am I right?" Sherry said.

"Hailey knows everything," Nate teased.

"I'll never tell," Hailey said and laughed along with him.

It was a relief to see Hailey relax. Home for just a few hours, Hailey was already starting to sound more like herself. The desolate tone that Sherry had heard in her voice for these past few weeks was easing, even if just temporarily. It was going to be hard, then it was going to get better. So many people would be alone in this situation, but Hailey wasn't going to have to do this by herself.

Once Maya finished eating, she wandered away from the table, and Hailey followed her into the living room, where Sherry had set up the bin of Barbies that were once Hailey's, along with the vast wardrobe of doll outfits and tiny rubber shoes that she'd saved for grandchildren so she could feel that time traveled not in a relentless line but a comforting loop.

At the table, Sherry lowered her voice. "Hailey didn't call the lawyer like she was planning to. And she told Jonah to take whatever he wanted from the house. For all we know, he's going to empty out the place," she said to Sol and Nate.

"I don't think Jonah would do that," Sol said.

"He left her, completely out of the blue, so at this point, I wouldn't put anything past him," Sherry said.

"Has she been in touch with him?" Sol asked.

"He keeps texting her. Did you see the look on her face every time her phone beeped?" Sherry said.

"Hailey just has to get used to the reality that this is happening, then she's going to be fine," Nate said.

"We need to help. She doesn't have to go through this on her own," Sherry said and glanced again at the family picture—it felt almost like Jonah was present, able to hear what they were saying.

"We need to think carefully about how to approach this," Sol cautioned. "We don't want to make Jonah the enemy. The last thing we want is for this to escalate."

"I would say leaving her is pretty much an act of escalation," Nate said.

Grateful for Nate's agreement, Sherry turned to him. "No one wants this to escalate, but we need to be sure that Jonah doesn't walk all over her. I don't want her to give in to whatever he wants just because that's what she's used to doing."

"Obviously she needs to hire a lawyer, and she should get access to all their financial information," Nate said. "She's going to want to make sure he doesn't try to drain the bank accounts or start moving money around."

"We have no reason to think he would do that," Sol said.

"We need to be ready, just in case. And we need to be sure that Hailey has what she needs," Sherry said.

"The faster we get this done, the better. Like ripping off a Band-Aid," Nate said.

"We do not want to let this get out of control," Sol protested.

"We are not going to stand by and do nothing," Sherry said.

Sherry could see Sol bristling, but her thoughts were already starting to turn, powering her into action. Over the years, there were teachers or other parents or even Sol who considered Sherry over-involved, but if she was guilty of anything, it was of loving Hailey too much. There were moments—surely this was one—when you had to stand wholly on the side of your child.

In her childhood bed, Hailey tucked her yellow bedspread around her, wishing she could rewind to the nights she'd lain in this room with everything still ahead of her. The room itself was perfectly intact—above her desk was the collage she'd made of her high school friends, and pinned to her bulletin board were pale pink corsages pressed and preserved. Her closet was lined with white plastic bins in which her mother had saved all her report cards and poems and stories. In this house, it felt possible to become a child again.

After dinner, Hailey had put Maya to bed in what had once been Adam's bedroom. Though Hailey would have expected her mother to avoid the room, she knew better than to mention it outright. There was an unsaid agreement that, except for the occasional comment Nate liked to make, they weren't going to talk about Adam. Next to Maya, she had tucked Bunbun, the small lavender stuffed animal her mother had given her a few years earlier and which had turned gray and matted from love. Last year, the bunny's ear came loose, so when they were visiting, her father brought supplies home from the office and stitched it back on.

Hailey had lain down next to Maya, who was so wound up she couldn't stop talking. "Tomorrow Grandma and I are going to plant magic flowers in the garden," she said, and Hailey laughed. For an instant, she had the impulse to take out her phone and share with Jonah what Maya had said. It was hard to admit now, but she'd always loved how effusive he was in his love for Maya. Often she'd catch sight of Jonah in the backyard, lifting Maya on his shoulders and running around. He made up elaborate stories, all starring Maya as an adventurer who lived with the animals, who captained boats across raging seas. It was too painful, though, to think about his good qualities, safer to reside in the anger, especially when, all day, her phone had buzzed with texts from him, reminding her that she needed to find a lawyer and agree to a temporary parenting plan. Already in her mind, different versions of Jonah were gathering. Two months ago, she would have said that she loved him, and now she was on the precipice of hating him.

Slowly, Maya had grown drowsy, and Hailey felt the desire, as she often did, to peer behind Maya's eyelids, to glimpse the bustling world that lived inside her head. She hadn't wanted to tell Maya about the divorce right away, but Jonah was adamant, moving everything at too fast a pace and giving her no time to accept the fact that this was actually happening. A week after he told her that he wanted a divorce, he had a list of the tasks they needed to take care of and started to make plans to move out. Before she had time to digest it herself, they'd sat down with Maya, who looked at them in bewilderment as they cut her life into two.

When she first met Jonah on Jdate, she was twenty-five and had recently moved into a small New York City apartment with two friends from college and was working as an editorial assistant at *Allure* magazine and taking an evening fiction-writing class at the New School. She'd gone to the University of Miami and because this was the first time she'd lived so far from home, she was overwhelmed by the prospect of being on her own. She was still learning how to read the subway map, which to her looked like an abstract painting, and so she was late to their first date. Jonah grew up in the city, in Morningside Heights, a few blocks from

Columbia University, where his parents were both professors. He left the city to go to Yale, then returned to get a PhD at Columbia, in American literature. He laughed when she told him that she mistook the direction of the B train, and he drew a map of the city for her on a napkin, promising that it was impossible to get lost once you understood how the grid worked. He had angular features and a slight cleft in his chin and dark hair that fell over his forehead. He was only a little taller than she was and slight, as if all his intensity was compressed. After seeing his Jdate profile, she had googled him and saw that he'd written a highly successful novel. She read reviews, which described his book as an intellectual thriller, a quest to understand the push and pull of family ties. She read profiles that described his immense discipline that enabled him to wake up at five every morning to write, before he turned to his work on his PhD. She read that he considered the book to be an homage to his mother, who died when he was a freshman in college, and how he felt like he could keep her alive through his writing—on the page, he stayed close to her. In her mind, Hailey was already falling in love with him. Once she was sitting across a table from him, she liked how, on any subject that came up, he'd read two articles and formulated his own, usually contrarian, opinion. She was often beset with the feeling that it was hard to be sure what she really thought, but being around him eased the task of having to know things herself. She liked her job at *Allure*, but when she described how she managed the submissions coming in and participated in pitch meetings, she worried it would seem insignificant to him. When she told him about the writing class she was taking, she minimized how much it meant to her, afraid she would seem small and silly. Jonah was only two years older than she was, but he seemed infinitely ahead.

They left the restaurant and began to walk up Broadway, she trying to match her pace to his, which felt more like a jog. In college her friends joked that she, despite her easygoing nature, was always attracted to dark and stormy, and it was true. Even then, Jonah seemed a little terse, a little ornery, but rather than being put off by it, she was enticed by the feeling that he had complicated layers she could navigate. She didn't want to stop walking, not even when her feet ached in her high-heeled black suede boots, which she'd selected at her mother's advice—though she wouldn't admit this to someone like Jonah, she still asked her mother's advice about practically every aspect of her life. Anytime she felt unsure, she imagined what her mother would say. Jonah, she knew, would earn her mother's approval, which made her like him even more.

"You seem like someone who's always in a good mood," Jonah observed when they were almost at her building. Even after a few hours together, he seemed softer. Having pierced the outer layer, she was being ushered inside.

"Not all the time," she said.

"Most of the time?"

He'd smiled at her with curiosity that felt like a kind of wonder.

"My mother actually calls me 'Sunshine,'" she said.

"I like that," he said and kissed her.

She had no idea that the qualities in her that he was so drawn to would eventually be the ones he came to despise.

Hailey was still awake a few hours later when Nate walked into her room. He'd left soon after dinner, claiming he had somewhere he needed to be, which she took to mean that he was dating someone, probably one more short-lived relationship he was always launching into, then trying to extricate from. He'd promised to come back to the house, but she didn't believe that he would.

"What are you doing in bed? The night is young!" Nate said.

"Please," she said as her phone beeped. She groaned and pulled her pillow over her head.

"Who's texting you?" Nate asked.

"Who do you think?"

"Give me the phone," he said as it beeped again. "I have a few things I'd like to say to Jonah."

"You wouldn't dare," she said.

"I think you know better than to dare me," he told her, and she laughed. Once an idea took hold, Nate felt compelled to follow it. It was why he'd so often been in trouble when he was young, for speaking back to teachers, for playing practical jokes that were funny until they weren't. But while that was the side of him most people saw, she knew that no one was more loyal or loved her more absolutely.

"Let's go for a swim," Nate suggested.

She groaned again. "Do you ever sleep?" she asked.

"Who needs sleep?" he said.

She put her bathing suit on and met him in the living room, where Maya's toys were scattered across the floor. When she and her brothers were young, her mother had complained about messes in their rooms, but when it came to Maya, she was entirely indulgent. On the living room wall, there were framed pictures of her and her brothers: graduations and recitals and family events, her brothers at each of their bar mitzvahs, in navy suits and ties, yarmulkes perched on their heads, tallises draped around their necks. There were pictures of her at dance recitals and school dances and at her bat mitzvah, where she wore a pale pink satin dress, her long hair piled on her head in an elaborate arrangement. In all of them, she was smiling so broadly that even now she could remember the ache she'd felt in her cheeks. In the center of the display, there had been a large bridal photo with the same enormous smile, but now the picture was gone.

"What happened to my wedding photo?" she asked Nate.

"You missed Mom's garden bonfire last night," Nate said.

"I hope that's a joke," she said, but actually, she liked the idea that somewhere deep inside the garden, her wedding relics had gone up in flames.

They had been dating for six months when Jonah told her that he wanted to marry her. "We belong together," he said, and his decisiveness eased any doubts she had. She heard how dismissive he could be about other people, quick to note any perceived flaw, but she allowed herself to believe that if he loved her, she would be protected from that. Though she introduced him to all her friends, they mostly spent time with his friends, who'd gone to Yale together and now lived in the city and seemed to all be engaged in a competition over who could start a foundation at the youngest age, or clerk for the most prestigious judge, or write books about the most esoteric topic. She knew that Jonah had dated some of the women she met, and she tried to pry from him details about those prior relationships, worried that he would compare her to them. Anytime she was going to see them, she took extra time applying makeup, blowing out her hair, getting dressed up—if nothing else, at least she would look good. Outwardly, his friends were nice to her, but once she'd overheard his roommate, Max, talking about her. "I see the appeal, but she's not who I imagined Jonah would end up with," he said. Mortified, she hurried away, but she was already filling in what else he thought: she wasn't as smart as Jonah, or as accomplished. When she told Jonah what Max had said, Jonah took her in his arms. "You have nothing to worry about. You are the nicest person I have ever met."

A few weeks before she and Jonah got officially engaged, her parents flew to New York to meet him. Her mother was eager to meet Jonah ever since they first started dating, but Hailey had managed to put her off until now. She thought the dinner with her parents went well, but on the subway home, Jonah surprised her by commenting how different she was from her mother. She didn't ask what he meant, but it was obvious that he thought he was bestowing a compliment. Back then, Jonah found it sweet that she talked to her mother as often as she did—he said it made him realize how much he missed his own mother. Jonah didn't like to discuss his family, but she knew that soon after his mother died, his father had remarried and moved to Arizona, into a new marriage and a new life that had little place for him. He and his father spoke every Sunday night, perfunctory conversations that to her sounded like news reports, and they saw each other a few times a year, which seemed to be enough for both of them. It was so different from her own family, where there was no such thing as enough. "Promise me that you'll love them," she said to Jonah that night about her parents and he had. Now it felt naïve, but at the time, she was so excited to share her family with him.

Once they were planning the wedding, she and Jonah started to have small disagreements, usually about the fact that her mother was extremely eager to pick a date and a venue. "Why don't we have a small wedding?" Jonah suggested. "Why do your parents need to invite every single person they've ever met?" In her presence, he complained to his friends about the wedding plans. "It's not Hailey who wants this, it's her mother," Jonah explained. They all laughed, but she burned with shame on her mother's behalf.

"Why can't you just tell her no?" he'd ask repeatedly.

"It's not that easy," she'd answer, wishing she could make him understand that, yes, her mother was very involved in her life, and yes, sometimes she wanted to say no without feeling guilty, and yes, sometimes her family was tied together too tightly, but at least it was with the bonds of love.

On his first visit to West Palm, Jonah took an intense dislike to Florida. They went to Riviera Beach, where she'd spent every weekend of her childhood, and she told him how she and her brothers had buried each other in the sand, and piled seaweed on themselves, pretending to be sea creatures. But there was no way to make him see West Palm as she did. To her professions of how much she loved being there, he sneered in a way that made her feel like she had to defend not just her family but the whole city, the entirety of the Atlantic Ocean. He hadn't worn enough sunscreen, and his neck and his cheeks were pink as he carried on about everything he hated about West Palm—not just its suffocatingly hot weather but its politics and lack of culture and lack of seasons and its abundance of overly manicured parks and strip malls. Outwardly, she agreed with him, because she didn't want him to think she was too shallow to see what he did, but privately she wondered if it was possible to recognize the flaws yet love it anyway.

Their swimming pool drew Jonah's greatest ire, with its ornate marble statue of an unnamed goddess installed on one side.

"Aphrodite in West Palm Beach," he said, expecting her to laugh.

"My mother grew up with nothing. It means a lot that she can have this," she said, hoping to appease him, but he was determined to keep pressing on the parts of her that were already tender. She loved the pool and the garden surrounding it, but when she saw it through Jonah's eyes, it became embarrassingly lavish.

At the end of the weekend, during which she was almost giddy with relief any time her mother and Jonah had a nice conversation, she drove Jonah to the airport—she was going to stay in West Palm for a few more days to take care of wedding details at her mother's behest. "Can we please not fight about my family anymore?" she implored him as they approached the airport, anticipating how unsettled she would feel while he was in the air and she'd be unable to call him and convince herself that they were okay.

He gave her a long, surveying look. "When you're with your mother, you seem like a different person. Even your voice changes," he said, and she understood that he loved her most when he could assure himself that she was nothing like her family.

As soon as Jonah got out of the car, she called Nate; he was the only person in whom she could confide her unease. "I'll meet you in twenty minutes," Nate said, though he was in the middle of his residency and had been awake all night. When Nate and Jonah met a few days earlier, they made polite conversation but didn't have much in common. It was one more reason to worry: she was on the verge of marrying someone her brother barely knew.

"Are you going to tell me what happened?" Nate asked when they were sitting at Benny's on the Beach, her favorite place for brunch—built on a pier, it gave her the feeling of being magically suspended over the ocean. She told him that she and Jonah couldn't have a conversation about the wedding without it ending in a fight and that she couldn't say anything about her family without Jonah rolling his eyes.

"You might have to cut the guy some slack. If you're not used to Mom, she can be a bit much," he said.

"I know, but Jonah won't even give her a chance. He only sees her worst side and he hates it when I defend her. I didn't realize how unforgiving he can be."

"Are you seriously surprised to discover things you don't like about him? You've known him for approximately twenty minutes. You do realize that everything fades with time," Nate said.

"How would you know? You haven't dated anyone longer than twenty minutes."

"That's my strategy. I would never let myself be trapped."

"Can you be honest? What do you think of Jonah?" she asked as she devoured the banana bread French toast she ordered every time they came here, even though she was supposed to be worried about fitting into her wedding dress.

"I barely know the guy so I'm not sure I'm the best one to ask," he said.

"Please, Nate. What do you think of him?"

"I think that Jonah doesn't deserve half of you, even your worst half. But the real question is, what do you think?"

"I worry that he can be kind of harsh," she admitted. "He has these absolute opinions and a very particular way of seeing things and he doesn't back down. Sometimes I feel like I could talk all day long but he's not going to hear me."

"There you have it, ladies and gentlemen. Hailey Marcus, officially deemed the nicest person in the entire universe, has said something mean."

"Please. I'm not that nice," she said, regretting that she'd relayed to Nate what Jonah had said about her, because now it was one more of his jokes, repeated until she never again wanted to hear anyone say she was nice.

"I'm making a prediction. One day, you're going to erupt."

"You're crazy," she said, but was intrigued by the possibility that she was in possession of a dark, alternate self.

"I've made a decision. Instead of giving you a wedding present, I'm setting up a divorce account. Every year I'm going to put money into it," Nate said.

"That's terrible," she said, but it was just the kind of outrageous joke Nate loved. She regretted saying anything mean about Jonah. It wasn't true that she harbored some ridiculous fury. And the fight with Jonah wasn't as bad as she'd thought. He didn't mean to come across terse or a little arrogant. Once you got past his outer edge, he was funny and playful and loving; it was only a matter of time before he acted that way with her family. Apart from Jonah, even for a few hours, it was easy to forget all the good things. Once she was back in their apartment in New York, she would remember how they loved to walk down Broadway together, he like a tour guide, she the grateful participant. And how he had a way of stopping whatever he was saying, staring intently at her and asking, "What do you think?" In those moments it didn't matter what his friends thought of her, just as it didn't matter what he thought of her family. What mattered was how, when she said something that made him laugh, she felt electric with happiness; and how, in his presence, she felt like she could become a stronger, more confident version of herself; and how, when he read, he tilted his head slightly to one side and his mouth hung open the smallest amount, which was the same way he looked at her when they were in bed, he on top of her, gazing with such intense concentration as if there were words written all over her body that he alone could read. In those moments, she liked to pull the blankets over their heads and block out the world. They were happy as long as they were on their own.

Outside, Hailey turned on the floodlights, which illuminated the pool, and Nate dove into the water. Night swimming with her brothers had once been her favorite activity—they squirmed onto Sherry's floating chaise, pretending to be lost in a swamp, and together they navigated their way to safety.

"Come on, you know what you have to do," Nate said as Hailey was about to lower herself into the pool.

"Aren't we too old for that?" she protested.

"You're never too old to rock the pool," Nate said. When they were young, Nate had a habit of coming up with outlandish games, and though she rarely misbehaved on her own, she usually ended up in the role of accomplice. This was one of his more benign ideas, which involved repeatedly cannonballing into the pool. He claimed that they could make a wave pool, but she worried that the water would flood the surrounding garden, then keep rising and overtake the house.

With Nate still staring at her expectantly, she gave in, as she always did. After a running start, she cannonballed into the water. When she resurfaced, he was clapping.

"Apparently I still listen to everything you suggest," she said as she floated on her back and gazed up at the palm trees that canopied over the edge of the pool. Every time she came home, she was astonished by how hot West Palm was in the summertime, how thick the air was, even at night.

"When have I ever steered you wrong?" Nate asked, and they both peered at the statue.

This game had also started out relatively harmless. Nate was throwing her a tennis ball that she had to catch in midair while jumping into the pool. Adam had come outside and wanted to play. To her surprise, Nate allowed him to join. "Here we are at the gold medal round," Nate intoned each time he threw the ball. At first they were just having fun, but Nate started to throw the ball harder so that Adam would miss it. Adam complained, and the next time, with no warning, Nate turned and pitched the ball as hard as he could at the statue. Stunned by the sound, the three of them quickly got out of the pool. Sherry came running, and right away, she noticed a crack along one side of the statue. Hailey was afraid she was going to be upset, which, in her mind, was the worst thing that could happen. The few times she had seen her mother crying—usually when Adam and Nate wouldn't stop fighting—she was riveted and horrified, the natural order of the world undone. As a child, she had often repeated "I love you, I love you, I love you" to her mother, as if a hole existed inside her so deep that it reached the center of the earth, and she, like a child with a plastic shovel, kept futilely trying to fill it. Though Hailey had the impulse to confess what happened, she quietly stood between her brothers. "I think it was a bird," Adam claimed. "Or maybe a coconut," Nate added. She nodded vigorously to both suggestions as Adam and Nate looked at each other and started to laugh. To her amazement, her mother laughed too. She went back inside and returned with cookies and orange slices, and she stayed out by the pool to watch the three of them swim. A week later, a workman came to repair the statue, but no one asked again what had happened.

That memory stood out because it was the exception. All too often, Adam and Nate fought relentlessly, and in the aftermath, they all retreated to their bedrooms—this house, which they'd moved into when she was five, was bigger than what she was used to, and on nights like that, she'd wished for their old house, where no one was ever that far away. Even once she got used to the new house, she sometimes worried that she'd wander the hallway and never find any of them, an endless series of doors, and all of them shut. To calm herself, she would go to her room and write in her pink hardcover diary that had a small gold lock. Mostly she logged the details of her day, but the real pleasure of writing was when she divulged what she really thought. In her tiny impeccable handwriting, she wrote that Nate could be so mean sometimes and so nice other times, and that she felt sorry for Adam, who was so awkward that she felt embarrassed in front of her friends. She wrote that her father was never around and that most of the time she wanted to do what her mother asked of her, but sometimes she felt like it could never be enough. At the sight of her words, Hailey felt thrilled, then afraid that every sentence might set loose another and then another and another, until she had no control over the truth that spewed from her.

On those nights, when she no longer wanted to be alone, she'd go into Adam's room, where he'd be lying on his bed reading. Sitting next to him, she feigned an interest in his books about outer space or animals. At the prospect of her attention, he talked so quickly that it was hard to understand. She stayed because she didn't want to hurt his feelings, but as soon as she could escape, she went in search of Nate. She felt bad because she was supposed to love her brothers equally—only in her diary and in the deepest trenches of her heart could she admit that she loved Nate most of all. Nate was usually in his room with the door closed, but he allowed her in, and she sat with him as he played video games or smashed his basketball across the room into the small net that hung on the back of his door. She wished she could have asked him why he had such a need to provoke their father and Adam, but he acted unbothered by the fighting, joking about how one day she was going to crush him at tennis, even though she'd just started taking lessons, and pretending not to remember the names of her friends.

By the next morning, her mother was bustling around the kitchen getting everyone ready for school as if nothing had happened, making her wonder if the night was as bad as she'd thought. When she flipped back to the diary entries, her guilt surged: What if she died and her family read her words? She couldn't bring herself to cross it all out, but she put an asterisk next to what she'd written, and at the bottom of the page, she added an explanation. "I didn't mean this. I wrote it when I was mad."

"How were Sherry and Sol after I left?" Nate asked as he swam beside her.

Hailey laughed, as she usually did when he called them by their first names, managing to blend mockery and love.

"Dad seemed tired, but Mom entertained Maya all night," she said.

"Don't you think that, on some level, Mom loves the fact you're getting divorced? She gets to have you all to herself," he said.

"I hate it when you say things like that."

"I'm fairly certain that you love when I say what you're thinking but would never dare say."

"I wish I didn't have to go back to Binghamton at all," she said. A cloud of gnats swarmed her face. Though she didn't feel them biting, she knew that in the morning she'd wake up with tiny red marks.

"You could move back into your old bedroom like you never left," he joked.

"What if I really did that? Maybe once the divorce is over, Maya and I could move to West Palm."

"Do you think Jonah would let you do that?" Nate asked.

"Probably not, but I only agreed to move to Binghamton in the first place because of how badly Jonah wanted the job. I was willing to do anything to please him."

"I know it might not feel this way now, but the divorce is going to be a good thing in the long run. You didn't want to spend the rest of your life with that asshole, did you?" Nate said.

"He's going to expect me to go along with whatever he wants. Jonah can be so . . ." She paused, wishing she knew how to explain him. "He doesn't change his mind. Once he decides to fight for something, he doesn't let up. I think it's almost like some kind of game for him."

"I know you've spent your entire life doing what everyone expects of you, but this is your chance to shake things up," Nate said.

"Maybe it's time for that grand eruption you used to tease me about?" she asked.

"It's way past time," Nate said. "Look, Hailey, sooner or later, things break apart. I understand that it's hard, but we both know you weren't that happy. Even if you never told me exactly what was going on, I could tell something was wrong. Do you have any idea how often I wondered if you were going to wake up and leave him? At least this way you get all the sympathy, which I hope you intend to milk for all you can. I know you don't want to hear it, but most divorces are shit shows, and you're just going to have to get through it. And once it's over, we're going to celebrate. I'm making a list of ideas."

"You're not going to take me on one of your vacations, are you?" Hailey smiled. Nate loved to travel to remote spots, seeking out the most arduous of treks and outrageous of adventures. From every trip, he sent her pictures of himself strapped into a harness or jumping off a cliff. A few times, he had invited her and Jonah to join him, but even if Jonah had agreed to go, she would have been too afraid to attempt any of those feats.

"You never know. The new and improved Hailey Marcus Gelman might become an intrepid explorer. I might come up with an idea that's going to change your life."

"Surprise me," she said.

The days ran together. Hailey slept late, while Sherry got up early with Maya. She tried not to think about how fast the week was passing. She meant to call her high school friends who still lived in the area, many of whom she was still in touch with, but she felt embarrassed to tell anyone about the divorce. Jonah texted multiple times a day, reminding her of some divorce-related task she urgently needed to take care of, but she ignored him. In her parents' house, the divorce wasn't happening because she wasn't yet married. Here, she was still a child with nothing of her life yet determined. Every day, she swam with Maya and her mother. Until this visit, she hadn't realized how much she missed the chance to swim so regularly. If there was any place where you were no longer yourself, surely it was underwater, where everything solid could shift and change and flow freely.

On their last day in West Palm, Hailey woke to more texts from Jonah. She was still in bed when her phone began to buzz frantically.

Reminding you again that I still need the name of your lawyer.

It was a relief that her parents had offered to help her find a lawyer, and even more so that they'd offered to pay, but she heard Jonah's ever-present opinion in her head: she was too dependent, she was an overgrown child, she was never going to wrest herself free. He would hate the fact that her parents were involved, but now, she wouldn't have to worry about that anymore. The feeling of being caught between them was over.

I would appreciate it if you responded to my email about my proposed parenting plan for the rest of the summer.

She began typing a response, but paused. The fact that she didn't have to listen to what Jonah wanted felt like a revelation.

Actually, I want to stay in West Palm a little longer

It was an idea she'd had many times during the week, but she hadn't realized she was serious about it until she was hitting send. For a few more days, she could remain in this house that still felt part of an ordered, recognizable world.

We had an agreement that you were just going for a week

She closed her eyes and didn't answer, which she knew would aggravate him: Jonah hated when anyone, especially her, kept him waiting.

Hailey

Hailey

Hailey

He did the same thing in person, repeating her name when he believed that she was being unreasonable. Before, she was able to tolerate it, but now she didn't understand how she had. With the love scraped away, every flaw of his was magnified.

I'm just talking about staying for another
week. Why is that such a big deal?

I think it's best if we follow our prior agreement.

I don't think you're one to talk about keeping an agreement.
Why am I even in Binghamton? There's nothing for me there.

This is where we live. This is where Maya lives.

You said that if I hated it after three years we could move

I have no idea what you're talking about.

She tossed her phone onto the floor and pulled the blanket over her head. Was this what it meant to get divorced—everything she knew to be true now called into question, no longer one set of facts to which they both agreed?

By the time Maya was born, Jonah had finished his PhD at Columbia, but was struggling to finish his second novel. He rarely discussed it with her and never let her read any of it, but she could tell by his ever-present bad mood that it wasn't going well. He started to talk about getting a job teaching writing outside of the city. It had taken a few years, but she had come to love New York—even the wind tunnel alongside their building that nearly toppled her when she walked outside, or all the times she stepped off a curb into what she thought was dry land only to have her foot plunge into a filthy pool of slush.

"How can we possibly afford to stay here?" he asked when she protested that she didn't want to move.

"I have a job here. And my parents are willing to help us, just until you finish your book," she said.

"I'm not going to take money from them," Jonah insisted.

"They're just trying to help," she said.

She was still working at *Allure* and had been promoted to staff writer. She was assigned small articles that ran under her byline, and she was in charge of the Best Of . . . lists that they ran each month, which she sent to her mother, who emailed them to all her friends. She still harbored the desire to write fiction, but she didn't have Jonah's confidence or ambition. Whenever she began to work on a story, she felt a rush of self-doubt. "You should write about your family. You have plenty of material," Jonah often said, which he probably intended as encouragement, but at the thought of hurting anyone she loved, her desire to write switched off. It was one more way she and Jonah were different. He wasn't afraid to provoke; on the contrary, he was energized by the prospect of a confrontation. Once, Jonah read an early attempt at a short story where she tried to shield and soften, and he all but patted her on the head. "If you want to be a writer, you have to be willing to go dark."

After applying for jobs, Jonah had two offers to teach in creative writing departments, one at Binghamton University, the other at the University of Miami. If she had to leave New York, she was excited by the possibility of Miami. She loved the sun and the beach and the fact that she never had to wear a coat. And though Jonah made it seem like a character flaw, she wanted to live close to her family. She would have help with Maya whenever she needed. Maya would have her grandparents as a part of her daily life.

She didn't tell her mother about the job offer in Miami, afraid that she might say something to Jonah that would turn him against the idea. Though she'd hoped that the tension between Jonah and her mother would ease, he still complained that her mother was always calling, that she was always trying to pin down a plan to see them. He said that he felt like he was married not just to her but to all of them. He pointed out that her overattachment to her mother made him afraid that he would be overly attached to her as well. In angry conversations any time they were about to see her parents, and in hushed, furious fights behind closed doors on the occasions when they did, he claimed that he had to be on guard in her mother's presence so that she didn't consume them whole.

Hailey told him that he was exaggerating, he was being unfair. "Can you please listen to me?" she interrupted his diatribes, holding her hand up like a stop sign against an oncoming onslaught of traffic. She said that he was so hell-bent on saying no that he couldn't recognize that some of what her mother wanted was reasonable. She said that they didn't have to be as involved as her mother wanted, but she didn't have to cut her family out of her life altogether. She said that she wished he could regard them as she did, as family, where there were always faults, but those didn't have to overshadow the love. She tried to explain that the more Jonah railed against her mother, the more loyal she became. There was no room for her own complicated knot of feelings.

For the most part, her mother seemed unaware of Jonah's disdain—not because he was good at hiding it but because Hailey had become an expert in recasting or reframing whatever he said so that it didn't sound too sharp or sarcastic. Once, though, her mother pressed her about why Jonah seemed to want so little to do with them and speculated that maybe he was afraid that if he were close to her family, he would feel like he was replacing his own mother. In a fight, Hailey made the mistake of repeating this to Jonah, who laughed caustically. "Please tell your mother that I don't need her to psychoanalyze me."

It was a mistake she wouldn't make again. She learned to screen what she said and called her mother only when Jonah wasn't home. But Jonah found a way to bring her mother up anyway. He claimed that if they gave in to anything her mother asked, there would only be another request—every yes spawned three more demands. If he budged the smallest amount, he would be forever entrapped.

"I know, but—" she protested.

There was no seeing it from any other side. Jonah dredged up things her mother said months before, pinning every word to a board and peering at it under a magnifying glass for any fragment of offense. He criticized how her mother was with Maya—too effusive, always strategizing for how she could see her next—as if he couldn't bear to acknowledge that she was part of them and they a part of her. He carried on about Sherry's habit of referring to Maya as "my Maya," outraged that she dared to lay claim. "Why can't you come for a visit?" her mother asked her with increasing regularity. "Why can't she take no for an answer?" Jonah said to Hailey in response. Yes, she told her mother, she knew that most people would be happy to have parents offer to babysit/take them out to dinner/take them on vacation. Yes, she conceded to Jonah, she understood that her mother could sometimes be controlling/intrusive/opinionated/needy, and yes, she apologized to her mother, she was sorry they couldn't come for the birthday/weekend/holiday, as she had hoped. Yes, to both of them. Yes and yes and yes.

It was a good thing she hadn't mentioned the Miami job because Jonah was intent on taking the position in Binghamton and had numerous arguments for why it was a better opportunity, all of them seemingly bulletproof.

"But you know how much I'd love to live in Miami," she said.

"They would overrun us. They would completely take over."

"We'd see them obviously, but we would have our own lives."

"I am never going to live near your parents," he said.

She started to speak, then stopped, aware of standing at the edge of something dangerous. At her silence, he reached for her. "I want it to be you and me and Maya. All we need is the three of us." It was easier to be swayed by this Jonah, who lovingly assured her that they would both be under less pressure. He told her that she'd have a chance to pursue her own writing, which she'd mostly forgotten about. And he wanted to take the money they'd gotten from their wedding and use it to buy an old house that they could fix up together. "I think you would enjoy that," he told her, and though she'd never had that interest before, she loved the idea of a project that could fill the cracks opening beneath them.

"And if you hate it after three years we can move, I promise," Jonah said.

By the time their marriage fell apart, they had been living in Binghamton for close to three years. She was offered a part-time job writing for the alumni magazine, to sweeten the deal Jonah had received. When she wasn't working, she took walks with Maya on the campus, but once it grew cold, she hated to leave the house. Even though Jonah insisted that the weather was the same as in New York City, she was freezing all the time. She had always made friends easily, but she felt isolated. Sometimes they went out to dinner with Jonah's colleagues, but she couldn't think of anything smart or interesting to say. It was easier to let Jonah hold forth, which he did expertly, everyone at the table leaning toward him to hear an anecdote or opinion. During the days, she saw other mothers with kids Maya's age, but they seemed to exist across a plain she couldn't traverse. In the city, she had loved to walk for miles with Maya, stopping at parks and cafés. In Binghamton, she mostly stayed inside because no matter how much she bundled up, she could never get warm.

When she talked to her mother, she sometimes complained about the weather, but mostly she gave an accounting of the various activities she'd done with Maya, as if they could be admitted as evidence of happiness. She didn't mention that she felt like she'd entered some internal state of hibernation; or that sometimes she woke in the middle of the night with a panicked feeling that her marriage was not okay. "What's the matter?" her mother asked, able to detect, with a special sonar, her unhappiness, but Hailey assured her that she was fine. She knew how badly her mother wanted her to be happy and didn't want to mar the image of her life that her mother had constructed. And she knew that if she told her mother how lonely she was or how much she hated Binghamton, she might end up telling her about the job Jonah had turned down in Miami, which would lead her to explain why he had been so adamantly opposed to it, which would lead her to tell her everything. Nate was the only one she could confide in, but even with him, she glossed over what she shared. If she told him the full truth, she would have to believe it herself.

She'd waited for Jonah to notice her unhappiness, but he was enamored of his new job and rarely home. He loved teaching, loved being surrounded by students, loved being asked to give readings and attend faculty dinners. Worried that he would think badly of her, she tried not to complain, but then, all at once, her unhappiness would erupt from her—she hated it here, she wanted to move, back to the city, back to Florida, anywhere but here. "Give me one good reason why you don't like it," he demanded, and all she could come up with was the fact that it was freezing. Jonah claimed that she wasn't going to be happy anywhere but near her family. He dismissed her complaints about her job. "If you don't like your job, then find something else you want to do. Take charge of your life," he would say and look at her like she was a stranger he was inexplicably yoked to.

One night, she made dinner and bathed Maya and read to her. She had been waiting for the right moment to raise the subject of their summer plans with Jonah—it was the end of May and her mother had asked several times when they were coming to visit. But increasingly there was no right moment for any subject—every word was capable of igniting a fight.

"Why is it so impossible to see my granddaughter?" Sherry asked her on the phone, and for the first time, Hailey was on the verge of telling her the truth.

"I'll know tomorrow," she promised.

Once Maya was asleep, Hailey went into the kitchen, where Jonah was sitting at the table, working on his laptop.

"Can we talk about when we're going to West Palm?" she asked.

"Don't you think it's a little hot there in the summer?" he responded.

"You know I want to visit my family."

"Why do we have to discuss this now?" he said.

He knew, but wanted to make her say it.

"Because I want to know what we're doing . . . And my mother wants to know when we're coming."

His expression was victorious, as if he'd forced some appalling admission.

"I'm teaching at a writer's conference that week," he said when she told him the week she was hoping to go.

"So we can go a different week."

"I'm not going."

"This is my family."

"Then you go," he said.

She was still standing there when he turned back to his work. All at once, she wanted to shake him from his infuriatingly calm demeanor, and she wanted to be taken in his arms and assured that everything would be all right.

She didn't believe him about the conference, which was why, the next morning, she decided to read his email—his password was MayaMaya, the same as hers. She had never done something like this, but she couldn't shake the desperate feeling that things were coming to an end and she had to know the truth. And there it was, in the emails to his college roommate, Max, that were paragraphs long, where he said what he really thought. It had been a long time since she'd heard Jonah so effusive—it was like gaining access to a hidden side, or at least one that was hidden from her. He wrote about his new book, details he never shared with her. He wrote about how much he couldn't stand his mother-in-law, all things she'd heard him say many times before, but seeing the words in print—intrusive, over-involved, controlling—made her hands shake. When she came to the emails about her, she wanted to throw up. He accused her of not being serious enough, a lightweight, he wrote. "There's a reason Hailey's mother calls her 'Sunshine.' She can't handle anything dark," he claimed. It was like being forced to stare at herself in an awful funhouse mirror. "She's completely under her mother's control. I should have known what I was getting into when I met her mother. I thought she was different, but the truth is, Hailey is exactly like her."

Each sentence fired its own bullet.

"I'm trapped. I don't know what to do," he'd written.

"You don't have to stay in something that doesn't work. You're allowed to be happy," Max had responded.

Hailey crouched on the floor, her arms shielding her head, her breaths emerging in short gasps. For one moment, she felt relief: at last, she knew what Jonah really thought. But then she felt the mortification. In his eyes, she was the worst version of herself. The person who was supposed to love her most didn't love her at all.

Before logging off his email, she printed out the messages—maybe she could make sense of them if they were tangible objects to hold in her hand. All day she stared at them, until she nearly memorized them. That evening, when Maya was asleep, she spread the emails out on the kitchen table. When Jonah came into the kitchen, she was waiting. Her eyes were rimmed in red, but somehow, she managed to sit there without crying.

When he realized what the papers were, he did a double take and gave a slight grimace. And then—she caught it passing across his face—he looked relieved.

"I'm sorry, I really am, but I can't do it anymore. I'm tired of being miserable," he said.

She remained frozen as Jonah said that he wanted a divorce. He was sorry, very, very sorry—he kept repeating that as if it would make her feel better—but he didn't love her as he should. He was tired of their fighting. He needed to be with someone he could really talk to. He needed to not feel so trapped. As he spoke, she tried to understand what he was saying, but the words couldn't penetrate her frozen exterior. All she could think was that she needed to get out of the kitchen, out of the house. She grabbed her cell phone and ran into the backyard and stood near the flower garden that her mother had planted one of the few times she came to visit. Even in late May, it had barely started to to bloom. Hailey called her mother, and at the sound of her voice, she finally melted into tears.

"We are here for you. We will do whatever you need," Sherry said, and all she wanted was to go home.

Because it was their last day in West Palm, Sherry had a long list of things she wanted to do. Hailey could hear her downstairs with Maya, playing happily. It wasn't true what Nate said about her mother loving the fact that she was getting divorced, but in some small way, Nate was right that she did crave any chance to have them to herself.

Hailey got out of bed and into the shower, turning the water as hot as it would go. She took her time getting ready, knowing that her mother would appraise her appearance: a quick, wordless inspection. There was nothing she could do about the lines of red along both her eyelids, but at least she could focus on her long hair, which her mother liked to claim was the most beautiful thing in the world. Sometimes, at these exclamations, Hailey felt the urge to cut her hair short, though she would never admit to that rebelliousness out loud. When she was a teenager, she was astonished at how easily her friends excoriated their mothers; if she said half as much, she would have been crippled with guilt.

When she picked her phone up again, more texts had accumulated.

You know very well we only agreed that you would go for the week.

I need your assurance in writing that you will return as planned.

Instead of responding, she went downstairs into the kitchen, where her mother and Maya were making heart-shaped chocolate chip pancakes. Maya was standing on a chair that Sherry had pulled up in front of the stove, both of them with spatulas in hand.

"I thought those were only for our birthdays," Hailey said, which was what her mother told them when they were growing up. It was a family tradition from Sherry's childhood, though she once shared with Hailey that, for her, as a child, it was a rare luxury.

"Maya loves them so much I decided we didn't have to wait," Sherry said.

Hailey's phone beeped again, and she glanced at it.

"Is it him?" Sherry whispered so Maya couldn't hear.

Hailey nodded. "I can't believe I'm leaving tomorrow. I wish I could stay here permanently."

"Do you really have to go back yet?" Sherry asked.

Once Maya was at the table, eating the pancakes, Hailey showed her the latest text from Jonah.

If you are not back as planned, I will be speaking to my lawyer about what I consider a deliberate act of escalation.

"I don't know how you can stand it," Sherry said.

"I can't, but what am I supposed to do?" Hailey asked.

"You have to get angry, Hailey. It's so much easier to be angry than to be sad," Sherry said.

Her phone beeped again, again.

We both know that your mother is the one trying to convince you to stay.

I highly suggest that you do not involve your parents in our divorce.

"We should have been living here in the first place," Hailey said. "Jonah had a job offer at the University of Miami, but he wouldn't even consider it."

The words had emerged before she could stop them, and now her mother was staring at her in disbelief.

"But why not?" Sherry asked.

She could still turn back—say she didn't mean it, try to reframe, recast as she always had—but her phone beeped again.

"Jonah claimed we wouldn't have our independence if we lived here," she admitted.

Sherry digested what she'd said, but the shock on her face remained.

"Is this why you never visited?"

"We had a fight anytime I wanted to come."

"Do you have any idea how I bent over backwards so that everyone would get along? Do you know how much I worried that I was doing something wrong? All I wanted was for Jonah to be part of our family," Sherry said.

"I tried, but he wouldn't budge," Hailey said.

"Tell me the truth," Sherry said. "He hated us. No, he hated me, right?"

Hailey took a deep breath. She would tell her mother everything. The time had come, Nate had said, and now it was all going to break apart.

MAINE, 2019

In the morning, the bitter cold wakes me. My body shivers under the blanket, and for a moment, I have no idea where I am. Then it dawns on me, why I am in this room, which is empty except for the bed and a small wooden desk; why I am lying next to Maya against a wall made of knotty pine. Sometimes, as I lie here, my hand is drawn to touch what looks like a dark, seeping wound.

Maya is still asleep when I pull on jeans and a fleece sweatshirt and slip outside, where the cold creates a burning sensation against my cheeks. It's just starting to get light, and the only sound is the rustle of bare tree branches and the crunch of my footsteps as I walk across the hardened snow. Everything lush and green has been stripped away.

The dogs bark as soon as they see me coming and crowd the edge of the pen. A few of them rise up on their hind legs, their front paws resting on the fence, tongues out, tails wagging. I stand there, unsure how to greet them.

"Hi there," I say. The dogs gaze searchingly at me, and I wonder if it's true that dogs can sense fear.

The kennel in front of me is a peeling barn that was probably once red and is now a weathered, dull brown. Its sloped gray roof is piled with snow, and firewood is neatly stacked along one side of the barn, where the exterior is nearly rotted through. On the other side, there is a grassy enclosure in which the dogs run freely.

"I didn't expect you to be out here this early," I hear and whirl around to see my brother Adam walking toward me. At the sight of him, the dogs begin to bark, in a state of delirious joy.

When we arrived two days ago, I told Adam that I wanted to be put to work, in search of anything that might chip away at my guilt. In response, Adam had regarded me skeptically, as if he couldn't imagine what I could possibly do. I'd insisted that, at the very least, I could help with the dogs, and warily, Adam had agreed to show me how to feed them in the mornings.

"No one else will ever be that happy to see me, I can promise you that," Adam says as he opens the rickety wood gate. Together we go into the enclosed pen and now the dogs are upon us, their paws on my thighs, my chest. My instinct is to recoil, but aware of Adam watching me, I don't allow myself to cringe at the sniffing of their snouts, at the slobbering wet of their tongues. I'm afraid that if I pull away, Adam will remember how, as a child, I was terrified of dogs, crossing the street if I saw one coming toward me, clinging to whomever I was with, sure that at any moment, the animal would lunge. I'm afraid that Adam will regard me as someone who is still afraid of what is hard or dark or true.

Soon most of the dogs lose interest or decide that I'm not a threat and they wander away, some back inside the kennel, others to romp at the far end of the enclosure. But one small dog, with long, drooping ears and mottled tan fur, places a paw on my leg and stares up at me, as if trying to tell me something.

Adam bends down and brings his face close to the dog so that she can lick him, then gently touches her belly. "Daisy's pregnant," he says. He points out the swelling in her nipples and belly, and I feel an urge to scoop her up and protect her.

Adam is wearing scuffed brown boots and an olive coat that is only partially zipped, as if he's immune to the cold. His dark hair is long and curly and falls to his shoulders. Peering out from all that hair are his bright blue eyes, the same shade as mine. It's hard not to stare as I try to unearth the person I once knew. In all likelihood, he's marveling with the same disbelief at how different I appear. My eyes, I know, are ringed with exhaustion, my lips feel frozen into two straight lines, and my hair is chopped artlessly short, darker than it has been in years. I'm wearing a nearly identical coat that Adam found in his closet because the light jacket I'd brought with me was no match for this weather and a pair of his old boots, which are too big. When I glance in the small mirror hanging from a nail in his bathroom, it's hard to recognize myself.

"A few weeks ago, someone I know found Daisy wandering about twenty miles from here, with no tags. If she'd been taken to a shelter, in all likelihood she would have been spayed and the puppies put down," Adam says plainly, but I hear his outrage.

As he sets out the food, the dogs come running. There are eight in all, two being boarded for a month while the owners are away, and six here permanently, because, Adam explains, people think they want a dog, but it's not what they expect. Or because the owners get old or sick and have no one to take care of their dogs. Or because the dogs are injured or aggressive and unlikely to be adopted—all of them wounded in one way or another.

"Will they stay here if you can't find anyone?" I ask.

"I'd like to think that there's a person out there for each of these dogs. But if not, then I'm that person," he says without meeting my eye.

"And who's that?" I ask, pointing to a dog who is missing a leg.

"That's Ruby. She got caught in a hunter's trap," Adam says and tells me a story about another dog who, after getting lost in the woods, arrived home a week later with gnarled white bone protruding from the bottom of his leg. Presumably, he had escaped the trap by chewing his paw off.

"A dog will do whatever it takes to get free," he says.

Once I knew I had to leave West Palm, I called Adam and asked if Maya and I could come stay with him for a while. Adam and I had spoken a few times on the phone since Jonah died; it was the most contact we'd had since my wedding. We exchanged specific facts about our lives, but if the conversation hovered close to more complicated subjects, I quickly said I had to go, and Adam, not one to press, said goodbye and hung up. When I told Adam I needed to get away, I heard his hesitation. "I don't know if it's a good idea for you to come here," he stammered. "Please," I begged. I had nowhere else to go.

I'd fled West Palm with the urgency of someone being chased. I'd grabbed a few things and threw them into my car—some clothes for Maya and me and a few of Maya's favorite toys. I ignored my mother's entreaties, didn't so much as glance in the rearview mirror as I drove down the street. To turn back might have rendered my leaving impossible. It had just started to rain, and the lack of visibility made me feel that I could drive off the edge of the road, into the mouth of the ocean and be swallowed up. I'd tried to act calm so as not to alarm Maya, but I couldn't shake the feeling that no matter how fast I drove, I could be apprehended at any minute. Only once I'd left West Palm and was safely on I-95, one car among so many others, did my heart stop pounding and my breath begin to slow.

On the long ride, Maya had asked several times where we were going. "To see someone in our family you've never met," I said, trying to sound composed. I glanced constantly at Maya in the rearview mirror—she was wearing her favorite T-shirt, emblazoned with a glittery yellow sun, and looked so small in her booster seat that I wished I could bring her into the front with me, to curl on my lap as I drove. I pointed out whatever sights we passed, tried to think of subjects we could safely talk about, wanting her to still believe that everything would be okay. There was no way I could fool her, but I also had no idea how to explain what I couldn't understand myself. She didn't press for more details, though sometimes she had a cryptic expression on her face, on the verge of asking more. But then, perhaps sensing my fear, she grew silent, which unnerved me as well.

I worried that she could see through me, that somehow she knew the truth—had known all along.

I drove four long days. Eight-lane highways gave way to mountainous foggy overpasses and back again. I plied Maya with potato chips and fluorescent gummy candies that I bought at gas stations and played her favorite music to keep her entertained. For the most part, she was quiet. For all the time we'd been in West Palm, an unnerving silence had replaced the raging fits she'd had in the immediate aftermath of Jonah's death. It was the middle of February and still hot in West Palm. As we made our way north, it grew colder, which somehow made it easier to breathe. I turned on the heat in the car only once Maya complained. I called out the states we drove through, eager to be as far away as possible. Georgia. South Carolina. North Carolina. Virginia. Maryland. Pennsylvania. Each new state I entered was a border being erected in me, one more mark of separation.

When my eyes grew heavy and the road became a blurry haze of light and speed, we stopped in motels. While Maya slept, I took out the notebook I kept buried in the bottom of my bag and considered where to begin: With my marriage, with my divorce, or with everything that had come before? I felt the urge to write in a way I hadn't since I was a child keeping a diary. Whether this was a confession or an accusation I wasn't sure yet, but I needed to write unimpeded. To write was dread and exhilaration and, most of all, the certainty that this was the only way I could arrive at the scalding truth. My heart burned with fear, my fingers burned with words.

Finally, we drove over the New Hampshire border into Maine. On either side of the highway, there was a forest of bare trees, but in the distance,

I could see the green fringe of pine that withstood the cold, and farther off, the snowcapped peaks of mountains rising defiantly against the sky. It was late afternoon, and I sped so that we could make it to Adam's before it grew dark. We turned off a mostly deserted highway onto a side road that was completely empty. Out of range of the GPS, I had to rely on the hastily scribbled directions Adam had given me, unable to know if I was going the right way. I tried to tamp down the fear that, at the end of the road, I would arrive at an impassable forest and discover that Adam had sent me to the edge of nowhere. "We're almost there," I assured Maya and checked her face in the rearview mirror, but she had fallen asleep.

Finally I saw the rocky driveway that Adam had described and, in the distance, a glimpse of the barn. At the sight of it, I woke Maya. "We're here, honey," I said, realizing that she had no idea where *here* was. As I drove closer, I saw Adam standing with two dogs, watching us. He couldn't have known when exactly we'd arrive, but his expression remained eerily calm. I jumped out of the car, about to rush toward him and hug him. But he recoiled, giving only a half wave, and I felt an inclination to return to the car and keep driving, but had no idea where else I might go.

Maya was undaunted. As soon as she saw the dogs, she darted toward them and they jumped on her in greeting. Quickly, I moved to protect her, but realized that she was enjoying the robust welcome. It had been so long since I'd heard Maya's carefree laugh that I had wanted to cry with relief. For one moment, my child was restored.

"Do you think Daisy knows she's going to give birth?" I ask Adam now as I crouch down to pet her head. She rolls over and, with a surprising amount of trust, waits for me to rub her belly.

"It depends what you mean by 'know,'" Adam says. "It's a mistake to attribute human emotions to dogs."

"Do you ever feel cut off out here?" I ask.

He shrugs. "People find me when they need me."

I try to catch his eye, but he looks away. There are so many things I want to ask him and so many things I don't want to say. A gust of freezing wind stings my face. I bury my hands in the pockets of my jacket, which is so big on me that I could almost disappear inside of it. If Adam is bothered by the cold, he shows no sign. His cheeks are red, but he doesn't shiver as I do. Behind him, the sun is blinding against the snow, and I have to squint to see him.

"I didn't expect you to be that interested in the dogs," he says.

"I think I prefer dogs to people right now," I say and try to laugh.

He doesn't respond, and in the ensuing silence, I can only imagine what he must suspect.

In the office, Nate had patients waiting, but he couldn't stop staring at the October issue of *Palm Beach Illustrated*, which had its annual feature on the area's top doctors. For the first time, he was included. "Can Dr. Nate Marcus Discover the Fountain of Youth? His Patients Certainly Hope So," read the headline of a small article, with a full-page photo of him standing outside the office, wearing scrubs, the sun glinting off his hair like he had a halo. Nate had known since August that he was going to be featured, but told no one. For the past few months, his family had been consumed by Hailey's divorce, and he decided to wait to share the good news until things were calmer. He assumed that everyone would be happy for him, but that was because he didn't know that, for the first time, his father wasn't on this year's list. He felt a pang of guilt, as if the omission were his fault.

"Don't tell me you're still looking at that magazine."

Nate quickly looked up. Tara, the office manager and everyone's favorite person in the practice, was standing in front of him with a look of bemusement. She was barely five feet tall and maybe twenty-five years old. Her blond hair was pulled back into a ponytail and she was wearing dress clothes and heels that gave her the air of a kid playing dress-up, which was something he understood. Whenever he incurred his father's displeasure, he felt like a kid cloaked in someone else's scrubs.

"Given that it just came out this morning, I think I'm entitled to enjoy it for at least another few minutes," Nate said but was embarrassed to be caught in a moment of vanity. For the twenty years that his father was named the area's top melanoma specialist, he'd acted like *Palm Beach Illustrated* was an accolade no serious physician would care about. Even so, his mother framed each issue and hung it in the office, claiming that the patients wanted to know their doctor was the best.

Tara came up behind him and read over his shoulder. "There is a bright new future for the prestigious office of Marcus Dermatology," the article began. When Nate was interviewed, he talked about the charity auction he emceed for Dermatology Medical Missions and about his plans to expand his cosmetic practice and offer laser treatments, chemical peels, and microdermabrasion. "Botox is only the beginning," he'd said.

"I didn't know your father agreed to that," she said.

It would be easy enough to claim that his father had come around. Tara was appealingly gullible, but maybe her appearance of naivete just meant that she was very young and he no longer was.

"Not yet, but he will after the presentation I'm going to show him later today," he admitted.

"Are you sure? I'm pretty sure he's dead set against the idea."

Of course Tara was right, but Nate was determined not to be waylaid by his father's opposition. Cosmetic dermatology was a thriving field. Some practices were opening separate medi-spas and expanding into realms previously regarded as plastic surgery. He began researching Laser Genesis machines and Fractora. He drafted a proposal to show his father what they could do. Every time he stepped into the office, he saw what it could become.

Three years earlier, Sherry had first broached the idea to Nate of joining the practice. "Does Dad think it's a good idea?" he'd asked, afraid that his voice would give away how badly he wanted the answer to be yes. "Of course he does," his mother said in that overly cheerful voice she used when she wanted to obscure the truth. She would never openly acknowledge what they all knew to be true: his father didn't trust him. But a month later, his father made him an offer, and though Nate had intended to make a show of hesitation, he immediately said yes. On his first day, he and his parents stood in the office parking lot next to the sign for the practice where, underneath DR. SOLOMON MARCUS, in smaller letters, DR. NATHANIEL MARCUS had been added. To celebrate, his mother bought a chocolate cake, like it was a kid's birthday party, but instead of expressing his gratitude or excitement, he felt compelled to make a joke. "Sorry, Dad. Now you can't use the office to escape." But that night, when everyone went home, Nate stayed late. He had finally been admitted to the inner sanctum.

They agreed that he would start by seeing some of his father's patients as he grew his own practice. "And then one day, when I'm ready to retire . . ." Sol said, dangling the possibility that he might eventually take over altogether. In the meantime, Nate was determined to show his father what he was capable of. He came in early and stayed late. He networked to cultivate referrals. He befriended the nurses and the drug company reps and the building manager and people who worked in the billing office. After a year, his schedule was packed. Many patients now requested to see him instead of Sol. Some of them were friends of his mother, and if they remembered him as the wild, misbehaving son, now they exclaimed how wonderful he was. But apparently none of that mattered to his father, who'd recently started to complain that Nate ran behind schedule because he talked to the patients for too long, or failed to notify Tara far enough in advance of his vacation plans, or joked around in a way his father deemed unprofessional. But as far as Nate was concerned, it wasn't always necessary to adhere to the letter of the law as long as he took care of what needed to be done. It was fine to bend a few rules every now and then. There was no requirement that the office had to feel so stiff and uncomfortable. There was a reason Solomon was always called Dr. Marcus, while everyone referred to him as Nate.

Nate was about to turn back to the proposal he'd been preparing, but Tara was still standing there.

"Can I ask you something?" she said.

"I'm an open book," he responded.

"Maybe I shouldn't say anything, but have you noticed that your father isn't totally himself? I didn't want to mention it to your mom because I know how worried she is about Hailey, with the divorce and everything. But yesterday, I thought that he made a few mistakes in one of the charts, and when I came into his office to ask him about it, he was just staring off in a weird way. I thought maybe he was asleep, but his eyes were kind of open."

"I haven't noticed anything, but I'm the last one he'd tell if anything was wrong," Nate said.

"That's not true," she said.

"Come on, Tara. We all know that you're his favorite child," Nate said, and Tara laughed. It was something he'd said many times, mostly as a joke, but it was impossible not to see how much his father liked Tara. Sol was reserved with almost everyone, but was effusive about her. He talked about how, when he hired her, she had no office experience, but he recognized how smart she was. He commented, far too many times, that she had a work ethic that was rare these days, and Nate didn't think he was imagining the pointed look his father cast in his direction. His father also extolled the fact that, after a few months, Tara put the scheduling and billing online and computerized the medical records and updated the bookkeeping files, as if she had performed some miraculous feat. After a year, he promoted her to office manager and paid for her to take college classes at night. Nate knew he was too old to be hung up on this, but it was hard not to wonder why his father could be so giving in certain instances, so withholding in others; why, no matter how hard he worked, he could never earn half that amount of approval.

Nate had wanted to be a doctor since he first discovered, at the age of ten, the books lining his father's study. He wasn't supposed to enter his father's private hideaway, but that rule only guaranteed that he would. On his father's desk, everything was laid out just so, the black fountain pens and the pile of Post-it notes and the little metal container of paper clips and the yellow legal pads. The orderliness stoked Nate's compulsion to move things around, enough that the disorder would be felt, but not so much that it would be obvious there was an actual culprit. Nate had always gone out of his way to anger his father. As a child, he ran around the house, making messes, making as much noise as possible. By the time he was in middle school, he had honed his ability to get a rise out of his father. He would do an imitation of his teachers, his tennis coach, but most of all, his father, with his slow cadence of speech, his measured mannerisms. It started as a joke, but he felt compelled to keep going even when it was no longer funny. Sometimes he skipped the part about trying to make people laugh and went straight for the anger. That could be as simple as swearing—emit a single *fuck*, and his father would tell him to watch his mouth. "What's wrong with you? Why don't you know when to stop?" his father would yell when Nate swore a second time, with more gusto. Nate would wait until his father assumed that he had been quieted into submission. Then the word would form again in his head. *Fuck.* He'd utter it once more and revel in the moment when his father finally erupted in anger.

Among the medical texts and journals in his father's office, Nate had come upon a book whose cover showed photographs of various deformities: a baby's face covered with a red rash; lips that were burnt and blistered; a hand with an oozing pink welt. Adam and Hailey were both squeamish, but he had no problem staring at the images. He studied the names listed inside the book: Pemphigus vulgaris. Syphilis chancre. Necrobiosis lipoidica. Entranced by the awfulness, he couldn't look away.

One time, Nate stopped reading and found Adam standing there, watching him. Adam was only a year younger, but almost a foot shorter and preternaturally pale—Nate's favorite insult was that he was one of those kids allergic to the sun.

"You're not supposed to be in here," Adam said.

"As if you're allowed to be?" Nate asked.

"Dad says I can because I don't make a mess," Adam said. "And because I can actually read the books in here."

Nate forced a laugh. Though Adam was younger, he was a far better reader, a fact that Adam made sure to point out because it was one of the few arenas where he could beat Nate. At school, Adam kept to himself. He read a book as he walked through the halls and sometimes talked to himself and had none of the ease Nate did when it came to sports. Determined to use whatever ammunition he could, Adam would sit smugly beside Nate with a book and quietly tell him how much he would love it if only he could read it. While Nate was mean to Adam out in the open, Adam preferred the stealth attack. Nate acted like he didn't care, but it bothered him every time he came upon Adam and his father studying Adam's favorite book, an enormous volume called *The Illustrated Encyclopedia of Animals*. As far as Nate knew, his father had no interest in animals, but that didn't stop him from listening to Adam explain every detail about every species. At the sight of them, Nate wanted to rip the book from their hands.

"Did you see this?" Nate asked Adam and showed him a full-size, color picture of a patient infected with a flesh-eating bacteria. "I bet I can stare at it longer than you can."

Adam immediately squeezed his eyes shut, which was too easy a victory, so once Adam opened his eyes, Nate pretended to study something on the back of Adam's arm.

"Has that been there a long time?" Nate asked.

"There's nothing there," Adam insisted, blinking rapidly, as he did whenever he was upset.

"I don't want to scare you, but there really is something on your arm just like in the book. The only option," Nate pretended to read, "is to amputate the infected limb."

Adam couldn't have believed him, so why would he beg Nate to admit it wasn't true? It was something about Adam he would never understand—why did Adam seek him out when he knew how the interaction would end? It was almost like Adam wanted to be made to feel bad.

Nate looked from Adam's arm to the book. "No, it's a definite amputation. Otherwise, your entire body could be consumed."

Adam burst into tears, looking at him with such desolation that he wished Adam would fight back—anything but stand there so meekly, so weak.

"I was just joking," Nate called as Adam ran from the room, but it was too late. He tried to tell himself that it wasn't his fault that Adam was hypersensitive, but the guilt set in anyway. What was wrong with him and why did he have to be this way, and why didn't he know when to stop? Nate knew he should have gone after Adam to apologize, but he told himself he didn't care what Adam thought, he didn't care what his parents thought, he didn't care about anything. In the office, he scrutinized the pictures, in search of the most grotesque. A nose inflamed with boils. A penis covered in welts. Sores like small mouths, orifices opening and oozing. Even that young, he'd sensed that he was stumbling upon a great awful truth. Everyone was damaged. Only some people bore evidence on the surface.

A few minutes later, Nate heard footsteps and looked up to see his father standing there—he assumed that he had come to rebuke him. But instead of being angry, Solomon looked pleased to find him engrossed in one of his books. In the glow of his father's interest, Nate's guilt dried up. He showed his father the book, and Sol told him about a patient he'd treated with one of those ailments and Nate tried to hold on to every word, as if he might be asked to recite them back.

"If you think that's interesting, let me show you something," Sol said and took from his briefcase a videotape and played it on the small TV on the bookshelf.

Together, they sat on the love seat, and Nate was afraid to move, not wanting his father to take away his hand, which rested lightly on Nate's arm. On the video, Sol, in scrubs and surgical mask, was calmly excising a mottled black lesion from a patient's cheek. Nate was mesmerized that his father, seemingly this ordinary man, could do something so wondrous.

"In the operating room, you're completely in charge. There might be other people present, but the patient's well-being rests in your hands," Sol said, trying to act nonchalant, but Nate could hear his pride.

"I want to be a doctor," Nate declared.

Sol studied him, as if seeing all that he was lacking.

"Do you have any idea how disciplined you have to be? Do you know how hard you have to work?" he finally said.

It was a fait accompli the minute his father doubted he could do it.

The first time Nate applied to medical school, he didn't get in. Consumed with shame, he took a year off and traveled solo through Central America, making use of his high school Spanish while nursing his wounds. He didn't want to think about the look on his father's face when he had broken the news that he didn't get in—there was sympathy, but also a glint of satisfaction at having been right. Nate rappelled three hundred feet into caves with hidden waterfalls. Ascending a steep summit in blazing heat, he learned to shut down the parts of himself that experienced pain. At the end of the year, he contemplated getting a job as a bartender in Belize and never going home—for as long as he could remember, his plan was to one day move far away. He didn't have a specific locale in mind, just as distant from Florida as possible. It was an appealing fantasy, but he eventually returned to West Palm, to a job in a lab that his father got for him. He lived at home while his mother hired tutors to help him with the MCAT. When the time came, his father made a phone call to a friend at the University of Miami medical school and asked him to write a letter on Nate's behalf. He was grateful for the help, but ashamed that he needed it. "Find me a parent who wouldn't do anything to help their child," his mother assured him. His acceptance to the University of Miami confirmed his mother's belief that things worked out in the end. For his father, it was one more piece of evidence that, on his own, he would never measure up.

In medical school, Nate stayed up all night, memorizing the names of the muscles in the hands, the characteristics of the columnar epithelium of the small intestine, and the interactions between anti-epileptic drugs and oral contraceptives. He would never feel that sense of failure again. When he started rotations in the hospital, he didn't mind being awake all night. He loved talking to the patients. Sometimes he could ease a patient's fear just by sitting down at the side of their bed to listen instead of rushing to leave, as many residents did. Initially, he wanted to be a surgeon. "The chance to cut is a chance to cure," his attending liked to say, and Nate understood it to be the truth. Yet when it came time to pick an area of specialty, he selected dermatology—less a decision than a feeling of being overcome by a force he couldn't control. As he expected, his father was taken aback when he told him of his choice. "Not once did I ever anticipate this," Sol said, and the plates shifted, a new familial landscape taking shape. Nate stayed at the University of Miami for his residency, where he treated patients suffering from flesh-eating bacteria and disfiguring lesions that covered their faces. The patients were pocked and mottled, but Nate didn't look away.

With a few minutes until his next patient, Nate went out front, where Sherry and Tara sat at a long desk overlooking the waiting room. It looked the same as it had when he was a kid, with chairs covered in a speckled maroon fabric that could have doubled as industrial carpeting and a tropical fish tank that his father often stared into, seemingly mesmerized by the colors and the gliding motion. His mother's desk was a Shutterfly extravaganza, with a calendar made of family photos and a mug with a picture of her and Maya, emblazoned with the words BEST FRIENDS FOREVER.

"The signed charts," Nate said and presented them to Tara with a flourish.

"I never thought I'd see the day," Tara said. On her desk, she had a few pictures of her kid, Caleb, and one of her with a guy named Kevin, whom she sometimes described as her boyfriend and sometimes as her fiancé. Nate and Tara joked around all day, but he knew little about her actual life. His mother, on the other hand, liked to proclaim that she considered Tara not just an employee but part of the family. Like Sol, she talked about how the office couldn't run without Tara, and sometimes she hired her to do other jobs and errands for them. She bought gifts for Tara's son and invited them to come swim anytime. Nate didn't listen carefully to the stories his mother told about Tara—when she launched in, he dubbed it the Tara Report and teased her about her need to get involved. But even without paying attention, he was pretty sure that there was more to the story than Tara's pictures displayed. He knew that Tara worried about Kevin for reasons she was reluctant to share but that made Sherry proclaim, in that caring yet all-knowing way she had, that she had a bad feeling about him.

"One magazine piece and look at him," Sherry said to Tara. She might have been joking, but he could easily see how proud she was. No matter what he did, his mother's approval had always felt boundless, which was maybe why he'd valued it less.

"Has Dad seen it yet?" Nate asked Sherry.

"He's been with patients all morning, but as soon as he comes out, I'm going to show him. He's going to be very proud," she said.

"Do you actually think that's true?" he protested. He often joked about his mother's ability to deny anything that she didn't like, though it bothered him more than he let on. She filtered out what she didn't want to see, magnified those parts that she did. She made constant proclamations about what a close, special family they were. If anyone else said those things, he might have let it go, but he felt the need to goad her into acknowledging that a small disagreement was really a bad fight, that what she called a perfect day was anything but.

"Of course it's true. Dad just needs time to get used to the idea of offering more cosmetic procedures," Sherry said.

"Right. I'm sure that's all it is," Nate said.

"Maybe I shouldn't say anything, but we do get a lot of calls asking if we do them," Tara chimed in.

"See, Tara agrees with me that we should create a state-of-the-art cosmetic dermatology center," Nate said.

"You can look into it. It won't hurt if you start to gather information," Sherry said.

"What do you think I've been doing?" he asked.

Sherry's phone beeped. She read the message, then quickly typed a reply.

"Have you talked to Hailey?" Sherry asked him.

"Tell me the truth. Does my mother ever work or does she drive you crazy talking about Hailey's divorce all day?" Nate asked Tara.

"It's fine. I want to hear about it," Tara said.

"Did I tell you that she's meeting with her lawyer this afternoon?" Sherry asked. "Hailey is serious about moving to West Palm. She knows it might be hard to convince Jonah, but she's going to try."

"You've told me that at least ten times and I'm sure you've told Tara even more," he said.

Sherry ignored his comment. "It makes sense for Hailey and Maya to live here. She has no one in Binghamton. She and Maya are all alone there."

"You know I'd love it if Hailey was nearby, but I would definitely not get your hopes up that Jonah's going to let her move here with Maya," Nate told her.

"They never intended to stay in Binghamton. She only moved because Jonah wanted to, but it hardly seems fair that she should be trapped there for the rest of her life," Sherry said.

Nate perched on the edge of his mother's desk. Once this vortex of conversation started, it would be a while before it wrapped up. In the three months since Jonah moved out, the divorce had become his mother's favorite topic of discussion. He overheard her telling her friends how Jonah ambushed Hailey with his plans to divorce her, how he was gearing up for a prolonged battle, and how she'd had reservations about Jonah from the start. It wasn't that he disputed his mother's version, but you couldn't take everything she said as the literal truth. He heard the small tweaks each time she told the story. In her renderings, Jonah was the villain for leaving—*Out of the blue! For no reason at all!*—but Nate understood that his mother was hardly objective. He didn't have to be getting divorced to understand that rarely did you know what went on between two people; there were always two sides, and it just depended on whose you were willing to believe. He wouldn't say it outright, but he was certain that if Hailey were the one who'd left, Sherry would still only see her side. He would also never say this, because he didn't want Hailey to think he was disloyal, but he almost felt bad for the guy. He and Jonah had little in common, yet if, in some alternate universe, he inexplicably found himself unhappily married, he would surely employ drastic measures to free himself.

He'd only met Jonah a few times before the wedding, and as far as he was concerned, Jonah was no worse than a lot of guys Hailey could have married. He seemed a little aloof, a little arrogant, but what struck him most was how intently Hailey tried to please him. Maybe they were a good match because Jonah seemed to get off on how adoring Hailey was, how she treated every word he said like it was a perfectly formed nugget of gold. But Nate missed how funny and relaxed Hailey could be—though rarely irreverent herself, she always laughed when he was. Everyone talked about how nice Hailey was, but he understood that some of it was due to her willingness to bend to what others thought. It was hardly a mystery why she'd been drawn to how domineering Jonah seemed to be. For all he knew, this was her attempt to get out from under her mother's control. Frying pan, fire, whatever the expression was. A few months before the wedding, she came to him upset after a fight with Jonah, and he should have asked her if she was sure, very, very sure; he should have reminded her that, yes, everything could be undone, but it always left scars. Instead, afraid of upsetting her, all he did was joke about how it wasn't too late to run. Over the years there were other times when he heard the sadness in her voice, and if he pressed, she sometimes confided that things were hard with Jonah. "I think he's disappointed in who I turned out to be," she once said. "You know that you don't have to put up with being treated that way," he said as gently as he could. But apparently that was too much because she quickly backtracked, her voice taking on a higher pitch as she claimed it wasn't a big deal and she was probably overreacting and it was all going to be fine. You couldn't make someone see what they didn't want to, but at the very least he should have reminded her that he would stand by her no matter what.

It was one more failing for which he bore the blame. He couldn't undo the past, but he could ensure that Hailey never doubted that he would stand by her in the future. He would let her know that she could call him any time, day or night. He would fly to Binghamton and spend weekends with her so she wouldn't have to be alone. He and Hailey often joked about his fear of commitment, but she was the one person for whom he would always be there.

While Nate was talking to Sherry and Tara, Solomon had come out of an exam room and was quietly watching them.

"Did you see this? Nate is in it, for the first time!" Sherry said, holding up the magazine.

As Sol glanced at the picture, Nate watched him hopefully. Apparently he was never going to outgrow the desire to be patted on the head and told he was doing a great job.

"Congratulations," Sol said blandly.

And that was all. For a moment, Nate was immobilized, then mortified. He glanced at his mother, whose smile hadn't wavered. Tara was watching him closely, trying to gauge his reaction.

"It's not a big deal," Nate said and grabbed the charts. "Back to work."

In the exam room, Nate had a new patient, here for a routine skin check, but also to inquire about the spidery red lines on the side of her nose and the papery layers of skin under her eyes. If he waited long enough, all his patients eventually confessed something about their skin that bothered them: wrinkles or brown spots or oversized moles, patches of scaly skin, red trail maps of broken blood vessels, or legs with varicose veins like someone had marked them in ink.

"In a few months, I'm going to offer a laser procedure that will make these disappear. You're going to look so young your own husband isn't going to recognize you," Nate promised, and his patient gazed at him as if he possessed a magician's powers. He wasn't going to deny it. He got a high from all the love. With the right tool, he could fix anything.

After a day of seeing patients, all Solomon wanted was to be left alone. But just as he was starting to relax, Nate walked into his office and sat down in the chair across from his desk.

"I have something to show you," Nate said.

With an air of grandiosity, Nate pulled out a report he'd prepared, with charts and figures showing what it would take to expand the practice. As Sol glanced at the pages, Nate looked at him expectantly, acting like he'd toiled for weeks, when in all likelihood he'd probably spent a few hours. Nate had on light blue scrubs, the neck dipping low enough that the hair on his chest was visible. It bothered him that Nate wore scrubs to the office every day, intent on giving the impression that he'd just come from the operating room, instead of what was likely the truth: he was too lazy to put on dress pants and a tie. It was the same annoyance he felt when Nate gave lavish holiday gifts to everyone in the office or issued impromptu invitations to take all the nurses out for dinner or acted like the patients were his best friends.

"We could either start slowly and hope word gets out, or we could make a big splash. I've already priced the new equipment," Nate said and leaned forward to show him where he'd listed the amounts.

Sol feigned interest, but he had no intention of changing the direction of his practice just because Nate wanted to. Earlier in the day, when he congratulated Nate on being included in the Best Doctors list, he felt his customary mix of caution and irritation. Sherry would admit nothing negative into her view of Nate, but he couldn't forget how Nate had always kept them on edge. Even this many years later, it was hard not to remember all the times they'd been called by the school principal and informed that Nate had been kicked out of class for clowning around or for orchestrating a coup against a substitute teacher. Or to think about the time Nate crashed Sol's brand-new car, which he wasn't supposed to be driving. Or the time he threw an unsanctioned party with at least a hundred kids that ended with the patio furniture floating in the pool and the neighbors calling the police. "Nate said he didn't mean for it to get so out of hand. The only reason he invited so many kids was because he didn't want to leave anyone out," Sherry explained, in line with her perpetual claim that Nate never intended to cause harm. Maybe so, but Sol would never have dreamed of acting so irresponsibly when he was younger. Even if he had the inclination, he didn't have the luxury of making so many mistakes.

Solomon set the pages down. "This isn't the direction I want to go in."

"Do you know how many patients we lose every week because we don't offer cosmetic services? Has Tara told you about all the people who've called?" Nate asked.

"Somehow I've managed to keep the practice running all these years without your help," Solomon said.

"You're not even going to consider it? It would be a real service for our patients, and do you not understand how lucrative it could be?" Nate argued—as if *no* were a word he'd never heard before.

"I understand perfectly. I just see it differently," Sol said, but that wasn't enough to quiet Nate's protests. If Sherry were here, she would try to persuade him to let Nate do what he wanted. She would take his enthusiasm as reason enough to say yes. Her method of parenting was a world away from how he'd grown up, with no one to hand him anything. Like Sherry, he was an only child, and nothing came easy for his family. His mother was a quiet, hardworking woman. His father worked long hours in a butcher shop off Blue Hill Avenue in the Boston neighborhood of Mattapan. The store belonged to his father's older brother, and his father was resentful that he didn't have something of his own. Because his anger needed a place to go, he berated Sol for any perceived infraction. Sometimes, when he decided that Sol had behaved particularly egregiously, he rose from his chair and reached for his belt. His father died the summer before Sol started high school, and Sol obligingly went to synagogue every day before school and recited the kaddish, but after the year was up, he wanted nothing to do with his parents' notions of God; he had no use for ritual or prayer. He believed in being self-sufficient. He believed in hard work. The only way to get ahead was to be smarter and more determined than everyone else. Sometimes he took the T into Cambridge and walked through Harvard Yard, and when he got home, he worked even harder. He didn't stop until he was admitted into the Harvard class of 1968. He worked his way through college, dependent on no one. He worked his way through medical school too. When he met Sherry, it was one of the few nights he allowed himself time off from his studies. He was shy when he asked her out, but on their first date—at Jack and Marion's deli in Brookline, where they ate oversized corned beef sandwiches and shared a banana split for dessert—he recognized right away that they complemented each other. She was outgoing and vivacious, he studious and quiet, but they came from similar backgrounds—the fact that neither of them had siblings had felt like the most intimate of discoveries. She told him how she was about to leave for college, at Barnard in New York, and how hard she had worked to get in. She confided that her mother was quick with criticism and only saw the worst in her. He revealed little, but enough to make clear that he too didn't wish to replicate the family he'd come from. The fact that she was leaving for

Barnard didn't dissuade him. On that first night, he understood that they could build a life together.

When Nate was born, Sol held his son for the first time, and the rush of love he experienced felt like a rebuke to his own father. Sherry assumed he would want to name his son after his father, but Sol decided against it. He didn't want his child to be saddled, or to have his own experience of being a father interlaced with how it felt to be a son. Solomon never wanted any of his children to feel as alone as he had; yet in giving them so much, he and Sherry had also taken something away. His own children would never arrive at the realization that they only had themselves to rely on.

Though Solomon planned to work for another hour, his exhaustion overtook him. Nate's report was still on his desk and he looked at it again. All those colored pie charts, all those eager graphs. It wasn't just that he thought Nate didn't have the discipline to follow through on his ideas. He sensed that Nate was trying to usurp all that he'd worked to build. This might indeed be the direction in which the rest of the field was shifting, but Sol was content to stand alone.

Holding the paper, Sol felt a weakness in his hand. Apparently even the thought of Nate trying to expand the practice undid him. He stood up, ready to go home, but had the same sensation that his legs couldn't quite support him. He grabbed his desk, but as quickly as it had come upon him, the feeling passed. If he were to tell Sherry about it, she would worry, but he assumed that his unsteadiness was due to the stress of the past few months, in which Hailey's divorce had become their main topic of conversation. When Sherry was upset, it was hard for her to stop talking—even when he agreed with her, he had little patience for discussions that went in circles. He preferred to rationally consider the possible courses of action, then make a decision about what to do.

Sol began the drive home, in this city where he'd lived for thirty-five years but still didn't feel like his own. From the car window, he should be seeing autumn foliage, but instead there were palm trees and endless, excessive green. As manicured as it was, sometimes it seemed like a matter of time before an act of nature intervened and it all reverted to swamp. When they'd first moved to Florida, he'd assumed that, sooner or later, the right opportunity would arise and they'd move back to Boston, where he'd spent his time entirely absorbed in his lab. His area of research focused on skin cancer cells, and the way two separate factors were required to cause a malignancy. The two-hit theory had been developed by other scientists, and his work was understanding how it applied to melanoma. Two graduate students worked with him, isolating the mechanisms with which a second hit caused a cell to become malignant. Every day, he held out the hope of a discovery. In the lab, he lost track of what time it was, what day. Sherry claimed that when he came home, he looked like a captive stepping out of a dark room, and she wasn't wrong, except he'd hardly been held against his will.

After years of work, Sol finally reached a breakthrough. Ready to publish, he offered to list his department chair as the last author as a courtesy. On the day the paper was submitted, there was a blizzard, but Sol went to work after shoveling his way out. He was only there a few minutes when he learned that his department chair had sent out a press release highlighting Sol's discovery as his own. He gaped at the piece of paper in disbelief. He read it over, as if the words might rearrange themselves. But no, it was true. His work had been stolen. Somehow, Sol staggered outside and walked the miles home, the falling snow making it hard to see, but he needed the time to devise a response. He should have stayed out longer, because when he came inside, Nate was screaming, "Stampede" with Adam chasing him, screaming as well. "Why can't the two of you get along?" Sherry was yelling amid a slew of plastic animals scattered around the room. It was the sort of chaos he walked into countless times, but on this night, it felt intolerable.

"What's wrong with you?" Sol screamed at Nate.

At the sight of Sol's anger, Nate's expression became more determined. In most situations, Solomon was able to maintain his composure. He could sit calmly with Adam, who asked little of him, wanting only to read a book or play a game. With Sherry, he could walk away from a fight, choosing silence over argument. Only with Nate did he come out of the grip of his rational self.

"Please, stop fighting," Sherry begged.

"Apologize right now," Sol screamed at Nate, angrier than he should have been, but he was sick of Nate's determination to push him over the edge, and he was sick of how weak he had been in the face of his own father's rage and he was sick of how powerless he was at work.

His hand was raised in anger, but Sherry grabbed him. "You said you weren't going to be like your father, but you're exactly like him," she said.

He left the house and walked for an hour, hating himself for losing his temper. The strong knew how to contain themselves. Only the weak lost control. The next day, when he came home from work, he told Sherry he was taking two weeks off and they were going on vacation to Florida. They drove the whole way, twenty-two hours over three days, Solomon at the wheel for most of it, Sherry taking short stints so he could rest. Sherry and the boys played I Spy and searched for license plates from the farthest states, and she seemed so happy that he wished he'd done something like this sooner. In Miami Beach, they walked along the boardwalk to the Fontainebleau hotel, which Sherry had longed to visit ever since she'd seen pictures of it, newly refurbished, in *Travel & Leisure*. The neighborhood looked seedy, but even so, Sherry was thrilled to sit at a thatched-roof bar and sip piña coladas with pink paper umbrellas while the boys drank virgin strawberry daiquiris topped with maraschino cherries.

While they were there, Solomon got in touch with a former mentor who had a dermatology practice in North Miami Beach and he told

Solomon to let him know if he was ever interested in relocating. He didn't take it seriously because he never intended to leave Boston, but Sherry seized onto the idea. "Let's move to Miami," she said that day, and every day for months. A few months after their return, he received an invitation to a Harvard research symposium where his department chair was given an award for the work Sol had done. The department chair thanked all the members of the lab, but not Sol. Sitting in the audience, Sol remained perfectly still, his expression giving nothing away. Let everyone around him think that he was undisturbed. Anger was far more powerful when it was ice-cold.

When the program ended, Sol pushed his way through the crowd, ignoring his colleagues, who tried to talk to him. They were aware of what the chair had done, but none of them were willing to risk the potential repercussions of speaking up on his behalf. They might have claimed to be a team, but in times of actual duress, everyone looked out for himself. Sol went back to his office and shut the door, sitting alone at his desk for the rest of the afternoon as he contemplated what to do.

That night, he came home and announced, "I took a job in Miami."

For Sherry, it had been the fulfillment of a dream. They joked that she was a native species, but he knew that he belonged elsewhere. It was true, as Sherry liked to point out, that he made more money than he had in academic medicine and no longer had the pressure of research. These were consolation prizes, but not enough to erase the loss of what was stolen from him.

Sol was almost home when Hailey called. She and Sherry talked all the time, even more so since the divorce was underway, while he was usually put on at the end to say a quick hello. He assumed that Hailey knew he was there if she needed something, but they didn't have the same daily involvement.

"I met with my lawyer today and told her I want to move to West

Palm," Hailey said. "I've been talking to Mom about it, and she obviously thinks it's a great idea. And Nate thinks I might have some leverage because we never planned to be in Binghamton permanently."

When he'd overheard Sherry and Hailey discussing the possibility of her moving here, he immediately urged caution, mindful of how readily Sherry fixated on an idea, then came to see it as a done deal rather than a wish. For weeks, Sherry had been obsessing about Jonah hating her, revisiting slights that she'd previously ascribed to miscommunication. All the times Jonah didn't get on the phone to say hello. All the times Hailey said they couldn't come for a family occasion because Jonah had too much work. Most of all, the asides Jonah made with which she hesitantly laughed along, assuming they were intended in a loving way. At the time, Sol had reassured Sherry that she was overreacting, seeing animosity where there was none. For the most part, he had believed this to be true, but even more so, he hadn't wanted to listen to her perseverate. If he had acknowledged that, yes, Jonah did seem particularly prickly to her, that yes, he did seem intent on creating distance, he would have needed to entertain long, unwieldy conversations analyzing every interaction. And even with all the talk, Sherry wouldn't feel better; on the contrary their discussion would only make her hurt grow.

"Tell me what your lawyer said," Sol said to Hailey.

"She says it's rare for a judge to allow one parent to move out of state if the other parent contests it, but there are exceptions, and if I really want, I can fight for it and see what happens. But I wanted to know what you think," Hailey said, sounding small and scared. As a child, she had been eager to please, the one enlisted to deliver snacks to her brothers, to go along on the family outings that Sherry planned and that the boys protested. Sol's regret surged. Exhausted by the boys' fighting, he had been less engaged with Hailey than he should have been. It was all too easy to regard her as belonging solely in Sherry's domain.

"When do you have to make a decision?" he asked.

"There's a pretrial hearing in February. She said we can put forward the motion and see what the judge says. If it doesn't go well, we can always drop it."

"And how do you think Jonah will react?" he asked.

"Badly. He keeps saying there's no reason we have to fight, but that's only as long as I do everything he wants."

"He's going to have to accept that he can't get everything he wants—no one will," Sol said. Perhaps it was a matter of recognizing a shared character trait, but he understood that because Jonah was so sure of what he wanted, he had a much better chance of getting it. When he and Sherry first met Jonah, he was impressed that Hailey had chosen someone ambitious and serious. He understood that Hailey was a lot smarter than she gave herself credit for, and could do a lot of things if she discovered what she really cared about. He had assumed that she and Jonah were happy until, a few years earlier, when they'd succumbed to Sherry's pleas to come for Passover, though from the expression on Jonah's face—something between unease and distaste—it was clearly against his will. Sherry tried to act like they were having a great time, while Jonah kept to himself, claiming he needed to work, and Hailey nervously offered excuses for him. At the seder, which Sherry spent hours preparing, Jonah barely said a word, leaving the table before it was over. It was best when they focused on Maya, who toddled happily around the house, oblivious to any strain. The one thing they all had in common was their love for Maya.

On the final day of their visit, Sherry was in the pool with Maya, while Hailey and Jonah were in the living room. Sol was coming down the hallway when he heard what sounded like an argument. Hailey was speaking softly, so he could only hear Jonah's outraged response.

"Why are you so mad? I didn't say a word," Jonah was saying.

By then, Sol was right outside the door. He didn't intend to eavesdrop, but he couldn't bring himself to move.

"You know what I'm talking about," Hailey said.

"How long was I supposed to listen to that? Has she ever said one interesting thing in her entire life? I don't know how your father can stand it," Jonah continued.

Sol waited for Hailey to push back, but all she did was meekly protest that Jonah was being unfair. In the absence of Hailey's response, Sol's own inclination for restraint evaporated. He wanted to storm in and throw Jonah out of their house. He wanted to go outside to the pool, to Sherry, and wrap her in his arms. It might be easy for Jonah to locate Sherry's flaws, but Jonah had no idea how loyal she was, how dedicated. Sol had never met anyone in his life so committed to the ones she loved—if you were ever in need, she was the person you would want coming to your aid.

At the time, though, Sol only cleared his throat and walked into the room. Before Hailey rearranged her face, he saw her looking at Jonah with an unhappiness that bordered on desperation. Jonah, however, seemed oblivious or uninterested in her distress. Sol had a flash of insight. It wasn't just that Jonah didn't want to be in West Palm and not just that he didn't want to be part of their family. He bore the agitated, impatient air of someone who didn't want to be in the marriage. Sol felt a certainty that he couldn't shake. This marriage was not going to last.

Now, on the phone with Hailey, a surge of regret overtook him. It was easy to portray his distance as a noble dispassion, but there was cowardice laced in too. At the very least, he should have asked Hailey if she and Jonah were okay. It was so basic a question, yet at the time, it had seemed like a private matter into which he shouldn't intrude.

"We need to pick our battles carefully," Solomon advised Hailey now, starting to map out the best course of action. "But at the end of the day, a divorce is a negotiation, and if this is what you really want, then we'll fight for it."

It was too late for a lot of things, but it wasn't too late to become more involved.

MAINE, 2019

Every night I am pulled, moth to light, toward the screen.

Two weeks since I arrived in Maine. Five months since Jonah was killed. Maya is asleep in the bed next to me as I scour the news stories and blog posts that detail the timeline of the murder, his whereabouts and mine, the kind of gun that was used, the trajectory the bullet took. I read profiles of Jonah and of me and of my family, testimonials from friends and former friends, theories spun out by experts and strangers.

I watch an interview with Jonah's father, his face grooved with pain as he describes being notified by the police, his voice shaking as he talks about flying to Binghamton to identify the body of his child. As much as I want to look away, I force myself to take in his every word.

What if I were to call him and offer a confession?

What if I were to show up at his door, Maya in tow, and ask for shelter?

I take in the photos: Jonah smiling, on skis, no older than Maya is now; Jonah in his gown, graduating from Yale; Jonah at a reading when his book came out; Jonah carrying Maya in a hiking backpack, both of them with wide smiles, their resemblance striking. It feels merciful that I am present in none of the pictures, as though it might be possible to construct an alternate version of his life in which I don't exist.

I read about other cases deemed similar: the cardiac surgeon in

Virginia whose wife was found strangled in the pond behind his house. The woman who supposedly hired someone to kill her husband, then two weeks later, posted pictures of herself on vacation with her boyfriend. The mother in Nevada who ran her husband over in the grocery store parking lot, her son in the car beside her.

"What's there to understand? Obviously he's a psychopath," says a comment under the article about the surgeon.

I read about a mother in California who went missing amid a contentious divorce. Despite the ex-husband's ardent disavowals, no other possible reason for her disappearance seemed to exist.

I try to imagine each of them, the victims of course, but the perpetrators most of all. Does doing so, I wonder, implicate me further? Is it better to remain safely inside the company of those who believe *Not us, never us*?

I read about a book called *The Murderer Next Door*, which claims that 84 percent of women and 91 percent of men have, at one point in their lives, fantasized about committing a murder.

I wonder about all those who admit to having harbored such a fantasy. Is the gap between imagining such a deed and actually doing it enormously large or immeasurably small?

In the Virginia case, the surgeon, who by all accounts had been a kind, reasonable man with no known history of violence, confessed to strangling his wife, then filling her pockets with rocks before dumping her body into the pond.

Was there a moment, I wonder, when he was shocked at what he was capable of? When his hands were wrapped around his wife's neck, did he feel like he was watching himself from a distant vantage point? Was there any relief, I wonder, in confessing? Did telling the truth ease his memory of the desperation on her face as she struggled to get free? Having said the words out loud, was he any less haunted by the way her dead body must have sunk under the surface of the water?

"Clearly he fooled everyone," says one of the comments.

"He just snapped," says another.

I want to add my own thoughts, but I don't dare. Privately, I wonder what mysteries in these commenters' own lives can never be solved.

In the California case, a few days passed with no sign of the wife. Then news leaked that drops of blood had been discovered in the husband's car. With his arrest imminent, the husband tried to hang himself. He was rushed to the hospital, where he eventually died.

"His death should in no way be considered a confession," said the man's lawyer. On the same day, the husband's family issued a statement: "We mourn the loss of our devoted son, brother, and father. He was never a murderer. In the rush to judgment, he never had a chance to tell his side of the story."

"Bad people get what's coming to them. He'll pay for what he did, if not in this world, then in hell," read the first comment.

"What a shame. I would have liked to see the asshole fry," said another.

It's late and I should sleep, but I return repeatedly to the scene of the crime. I search until I come upon a simulated reconstruction that a local Binghamton station ran on the three-month anniversary of Jonah's murder.

After checking that Maya is still asleep, I put on my headphones and hit play.

In sepia tones, with a hazy filter, there is a shot of the Binghamton campus, with its brick and glass buildings, its green clock tower. The camera follows a man walking from a building, carrying a small stack of books. The man who plays Jonah has the same black hair and slight build, though he's at least five years too young. In the video, this Jonah waves to students as he walks across the campus. Once he gets into his car, foreboding music begins to play. There is a faint thumping sound, like the beating of a heart.

Though it's not real footage, my body starts to shake, and to calm myself, I dig my nails into my arm, indenting small half-moons into my skin. I hit pause, but all that does is freeze a close-up of Jonah's face on my computer screen.

The pretend Jonah drives down a small street, singing along to the song on the radio—which he would never do—then checks his phone as he waits in traffic—which he would often do. The more I look at him, the more I realize how he diverges from the actual Jonah: Jonah's hair was thicker and his walk was never that languid. But even so, as I watch the re-creation, Jonah is in this room with me, more real than he has been in months: not just the Jonah of the divorce, but the long-ago Jonah whom I loved.

The Jonah the night we first met.

The Jonah I kissed, my body leaning hungrily toward his, with no idea how any of this would end.

Jonah fills my mind. Like being in a hall of mirrors, in any direction, there he is.

Before, it was impossible to imagine any of this from Jonah's perspective, but now I force myself to do so, even though it feels like turning my mind inside out, like forcing my limbs into pretzeled contortions.

How, I wonder, would Jonah tell the story of what happened between us? Would he start with what it was like to wake up beside someone—me—and feel the growing certainty that this was not where he wanted to be? Would he describe what it was like to try to dredge up a disappearing love?

Who would I, my family, become in his rendering? Unrecognizable, surely, to ourselves. Our versions would have little in common, except for the uncanny presence of a child named Maya.

In the video, Jonah pulls into the driveway. The beating heart grows louder as he walks to the front door, unaware of the white car parked across the street.

Don't do it, I want to scream to him, to all of us.

As if this were an ordinary day, Jonah unlocks the door and goes inside. A few moments later, on the screen, a hazy blurred figure wearing jeans and a dark gray shirt darts from the parked car and knocks on the door.

There is a pause. Maybe Jonah won't come to the door. Maybe he will barricade himself inside, or escape out the back. But no, there he is. In an instant, his relaxed demeanor vanishes and his eyes widen in alarm.

I try to envision when Jonah first saw the gun, when the shot was fired, when the bullet pierced his body. In the moments before he died, did he have any flash of awareness—that one instant divided into a hundred smaller instants? What was he thinking about on that final drive home? What were the last words he said to Maya? What hope, if any, might he have harbored that we would eventually find a way to get along? What fear besieged him when he was filing motions, when we were screaming at each other on his front lawn—that Maya would be taken from him? Did he have the same nightmares as I did, of her being snatched from his arms, of her perched in a small boat while a current whisked her away?

After Jonah answers the door, the camera shakes. The screen goes black, but we hear the gunshot.

The scream comes not from my computer but from Maya beside me. I slam shut the laptop. Maya is in the grip of a night terror. Her eyes are open but she's caught in the state between asleep and awake.

She has been having these night terrors since Jonah died. The first time I'd heard her cry out in the middle of the night, we were still in Binghamton, where I too felt trapped inside a nightmare from which there was no waking. I'd sprinted to her, afraid that the same person who killed Jonah had returned to harm her as well. When I saw her thrashing, her eyes open but still unreachable, I'd thought she was having a seizure.

"No. Please, no," Maya is saying now, pleading with someone who exists only in her mind.

"Can you see me? I'm right here, Maya," I say.

But she neither wakes nor falls into a deeper sleep, and before I can stop her, she gets out of bed and runs around the room, screaming. I reach for her and gently shake her, but there is no way to rescue her. Her face is ghostly pale. Her eyes are panic-stricken circles.

"It's Mommy, I'm here," I repeat, wishing I could transform my words into an outstretched arm that will guide her to safety.

"No," she whimpers.

I worry that the images on my screen have seeped into her dreams. I worry that she's running from me.

I kiss her hair, which is clammy with sweat. As I wrap her in a hug, I feel the dampness of her pajamas and realize that she has wet herself. She struggles and flails, but I gently restrain her until her resistance gives way and the weight of her body leans into mine.

"It's okay," I whisper as I walk her to the bathroom, as I change her into clean underwear and pajamas. "You're safe."

We return to the bedroom, where I change the wet sheets, then sit on the bed with her and rock her in my arms. Slowly, her body relents. Her breathing slows and she falls back to sleep. In the morning she will remember none of this. She will wake, eager to play with the dogs.

The realization hits me again, again. There will come a time when Maya will want to know what happened to her father. As much as I'll want to protect her—as much as I'll want to protect myself—I silently vow that I will always tell her the truth.

Outside our bedroom, Adam's footsteps creak on the wooden floorboards and he knocks lightly on the door. When I open it, he is standing there, Daisy dutifully by his side.

I'm surprised to see him. In the time that we've been here, Adam has left us largely to ourselves—a few words of greeting in the morning, practical discussions about meals, polite inquiries as to whether we need anything, but he has avoided prolonged conversation. When he's not hiking with the dogs or working as a trainer in town, he takes refuge in his bedroom. I haven't heard him on the phone even once or make reference to a friend, to anyone. Except for the company of the dogs, he seems content to be alone.

"Maya had a night terror," I explain.

"Is she okay? It sounded pretty bad," he says.

"She's been having them since Jonah died," I say. "She's not really awake and thinks someone is chasing her."

"I'm glad she's okay," he says as we both turn to look at her, peacefully asleep under the blankets.

"You didn't know her before, but she's more relaxed here than she's been in a long time. When we were home—"

At that word, Adam winces and I wish I could take it back, pretend that it doesn't exist anymore. Instead of looking at Adam, I glance down at Daisy, whose eyes meet mine. I know I'm ascribing human emotions to her, but I feel little doubt that some form of compassion is being offered.

"Are you sure it's okay that we're here?" I ask Adam. "I know how it must look."

Adam touches my hand and I flinch in surprise.

"You can stay as long as you want," he says.

Maybe it's the sight of Maya or maybe it's the distress on my face. Maybe he, for a moment, is remembering when we were kids. Whatever the reason, he meets my eye and I don't look away, wanting to keep him here for as long as I can. Even though every word I say to him feels like a risk, I hope that we might find a way to start anew.

Sherry was in the pool, swimming laps. It was January and the divorce was still all she could think about. Even when she was at work or with her friends, she was focused on Hailey. Every time her phone beeped, she jumped.

Just before she'd started to swim, she had called Hailey to check in. Sometimes when they talked, Hailey was in good spirits, but today, she had started to cry.

"I feel so alone," she said, calling right after dropping Maya off at Jonah's and driving back to an empty house.

"You're not alone. We're here for you," Sherry promised.

It was a lesson you learned so many times as a parent, and each time was as hard to accept as the last: there was no way to protect your child from pain.

Sherry swam to the far edge of the pool and touched the tile, then turned around. In vain, she tried to relax. It was unbelievable that for all these years, she had talked herself out of seeing what was in front of her. It would have been easier if Jonah were openly hostile. Instead of the second-guessing and the trying so hard, she could have talked to Jonah directly; she might have forged some kind of understanding. Now all she could do was worry. What terrible things had Jonah said to Hailey about her? And what did Hailey say in return? Did she defend her or—the very thought scalded her with shame—did she agree?

Sherry swam faster. She wanted to believe that she had done nothing to deserve Jonah's hatred, which now felt like a glaring light shining on her, exposing only her worst parts. Had she wanted too much, had she tried too hard, had she come across as demanding when all she meant was to offer her love? When she felt Jonah pulling away, taking Hailey and Maya along with him, she had believed that if he saw the degree of her love, he would relent. In the face of his refusal, she held on more tightly—because how could she have just allowed them to slip away?

With each stroke, she consoled herself. She didn't intend to cause harm. She had tried her best. She had wanted simply to be close. With each stroke, it became clearer. Yes, there were things she could have done differently, but Jonah had no interest in being part of their family. He wanted Hailey all to himself. He would have hated her no matter what she did.

As Sherry reached the end of the pool and turned around, she felt an easing in her mind. She didn't have to see herself through Jonah's eyes. She didn't have to allow Jonah to encroach into her day. What she needed—what they all needed—was something to look forward to. As soon as the divorce was over, they could go on a celebratory trip, maybe even re-create the Grand Canyon vacation they'd taken when the kids were young, except this time, it would be Nate, Hailey, and Maya in the back seat. She'd never been out west before that trip and always longed for them to be a family who took vacations together. Neither she nor Sol had those opportunities growing up, but she was determined to give her children more than she'd had. She only hoped that they appreciated it. So many times she'd listened to Nate tell the story of that vacation: "We traveled across the country to spend twenty minutes looking at a big hole," he'd say in search of a laugh, but that captured nothing of how she'd experienced it. Kids made a point of claiming that you didn't know them, but the truth was that they had no idea who you really were, either. They'd stood beside her, sweaty and cranky and more enamored by the prospect of popsicles than any great wonder of the world, oblivious to how enraptured she was by the majestic beauty before her; unaware that she was nearly overcome with gratitude that she could bring her family here to witness it.

Sherry had one more lap to go. Nearly out of breath, she swam the last stretch, her arms like oars, her body perfectly aligned. This hard time would soon end. With the force of her love, she would propel them forward.

Sherry was sitting in the chaise lounge, drying in the sun, when the sliding glass door opened and Solomon came outside.

"Why are you home?" Sherry asked in surprise. While she didn't go into the office on Fridays, Sol almost never took a day off, which was a point of contention. For so many years, he put his job first, and she went along with it, but now that Nate was available to cover for him, it was time to cut back.

"I need to tell you something," he said.

At the distress on his face, her mind flooded with possibilities. Though it was hot out, she shivered and had the urge to dive back into the water, to forestall whatever he was about to say.

"This is going to be hard to hear, but I've been to a neurologist. After a series of tests, he believes I have Parkinson's," Solomon said.

Sherry jumped up and in a state of disbelief, she rushed to hug him.

Sol told her that he'd noticed that his right hand sometimes shook, but there were many possible explanations. In the past month, he'd experienced other symptoms, primarily a debilitating exhaustion that made it difficult to move. Sherry thought back. A few times, she'd wondered if his hand was trembling, but she'd pushed away the possibility that anything was seriously wrong. It was because of the divorce, because they were stressed.

"When did you find this out?" she asked.

"A few days ago," he admitted.

Every evening this week, they ate dinner together. Every morning, he woke beside her and didn't say a word. She had so many things she wanted to ask, but couldn't formulate any of it into specific questions.

"I don't want anyone else to know yet," he said.

"How can we not tell the kids?" she exclaimed, though she wasn't surprised. Sol preferred to handle anything painful on his own, while in a moment like this, all she wanted to do was pull people toward her so she wouldn't have to bear bad news alone.

"They'll have to know soon enough, but not yet. For now, can you tell Tara that I need to move the patients for Monday and Tuesday? You can say I need a few days off," he said.

He went upstairs to their bedroom, and though she would have once implored him to share what he was feeling, she let him go. It was one of the truths of her marriage, maybe any marriage, that she'd long ago learned to accept. Just because you spent your life with someone didn't mean you knew them entirely. There would always be aspects of him she couldn't understand.

They were supposed to be meeting her friends Judy and Eleanor and their husbands for dinner that evening, and steadying herself, Sherry called them to say that Sol was coming down with a stomach bug. She wouldn't have expected to easily be able to hide something so awful from them—it was an old argument between Sol and her that she didn't possess the ability to keep any news to herself. Maybe that was true in the past, but on the phone now, she did as Sol asked. If her friends heard a quiver in her voice, they were both nice enough not to mention it. They asked her only if she needed anything, said that they hoped Sol felt better soon. Afraid that their kindness would compel her to say more, she rushed off the phone and called Tara. Cheerfully, she said that Sol needed to take a little time off and asked her to move the nonurgent patients and schedule Nate to see the ones who couldn't wait.

"Is everything okay?" Tara asked, aware that Sol rarely missed a day.

Sherry's voice cracked, and she wished she could confide in Tara. In the five years that Tara had been working in the office, Sherry had grown accustomed to telling her everything. She often said that Tara was like family, but in a moment like this, there was an enormous difference between being like family and being family.

"There's nothing to worry about," Sherry said.

Sherry went upstairs. Sol was lying on top of the blankets in their bedroom. His eyes were closed, but she didn't think he was asleep. She knew him better than anyone, yet she was afraid to say the wrong thing. The only sentiment she could think of, which also might be wrong, was to tell him how much she loved him. It was impossible to envision her life separate from his. She didn't know how she could exist in his absence. If he were gone, surely she would grow smaller and smaller until one day she disappeared altogether. When they first met, she had just graduated from high school and was awarded a scholarship to Barnard. She had worked feverishly, locking herself in her tiny bedroom to study. She prided herself on not overlooking a single assignment or turning in a paper without first scrutinizing it for errors. Every A she received felt like a promise. At the start of her senior year, her English teacher stopped her in the hallway and asked what she was doing the following year. She was considering Lesley, a school close to home and within her reach, but the teacher handed her a glossy pamphlet for Barnard. She applied without telling her parents and was accepted with a scholarship. When she finally told her mother, she was stunned, then hurt that Sherry wanted to go so far from home. All these years later, Sherry still remembered how, if she had ever dared to want too much, her mother, who suffered from her own pain and hardships, managed to make her feel bad.

A month before Sherry was supposed to leave for Barnard, she agreed to go on a date with Solomon. He seemed so steady, so responsible, already an adult, and in his presence, she had the feeling that she would always be taken care of. Swept up after just a few weeks of dating, she had thought about backing out of Barnard, but he encouraged her to go and promised to come every week to see her.

She'd worked tirelessly to get to Barnard, but once she was there, the classes were harder than she'd anticipated. She was shy around the other girls, who seemed so worldly. As promised, Sol visited every weekend—his car pulled up in front of the wrought-iron gate, and in his presence she was returned to herself, full of energy and life. They went to Broadway shows and to visit his friend at the Einstein College of Medicine in the Bronx who was married with a six-month-old baby boy. The wife served brisket on their white wedding china and seemed more of an adult than the girls in school who, even with their sophistication, seemed just that, girls. The baby was asleep in the bedroom, but as they were about to eat the red velvet cake the wife made for dessert, he woke up and she nursed him right at the table. At the sight of this mother giving her child what he needed, Sherry felt certain that nothing anyone did would ever matter more. She decided that instead of staying at Barnard the following year, she would transfer to Lesley. That night, in Sol's car in front of the Barnard gates, he took a small box from his pocket and showed her the diamond engagement ring he'd bought and softly asked her to marry him; even back then he had never been one for grand displays of love. "I want to give you a beautiful life," he told her when she accepted his proposal, and she allowed herself to believe that life was a gift you could wrap up and hand someone.

Sol had fallen asleep as Sherry lay beside him now. Even though she risked waking him, she ran her hand gently across his face, then slipped downstairs with her cell phone. To calm herself, she scrolled through pictures on her phone of Maya in the pool and at ballet class. She enlarged them to take in her expression, then made them smaller to see all of her.

The house felt unbearably empty. Before she met Sol, she so often felt lonely—in such a vastly populated world, there were so few people who would drop everything and come to her in a moment of need. Was this the kind of alone she would one day face every night? She wished she had something to pray to, a consoling belief to which she could attach herself. When the kids were young, Hailey in elementary school, the boys in middle school, she'd insisted that they have Shabbat dinner together, one of the few vestiges of her upbringing she wanted to retain. Solomon had no interest in anything to do with religion, and sometimes she could feel him trying to steer the kids toward his disdain. But even if she didn't quite believe, she still hoped that a spirit of peace and calm might spread over them—she hoped it might give her the feeling that she belonged to something beyond herself. She filled small silver cups with grape juice, one for each of them, and before they all sat down, she lit the candles, reciting not the specified prayers but her own private one, that her children be protected, that her family be safe. Eventually it was too hard to cordon off those nights, when there were tennis tournaments and dance recitals, then tutors and friends and more and more. But if she had stuck with it, would she feel something other than this dark void, with nothing to keep her or catch her?

The news of Sol's illness was too heavy to bear on her own. She felt a yearning to call Adam and tell him the bad news, but he wouldn't answer and then she would feel even more alone. She could call Hailey, but it was late and she didn't want to upset her. The divorce hearing at which she would present the petition to relocate was a few weeks away. They were so close to this being over, and she didn't want Hailey to worry about anything else.

She decided to call Nate. She felt a pang of guilt, but also a growing certainty that Nate needed to know. In recent months, there had been a newfound tension in the office as Nate became intent on asserting his independence. In response, Sol more forcefully put down any suggestion

Nate made, then retreated, as he always had, into his own office. Especially now, she didn't want Nate working in the office to become one more failed attempt for them to get along. She didn't want to live with the possibility that in trying to help them become closer, she had caused the opposite to occur.

Nate didn't answer when she called, but he rarely did the first time.

"What's up?" he said on her second attempt, his words nearly drowned out by the high pitch of voices and music. It was Friday night and he could be anywhere.

"I just wanted to see how you're doing," she said.

"What's the matter?" He must have sensed the alarm hiding in her voice because the background noise quieted.

"It's Dad," she said and felt the impulse to turn back, but it was already too late. "I'm not supposed to say anything, so please don't tell him I told you, but he's sick."

"What is it?" he asked.

"He has Parkinson's." Even as she said the words, she was still in a state of disbelief. She had the feeling that, inexplicably, she was making this up. Surely Nate would admonish her that there was no way this was true.

"I'm on my way."

When Nate came into the house twenty minutes later, Sherry burst into tears. Usually she hated the speed at which he drove, but now she was thankful not to endure an extra minute alone. She was so accustomed to Nate wearing scrubs all the time that it was surprising to see him dressed in nice jeans and a white button-down shirt, left open at the neck. She hugged him and felt a renewed gratitude that she got to be with him almost every day.

"He's been going to a neurologist and didn't say a word to anyone. I can't believe he preferred to deal with this alone," Sherry told Nate once they were seated at the kitchen table. She lowered her voice, even though Sol was upstairs, asleep.

"Tell me exactly what he told you," Nate said, and she relayed what little information Solomon had given, each word stoking her guilt that she was breaking Sol's confidence.

"Have you noticed anything?" she asked.

"Not really," Nate said. "A few months ago, Tara asked me if anything was wrong with Dad, and once I was looking for it, I did notice a little tremor, but it didn't seem like a big deal."

"I was worried that he seemed unusually tired, but I thought it was because there's been so much going on," she said. "I should have realized something was wrong."

"You couldn't have known what it was. If anything, I should have been the one to see it," he said.

"I'm not going to tell Hailey yet. I wasn't supposed to tell you, but I couldn't hold it in," she said.

"It's okay. I know Dad is so private about everything, but how long do you think you could have hidden this from me?" Nate asked.

"Please don't tell him I told you. I don't want him to be mad at me, especially now."

"I won't say anything, but eventually we're going to have to talk about it. This is not the kind of thing you can keep secret in the long term."

"I know. We will, I promise. But in the meantime can you just . . ." She didn't say it outright because she didn't want to risk angering Nate, but she hoped that he would hear her silent plea to go easy on Sol, to tread more lightly. Underneath Nate's need to push back against any rule, there were still deep wells of loyalty. She trusted that he loved Sol, he loved them all.

She started to cry and Nate hugged her. He was her child, yet she was never so in need of his comfort. When he was a teenager, he was intent on evading her questions about where he was going and when he would be back. Yet there were times when she and Nate, both night owls, were the only ones awake and, miraculously, he wanted to talk. She'd make him a grilled cheese or a steak on the grill and, at the same table where they sat now, she'd ask about his friends and his tennis games and revel in each answer he was willing to give. She wouldn't push too hard for fear of shutting him down—sometimes it felt like trying to assemble a complex sentence in a language she barely spoke. She wanted so badly to say the right thing.

"What are we going to do?" she asked.

"From what I know, this can progress a bunch of different ways. There are all kinds of new treatments, but he's going to need some more tests before we jump to conclusions. I can look into some things in the morning," he said.

Already Nate was taking charge, just as Sol would have, were the situation different. It was true that Sol and Nate fought, but it was also true that the two of them were so much alike.

"You know I'm going to be here for you and Dad," Nate said.

Despite what Sol had requested of her, she had done the right thing in telling Nate. Solitude could be a hard habit to break, but in a crisis, all you could do was summon those you loved and hope that there might be safety in numbers.

On a playground in Binghamton, Hailey was watching Maya while reading an email from her lawyer detailing her latest offenses. She had been late to drop off Maya at Jonah's house. She had not allowed Jonah to FaceTime sufficiently with Maya when he wasn't with her. She had failed, twice, to include Bunbun, Maya's favorite stuffed animal, in what she packed for Maya's weekends with Jonah, which was a necessary requirement for Maya to fall asleep.

Hailey waved to Maya as she climbed up the slide. Bundled in her coat and scarf, Hailey shivered. It was unseasonably warm for the beginning of February, which was why so many kids were here, but to her, it felt frigid. "Once a Florida girl, always a Florida girl," her mother liked to quip, and she was starting to agree. Hailey tried to concentrate on Maya, but she was drawn to her phone. Ever since Jonah learned that she wanted to move with Maya to Florida, they had entered a permanent state of battle. With the pretrial hearing a week away, Jonah fired off one missive after another to her, all written in a formal tone as if they were business adversaries or strangers. *I can only presume that you are on your way. Henceforth I will expect you to arrive at the agreed upon hour.* Before, in what felt like an entirely different era of her life, she had no idea how much of her time and attention the divorce would take up—everything in her life was divided in half, even her own mind.

Hailey's phone rang, as though, from miles away, her mother sensed that she needed bolstering.

"What's going on? What's happening?" Sherry asked, in search of the divorce update. Even if Hailey didn't feel like talking about it, she ended up sharing every detail. She told her mother the details of the temporary parenting agreement they were trying to negotiate, arguing about the exact time that Maya would change hands because neither of them wanted to relinquish a minute. Her lawyer often referenced stories of normal people who went a little crazy in the midst of a divorce, and Hailey wondered if she was at risk of becoming one of them. Some days, she could envision herself capitulating in order to keep the peace. And she could also envision herself saying no to every single thing Jonah asked—not just to the request before her, but to everything she'd ever ambivalently agreed to. In the meantime, the thirty-minute difference between their positions was costing thousands of dollars. Every time she got another bill from the lawyer, she felt sick. Her mother tried to allay her worry, assuring her that the divorce would be over before she knew it. Every morning, she texted Hailey an inspiring quote she found online about the importance of persevering. This past week, a package had arrived, a wood placard painted with the words *difficult roads lead to beautiful destinations*.

"I just heard from my lawyer about the fact that I was late bringing Maya over to Jonah's last week," Hailey told her mother now.

"Jonah can wait a few minutes."

"Apparently not."

"Please tell me he didn't send you another angry email," Sherry said.

She regularly forwarded Jonah's emails to her mother and to Nate, which was probably a mistake because Nate had started to imitate them. "I henceforth expect you to surrender the aforementioned bunny rabbit as mandated by our agreement," Nate would now text her. "I heretofore beseech you to comply with my every decree." When she was married, neither Nate nor Sherry said anything bad about Jonah, but she knew that they were just holding back. Now they enjoyed the freedom to say what they'd been thinking all along.

"Did you tell your lawyer? What did she say?" Sherry asked.

"She said there's not a lot I can do, but if I really wanted to, I could file a motion claiming he's harassing me," Hailey said as she watched Maya, who was now on the swing, expertly pumping and singing a song to herself.

"I think you should. We don't want Jonah to feel like he can intimidate you and get away with it. Remember, he's the one who wanted the divorce in the first place. You're allowed to fight for what you want."

"I am fighting," Hailey said. The idea to move home had initially been hers, but her mother had seized on it with such enthusiasm that it felt like she was the one who'd come up with it. As it had so many times growing up, it felt easier, almost, to cede to her mother's wishes than try to determine her own.

"I know, but please—don't let Jonah scare you into backing down," Sherry said. Her voice cracked, and immediately Hailey felt bad.

"You sound funny. Are you okay?" Hailey asked. For several weeks, her mother had sounded worn down, but when she asked, Sherry claimed that nothing was wrong. Usually Hailey could count on Nate to tell her what was really going on with their parents, but he acted like he hadn't noticed anything. It was like being a kid again, when she often felt purposefully kept in the dark—so many times, she heard her parents whispering in urgent, hushed tones, but as soon as they saw her, any sign of conflict was hidden.

"I'm fine," Sherry said.

Hailey's phone beeped, and her heart plummeted.

Please confirm that in accordance with our agreement,

you will arrive at my residence by 6 pm

She knew it was best not to respond, but couldn't help herself.

Are you actually turning Bunbun into a legal issue?

She could see that Jonah was typing, then stopping, probably calculating each word. He could complain to his lawyer all he wanted, but to save his life he couldn't pick Bunbun out of a lineup of other bunnies.

Perhaps you're not aware that in a custody

dispute, everything is a legal issue.

"Watch me," Maya screamed from the climbing structure.

"Good job!" Hailey called back. "Ten more minutes, okay?"

She put away her phone. The last thing she wanted was another fight—then she would spend the rest of the night parsing every word of every text. She had fifteen minutes to get to Jonah's. The calendar was now bisected with seemingly infinite lines. Now Maya had a small bag in which they passed her necessities back and forth. She had duplicates of some things. She referred to her mommy blanket and her daddy blanket, her mommy toothbrush and her daddy toothbrush—her world, down to the smallest of items, was divided.

Maya came running over, her coat stained with chocolate she'd eaten earlier in the day, but there was no time to do anything about it. Once Hailey was buckling Maya into the car, Maya's playful demeanor vanished. Hailey smiled, trying to act like everything was fine, but Maya had recently developed a seismographic ability to detect every shift in her mood. Hailey remembered all too well being a child able to read her mother's face. Even if she didn't know what was wrong, she'd felt the unease.

Hailey sped through the streets. She was going to be more or less on time, so long as no one was clocking her arrival with a stopwatch, which, she realized, Jonah probably was. But, *Oh my god. Bunbun.* She'd forgotten again. They were a few blocks from the house, and normally Hailey would keep going and hope Maya could survive the night without the bunny. But given the lawyer's missive, she turned around.

Running a few minutes late. Have to find Bunbun

With Maya, she hurried inside the house. Her parents had bought Jonah out of his half of the equity so that she could stay there. She felt bad taking the money from them when she was already taking so much, and she promised to pay them back one day. "It's fine. We'll figure it out," her mother assured her. "For now, you need stability. You want to be the place Maya thinks of as home."

"Maya, honey, can you remember where Bunbun is?" Hailey asked.

"He's hiding," Maya said.

Hailey crouched down to Maya's eye level. "Please, Maya. Don't you want Bunbun to come with you to Daddy's house?"

Maya turned away and wouldn't answer. For the first few years of Maya's life, Hailey had barely been apart from her for more than a few hours at a time. To pass a night without her had seemed impossible. Now Maya cried when she dropped her off at Jonah's, and once she was alone, Hailey cried too. On those nights, she heard the phantom cry of "Mommy?" She harbored the irrational fear that Maya might never come back.

Bunbun wasn't under the bed. He wasn't in the toy bin or in the closet. Hailey was on the brink of tears, but didn't want Maya to see. Finally, she opened the hamper and there he was. Hailey grabbed the bunny and hugged it in relief.

"Okay, we have Bunbun! Let's go," Hailey said.

"I'm hungry," Maya said.

Hailey grabbed a package of goldfish crackers and they were on their way. Jonah had moved a few streets over, to a ground-floor apartment carved out of a larger house. It was on a street she'd driven down countless times, but never imagined that it would come to feel like enemy territory.

She checked her phone to see if Jonah had texted again, but nothing yet. Maybe he hadn't noticed that she was late or maybe he was finally getting tired, as she was, of fighting.

Her relief was short-lived. When she pulled up, Jonah was standing in the doorway, glancing at his watch.

"I assume you brought everything," Jonah said as he stepped onto the porch. He was barefoot, even in this weather, and his pale, boyish feet felt like an intimacy she couldn't bear to see.

"It's all there," she said cheerfully and held up Maya's pink backpack.

Maya glanced warily from her to Jonah. When Hailey kissed Maya goodbye, she wouldn't look her in the eye. She gave a half wave and disappeared inside.

"You know I'm not trying to keep Bunbun from you," Hailey said to Jonah once the door closed and she was alone with him on the front porch.

In another world—in a different era—they would have laughed that such a sentence could be uttered. They would have looked at each other and at themselves and wondered who these strangers were.

"At this point, I wouldn't put anything past you," Jonah said.

Here was the man she'd once loved, the man she now hated. Depending on the angle, he could be either, sometimes both at once. He was wearing the gray sweatpants he often wore around the house, and a navy Yale sweatshirt she had washed and folded a hundred times that had a small hole under the arm and was fraying along the bottom edge.

"Jonah," she said. "Can we please stop? Why does it have to be like this?"

"I'm not the one who's escalated this into a legal battle. We could have settled this amicably."

"As long as I did everything you wanted," she said.

"There's no way I'm going to let you take Maya from me."

"I'm not trying to take her from you. I just don't want to live in this city where there's absolutely nothing for me."

"When do you think I would see her if you moved? She's my daughter too."

"You could also move to Florida."

"I have a job, or does that not matter to anyone in your family?" he said.

"I had a job in New York, remember?" she said.

"We both know that your mother is behind this," he said. "How many times have you said that she won't take no for an answer, that you're basically programmed to please her?"

Had she said those things? Not in those exact words, and never so angry, with all the love scraped away.

"This has nothing to do with my mother."

"Then who's paying for the protracted legal fight this is causing?"

"You know we said three years. Am I supposed to be trapped here forever?" she said.

"No matter how much money your parents throw at this, I will never agree to your moving Maya."

"I have a say in this too, or did that not occur to you? I only agreed to live here because I knew you would never listen to what I wanted."

I don't want to fight. I don't want to fight. She repeated that to herself, but her body felt too hot and her hands were starting to shake. It was so much safer to argue over text, with the illusion of distance and the ease of retreat.

From inside the house, Maya called for Jonah.

"I'll be there in a second!" he called back, as if he were in the midst of a friendly exchange. "Let me just say this. If you think your parents are going to control me, you are very wrong."

Despite her mother's certainty that she was almost at the end, it hit her again, again, again. Even when the divorce was over, it would never be over. Nearly half of Maya's life was going to take place away from her. She would always share the person she loved the most with the person she liked the least. Jonah might have left her, but she was still pinned to him.

"For our entire marriage, I did whatever you wanted and now I'm done," she said.

At home, Hailey looked around the house. In the fifteen minutes of searching for Bunbun, she'd created a mess. She started with Maya's room, gathering up her dirty clothes and throwing them into the washing machine. She made Maya's bed and lined up her small zoo of stuffed animals. At least when Maya came home, she would return to the semblance of an ordered world. Hailey went into the kitchen and began sorting through a pile of papers she'd left on the counter. She stopped when she came to a picture Maya drew at school, of a little girl with purple hair and outstretched arms, standing between two grown-ups, either pulling them toward each other or trying to keep them apart. At the sight of it, Hailey sank to the floor, suddenly exhausted. If she agreed to stay in Binghamton, at least the fighting would end. As hard as it might be, maybe she and Jonah could find a way to get along. Eventually Binghamton might feel like home. At the very least, she wouldn't exist in this state of constant battle and depletion. She wouldn't be one of the figures Maya drew, pulling so hard until they all came apart.

Hailey was washing the dishes when her father called. He had started to make a point of checking in every few days, for which she was grateful. She knew, in an abstract way, that her father was there for her, but when she was growing up, she rarely went to him when she had a problem. When he was in his study, it felt like he wasn't at home. She didn't know if there was a lock on that door, but it didn't matter because she never would have tried to enter.

"There's something I need to tell you, and I'm very sorry that it's not good news," Solomon said and told her about his diagnosis.

"Oh my god, Dad, are you serious? I'm so sorry," she said. She didn't understand how he could sound so calm, almost detached.

"I found out a few weeks ago. Obviously, it's not what any of us want to hear. I wasn't going to tell anyone until I had a better sense of how this might progress, but Mom told Nate, so I thought you should know too."

"I knew something was wrong. Mom hasn't sounded like herself lately, but she didn't tell me."

"I wanted to protect everyone for as long as possible, but now I need to focus on making sure you all have what you need."

"Should I come home? I could fly down in the morning."

"Get through the pretrial hearing next week and then you can come visit."

"I'll be there the minute it's over."

Her whole life, she'd had the luxury of knowing that her parents would be there for her. She knew, of course, that one day this would be reversed, but it never occurred to her that she might live far away when it did. Growing up, her mother's favorite saying was that they were a family who would do anything for each other. Nate liked to make fun of how she said it with such vehemence, as if they were under siege, and he proposed outlandish scenarios to determine if she really meant *anything*. Now Hailey felt the same urgency that she'd once heard in her mother's voice. She emailed her lawyer to say that she was ready for the pretrial hearing. Her family needed her. She was not going to change her mind.

Sherry wrapped her arms around Hailey and Maya as soon as they walked through the front door. Hailey tried to put on a brave front, but now that she was home for the weekend, Sherry could see the strain of the last few months carved into Hailey's face.

"We are going to have so much fun! And you won't have to worry about snow while you're here," Sherry said to Maya as she took her into the kitchen and gave her a plate of her favorite cookies, which she'd baked that afternoon. She'd asked Nate to pick Hailey and Maya up at the airport and now she had Nate carry their bags upstairs. Once they were settled in, she turned to Hailey for the news she'd been waiting for. The pretrial hearing had been that morning in Binghamton, a few hours before their flight. All day, Sherry had waited in agony to know what the judge had said, but she didn't call Hailey, afraid of bad news. It would be better to find out what happened once Hailey was home.

"The judge said it was unlikely that she would allow a move, unless I can show extenuating circumstances," Hailey said.

Trying to hide the crush of disappointment, Sherry reached for Hailey's hand. "We can still fight for this," Sherry assured her.

When Nate came back downstairs, she reminded him about the

small job she needed him to do, and asked him to go out to the car and bring in a large, wrapped picture.

"This is a two-person job," Nate said and recruited Hailey to help carry it into the dining room.

The wall had been bare since Sherry had taken down the family photograph from her sixtieth birthday that Jonah had ruined. For the past few months, she'd been unable to look at it without thinking about the fact that Jonah hated her. Every time she saw his red tie, she felt his mockery.

Sherry removed the brown paper, revealing the new-and-improved photograph. "It's perfect," she said.

In the picture, Sherry and Solomon, Nate, Hailey and Maya were all still there. In the spot where Jonah once stood, there was now a flowering plant.

"I can't believe you did this," Hailey said, looking over her shoulder to ensure that Maya was absorbed in her toys and unable to hear her.

"Hailey, your soon-to-be ex-husband has been downgraded to a hibiscus bush," Nate said. "I don't know how Jonah is going to react to this. I'm pretty sure his next book contract stipulates that he has to be featured as a more important plant."

"I wouldn't be sure he's ever going to finish another book. He's too busy fighting with Hailey," Sherry said as she studied the photo. The photographer had done an impeccable job. Except for the subtlest suggestion that Hailey was leaning into the plant, Jonah might never have existed.

"You better hope he never finishes, because I guarantee you that his next book is going to be all about our family," Nate said.

"Please tell me you don't think he'd really do that," Sherry said.

"Of course he would—he'll write whatever he wants and hope it upsets you," Nate said.

Surely Nate was joking, but it sounded exactly like the kind of thing Jonah might do.

As Nate was hanging the picture, the front door opened and Solomon came inside. Hailey hugged him, but if he was happy to see her, he barely showed it. Only Maya, who stopped playing and ran over to him, received a smile. Ever since Solomon's diagnosis, Sherry was keeping herself as busy as possible, researching second opinions and alternative treatments, holding on to anything that offered hope. One night, as they were getting ready for bed, she'd confessed to Sol that she'd told Nate about the diagnosis—she hated the heaviness of carrying a secret and the worry every time Nate acted uncharacteristically deferent to Sol in the office.

"I'm sorry. I was so afraid, and I couldn't keep it to myself," she admitted as they lay beside each other.

"I should have realized there was a reason Nate has been so well-behaved," he said, annoyed, but not unduly so. He understood that she hadn't intended this as a betrayal of his confidence, but had acted from a place of love.

"I still don't understand why you wouldn't want the kids to know," she said.

"I didn't want everyone to see me as sick," he said.

"I don't want to lose you," she whispered.

"I'm going to take care of everything," Sol assured her. Even if she knew it was a promise he could no longer make, she allowed herself to believe it was true.

"Did something happen at work?" Sherry whispered now to Nate when Solomon went upstairs to lie down before dinner. Over the past week, Sol's gait seemed slower, and he'd lost so much weight that his pants hung from him. Maybe these symptoms were present all along, but she'd chosen not to see them.

"It's not a big deal," Nate said. "All I did was lease some new equipment that was delivered today."

"I thought you were getting along better now that—" she said.

"I ordered it before I knew he was sick. And I was going to tell him about it. I was just waiting for the right moment. Obviously I didn't think he would be in the office today when it came."

"Can we at least have a nice dinner?" Sherry requested.

To her relief, Nate agreed. He went into the kitchen to unpack the bags of takeout she'd ordered, and she felt a renewed sense of gratitude. Though she never would have anticipated that Nate would be the child most present for her, she was growing dependent on him.

"Dinner is served," Nate called from the dining room. Sherry went upstairs to let Solomon know that they were eating, and he came to join them.

"I don't know what we would do without you," Sherry praised Nate as he passed the food around. "Nate is going to move in with us, right?"

"Just what you always wanted," Hailey joked to Sherry.

"Just what I always wanted," Nate said.

They all laughed, except for Solomon. "No one is moving in with us. We don't need anyone's help," he said.

Quickly Sherry changed the subject. She asked Maya about her upcoming ballet recital and Hailey about her job, which Hailey seemed apathetic about, at best. Sherry had always believed that it was a shame Hailey had given up her job at *Allure*, which she'd loved and been so good at. And she had always wanted Hailey to pursue her own writing, not just tuck it away in the face of Jonah's more public accomplishments. At the time, Sherry had more or less held her tongue, afraid of incurring Jonah's resentment, but she should have said what she thought.

"Did I tell you about Tara?" Sherry asked. "Apparently her boyfriend, Kevin, left his job again, the one I helped him get. Tara is trying to act like she's okay, but I can see how upset she is, especially because now he's back in Winter Haven with his brother, Sam. He's done this before—he takes off and goes to stay with Sam, and Tara is just supposed to put up with it. He said he would only be there for a week, but it's already been close to a month."

Sherry glanced at Sol, who was quiet. He was as close to Tara as she was, but recently, he was keeping his distance from everyone. She hadn't told Tara about his illness, which made it hard to sit beside her every day, especially when Tara could sense that something was wrong. Every time Tara asked if Sol was okay, Sherry changed the subject, plying her with questions about Kevin and Caleb, offering advice and looking for ways she could help. It was nice to be needed and a relief to worry about someone else's life; at least when it came to Tara, she felt like these were problems she could solve.

"Has Tara said anything to you about Kevin?" she asked Nate. She'd noticed that the two of them had grown closer and she was glad, wanting everyone to get along.

"Not a word," Nate said.

"Tara still believes that he's going to change. I haven't said this to her because I don't want to upset her, but I'm pretty sure that she's fooling herself," she said, and in the lull that followed, she turned to Maya, who had finished eating. "Do you want to go play? I set up the dolls that you love in the living room."

Once Maya was out of earshot, Sherry turned to Hailey. "Tell us exactly what the judge said."

"She made it clear that this is how she would rule unless we can come up with 'extenuating circumstances,'" Hailey said.

"What kind of extenuating circumstances?" Sherry asked.

"I have no idea, but at this point I can either agree to stay in Binghamton, or I can keep fighting and probably lose," Hailey said.

"If the judge said she would consider extenuating circumstances, we just need to come up with the right one," Sherry said.

"That's probably a standard thing to say," Solomon said.

"It doesn't hurt to try. There's a chance that the judge will allow it, and there's also a chance that Jonah will give in," Sherry said.

"I assume you know that this is highly unlikely," Sol said.

"You never know what a judge is going to do. And it might not even come to that, because at some point, Jonah is going to understand that we're not backing down and he's going to realize he doesn't have the money for this kind of fight," Nate said.

"My lawyer said that if we don't come to an agreement, it could take months, maybe longer. If we go this route, it means we'll have depositions and go to trial," Hailey said.

"Would that be the worst thing?" Sherry asked.

"This does not need to go to court," Solomon protested. "This is exactly the kind of escalation we want to avoid."

"You know what you should do?" Nate said to Sherry. "You should kill him."

She laughed. "That would certainly create an extenuating circumstance."

"Sherry Marcus. Medical secretary by day, murderer by night," Nate intoned. "Come on, Hailey, you have to agree that it's not the worst idea for Mom to get rid of him. She can bury him in the garden. No one will ever know."

"You are so crazy," Hailey said.

"Sometimes you have to take matters into your own hands," Nate said.

"That's enough, Nate," Sol said.

"I'm not saying Mom has to do it herself," Nate said and turned to Sherry. "I'm sure you could hire someone. Maybe Eleanor or Judy knows someone."

Solomon slammed his hand down on the table. "What is wrong with you?"

Nate startled and held his upturned palms in the air in a guise of surrender, the same way he had as a child. "I have no idea what you're talking about," he claimed.

"Did you think, 'My father is sick, this is a good time to do what I want'?" Solomon said.

"Do we have to talk about this now?" Sherry pleaded.

"All I did was lease one machine," Nate said.

"I told you no," Solomon said.

"Please," Sherry begged, but they didn't listen. She looked at Hailey, who gave a small shrug and excused herself to go find Maya. Sherry wished she could follow her. The three of them could flee and seek shelter far away.

"For however much longer, it's still my practice and I am going to run it the way I want," Solomon said.

"I'm sorry. Okay? I'm sorry," Nate said. In the past, Nate would have forged ahead with arguments and excuses, but now he looked stricken with guilt.

Solomon stood and shuffled from the table. The back door that led to the pool area slammed shut. And with that, dinner was over. Within seconds of getting up from the table, Hailey and Nate disappeared; Hailey to get Maya ready for bed, and Nate to hide somewhere with his phone. In the kitchen, Sherry put away the food, rinsed the dishes and loaded them in the dishwasher. How many times had she performed this exact routine, trying to restore order after the night was ruined?

All these years later, it felt hard to admit that the fighting had been a fixture of their family life. Even now, she wished for a way to expunge it from her memory. On so many nights, over so many years, she chided Sol not to react to Nate's provocations, to be more patient, more present. She urged Adam not to run from the table at every slight. She implored Nate not to start up with Adam, not to go out of his way to anger his father. But no matter what she said, no one listened. Sometimes she wondered if the intensity of her desire for them to get along was why they always chose the opposite—but was she supposed to stop trying? Sol solved the problem by being less present, but the rest of them didn't have the luxury of absence. Instead of mellowing as they got older, the fighting between the boys had grown worse. In middle school, Adam was painfully shy and lost in his own world. Sometimes he talked to himself, which Nate seized on, imitating him even after she rebuked him. Nate had become an exceptional tennis player, and when he was on the court, he displayed none of his high-spirited antics. His seriousness and focus were absolute. Once he was in high school, the house was filled with his friends, who were as boisterous as he was. She encouraged Adam to have people over too, to join a club or try an activity, but he balked at any suggestion.

Only once Nate left for college did Adam emerge from his room, full of fury. He played obscure music, grew his hair long, and posted signs in the kitchen demanding that they stop eating meat and having the garden sprayed with insecticide. He declared the pool a colossal waste of water and refused to swim in it. He had few friends and, as far as she could tell, little interest in making any. All of a sudden, Adam hated everything. He hated West Palm. He hated his school and the family activities she planned. Most of all, he hated her.

She tried to talk to Adam about what colleges he wanted to apply to, but he had no interest in the conversation. He accused her of wishing he was more like Nate. He claimed that she made him feel terrible about himself. She tried to listen, but was too stunned by the ferocity of his anger. She protested that she had done everything for him, for all of them. She said that she had tried to give and give, and that it wasn't enough, or it was too much—either way, whatever she did was wrong.

After that, Adam closed himself off. The only conversations were perfunctory. He remained in his room whenever he could. One night, in the fall of his senior year, Adam pulled out a poorly photocopied pamphlet that looked like it was made by kindergarten children, with blurry pictures of students squatting in green fields alongside crops and animals. Instead of going to college, he was planning to do a farming internship.

"You have to go to college," she protested.

"Just because that's what people do?" Adam challenged her.

In the wake of Adam's anger, she glanced at Solomon, who was sitting beside her but had a disengaged expression and didn't join in the conversation. Surely he wasn't okay with Adam's plan any more than she was, but he had the demeanor of someone who intended to sit this round out. As always, she was pulled into the fighting, while Sol remained safely out of the fray.

For weeks she'd argued with Adam, but it was futile, because a month later, Adam lost interest in the farming internship and instead wanted to attend a college that met in the California desert, where the classes were all manual labor. She worked hard to suppress her reaction, part bemusement, part dismay. Her father had owned a fruit store and unloaded and unpacked crates all day, his hands calloused, his back irreparably strained. Her father's father worked seven days a week in a crowded, unventilated factory. If given a choice, they would have seized any opportunity to do something else. If they could have glimpsed her life, they wouldn't have believed her good fortune.

Finally, Adam had come up with an idea that they could all live with. He would apply to Sterling College in Vermont, where he could get a degree in animal science. This wasn't what she had imagined, but at least it was an actual college that conferred a degree. She told him she was excited about it, but the distance remained. Once Adam was in college, he never wanted them to visit. When he came home for vacations, he kept to himself, like a stranger they were inexplicably housing. "He just wants his independence," Sol often said, and she tried to believe that eventually Adam would relent and they would find a way to talk to each other. In the meantime, she focused on Hailey, who was in high school and had a busy schedule of friends and dance recitals. The two of them went shopping and to the beach, where she listened to details about Hailey's classes and her friends and the boys she liked. Sherry had pitied the mothers bemoaning teenage daughters who had become unrecognizable to them. But Hailey had never strayed. She remained who she always was.

In the middle of his junior year, Adam called to announce that he was dropping out of Sterling.

"You're almost done. Why can't you just finish?" Sherry asked, but all he said was that school wasn't for him. Instead, he was planning to work on a farm collective.

She tried to argue, but he wouldn't listen. She looked to Sol, but he refused to get involved.

"We're not going to pay," she said finally to Adam—the threat a weapon of last resort.

"I didn't expect you to," he said.

"Please, Adam, what is this about?"

"I'm not like all of you. I can't stand how I feel when I'm home," he said.

"All I wanted was for us to be close," Sherry said, but it was too late. After that, Adam rarely came home. In every phone call, she tried to fill the conversation with updates about Hailey and Nate, but inevitably they wound back to his litany of complaints. No one in the family was honest with each other. No one talked about anything real. They were expected to adhere to a code of loyalty, regardless of how anyone felt. "That's not the way it is," Sherry objected. He was rewriting the past, describing a family not their own. Later, she realized that she should have just listened, but at the time, her entire life seemed to be under attack. She offered to find him a therapist. She tried to convince him to come home and work this out, or at least to go on vacation with them so they could forget about the past and have a nice time together. She apologized for whatever she'd done wrong. She wrote him a letter in which she enclosed a picture, now yellowed with age, of her holding him as a baby, the two of them gazing at each other, and told him how much she loved him.

But she couldn't hide from the knowledge that her own son didn't like her.

• • •

When it was bedtime for Maya, Sherry went in to say good night. As she kissed her on the forehead, Maya gave her a concerned look.

"Why are you sad?" Maya asked.

"Don't worry, sweetie. It's nothing for you to worry about," she said.

"Is it because we're leaving soon?" Maya asked.

"If it were up to me, you would live here and I would see you every day."

"Would we live in your house?"

"If you wanted to. Wouldn't that be fun?"

"What if we built a house in the garden for me and Mommy?" Maya asked.

"We could do that!" Sherry said. "A special little house right in the middle of the garden."

"Can we make it out of flowers and grass?"

"We can make it out of anything you want!"

It came over her, how quickly time was passing. It felt so long ago now, but she'd once dreaded the day Hailey would leave for college. Somehow she'd allowed herself to believe that the moment would never arrive—an end point in an ever-receding distance. Hailey was the kind of child who felt not just part of her body but like a sliver of her soul, yet when the time came, she was supposed to let her go as if it were the easiest thing in the world. When the day finally arrived, they loaded up her car and she drove Hailey to the University of Miami campus in Coral Gables. It was just the two of them because Sol didn't want to take the day off from work. "She's going to school ninety minutes away. We're going to see her all the time," he said, not grasping the enormity of the change. Sherry helped Hailey set up her dorm room, and when it was time to leave, she forced a smile, but felt hollowed out. She walked to the car, but instead of driving home to her empty nest, she sat there and cried. She had no one who needed her, nowhere she needed to be. No matter what, the kids left you in the end. One day, Maya too would grow up and be gone.

When Hailey came in to say good night to Maya, Sherry left the room, longing for her children's younger selves. Even when she was with them, it was still possible to miss them.

Sherry sat at the kitchen table and waited for Hailey. Either Maya was taking a long time to settle down or Hailey had fallen asleep next to her. She considered going to check on them, as she had when the kids were little, cracking open their doors to ensure that they were safe.

Every day since Solomon told her about his diagnosis, she'd wanted to call Adam, but dreaded the rise of hope, then the descent into disappointment. But surely there had to come a time when the past was forgiven. Time and distance will have done their job and what had seemed like a permanent wound will have healed. Upon hearing the news, Adam would rush to the airport and come home.

Sherry picked up the phone. Twice, she hung up before she finished dialing. On her third try, she completed the call. It rang until she was prompted by an electronic voice to leave a message.

She had planned what to say, but even so, she fumbled with her words. "Dad is sick. He has Parkinson's. Call me. Please," she said and sat at the table, waiting.

"Do you need anything?" Hailey asked. She was standing in the kitchen doorway, her hair rumpled, her eyes bleary.

"I left Adam a message," Sherry said. "He needs to know about Dad."

"Do you think he'll call back?" Hailey asked.

"I have no idea, but if he doesn't, will you call him?"

"I can try," Hailey said.

"Do you ever talk to him?" Sherry asked.

"Not in a long time. I sent him some pictures of Maya a few months ago, but he doesn't seem that interested in being in touch."

It felt bad to admit, but Sherry was relieved. She worried that behind her back, the rest of the family carried on as normal, while she alone was made to pay for what Adam considered their failings. She worried that Hailey or Nate would come to see her as Adam did, all of them turning against her, creating a portrait of her that would be unrecognizable to her own eyes.

Once, years ago, after a fight with Adam in which he'd again refused to come visit, she was in the living room crying as Hailey arrived home from school. Usually Hailey was surrounded by a pack of friends, but this time, mercifully, she was alone.

"Mom, are you okay?" Hailey had asked in alarm when she realized that she was crying. Normally she tried to protect Hailey from anything painful, but gutted with grief, she confessed to Hailey that Adam had no interest in coming home.

"Am I as awful as Adam says?" Sherry asked.

"Oh my god, of course not. You're the best mom ever," Hailey reassured her.

"I hope you never know what it's like to lose a child," Sherry said.

"You will never lose me," Hailey whispered with so much kindness that Sherry had started to cry all over again. Your children weren't supposed to be the ones to comfort you, yet Hailey had said exactly the right thing. Now those were the words Sherry longed to hear again. Even now, when Hailey was all grown up, Sherry felt the same urge as she had then, to take hold of her and never let go.

"I know it's hard, Hailey, but I really think you should keep fighting to move here," Sherry pleaded.

"I don't know, Mom. I'm starting to think that it's time to give in."

"But what do we have to lose if we keep going a little longer?"

"I really can't let you and Dad spend this kind of money," Hailey said. "I feel terrible about how much it's costing."

"Let me worry about that," Sherry said.

"I appreciate that. I really do. But I'm worried that it's going to make everything worse. I'm afraid this could get out of control," Hailey said.

"Please," Sherry begged. "I know you're ready for this to be over, but we're so close. We don't want to look back one day and wonder if we could have done more."

"But we could spend all this time and money, and the odds are still unlikely. And even if I can't move, I'll come all the time. And you'll visit us too."

"How often will you really come? And if Dad is sick, how easy will it be for me to get away? I'll be all alone."

Sherry knew she was pushing too hard, but she couldn't stop herself. When Hailey first broached the idea of moving to West Palm, she tried to keep her hope in check, but by now, the possibility felt like reality. In her mind, it was already happening.

"I guess I can keep going for a little longer," Hailey conceded.

A strand of Hailey's hair had fallen into her face and Sherry gently brushed it back. She kept her hand on her cheek, as she had when Hailey was a child and her face seemed like the most beautiful sight she would ever see.

"You won't regret this," Sherry said. Even if Hailey didn't seem entirely convinced, she would come to see that it was the right decision. She would understand that there were times you had to try everything, no matter the cost. Sherry hugged Hailey tightly. She had spent her life crafting a small boat inside of which Hailey would eventually set sail. But sometimes the tide turned and the winds changed, and the ones you loved most came sailing back into your safe harbor.

Once Sherry went to sleep, Nate took refuge in his childhood bedroom, which looked nearly the same as when he was a teenager, every surface covered with tennis trophies and faded notes from girls. He didn't know why his mother still saved his old stuff—if it were up to him, he would have trashed it all ages ago.

"I didn't realize how tense things were here," Hailey said when she came in to join him, sinking into the beanbag that had once served as a repository for his clothes.

"You have no idea. During the day, I see most of the patients, and when I finish, I bring dinner over to the house and eat with them. When I finally get home, Mom calls me approximately twenty more times. And at the same time, I have to keep the office running, because who's going to pay for everything if Dad stops working? Do you realize how much pressure that is? If the practice fails, what do you think is going to happen to everyone who works there?" Nate said as he sprawled on his bed.

"I can't believe you didn't tell me about Dad right away. I could have come sooner," she said.

"Mom didn't want me to, and you didn't need anything else to worry about," he said.

"I just told Mom I would keep fighting to move."

"Is that what you want?"

"Do you think I know what I want?" she asked.

"You're not a kid anymore. You're allowed to tell her no."

"You know it's not that easy . . . and I do hate the idea that Jonah still gets to be in charge. For the next fourteen years or so, until Maya's grown up, I'm in a state of entrapment."

"People murder and get less than that," he said.

"Is that supposed to make me feel better or worse?" she asked.

In the corner of his room, a small basketball had survived all these years, and Nate tossed it into the net that still hung on the back of his door. As a teenager, he'd smashed the ball into the wall next to it so often that, more than once, a contractor had come to replaster and paint.

"For what it's worth, I don't think it's the worst idea to keep fighting, at least for a little longer. Do you know how many times I've seen you back down? Maybe it's time for you to fight," he said. "And it would definitely be good for Mom to have something to focus on. At least it's something to obsess about besides Dad."

"I didn't realize how attached she was to the idea of my moving here," Hailey said.

"It's all she talks about," Nate said. "It's almost funny. Of all of us, I'm the only one still here."

"Mom asked me to call Adam," she said.

Nate squeezed the ball more tightly, then shot it too hard, so that it bounced off the rim. "No good is going to come of bringing Adam into the mess we already have," he said. He often made jokes about the fact that Adam wanted nothing to do with them, but any serious discussion about what had happened with Adam made him want to flee.

"Maybe it would help if Mom talked to him. It might make everything feel less awful."

"Do you think that's going to go well? If Adam wants to hide out in Vermont or Maine or wherever he is, then let him. I already have more than enough to manage here, so I'm going to have to save Adam for another day."

"I used to call Adam. I thought I could patch things up," she said and gave a small, sad laugh. "I didn't tell Mom because I didn't want her to feel bad. I know it's crazy, but I always had the feeling that it would be disloyal to Mom if I was close to him."

It was something Hailey hadn't told him, either, and it unsettled him. Not that he had any right to control who she spoke to, but he always assumed that her sympathies lay with him. He took it as a given that he and Hailey would always be on the same side.

She must have caught his unease because she gave him a reassuring look.

"Don't worry. He almost never called me back. And when he did, it was really awkward. I had to work hard to think of things to talk about, and eventually, it became easier not to call."

"Why won't he talk to you? I thought everything was my fault."

"No one thinks that," she said.

"Are you kidding? Everyone does. Do you know how many times Mom begged me to call Adam? She tried to act like it wasn't a big deal, but it was obvious that she wanted me to apologize to him."

"Why didn't you, just so that everyone wasn't angry all the time?" she asked.

"Do you have any idea how much you sound like Mom when you say that?" he answered, more sharply than he'd intended.

By the time he and Adam were both in college, they had become increasingly distant. If they were home at the same time, they more or less avoided each other. Nate might have made a few comments about Adam's choice of school, asking how the harvest was coming along, humming "The Farmer in the Dell," things like that, but he had mostly outgrown the need to start up with him. Nate knew how upset his mother had been when Adam started pulling away from the family, but as far as he was concerned, some people just weren't meant to get along. His mother would never admit this, but just because you were born into the same family didn't mean that you fit together. When they saw each other at the few occasions Adam bothered to attend, it was hard to believe that this almost stranger was the same person he'd once stood at the bathroom sink with every night, brushing their teeth, wearing the matching pajamas his mother loved to dress them in.

Nate was in Belize, running away from his medical school debacle, when he called home and his mother asked if he would apologize to Adam—she'd implied many times that he was the one at fault, but this was the first time she had explicitly laid the blame at his feet. It didn't matter that, as far as he knew, Adam's fury was directed primarily at her. It didn't matter that it had been years since he'd said a mean word to Adam. Everything bad that happened was apparently because of him. What was wrong with him and why did he have to be this way and why couldn't he stop? No matter how far he traveled, his father's litany of questions played in his head. Was the fact that he had been a kid enough of an excuse or was there never any excuse? No, he said every time his mother brought it up, no to any artificial attempt at patching things up, no to the suffocating pull of familial obligation. He thought that he meant it, yet sometimes he'd found himself at a pay phone in the lobby of one of the hostels he stayed at or on a noisy corner of a city he was visiting, nervously waiting to see if Adam would pick up, not sure what he would say if he did. If he handed him a hundred apologies, would that remake the past? He didn't need to worry, because Adam never answered the phone.

Only once it was too late, and only once he was no longer at fault, had he really tried. A month after Hailey's wedding, he called Adam again. "It's your long lost brother, Nate," he said to Adam's answering machine. "I'm just . . . I'm sorry about what happened at the wedding. Mom is pretty broken up about it, so maybe you could forgive her and we could all move on?" As soon as he'd hung up, he felt ridiculous. He didn't actually believe that anyone changed or really forgave anyone—they just decided to move on when it benefited them. Then too, Adam hadn't called back. One thing at least they were in agreement about: there was no use trying to undo the past.

Hailey was still sitting on the beanbag, the same as she had when she was little, only then she'd regarded him with complete admiration and now she was looking at him with disappointment.

"You know what, Hailey? You have no idea what it was like for me. You never did anything wrong. Everyone loved you all the time," he said.

Nate shot the basketball one last time before he tossed it into the closet. On his way out the door, he paused.

"Do you have any idea what it's like to know that you're the reason for all the problems, and nothing you do will ever make up for it?"

It was almost midnight when Nate got into his car. His mind was besieged. Home for too long, it was easy to revert—or maybe to realize you were still who you'd once been. He didn't feel like being alone in his condo or going to Duffy's, the sports bar where he was a regular. The thought occurred to him that he could drive to Miami. It had been too long since he'd been there. He used to make fun of his mother for acting like it was a considerable trek, but since he'd been working so hard, it had come to feel like a distant city for him as well.

He'd only driven a few miles when his interest in Miami faded. It was seventy miles away and for what? Until a few years ago, he and his friends went to bars and clubs as though they were still in their twenties. They had no intention of being pinned down, but by now they'd all caved. Married, they needed a furlough to go out on a weeknight. Now some of them had babies, which they held up like prizes they'd won at games he hadn't known they wanted to play. Sometimes he thought that if he found the right person he could get married and have a kid, but an internal warning was instantly triggered the moment he sensed anyone wanting too much from him. The prospect of endless obligation made him realize that he was happy with his life the way it was. He could work late, then go for a long run or to the gym without anyone expecting more. For a long time, he'd been talking about buying a boat. At first it was just something to say, but now he wished he'd done it so that he had a ready-made means of getting away.

Approaching the highway exit that would bring him to the office, Nate swerved across three lanes and took it. Once he was there, he unlocked the front door and flipped on the lights. He sat at his desk, which was cluttered with pamphlets for new machines and procedures and tossed them into the trash. Now his plans seemed futile, but he'd really believed that his father would go along with them. He'd begun the certification course needed to do laser treatments and told Tara to book appointments for a few months from now. A few weeks earlier—before he knew his father was sick—Tara had come into his office while he was researching what it would cost to lease the Laser Genesis.

"Let me ask you something," he said to her. "What if, theoretically, someone was considering a lease on a new machine? Would you be willing to not mention a monthly expense that mysteriously started to show up?"

"I'm worried that it's wrong," she answered.

"We both know that it's good for the office, so what does 'wrong' even mean?" he said.

"I don't know about that," she countered, but she was smiling.

"Is that a yes?" he asked.

"It's not a no," she said.

Over the past month, he and Tara had become closer, spending time talking during the day and texting after work. A few times, they went for lunch and stayed out too long, returning to the office to find patients waiting. He couldn't resist the impulse to seek her out during any lull in the schedule. He'd long sensed that she liked him, but until recently, it was an innocent game that added a fizz of interest to the day, an intriguing question hanging over every interaction. Obviously this was a bad idea, but it was exactly the sort of bad idea that he was drawn to.

At the end of one day, after his parents left and the last of the patients were gone, he had come upon Tara still at her desk. He was about to make a joke about her not wanting to go home, but then he realized that she was crying.

"Whatever it is, you can tell me," he said as he sat down beside her.

She looked at him with a combination of gratitude and embarrassment. "Kevin's still in Winter Haven with Sam. I don't even want to know what he and Sam do when they're together. I know I shouldn't say this, but I feel like every bad thing that happens to Kevin is because of him."

"What kind of bad?" he asked.

"I don't know. He says he works with Sam, but I know there's more to it. Whenever I tell him that I don't want him to be involved with Sam, he doesn't listen, so what's the point of saying anything? Maybe some things are better not to know?" Tara said and tried to laugh.

"Obviously I'm no expert in relationships—I'm always looking for any excuse to get away. But I'm pretty sure that if you're planning to marry the guy, this might be the kind of thing you want to know," he said.

"I've thought about leaving him, but I still hope that he can change. Maybe I'm fooling myself, but I have this idea that one day he's going to tell me that from now on, everything is going to be different."

"Do you really believe that?" Nate asked.

"It's not his fault that he's like this. He had a really messed-up childhood. He doesn't like to talk about it, but I know that Sam had to protect him from their horrible stepfather. For his whole life, the only person Kevin could count on was Sam. And now he has me, but that's it."

"I assume you know that whatever happens, we're here for you," Nate said.

"Your parents are the nicest people I know. Do you know how many times they've helped me?" she asked.

"It's not just my parents. I'm here for you too," he said.

The day after he'd ordered the new machine, his mother called to tell him about his father's diagnosis. In the wake of it, he'd been intent on getting along with him, all the while hiding the fact that he knew. It was only a few days before his father stood in the doorway of his office and, with barely a flicker of emotion, said, "I'm aware that Mom told you." Those few words, a curt nod, that was all. Any notion that they would cling to each other, that he would whisper consolations in his father's ear, was a ridiculous fantasy. After that, Nate decided not to cancel the order for the Laser Genesis machine, and now it sat next to his desk, much bigger than he'd expected. That afternoon, Nate hadn't realized his father was still in the office when the machine arrived. Certain there was a mistake, Sol had tried to refuse the delivery, and Nate had no choice but to confess that he'd ordered it. His father retreated to his office with a befuddled expression, and Nate wished that he'd gone after him to apologize. In the state his father was in, there was no pleasure to derive from angering him. It already felt hard to imagine that there had once been. He also wished that, months ago, when Tara first asked if he'd noticed anything wrong with his father, he took it more seriously. A different son might have been able to say something. A different father might have been able to hear it.

Too agitated to work, Nate went down the hall to his father's office and sat at his desk. On the walls, his father's Harvard diplomas were framed, along with citations from professional societies. Next to towering piles of the *New England Journal of Medicine* was a photo of his father as a child, wearing a sailor's hat, standing on a dock. His father rarely talked about his childhood. One of the few things he'd been told was that his father's father never took him anywhere—Nate could recite this fact as if it were a nursery rhyme. All his father had was this one memory of being taken fishing on Cape Cod when he was five. "Really? I never knew that. Why don't you tell us about it?" Nate said whenever the story was repeated. Maybe he should have asked more about why, unlike most of his friends, they didn't have webs of extended family. There was little talk about aunts and uncles and cousins on either side—he never probed because it didn't interest him, but he understood that the word *family* extended only to the five of them. And that was why his mother was so protective or over-involved or whatever else he might have chosen to call it. And this was also why the one time his father agreed to take two weeks off, his mother made such a huge deal about their vacation. For months all he heard about was the Grand Canyon. At his mother's urging, he and his father and Adam huddled at the dining room table, a map open before them. With his finger, Solomon traced the route they'd drive, while he and Adam mapped out every rest stop, every motel, every activity. He and Adam identified the most obscure tourist attractions and claimed a burning desire to stop at each one. Sol grumbled that they'd have to be gone a month to do all that, but he enjoyed the game, especially when he and Adam presented Sherry with the itinerary, and she acted delighted to drive a few hundred miles out of the way if it would make them happy.

Nate was thirteen when the first-ever Marcus Family Adventure got underway. They had flown to Denver and planned to slowly make their way to the Grand Canyon. He sat in the wayback of the station wagon they'd rented, the world whizzing by in reverse, while from the front seat his mother passed out snacks and proclaimed how much fun they were having. The day before they reached the Grand Canyon, they were all tired of being in the car, and he and Adam fought over who was making annoying breathing sounds and who had eaten all the potato chips, and soon they were trading the same insults and the same blame over who had started it. Hailey turned around from her spot in the middle row to shoot him a pleading look, and he wished that she could have rescued him from his own self. But he couldn't stop, not even when his mother begged, not even when his father screamed. The more Nate was told to stop, the more he was unable to do so. Sol was driving, but he kept turning around to rebuke Nate, which made Sherry yell at Sol that he was going to get them all killed, until finally Sol pulled the car over on the side of the highway. Sol got out and opened the back of the car where Nate was sitting and stood over him. Nate thought he was about to hit him, but that wasn't it. His father stopped screaming and stood in bewildered silence, as if after all these years of trying, Nate had finally broken him. Nate's tears welled, and he grew silent too. He had ruined the trip. He ruined everything.

The next day, his mother acted like nothing had happened. At the South Rim, they waited in a long line of cars, then in the sweltering heat for the trolley to the lookout point. How magnificent would the Grand Canyon have to be to make up for the fighting—large enough that the bad parts could be tossed in and disappear? At the sight of this massive crater, Nate tried to feign indifference. Instead of focusing on the view, he studied his mother. "I never thought I would see this," she marveled, and his resistance seeped out. At the sight of her awe, a feeling of wonder opened inside him as well, making him feel small and insignificant in the best kind of way.

Across the street from their motel was a Carvel ice cream, and as they were getting ready for bed that night, his father offered to take him. They'd ordered cones of soft vanilla ice cream with rainbow sprinkles, and as they walked back to the motel, Sol faltered first. "I was the same way with my father. I fought even when I wanted to stop," he admitted. At the corners of his eyes, Nate saw his father's tears. Of all the places Nate eventually traveled to—Patagonia and Bolivia, Nicaragua and Guatemala and Belize—that Carvel topped his list of the greatest wonders.

On Sol's desk, in a folder that Nate opened, were his father's medical records. Though he wasn't supposed to, Nate read through them and understood that Sol's disease had progressed far more than he let on. In the quiet of the office, Nate put his head in his hands, and for the first time since he was a boy, he sobbed.

Nate was walking out of the office when he texted Tara.

Are you awake?

I am now

I just left the office

It's so late! Why are you there??

Rough night at my parents. I didn't want to go home

Caleb's asleep and Kevin's still gone. Do you want to come over?

Do you think that's a good idea?

Probably not

On my way

Before he could think about it, Nate was in his car, on his way to an apartment complex in Lake Worth, just outside of West Palm. This late, it took only twenty minutes. All the units were nearly identical, with an air of neglect that was unlike the pristine, manicured neighborhood he grew up in, or the ultramodern glass high-rise where he now lived. In all these years of knowing Tara, not once had he thought about where she lived. Had his parents ever been here? he wondered. Despite his mother's claim that she was part of the family, Tara knew them far better than they knew her.

Nate knocked softly on her door. If she didn't hear him, he would get back in his car and drive home, and that would be the end of whatever this was.

When Tara answered the door, she appeared surprised to see him, even though she'd invited him. He understood, though, because he felt the same sense of dislocation. In black running shorts and a pink cropped top, she looked younger than she did in the office. During the day, she had a face full of makeup, but now her face was scrubbed clean, and she had a tiny spray of acne across her forehead.

He followed her into a living room strewn with magazines and dishes and clothes. The floor was cluttered with toys. He knew obviously that she had a kid, but when they were at work, it was possible to forget what that entailed. He stood awkwardly in the middle of the room. It was a mistake to have come.

"Just tell me what's going on," she said.

"You were right about my father. He has Parkinson's."

"I knew something was wrong," she said and reached for him.

They sat on the couch, close enough that he felt the warmth of her arm.

"You're the only one I can tell," he said. As much as he hated sharing anything personal, it was a relief to talk to someone who knew his parents nearly as well as he did. There was little he needed to explain. She might actually understand better than he did.

"I know that I should try to get along with him, but it's harder than it's been in a long time." His voice cracked. "He doesn't trust me. In his mind, I'm still the same irresponsible kid I once was, screwing everything up. Who knows? Maybe he's right. Maybe I'm just fooling myself that I think I can do a good job."

"Don't you think maybe you're being too hard on yourself?" she asked.

"I don't understand why he's nicer to you than he is to everyone else," he said.

"Maybe he sees something of himself in me? When I first started working for him, he would tell me how, when his father died, he knew that he was completely on his own. He decided to go to medical school and had no one but himself to count on. And then, even when he had a mentor, he realized that he couldn't trust him. I'm sure he told you this story a million times," she said.

Nate's first impulse was to pretend that he had, but at the understanding look on Tara's face, he realized there was no point lying.

"Actually I've never heard this," he said.

"His mentor stole his research and acted like it was his own? So that was why he decided to leave Boston, and it worked out because your mother really wanted to move to Miami. But even though he was leaving, he wasn't going to let him get away with it." She paused. "Should I not be telling you this?"

"I want to hear it."

"And so on his last day, when he went to clear out his office, he took this chemical from the lab . . ." She looked questioningly at him. "Something with a really long name that starts with a *B* and smells awful?"

"Beta-mercaptoethanol?" he said.

"Yes! And he put it all around the lab, and in his mentor's office, because he knew no one would be able to use those rooms for weeks. And even though nothing could give him back his work, he wasn't going to let anyone treat him that way."

Nate shook his head in disbelief. He didn't know if he should be amused or horrified. His father had his own way of doing things. There were parts of him he would never access.

"I shouldn't have come," Nate said and stood up.

"I'm glad you did," Tara said and looked up at him. He sat back down.

Her eyes issued a dare. There were so many reasons not to, but Nate touched Tara's face. So many reasons, but she leaned toward him and kissed him. An image of his father forced its way into his mind. You could try to do everything right and still somehow be in the wrong. Eventually you had to wonder why you would even bother. They leaned back into the couch and she was pulling off his shirt, fumbling with the ties of his scrubs. People liked to make all kinds of proclamations about what they would never do. But people did all sorts of things, and never was a very long time, and in his experience, people who said things like that lacked imagination. All it meant was that they hadn't yet found themselves in a situation where they might.

MAINE, 2019

Adam leaves early every morning to hike the dogs, while I stay in the cabin with Maya. We've been in Maine for almost a month, but the days still seem unsettled. I try to get Maya to share what she's feeling—cautiously, I ask if she wants to talk about Jonah or even my parents. But she turns away from me and acts like I'm not speaking. As much as I want her to open up, I have no idea what I'd say if she did. And so I try to create an illusion of normalcy, suggesting we go into town and get ice cream, or drive an hour to the rocky shoreline, which seems like an entirely different body of water than the one I was raised near. At each proposition, Maya shrugs and my own desire to leave the cabin wilts. As unlikely as it is that I would be recognized, the prospect of being around other people makes me uneasy. All I want to do is hide.

To assuage my guilt that Maya is missing school, Maya and I sit on the couch and I teach her to read and write. In an extra spiral notebook that Adam had, she traces the letters I make. At each word she completes, Maya holds up the notebook to show me her letters, which are wobbly and oversized, and I exclaim over them, as if my exuberance can somehow make up for everything she has lost. Eventually, I know, I will need to decide what to do, but in these moments, I allow myself the fantasy that we can remain here forever.

Daisy is curled at my feet, having located the one spot where the sun streams in through the window. When I reach down to pet her, she nuzzles against my leg.

"Good girl," I say, and she cocks her head to one side and studies me. Adam once explained that it's just a dog's way of focusing, but to me, this wordless communion seems like a sign of deep connection. I feel like Daisy can read my mind, like she alone can intuit what I can't bear to say. When I bring my face close to her, she licks my chin and cheeks. I had no idea I could love a dog so intently, but a new capacity has been forged inside me, a widening in my heart.

When Maya tires of practicing her letters, she plays with Daisy, throwing a ball to her and delighting each time she dutifully returns with it. With Maya occupied, I take out my notebook and read over what I've written. The words startle me, as if they've been forged by some hand other than mine. Despite my impulse to shield myself, I push closer to what I fear most. The facts feel bent and curved, and I struggle to lay them flat. During the day, when I write, I still hold on to the idea that I can make sense of this—I might eventually be able to understand. At night, though, nothing is comprehensible. My memories intertwine with my dreams. Every thought has the sheen of unreality. I am not in this bedroom, I am not in this cabin, I am not anywhere. I scrutinize the online re-creations of Jonah's murder and the video of me being interrogated, which continues to gain more views and comments. The woman on the screen no longer feels like me, but some other person crafted from a small rib of who I once was. In that interrogation room, I first had the sense that I'd ceased to be myself. Or maybe there were two of us, one watching as the other swam farther out to sea. I didn't know if she was forging an escape or dooming herself to drown.

Even before I hear the sound of a car, Daisy's ears perk up and she barks and runs to the door. Alarmed, I jump up, envisioning who might have come in search of us. My phone still lies uncharged in a zipped pocket of my bag, and the messages surely accumulating may as well be notes sealed in bottles and sunk to the bottom of the sea. Maybe one day they will wash up on a distant shore and be deciphered by people who know nothing of us.

I relax when I realize it's Adam, home earlier than usual. Instead of coming into the cabin, he walks around to the back—I catch sight of him through the window, holding the leash of a small brown and white beagle.

"Is Uncle Adam home?" Maya asks.

"He's outside. And I think he has a new dog with him," I say.

"Can we see?" she pleads.

Since we've been here, Maya has become enamored with Adam. She plies him with questions about the dogs and wants to show him the pictures she's made. Instead of asking why she's never met him before, she seems to accept the reality in which we now exist.

We put on our coats and go outside to the kennel, where Adam is crouched on the ground next to the new dog.

"Is it okay that we're out here?" I ask.

Adam nods, and Maya and I huddle next to him, our bodies so close that if we were to extend our arms, we would be hugging. I try to catch his eye, looking for assurance that he isn't bothered by our proximity. Since Maya's night terror, we have become more comfortable with each other. The small gestures he makes—bringing me a cup of tea at night, offering a small smile when I stand at the kitchen counter preparing Maya's food—have given me hope that slowly we are growing closer.

"Cody's going to be staying with us for a while," he says. He tells us that he's been training him for a family in Bangor who'd adopted him from a shelter. "But they're having a hard time with him and asked if I could take him for a while."

"Why can't he stay with his family?" Maya asked.

"Cody did some things he wasn't supposed to do, so they're not sure it's going to work out."

"What did he do wrong?" Maya asks.

Adam glances at me before answering.

"He bit someone," he says. "Actually, he bit twice."

"Why?" Maya asked.

"I don't know. But most dogs don't bite because they're aggressive. They bite because they're afraid."

"Why was he afraid?" Maya asks.

The face of this dog is so sweet that it's hard to believe he could harbor any aggression. I open my mouth to say that, but change my mind.

"Something might have happened to him in the past, but we'll never know for sure. If a dog bites once, a shelter will still take him, but with a second bite, no one wants the risk," Adam explains.

Crouched on the ground, Adam is giving commands in a low soothing tone and offering rewards. When he's with the dogs, he moves cautiously so nothing takes them by surprise. From a single word or precise gesture, the dogs understand what he wants. They know he is someone they can trust.

"Can I help?" Maya asks Adam.

"I don't know if that's a good idea," I interject.

"You don't have to worry. I would never let anything hurt her," Adam assures me.

My body is ready to spring forward in protection as they squat together beside Cody. Maya's face is furrowed in concentration as Adam gives a command, his voice firm, emotionless. He points his finger to the ground, instructing Cody to sit. "Good boy," he says when Cody does as asked.

"Sometimes, if a dog has been treated badly, it can take a long time to gain their trust," he tells Maya. "So we have to let Cody understand that we aren't going to hurt him."

Adam gives Maya the treat and she points her finger as he had. Adam is watching Cody intently, able to read his body language for any sign of danger. Each time Cody sits, Maya laughs. Every time she draws near to the dog, I tense. Adam attaches a longer leash to Cody and works on getting him to come when called. Over and over, he gives a command until Cody's resistance begins to bend.

"Should we take Cody for a walk?" Adam asks.

Maya looks at me and I nod.

The woods are behind the cabin, and sometimes, when Maya is with Adam, I have ventured into them, hoping that their winter starkness can somehow cleanse me. But the wish is always short-lived. No matter how deep into the woods I go, there is no respite. When I am far enough that neither of them can hear me, I bend down, my face close to the ground, and scream.

Together now, Adam, Maya, and I follow a barely visible trail up a small hill and over a footbridge. Instead of moving at a steady pace, Cody scampers back and forth, burrowing his snout in the snow that remains on the ground, sniffing every plant and tree as if this is the only way to truly experience it. Bundled in her too-small yellow coat, Maya walks beside Adam. She holds his hand as she stomps in the snow, her red boots leaving small footprints next to his larger ones. She harbors none of my fear that our newfound closeness to Adam could disappear at any moment. I trudge behind as Maya squats to inspect a pile of dried leaves. Adam points out the pine trees, whose branches arc toward the ground, weighted with snow. He shows her the animal tracks and knows which animals are asleep just out of sight, part of the teeming world beneath the white layer. Except for the occasional pine trees, all the bare branches draw stark lines against the sky and remind me of the forest of scratches I've been making on my arms. Each time I dig my fingernails into my skin, the pain is concentrated in a red streak and I feel a small measure of relief.

"What's this called?" Maya asks about each of the trees we pass.

"Birch," Adam tells her.

"Maple," he says.

Laughing, Maya runs ahead, and Adam and Cody chase after her—it's a sight I want to take hold of and somehow bandage on top of the pain.

"Once the snow melts, you won't believe all the things we'll be able to see out here. And when it gets warmer, you could learn how to climb one of these trees," Adam is telling Maya when I catch up to them.

"I wish we could live here forever," she says.

"I wish you could too," Adam says.

"Who knows? Maybe we will," I say.

They both look so happy, as if they believe what I have said, and I wish I could let myself linger in the fantasy as well.

Adam offers Maya the leash, and she takes it proudly. Overhead, a crow circles. A wall of gray rock juts out from the snow. There's a dead bird off to one side, and Cody bounds over, exuberantly trying to rub his face in it until Adam pulls him away. The woods grow denser, and any suggestion of a path is obscured by the snow. We come to a pond that is mostly frozen over, but there are parts where the sludgy water below is visible. If I were alone, I would be entirely lost, but Adam knows the way, taking us over a small tree that has fallen, its insides hollow and desiccated; past an enormous trunk that is splintered down the middle but still standing. The sky is slate gray. In summer, with the trees in full bloom, it's probably not visible at all.

As we're about to head back to the cabin, Maya turns to Adam.

"If Cody only bit because he was scared, why wouldn't his family forgive him?" Maya asks.

The buoyant feeling vanishes. I feel the urge to lie down in the snow and surrender. Adam glances at me before he speaks. When our eyes meet, I feel a jolt.

"Dogs don't hold grudges, but people do," he says, and Maya nods in a way that makes me think she understands.

Tara sat at her desk and tried not to think about Nate. Though it had been almost two months since the night he'd first come over, she still couldn't believe this was real.

I have some charts you might want to look at IMMEDIATELY

She smiled at Nate's text, though she tried to hide it. Nate was probably enjoying the fact that in front of his mother she had to act normal. But underneath her excitement, she felt the turn of anxiety. Surely this was going to blow up in her face.

Some of us are trying to work

Before sending her text, Tara added a smiley face, but that was only because there wasn't an emoji that could convey her complicated feelings. She was afraid this was a mistake and she felt guilty to betray Kevin, but also, she couldn't stop thinking about Nate. Even when she was at her desk or talking to a patient, a part of her was kissing him. She had started to make mistakes, sending the wrong form to the insurance company, forgetting to pull charts or book follow-ups, the way she had when she first started working here, with no idea what she was doing.

Before Nate joined the practice, he never stopped by the office, but she'd heard a lot about him from Solomon and Sherry. Their accounts diverged so much it was hard to believe they were talking about the same person. According to Sherry, Nate was the perfect son, fun-loving and loyal and energetic. Sol didn't say anything negative outright, but she could see how he clenched his jaw when Sherry carried on like that. A few years back, she had known that Sherry was trying to convince Sol to hire Nate, and while she didn't want to butt in where it wasn't her business, she'd hoped that Sol would agree so that she could see for herself what Nate was like.

Nate had joined the practice a few months after Caleb was born, and that was when she started to think about him even more. She knew it was ridiculous because he was too old for her and a doctor and Sherry and Solomon's son, and technically she was engaged to Kevin. But until she saw Nate every day in the office, she didn't know the degree to which you could be overcome by the force of wanting someone. She was sure that nothing would come of her infatuation, but sometimes on the nights when she doubted that Kevin was ever going to change, she pretended it was Nate who was on top of her. It was the first time she had allowed herself to imagine another way her life could be. Until then, she'd always believed that no matter what happened, she and Kevin would be together. Kevin needed her, and this meant, in some kind of twisted formulation, that she needed him as well. When she got pregnant with Caleb, she thought Kevin would be angry, but instead he proposed. She was only twenty-one, which was too young to get married, but also too young to have a baby, and somehow those two facts canceled each other out. He promised her that he would change, and she held on to this hope of a Kevin remade by her love.

By the time Nate texted that night and she invited him to come over, it felt inevitable. Every day leading up to that exchange, they talked by her desk or walked out together to grab lunch. All those weeks spent waiting for Kevin to come back, she lay awake, too anxious to sleep. By the time she pulled Nate on top of her, all her hopefulness was used up. She couldn't turn Kevin into the reliable person she needed him to be. She was done feeling like her body might explode from worry, like her heart was a bomb ticking inside her. Once Nate was in her apartment, she understood that she stood on a dividing line. For so long, she had tried to hold everything together and now she was going to see what happened if she let it fall apart.

Tara's phone beeped—Nate again—and she jumped.

"Are you okay?" Sherry asked.

She didn't know how long Sherry had been watching her, or what she could read on her face.

"I'm fine," Tara said, but she was a terrible liar, and Sherry gave her a probing look.

"It's nothing. It's just a little hard with Kevin away."

"I can't believe we still haven't met him. Why do I get the feeling that you're trying to hide him?"

"I don't know if you'd like him very much."

"Is he good to you? That's all that matters."

Instead of answering, Tara glanced down at her phone.

"Can I give you some advice?" Sherry asked. "If you're unhappy now, it's never going to get easier."

"I appreciate your trying to help, but it's kind of more complicated than that?" Tara said.

As soon as she said it, she worried that Sherry had heard her irritation. There had been so many times when Sherry and Sol were there for her. She could see why people might think that Sherry could be a little overwhelming, but she genuinely liked her and appreciated the way she tried to take care of her. When she'd told Sherry that she was pregnant,

Sherry had started to bring healthy lunches for her to the office. She bought her maternity clothes and offered to go with her to all the prenatal appointments and told her she could use their pool anytime. "Just show up, you don't even have to ask," Sherry would say, though she never did because she didn't want to discover that it was something to say, not to mean.

When she went into labor, she pushed for five hours, but the baby wasn't descending. "I'm afraid something is wrong," she'd said, but no one seemed to hear. Finally, the baby's head crowned, but the monitor began to beep, not the regular rhythm to which she was accustomed, but a piercing alarm that made it seem like someone was definitely about to die. The nurses were pressing down on her stomach and holding her legs to her chest. She was told to push, then not to push; she was torn open from the inside out. Caleb was whisked away before she could see him. Soon after the delivery, Kevin left the hospital to grab some food, but it was really because he couldn't deal with what was happening. She called him twice and he didn't pick up. She kept having this idea that she could rewind to the moment when she'd said that something was wrong—except this time everyone would listen. Rewind even further and Caleb would be returned to her body. She could birth him again. This time, he would slide from her, unscathed.

She called Kevin again and he didn't answer. Then she knew who to call. Sherry and Sol came right away. It had only been a few minutes, or maybe it was longer, she couldn't be sure because time was doing that strange thing where it slowed down, then sped up. At the sight of them standing in her hospital room with an air of authority, she wanted to hand herself over to them. Sol was asking for consults and specialists and second opinions, studying the lab results, calling the head of the NICU, who happened to be his friend, at home. "Don't worry, your baby is going to be fine. We will take care of everything," Sherry assured her, which were the most beautiful words she ever heard. She had only been a mother for a few hours and nothing prepared her for how swiftly the feeling had come over her: she would do anything for her child. Before that night, she sometimes believed Kevin when he said that Sherry and Sol were only nice to her so she would work hard. But after that, she started to believe them when they said she was part of the family. She understood for the first time how it felt to have a net below you, not the kind of net that could trap you, but that could catch you.

"Have you heard from Hailey yet?" Tara asked Sherry now, to change the subject. For weeks, Sherry had talked nonstop about Hailey's divorce deposition, which was scheduled for today. She relayed every detail of the proceedings, sometimes more than once, circling back to the fact that Hailey needed to move here, to the fact that Jonah would never back down. Nate was always joking that she heard more about the divorce than anyone, but she didn't mind. It was better to listen to someone else's problems than think about her own.

"The deposition was scheduled to start an hour ago. I talked to Hailey while she was driving there and she sounded nervous, but she knows she has to be strong," Sherry said.

Tara's cell phone buzzed again, but she ignored it, which made Nate come out front.

"Any word?" Nate asked Sherry.

"I was going to ask you the same thing," Sherry said.

"These things can take forever," he said. "Jonah probably has an entire treatise he's forcing her to sit through."

"I should have gone up there," Sherry said. "Even if I couldn't go into the deposition, I could have waited outside."

"Hailey's going to be fine. We've gone over everything they could ask her. You know that Jonah is going to bring up anything he can think of to make her look bad. But at the end of the day, the deposition doesn't matter. She just needs to get through it," Nate said.

At his reassurance, Tara could see Sherry relax. She'd heard plenty about how Nate was unpredictable and impulsive, but she didn't know that he could be so loyal and sweet. He listened when she described her fears about Kevin and promised her that everything was going to be okay. Even if it wasn't necessarily true, he had a way of making her feel better. Whenever he left the office, he came back with an iced caramel vanilla latte for her and he tucked pieces of expensive-looking chocolate into her desk drawer. She was pretty sure that this thing with Nate would soon run its course, but until that happened, she was going to enjoy it.

"The truth is," Sherry said to Tara once Nate went into an exam room, "I never thought Nate would be the one I would count on. But ever since Sol's diagnosis, he's been there whenever we need him. I know he likes to make a show of not caring, but he always comes through."

At least they could talk openly about Solomon's illness. Tara could only keep so many secrets at once. When Sherry finally confided in her, she acted like it was the first time she was hearing about it. To everyone else in the office, they maintained the illusion that all was fine, but quietly, they had lightened Sol's schedule. Nate had started to look over the charts of the patients that Sol saw, to ensure he didn't make a mistake.

"And . . ." Sherry said, looking over her shoulder to make sure Nate hadn't returned. "I think he's seeing someone. He has that look."

"Didn't he have a girlfriend a while ago?" Tara asked.

"That was ages ago and didn't last. I think he's still terrified of making a committment."

Tara kept her eyes trained on her computer screen, hoping Sherry wouldn't notice how curious she was. Over the years she'd heard all about Nate's various girlfriends and enjoyed being privy to the information. Sherry's stories were like a television show she faithfully watched—she heard about the wide array of problems everyone needed Sherry to solve in order to bring about the happy ending. There were times when Sherry and Sol were out of town, and they paid her to take in their mail or wait for a delivery or water the plants. She'd sit by the pool and snap a picture for Kevin, even though he made her feel silly for caring as much as she did, sometimes joking that he wasn't sure which of them she was in love with the most. She'd taken herself on a tour of the house and looked at Sherry's clothes and tried on her lipstick and then wandered into Hailey's old bedroom, where it was fun to imagine that she was the one taken care of and adored. She always ended up staring at the family pictures on the wall, enlarged like something in a museum. One in particular caught her interest: the whole family in front of what she figured was the Grand Canyon—she'd never been, but what else could that be? They were all smiling, but no one seemed particularly happy. The fact that nothing was as perfect as it looked shouldn't have given her a jolt of pleasure, but it did. For all the time that she'd worked there, Sherry talked only about Hailey and Nate, never about Adam, whose name and existence she didn't even know about until she saw the picture. It was pretty much true of Sherry in general: she didn't like to dwell on anything upsetting. A few times, Sherry's voice had grown softer and her face looked sad, like a storm was passing through, and she had confided that she wanted to see Maya more, or she would complain that Jonah didn't want her to be that involved. The moments never lasted long, because Sherry would force a laugh, like it wasn't a big deal. But Tara wasn't fooled. She saw the pain.

Don't you have some charts you need me to sign?

Nate, again. Tara made a show of gathering a stack of charts. She walked into Nate's office, but left the door open, which seemed less incriminating.

Nate was sitting, his feet propped up on his desk. "Do you know how hard it is to watch you all day?" he asked.

"I watch you all the time too," she admitted.

He came out from behind his desk and stood close to her.

"We shouldn't," Tara said.

"We definitely shouldn't," he said, but his smile made it clear he meant the opposite.

That first night, before Nate left her apartment, she'd stopped him at the door.

"Is it going to be strange in the office?"

"Only if we let it be," he said.

"Really?" she asked, wanting to believe him.

"No. It's going to be very strange."

In the hallway, Tara could hear the voices of the nurses and patients, and wished that she'd closed the door. Nate encircled her waist with his hands and she let herself be steered toward the wall. For the moment, all she wanted was the sensation of his body against hers.

"Why do I have the feeling that you want to get caught," she teased.

"What if I do?" he asked.

Up against the wall, he was running his hands inside her shirt. She knew she shouldn't be doing this, but that thought was like an alarm clock sounding somewhere in the distance when you were in the deepest state of sleep.

"Being brazen is the best way to avoid getting caught," Nate said, blue eyes sparkling. So often, she'd had the depressing thought that there was no point hoping her life might be different from how it was. But if anyone could make you believe it was possible to get what you wanted, it was Nate.

From the hallway, she heard footsteps and pulled away.

"I really don't want anyone to know . . . And I also really need to go talk to your dad," she said, trying to sound serious, but she couldn't stop smiling.

"He's still mad at me. He's barely said a word to me in weeks," Nate said. He always told her that he didn't want to talk about his parents, but he seemed unable to stop himself from bringing them up.

"I'm sure it's just that he has other things on his mind," she said.

"Has he said anything to you?"

"Of course not. I just know that he sees what a good job you're doing."

As soon as they started talking about Sol, the Nate she knew disappeared and was replaced by an insecure child. He acted like everything slid off of him, but you didn't have to be an expert to realize that he took everything his parents said to heart. If she were the one worrying, he would tell her not to get hung up on needing anyone's approval. But obviously it was a lot harder to do that when it was his own family.

After disentangling from Nate, Tara went into Solomon's office. In front of him, she'd been pretending that she didn't know he was sick, but she probably wasn't doing that good a job. Since she first noticed something was wrong, she felt the constant fear that something bad was going to happen. For all the time that she'd worked here, she'd known that she could go to Sol with a problem and he would tell her what to do. She liked how calm he was with patients, even when he had to deliver bad news. When Nate told her how Sol used to lose his temper, she had trouble imagining it—the Sol he described was nothing like the one she saw every day, but that was just another piece of evidence for what she was coming to believe: you could be more than one person at the same time.

"Can you explain why my schedule looks the way it does?" he asked her.

"What do you mean?" she asked, relieved that it wasn't Nate he wanted to discuss.

"I take it that you know that I'm sick?"

"I'm sorry. I know you didn't want to tell me," she said.

"I suppose there are some things you can't hide."

"Do you maybe want to talk about it?" Tara asked.

"Do you know what Parkinson's is?" Sol asked her. "On the most basic level, it means that nerve cells in my brain are starting to die, and are no longer able to produce the required amount of dopamine."

She nodded as he told her more. Sol had a way of explaining something so that even if she didn't fully get the science, she could still understand. The first time he explained melanoma to her, he talked about cells that, for a variety of reasons, began multiplying wildly, and the hairs at the back of her neck rose at the idea that there were all these disasters in your body, waiting for the right moment to make their presence known.

"What can I say? I've had a few months to accept the fact that I'm sick. There's nothing like a diagnosis to make you think about what really matters," he said. "When my father died, I was fourteen years old. We had a fight one morning before he went to work. An hour later, he was standing behind the counter, about to slice a side of meat, and slumped over and died of a heart attack."

"I'm so sorry," she offered, but didn't know what else to say.

"I'm just hoping for enough time to take care of everything," he said. "When you've worked your whole life to build something, it's not easy to accept that it's the end. That's why I wanted to talk to you."

"Of course. Anything you need," she said.

"What do you think of the job Nate is doing?" he asked.

"Actually, I think Nate's doing a really good job." she said, hoping that she wasn't giving herself away by blushing. "It's true that in the beginning he didn't do everything like he was supposed to, but he seems different now. He's totally focused on his patients and wants to grow the practice. Maybe I shouldn't say anything, but he really admires you. He wants to be close to you."

"There are things I wish I'd done differently," he said. "When it was hard at home, I stayed as far away as I could."

He looked so old to her so suddenly that she wanted to cry. "I think they know how much you've done for them," she said.

"It's Sherry I worry about the most. She still thinks I'm going to get better."

"She's scared. I guess we all are," she said.

"When I first met Sherry, all I wanted was to take care of her. We were young and knew next to nothing, but I promised her that I would give her a beautiful life. I know it's hardly a promise you can make, but I think she's believed it all these years,'" Sol said, and it was the first time she'd seen him look afraid.

Tara was about to leave his office when Solomon called her back. This time, she was sure that he was going to say that he knew about her and Nate.

"I hope you know that you don't have to worry. I'll make sure you're taken care of too," he told her.

By the time Tara got back to her desk, Sherry was on the phone with Hailey, obviously upset.

"Should I get Sol or Nate? I think they're with patients, but I could tell them that you need them," Tara asked, but Sherry was already rushing from the office.

"What happened? How was the deposition?" Sherry asked when Hailey finally called. All day, she had been sitting at her desk, trying to fight off a feeling of dread.

"It was terrible," Hailey said. "It went on for hours, and they wouldn't stop hammering me with questions. It was all about who does what for Maya, and why I think I should be allowed to move, but there were also things we didn't anticipate."

For weeks, the deposition gave Sherry something to focus on besides Solomon's illness. They had practiced Hailey's responses over the phone until she was ready. Say as little as possible, Nate urged her. Be hard and unwilling to budge, Sherry advised.

"What else did they ask?" Sherry said.

"There were a lot of questions about you. Obviously their strategy is to say that I'm under the control of my parents. They must have asked me ten different times if it's true that you have a vendetta against Jonah and if you're the one who came up with the idea for me to move to West Palm."

Sherry took a deep breath. It was exactly as Nate said it would be: Jonah would hurl whatever he could at them, to see what would stick. He would float accusations, try to make them look bad. She couldn't take any of it seriously, Nate had warned. They had to look past the outrage of the moment and keep their minds fixed on the outcome they wanted.

"But they also had some questions about Adam. They wanted to know—" Hailey said.

Sherry cut her off. "What did they say about Adam?"

"They wanted to know why he's not close to us," Hailey replied.

"I hope you didn't tell them anything."

"They wouldn't stop asking, so I finally said that Adam had certain issues with his upbringing and decided not to be involved in the family."

"Is that what you told Jonah?" Sherry asked. She hated that he'd been privy to what felt so personal—it was like discovering that a spy had been in their midst all along.

"We were married. Of course I told him what happened with Adam. And it was at our wedding. Obviously he was going to know."

There was something in Hailey's voice she didn't recognize. A vehemence. An anger. Not just at Jonah but at her. Before she said anything she would regret, Sherry got off the phone. She rushed past Tara, out of the office, and into the privacy of her car. She tried to take a deep breath. She tried to remember what Nate said. Steel herself. Stay calm. In the distance, she heard those admonitions, but her anger had descended too quickly and was too dense to see through. All she could think was that Jonah was going to use what had happened with Adam to take Hailey and Maya from her. Once you knew that you could lose a child, you couldn't escape the knowledge that you could lose more than one.

Hailey's wedding was the last time Sherry had seen Adam. While planning the wedding, she'd worried whether Adam would come. After he dropped out of college, he stayed in Vermont to work on a friend's farm, then moved to Maine, where he got a job as a dog trainer. Every vacation she invited Adam to join them was a no. Every time she asked to come to

Maine, to see where he lived, was also a no. But this was her child, and she would never give up. Once, Adam emailed them a picture of him with his two enormous German shepherds, his face pressed close to them, and a look of happiness so complete that she didn't recognize him at first. "Meet Gus and Luna," was the only thing he'd written. She replied that they looked like very nice dogs, but didn't know what else to add. "You and Dad have been replaced by his dogs," Nate teased, which she didn't find funny. By then, she had grown accustomed to the dull ache of having no children at home. Nate was busy, but at least he was close by, and she made sure to pin him down for regular dinner plans. She talked to Hailey on the phone every day and flew to New York to spend weekends with her. She never said goodbye without having another plan to see her in place. Each moment together was confirmation that she had been a good mother.

In the weeks leading up to Hailey's wedding, she'd left multiple messages for Adam, to confirm that he was coming. He'd missed so many family occasions, but the wedding was a once-in-a-lifetime event. If he didn't come, there would be a finality to that. Finally Hailey called him, and no one, not even Adam, could say no to her. "He's coming, but he sounds wary. He doesn't feel like seeing a lot of people and having to pretend to fit in," Hailey said.

"All he has to do is come," Sherry said.

"One thing you should know—he said he has to bring his dogs. Not to the wedding itself, but to Florida," Hailey said.

"As long as he comes, he can bring whoever he wants," Sherry told her. She offered to buy him a plane ticket, but he intended to drive because of the dogs. Nate thought it was hilarious that the dogs were attending the wedding. "You have to let them walk down the aisle. These are your grand-doggers," he said so often that finally she'd told him it was enough.

The wedding was held at the Mounts Botanical Garden in West Palm, which was one of her favorite places, with its winding pathways that were meticulously manicured, its seemingly endless varieties of plants, all of them perpetually in bloom. When Adam arrived, it took a moment to recognize him. He wasn't wearing a tux, and his hair was long and unruly, but none of that mattered. All she wanted was for him to know that he still had a place in their family.

"How was the drive? I hope it wasn't too bad," she asked, but before she rattled off any more questions she stopped herself. "I'm so glad you're here."

Adam gave what seemed like the start of a smile, and her hope flared. But when she tried to talk to him more, he kept to himself. Even when the photographer instructed them to stand closer, he remained apart.

"I don't see the dogs," she whispered to Hailey when she was having her makeup touched up before the ceremony.

"They're tied up in the front," she said.

Sherry looked out the window. Adam was coming back from walking the dogs and he was rubbing their backs, as loving as any parent could be toward a child. In spite of herself, she felt jealous.

And then it was time. Sherry didn't think about the peace she longed for in her own family, or about extended family she didn't have. She didn't focus on her wish that Jonah's father—that Jonah himself—was friendlier, or more appreciative of all she'd done to plan the wedding. At the sight of Hailey in strapless venetian lace, she drew in her breath. If this daughter was all she had, it would have been enough. As she and Sol escorted Hailey down the aisle, she looked from side to side, savoring the smiling faces of their friends and the swaying palm trees and Jonah waiting for Hailey under the chuppah, which was billowy and white. Most of all, she remembered Hailey's radiance—she beamed like the sun. All she wanted was for her daughter to be happy and to be loved.

The rest of the wedding passed quickly. In the white tent strung with tiny white lights, Jonah and Hailey danced. Watching them filled her with a longing to be back at the beginning, before anything was fixed in place. Toward the end of the night, Sherry sank into a chair. The dance floor was littered with confetti, the cloth napkins were stained, the cakes consumed. Her makeup was smeared, her hair uncoiled and flattened. She slid her feet out of her strappy gold sandals. Her toes were red, and blisters bloomed painfully at the backs of her heels. The guests were starting to leave, holding tiny boxes of chocolate truffles monogrammed with Hailey's and Jonah's initials. A few boxes were left behind on the table, and Sherry gathered them to take home as keepsakes. For months leading up to the wedding, she'd monitored every morsel that went into her mouth, but alone at the table, she opened the boxes of chocolate and devoured them all.

At the end of the night, she and Solomon stood by the parking lot with Adam.

"Will you at least stay until tomorrow?" she asked.

"I've got to get going. I'm just going to let the dogs run around for a few minutes before we get on the road," Adam said. The two dogs were by his side, unleashed but sitting obediently. She could understand a small cuddly dog, but not these, who came up nearly to her waist and had enormous mouths with slobbery wet tongues and wore chain collars as if they needed extra restraint.

She reached to hug Adam, but he stiffened. The dogs had a similar reaction: their ears perked up and she was sure that if she stepped any closer, they would lunge at her.

"Adam, please. I don't want it to be this way. I miss you. I love you," she said.

"It's just the way it is," he said and shrugged.

She hugged him goodbye, not knowing when she would next see him.

She and Sol had come separately because she'd needed to be there early for hair and makeup, so she left Sol standing with Adam and walked to her car. She glanced back. The two of them were talking, and she couldn't help but notice that, in her absence, Adam looked more relaxed. Her blisters were bleeding, not just on her heels but on the bridge of both feet, where the straps of her sandals crossed. Every step was another descent into pain. She took off her sandals and carried them across the dark parking lot. When she got into the car, she threw the sandals inside and slammed the car door. She had made a beautiful send-off for a child she never wanted to leave.

She was tired and crying and it was dark in the parking lot and it was hard to think clearly. She put the car into reverse and backed out. She felt a bump and braked.

When she got out of the car, one of Adam's dogs lay on the ground.

She had looked—of course she'd looked—but that didn't matter. The dog was by the car, alive, but barely. The other dog was barking furiously and Adam was screaming and then she too was screaming.

"She's not dead. She's not dead," she repeated.

Adam crouched next to the dog. "Come on, Luna, you're okay. You're going to be okay," he was pleading. Then he gathered up the dog and placed it in the back of his car.

"Tell me what we can do," she begged Adam.

Adam lurched toward her as if he were going to hit her.

"Sol, help, please," she begged as he stood beside her.

She waited for Solomon to say something, but he was silent and instinctively took a step away from her.

Adam grabbed the other dog, but before he hurried to his car, to drive to a veterinary hospital, he turned back.

"I never want to see you again," he said.

When Sherry got home from the office, her hands were still shaking from what Hailey had told her about the deposition. Once she was in the pool, the habits of her body took over, and after a few strokes, she began to calm down.

Hailey's wedding was more than seven years ago and she still thought about it every day.

In the weeks after the wedding, she rarely left the house. To her friends, she made vague references to the fact that it hadn't gone as well with Adam as she'd hoped, and her friends tried to say the right thing, but behind her back surely they wondered why her own child wanted little to do with her. She left messages for Adam, asking if she could buy him a new dog. She made a recurring donation to the Humane Society in Luna's memory. Months passed and she didn't hear from Adam. Before calling him, she'd script the perfect message, but once she was on the phone, she grew flustered and said too much, or said the wrong thing. She envisioned him listening to her messages—where did he sit as he listened to them? What did his room look like? She couldn't understand how her own child, once so soft and malleable, could have become this hardened.

In her mind, she brought the dog back to life. She never backed the car out. She waited all night, until the lot was empty, until the sun came up.

A few months after the wedding, Sherry went to their synagogue on Yom Kippur. For the first time in ages, she didn't have the energy to invite friends over for her usual break-fast of bagels and lox by the pool. But she did go to services. Every year, she derived comfort from the words of the prayers even if she didn't really believe in them. Even as a child, she'd loved the pageantry of the day, the Torah scrolls in their white coverings and the rabbi cloaked in white and the choir assembled of men and boys from her Hebrew school class who, dressed in their white gowns, seemed angelic and otherworldly. At the cantor's invocation of *Who shall live, who shall die*, she shuddered, believing that literally right then it was being decided, *Who by fire, who by sword, who at the right time, and who at an untimely end.* When the kids were young, she had made them go with her to synagogue on this one day, where they learned about the practice of asking one another for forgiveness: if you asked three times, and were turned down, the sin was no longer on you but on the one who refused to forgive. She took comfort in the idea of second and third chances, but of course Nate made a joke of it, teasing Adam so that he could then ask for forgiveness three times. When Adam refused, Nate carried on about how the sin was now Adam's, and he wouldn't be inscribed in the book of life, and on and on until she screamed at Nate that he was mocking something important. In vain, she tried to make them understand about the opportunity to start anew and the recognition that holding a grudge imprisoned you as well.

On this Yom Kippur, Sherry was desperate for any solace the prayers might offer. Over the course of the morning, the word *forgiveness* was repeated over and over. The rabbi told a story about how a broken vase could be expertly glued back together, but a crack would remain visible; when God forgave, however, the crack didn't exist. The rabbi reminded them, though, that God did not grant forgiveness for sins against one another until you made amends with the one you had harmed.

After services, Sherry stood outside the synagogue and called Adam.

"Will you forgive me?" she asked into his answering machine. She told him she had come from synagogue, where she thought of him the entire time and hoped there might be a way to lessen the gulf between them. Not all at once, she understood, but maybe slowly, one step and then one more.

There was no response.

A few days later, she called Adam again.

"Will you forgive me?" she asked. She said that she knew how much he loved the dog. She said that even though it was an accident, she took responsibility for what she had done.

The next day, she asked again. She said that she understood that his anger was about more than the dog. Into his answering machine, she admitted that she had tried to defend herself when she should have simply listened, that she hadn't been able to see his experience when it matched none of what she believed. She was sorry, she pleaded, before the inevitable beep on the machine cut her off.

Still she got no answer. She went out in the garden, where everything grew and changed. She uprooted old plantings and added new ones in their place. At each new blossom, she felt herself slowly coming back to life. She accepted that she wouldn't be forgiven. Even if she and Adam spoke once in a while, even if they occasionally saw each other, nothing could be undone. In Adam's mind, she would remain frozen in a block of ice, or tacked to a display board, a pin through her torso. That was when she started working in Sol's office. That was also when she started to swim. The pool was the only place she felt free. The garden was the only place she felt alive. She poured her energy into Hailey and Nate. Not one more person she loved would ever slip away.

Sherry didn't stop swimming until she was out of breath. When she climbed out of the pool, Solomon was standing there. She had no idea how long ago he'd arrived. Increasingly, she noticed that his voice lacked emotion, his face as well. Sometimes when she spoke to him, she had the feeling that no one was home.

"Did you hear about the deposition? It was all about Adam and what we—what I—did wrong," she said.

"I talked to Hailey. It's true that they mentioned Adam, but that was hardly the focus," Sol said, but she wasn't going to be made to feel like she was overreacting. How easy it was to offer advice when you weren't the one in danger.

"What if Jonah gets Adam to testify against me?" she asked.

"You're not on trial, so I don't know how that's even a possibility, but even if it were, Adam wouldn't do that."

"How do you know? For all we know, Jonah has been in touch with Adam. Maybe he was in on it."

"Adam has nothing to do with this. He has no desire to hurt you."

"He knows you're sick. I called him and left a message. And did he call back? Does he care?"

"He cares," Sol said.

"How do you know?" she asked.

"I've spoken to him, Sherry."

She thought she had misheard him. For so many years, she had craved contact with Adam. Any letter with a few scribbled sentences or a short phone conversation was treasured like the most valuable of family heirlooms.

"What do you mean? When did you talk to him?" she asked.

"He calls me," Sol admitted. "And I've helped him out over the years. He wanted to buy the property in Maine, to create a dog shelter, and he asked me if I would help him pay for it."

"But how?" she asked.

"I took it from my retirement account," he admitted.

"How could you not tell me?"

"Adam asked me not to. He didn't want anyone to know."

"How often do you talk to him?"

It was unfathomable. For her, Adam had become a series of memories and regrets. For Solomon, he continued to be a live person.

"Every week or so," he admitted.

"All this time . . . ?" she said.

"What was I supposed to do? Turn him away? What would you have done?" he asked.

She glared at him. She wanted to run, past the pool and along the path into the garden, where he might never find her. What would she have done if Adam had come to her alone? She knew, but couldn't admit it.

"Why do you think Adam and Nate were always fighting?" she screamed. "They wanted your attention, but you were never here. You let me take care of everything. When we needed you most, you were absent."

She expected him to stand there unperturbed, as if what she'd said contained no truth, but to her surprise, he looked gutted by her words.

Nate was working late, waiting for Tara to put Caleb to sleep and then call to let him know he could come over. At first, he had enjoyed the challenge of trying to hide their relationship, but by now, he was ready to drop the pretenses and just be with her.

Though it had only been a week since Hailey's deposition, it felt a lot longer. Every day, Nate talked to his mother and to Hailey multiple times, reassuring them that everything was fine, but the truth was, he was far more nervous than he wanted to admit. He had to hand it to Jonah. By bringing Adam into the mix, he'd found a way to make the divorce even more contentious. Of course, Jonah would claim that they were the ones escalating at every turn; surely if he were to tell his side of the story, it would be the equal and opposite of theirs. Not that it really mattered anymore what either of them would claim—everyone was going to fight as if their version was the only one.

Come over?

Finally. He had started to worry that at any minute Tara would end it between them. He didn't believe Kevin was ever coming back, but that didn't stop Tara from talking about how guilty she felt. "Guilt is a useless emotion. You can't let yourself think about it," he told her. "How can I possibly do that?" she asked, and he wished he could explain what he had long ago discovered: if you acted unbothered, sometimes you could even fool yourself. "You just tell yourself that you're not doing anything wrong. If anything, Kevin is the one who should feel guilty. He's the one who left." For a few days, she seemed less worried but her guilt inevitably returned.

On his way out of the building, Nate lingered in front of the dental office next door. He'd heard that they weren't renewing their lease, but afraid of upsetting his father, he hadn't mentioned it to him. He had little time anyway to think about the expansion he'd once cared so much about. Being so overrun with familial obligations confirmed his lifelong instinct to keep himself at a distance. Once you stepped too close, you were in danger of being swallowed up.

On the drive to Tara's, Nate called his mother back. She hadn't come into the office since the deposition, claiming she had a lingering cold, but he knew better. Each time they spoke, he'd encouraged her to return to work, or if she didn't want to do that, at least get together with friends or work on the arrangements for the sixty-fifth birthday extravaganza that they were supposedly throwing for her, but that in reality she was organizing herself.

"We have to do something. We need a plan," Sherry said.

"What do you want me to do? Fly up there and threaten to break Jonah's legs? Shoot him?" he said. The desperation in her voice scared him. She was sure that Jonah was intent on using Adam to hurt her, and there was no convincing her otherwise. She also truly believed that if they refused to back down, Hailey would eventually be allowed to move here. In the past, when he'd claimed that his mother only saw what she wished to see, he'd believed it was a game in which she just refused to acknowledge what, deep down, they both understood to be true. But maybe all these years he'd had it wrong, and she didn't actually see what she couldn't bear. She wasn't just reshaping her reality but living inside an entirely different one.

"Jonah hated me all along, and now he's going to do whatever he can to hurt me," Sherry was saying. "This isn't just about Hailey. Please tell me you can see that. He's hell-bent on trying to hurt all of us."

He was hoping Tara wouldn't fall asleep in the time that it took him to drive over.

"I know you don't want to hear this, but I really think we need to ask ourselves how ugly we want this to get," Nate said. "It's time to accept the fact that Hailey isn't going to move here. I would hate to spend all our money and energy fighting Jonah when we should be focusing on taking care of Dad."

"Why do you think I'm doing this? Our family needs to be together," she said.

"I know, but—"

"You need to promise me that you'll come up with a plan."

He hesitated. Every part of him wanted to say no and return to the time in his life when he thought nothing of letting his parents down. What had happened to that person who derived such pleasure in screwing up, then walking away?

"I promise," he said.

At Tara's apartment, Nate took the key from under the mat, where she'd left it for him, and went inside. Judging from the look of the place, she'd had a hard night. Toys and dishes were strewn and the kitchen was cluttered with empty containers. When he was Tara's age, he'd barely been able to take care of himself, let alone another person. In the beginning, he'd felt funny being at her apartment, but Kevin had been gone for four months, and surely there was some statute of limitations on how long she was expected to wait. He rarely asked Tara about him directly, but he knew that she and Kevin spoke on the phone. A few times, she'd driven Caleb to Winter Haven to visit him, but said that she refused to stay over at Sam's apartment. "Why do you put up with it? You realize that you don't have to, don't you?" Nate said to her, but she was crippled by a passivity he couldn't understand.

Nate opened the door to her bedroom. The blanket covered most of Tara, but one of her bare legs was on top. He got into bed beside her and ran his hands across her thigh.

"Here I am," he whispered.

"How was your night?" she asked.

He groaned. "You don't want to know."

More awake, she rolled to face him. He'd hoped that once he was with her, he would be able to get his family out of his mind, but apparently they were ever-present.

"My mother is obsessed. Instead of coming to the office, she sits around all day thinking about Jonah. And she's convinced that I'm going to come up with a way to magically fix everything," Nate said.

"She knows you're the one who's there for her," Tara said.

"Is that what she tells you?" he asked.

"It's clear how loyal you are. You're the most dedicated son ever. Even your father knows that."

"Hailey is the one I'll do anything to help. For as long as I can remember, she had this way of looking up to me that made me feel like I was a good person. Did I ever tell you that when she and Jonah got engaged, I told her I was setting up a divorce account for when she was ready to leave him? It was just a joke at first, but I decided to really do it. Hailey had no idea, but every year, I added money just in case. Then once she started telling me that things were hard with Jonah, I put more in. I was doing well, and I liked the idea that, behind the scenes, I was taking care of her."

"And the money is just sitting there?" Tara asked.

"Yes," he said. "And by this point, there's a lot of it."

"What if you used it to pay Jonah off?"

Nate laughed. "I don't think that's what my mother has in mind."

"Ask her. Sometimes you have to do things you ordinarily wouldn't, for the people you love," she said, as if it were simple, and maybe it was.

He pulled Tara on top of him. If she was still feeling guilty, he saw no sign of it. He hoped she was coming to recognize that you could compartmentalize guilt and carry on with your life. When they first started sleeping together, he had been sure that in a few weeks his excitement about her would burn itself out. If anything, he had worried about the fallout when he wanted to extricate himself, not what would happen when he wanted to stay where he was.

He watched as she fell back to sleep. Lightly, he kissed her goodbye.

On his way out, he noticed that the door to Caleb's room was slightly open, and he peeked in. Even in the toddler-sized bed, Caleb looked tiny. He was partially covered by a light blue blanket printed with red cars, and Nate could hear the soft sounds of his breathing. Though Nate didn't dare wake him, he wanted to pull the covers higher to protect him.

Nate put the toys away in the living room and went into the kitchen, where he washed the dishes and wiped off the table. He couldn't remember the last time he'd cleaned his own apartment, so he couldn't say that he did a stellar job, but at least in the morning, Tara wouldn't be bombarded by all that she needed to do.

Nate got back into his car, but before he started to drive, he took out his phone and called his mother. Yes, the idea of paying off Jonah was a little outrageous, but so were a lot of things. And yes, it was impossible to know if an idea like this would even work, but it was better than sitting around, helpless. The longer the divorce went on, the angrier everyone would become. Sometimes the best way to end something was to make a bold, swift cut. Sometimes the only way out was through.

"I'm coming over," he said to Sherry.

His parents' house was unusually dark when he pulled into the driveway. Sherry rarely turned out the lights, the house always blazing like a beacon, and privately, he wondered if she hoped that Adam might unexpectedly arrive home, see the lights, and know that she was waiting for him. He had no way to know if that was true, and while he joked about a lot of things that his mother did, this possibility felt too raw even for him.

When he went inside, Sherry was in pajamas, her hair unbrushed. It was rare to see her so undone.

"Let's sit outside," she said.

She flipped on the lights and they stretched out in two chaise lounges by the pool. Now that it was springtime, the bugs were out in full force. A mosquito buzzed in his ear and he flicked it away. The statue was lit up and even though he'd always hated the gaudiness of it, he felt a pang of guilt. It had been years, but he felt sure that if he inspected the statue, he would still be able to see the crack he'd made.

"No offense, but you look awful. Have you slept at all?" he said.

"I can't. My mind won't stop racing."

"Do you want to take something? I could prescribe it," he offered.

"I don't want to sleep."

"Then come back to work. The office is falling apart without you. And sitting at home all day isn't going to accomplish anything."

"I'm terrified that Jonah is going to prevent me from seeing Maya. I can't do anything. I can't even swim."

"You know you'd feel better if you did," he said, but she shook her head. Over the years, he teased her about her hobby and found ways to diminish it. But when she swam laps, he watched her transform into someone else, not his mother but an athlete who understood that you always had to keep going. In other contexts, this quality of hers was annoying, but when she was in the pool, he marveled at her determination.

"I have an idea that might make you feel better," he said.

"Please. Anything," she said and sat up and swung her legs around to face him.

"What if we pay Jonah to let Hailey move?"

He watched her closely, awaiting her reaction. She looked like someone who had been holding her breath, and now finally, was able to let go.

"A bribe? Are you serious?" she said.

"Not a bribe," he corrected her. "A settlement offer. And I know it might sound outrageous, but yes, I'm serious."

"Is it wrong?" she asked.

"Look, a lot of things are wrong. Jonah is convinced that Hailey is completely wrong to want to move here. And she's sure that he's completely wrong to leave her, then keep her in a city she hates. And it doesn't matter which one of them is right, because at this point, they're never going to agree. What matters is that, one way or another, this has to end."

"Yes. It has to end," she agreed.

Their eyes met. He had spent so much time wanting to extricate himself, but he'd had no idea how good it would feel to be the child who did everything right.

"How much are you thinking?" she asked.

"At least two hundred thousand. Maybe two fifty. It doesn't seem like Jonah has a new book on the horizon, and we know he must be spending a fortune on lawyers, so he might be getting desperate."

"There's no way I can pay something like that," she said.

"I know—but I can."

She looked at him with surprise. "How do you have that kind of money?"

"Do you remember how I used to tell Hailey that I was setting up a divorce account?"

"I assumed you were joking."

"I was completely serious," he said.

"I knew that if anyone was going to come up with an idea, it would be you."

"Look, I wouldn't get too excited just yet. There are things we need to work out. I don't think this is something Dad would approve of. Do you think you can keep it from him?"

"He keeps plenty from me," she said.

"Is there something I should know?" he asked.

"Nothing is the same anymore. He's not the way he once was."

He took her hand. "You know it's only going to get worse, don't you?" he said as gently as he could.

He expected her to deny it, but she nodded with an air of resignation. "Sometimes I feel like he's already gone."

"I know. I feel the same." His voice cracked, but he collected himself. "Look, I really think it's okay not to tell Dad about the money. He doesn't need to worry about this, on top of everything else. But we do have to tell Hailey."

"Do you really think she'd be okay with it?" Sherry asked.

"She's pretty angry. If we present this in the right way, she might be willing to try it," he said. "And we should make the offer to Jonah in person. I'm thinking that I could go up there one weekend and have a little chat with him."

"You convince Hailey, and I'll make the offer to Jonah," Sherry said.

Nate hesitated. "Don't you think it would be better if I did it?"

"I want to be the one to talk to him," she insisted.

Nate really hoped he wasn't going to regret this, but he said yes.

Nate called Hailey the next morning as he was driving to work. "What are you doing next weekend?"

"Nothing. Maya is with Jonah."

"Great. Then you're meeting me."

As far as Nate could tell, Hailey seemed surprised by the invitation, which made him feel even worse that he hadn't spent a weekend with her in Binghamton, as he'd intended. So consumed with being present for his parents, he hadn't paid enough attention to how much she needed him too.

"How about Miami Beach? I'm sure you could use some sun. And that's as far away as Mom is going to let me travel right now—she basically has me pinned to the office and the house," Nate said.

"Why don't you sound bothered by that?" she asked.

"You can get used to anything, right? For now, I'm trying to distract Mom. When in doubt, I ask her about her birthday party."

"That's not until August," she said.

"It's never too soon! You only turn sixty-five once," he said. "I assume you're hard at work on 'Sherry Marcus: The Musical Tribute' that you and I will be starring in at the party."

At the sound of Hailey's laughter, he had that same hopefulness he'd experienced the night before when he told his mother his idea. He hated how distant he'd felt from Hailey the last time he saw her, but now that unease was dissipating. It reminded him of when he was a kid, and everyone, himself included, was mad at him for spoiling what could have been a peaceful night. He would take refuge in his room and there would be a knock on his door, and Hailey would be standing there, her long blond hair cascading down her back like some kind of cartoon princess. In his room, she would tell him the details of her day, which he'd be happy to listen to, and she'd laugh at his jokes, even if they weren't that funny. In her presence, it mattered less how awful he'd behaved at dinner. So long as she was on his side, he couldn't be entirely bad.

"Are you really not going to tell me what the occasion is for our little getaway?" she asked.

"Why do I need an excuse to spend the weekend with my favorite sister? I'm buying you a plane ticket. Once Maya is with Jonah, you'll fly down and I'll take care of everything."

• • •

On Friday afternoon, Nate was about to leave the office and drive to Miami Beach when Solomon appeared in his doorway.

"It's time we talked," Sol said.

Nate followed him into his office and sat in the chair in front of his desk, where he'd always felt like a child in trouble at school.

"I have something for you," his father said and pushed a pile of papers closer to him. His hand shook and Nate had to resist the urge to place his own hand on top to steady him.

Nate startled. It was the signed lease from the building management for the office next to them.

"The space is yours," Solomon said. "You can do what you want with it."

Nate skimmed the papers. "Are you serious?" he asked.

"I intend to see patients for as long as I can, and I'll be available to help with the transition, but the direction of the practice is up to you," Sol said.

"I'm speechless. This is the last thing I expected," Nate said.

"I've accepted the fact that I can't keep working at this pace, and before I step back, I want to make sure everything is taken care of. It's not easy to accept that you're at the end of your career. Maybe one day you'll understand how that feels."

Were those tears in his father's eyes? It felt like a kindness to look away.

"If I know you, you're not going anywhere that fast. You're going to be checking up on me, to make sure I don't screw up," Nate said.

"You're not going to screw up," Sol assured him.

Nate stood up, which felt like wading through a thick slog of air, but he walked around his father's desk to hug him. How long had it been since he had done this? He remembered something he hadn't thought about in years. Before, he was so intent on making his father mad, he couldn't wait for him to come home from work. All afternoon, he would ask his mother how much longer it would be, until she stood with him in front of the clock and taught him how to tell time. He stood, transfixed, as the minutes dragged by. The waiting was unbearable. He'd had the urge to climb onto the table and move forward the hands of the clock. Between hearing his father's key in the door and him walking inside, everything somehow went wrong.

Nate was halfway out the office door when he heard his name. He turned back and waited.

"I wish it had been different," Sol said.

"You wish what had been different?" Nate asked tentatively.

"Our family. The way I was. I should have been there more."

Nate met his father's gaze, but he was afraid to speak. He was struck anew by the mystery of this man. He assumed he would always remain at a distance, but now he was being ushered closer.

"Congratulate me. I'm in charge," Nate said to Tara on the phone once he was on his way to Miami Beach. The other cars were impediments he sailed past. The open road was for him alone. When he got to the hotel, he would make a few calls, see if he could get a contractor in on Monday to look at the new space, and set up a meeting with an architect, who could start working on plans.

"Oh my god, Nate! That's great," Tara said.

"You should have seen my father. He was practically crying. I knew if I didn't get out of there, we would both be bawling," he admitted. It was probably for the best that he left when he had, but he was replaying every word and wishing he'd stayed until his father said more.

"See, I told you that you're the family hero," she said.

"I'm hardly a hero," he said.

"You know you love it," she teased, and he had to admit that she was right. He was aglow with the good feeling.

"We have to celebrate. You should come meet us in Miami," Nate said.

"Me and Caleb, you and Hailey? How exactly do you think that would play out?"

"Maybe we should just tell everyone about us," he said. He didn't think his parents would be that upset. His father would regard it as unprofessional, but he was pretty sure that his mother would overlook a lot if she thought that he was happy.

"Oh my god, are you insane?" Tara said. "I feel guilty enough as it is."

"End it with Kevin and we'll have nothing to feel guilty about."

"I'm serious, Nate. You know it's not that simple, so can you please not say things like that?"

"What's the matter?" he asked, hearing the shift in her tone.

"I don't know how to tell you this, but last night, I was talking to Kevin on the phone and he told me that he's coming back next week."

Nate sped past a car in front of him. He had the urge to swerve across to the upcoming exit and drive home to her. "And you believed him?"

"I don't know. Maybe? He was making all these promises about how it's going to be different from now on, and how he's really changed, and he just wants to take care of me and Caleb."

"Tara, how many times has he done this? It's been months. Tell him you've moved on," Nate said.

"You don't know him like I do. You have no idea what he's been through."

"What I know is that he left you alone with Caleb. He's done it before and he's going to do it again. How can you not see that?"

"We have a kid together, okay? You don't know what that's like."

"I know that he's not here. Doesn't that matter?"

"It does, but it's not that easy to overturn my whole life."

Her voice had softened and he hoped that he was starting to sway her. "End it with him. I want to be with you," he said.

“What happened to ‘I always want to get away’?” she asked.

“Maybe that’s how I used to be, but not anymore,” Nate said. “I’m going to be running the practice, and I want you to do it with me. I want you to do everything with me.”

“I don’t know,” Tara said.

“Promise me that you’ll at least think about it,” Nate said. An earlier version of him would have been flabbergasted by the promises he was offering, but with everything around him changing, he too was becoming someone new.

He was meeting Hailey at the Fontainebleau, which played a central role in the family lore about their first trip to Florida and how, sipping a tropical drink at the outdoor bar, his mother had a life-altering epiphany that she was destined to live here. When he’d told Sherry where he was meeting Hailey, he saw the longing on her face and for a moment he’d considered inviting her to join, but she was already more involved in the execution of the plan than he was comfortable with. He couldn’t control what his mother said to Jonah, but it would be much easier to convince Hailey if they were alone.

When Nate got to the hotel, he changed into his bathing suit and waited for Hailey by the pool. It was probably a bad idea to barrage Tara with texts, but he wanted her to know how serious he was. He sent her a selfie and wrote that he wished she was here. When she didn’t write back, he texted again and said she could still change her mind and meet them. At least it was something to distract him until Hailey came. After continually replaying the conversation with his father, his excitement was starting to dampen. It was a lot easier to want something when you didn’t think you were going to get it. Now, after all his talk about expanding the practice, he was afraid that he would make irredeemable mistakes that his father would have known how to avoid.

When Hailey came out to the pool a few hours later, she'd already put her bags in their room and changed into her bathing suit. For a moment, he didn't realize it was her. He always made fun of the fact that Sherry called Hailey "Sunshine," but it was true that she'd had a warm, bright disposition. Now he saw how brittle she seemed, too thin and not in a good way. The small lines around her eyes were more pronounced and her forehead was creased with worry. It was an occupational hazard. He couldn't help but notice people's flaws.

Hailey stretched out next to him, but studied her phone. "I have to text Jonah," she said.

"You're in beautiful Miami Beach—isn't he the last person you want to be in contact with?"

"I need to make sure he remembers that Maya is supposed to go to a birthday party this weekend. If I don't remind him, he claims I'm withholding information. And if I do, he acts offended that I didn't expect him to remember . . ." She trailed off. "I'm sorry. I don't know why I'm talking about him. Please kill me if I become one of those people who can only talk about my ex-husband."

"One shot, right through the heart," Nate said.

"Do you know that sometimes I still don't believe we're getting divorced? It's almost been a year since he told me he was leaving me, and I'm still not used to being away from Maya for a weekend."

"Can you at least try to enjoy yourself when you're not with her? You seem like you could use some fun."

"Do I look that bad?"

"Horrible," he joked. "Which is why, for this weekend, you don't have to worry about anything. I have every minute planned. And the first thing I'm going to do is make sure you don't have any contact with Jonah," he said and snatched her phone. "And the next thing I'm going to do is tell you about our jam-packed weekend." He presented the brochures he'd grabbed from the lobby display of local attractions. "Tomorrow, we're going to start our day by heading over to beautiful Monkey Jungle, and then we'll hit the Seaquarium."

"Please, just let me lie here," she begged.

"Because I'm so nice, I'm going to make a onetime exception and not force you to go to Monkey Jungle. But you do have to come into the pool," he said.

They entered at the shallow end and leaned against the edge, their faces to the sun. He was nervous, but didn't want her to see that—better to act like he had everything under control.

"Are you really not going to tell me what's going on?" she asked.

"I don't understand why you're so convinced there's anything going on."

"Because I know you," she said. "And you have that smile."

"I'm not smiling," he said, but of course he was. If anyone could read him, it was her.

"I know things have been hard, but I can't stand the feeling that you're pulling away from me," she said. When he started to protest, she continued. "No. Let me say this. I appreciate what you're doing for me, for all of us. I know that my divorce has been a strain on everyone, and I'm sorry if you've shouldered too much. And I hope you know that our closeness sometimes feels like the one thing I can count on."

His eyes met hers. "It's Tara," he said. "I was afraid to tell you, but I'm pretty sure I'm in love with her."

"Oh, Nate. I'm not sure I've ever heard you say that about anyone," she said with so much sympathy that he wished he'd confided in her sooner.

"I told you that you didn't want to know," he said.

"Is she still with that guy Mom is always carrying on about?"

"Officially he's her fiancé, but he more or less left in January. He claims he's coming back, but there's no way that's happening. Tara says she believes him, but I'm pretty sure that on some level she knows he's not."

"And Mom and Dad have no clue?" she asked.

"I don't have a problem with them knowing, but Tara thinks it's a bad idea. And they have more than enough to worry about right now. This afternoon, Dad told me I'm in charge of the practice."

"Nate, congratulations! That's great, isn't it?"

"You understand how sick Dad is, right? You do realize that he's not going to get better?"

"Is this why you wanted to meet me?" she asked, alarmed. "Is he getting worse?"

"Yes, he is, but that has nothing to do with why we're here," he said.

"Then what is it?"

Nate drew closer to Hailey and looked around. Only a few people were swimming past, but even so, he lowered his voice. He knew Hailey well enough to expect her to initially say no to what he was about to propose. But he also knew that as the idea settled in, she would consider it. In his estimation, the people who held things in eventually erupted with the most ferocity. All the times that, as a kid, he convinced her to go along with one of his practical jokes or questionable games, he'd had the feeling that he was enabling her to break some internal boundary and feel momentarily free.

"I know this is going to sound a little extreme, but all I'm asking is for you to listen for a minute and consider an idea we had."

"Why am I already afraid?" she said.

He paused, more nervous than he'd expected.

"Mom and I want to pay Jonah something in the neighborhood of two hundred and fifty thousand dollars to let you move," he said.

She looked stunned. "Oh my god. Please tell me that you're joking."

"Dead serious," he responded.

"There's no way Jonah would ever agree to anything like this. And even if he would, I can't let you spend that kind of money," she said.

"At this point I would pay anything to never have to talk about Jonah again," he said. "But seriously, a lot of it is your money. Your divorce account has done very well."

"I thought that was a joke."

"I told you I was going to do it, and I did, and now there's a lot of money sitting there. I know you might feel funny about it, but I want you to let us try," he said.

Hailey shook her head in disbelief, but he could tell that she was willing to listen.

"The way I see it, the risks are low—there's a good chance that Jonah is going to see this as a desirable option and he's going to come to an agreement with us. And if he says no, then he might be angry and try to use it against you, but what can he really do? There's no harm done. You can pretend like this never happened."

"I don't know. It sounds pretty insane to me."

"At this point it kind of feels like our only option."

"I really don't want to do something wrong," she said.

"You've been so good your entire life and where has that gotten you? Sometimes you have to play a little rough to get the outcome that's best in the long run. And in order to do that, you first have to accept that you're not in a normal situation."

"I don't know," she said, but had the wistful expression he saw whenever she was starting to sway.

"Look, Hailey, I know this isn't something you would ever imagine doing, and obviously we don't want things to escalate, but I'm concerned that the longer the divorce goes on, the more out of control it will become. The two of you are never going to see eye to eye, but I'm hoping that this will let everyone move on with their lives."

"I wish you could do it without me having to know," she said, only half joking.

"If you want, this can be the last conversation we have about it. Mom and I will take care of it and you can claim you knew nothing."

"Can I think about it?" she asked.

"You can do whatever you want," he said.

She lay on her back, floating, and he put his arms under her and steered her around the pool.

"You're on a long, long journey, miles from home," he said, as he had in the pool when they were young, pretending she was lost at sea. There always came a moment when he claimed they'd encountered choppy waters, or spotted a shark, and then he'd dunk her. Though she knew what he was going to do, she always played along.

"I can't believe I'm actually considering this," she said.

"It's going to be fine. I promise you," he assured her.

"How can you possibly know that?"

"Trust me," he said.

Solomon wasn't up to the trip, so Sherry flew alone to Binghamton for Maya's dance recital at the end of May. So many times she'd wished she could tell Sol about the plan to pay Jonah. In the past, she relied on his calm, rational thinking and enjoyed knowing that in the background, he was taking care of everything. Now she was quiet around Sol, afraid she might inadvertently give away what she was on the verge of doing.

Since Nate had first proposed the idea of paying Jonah, she and Nate had discussed little else. Even though he'd agreed to let her make the offer to Jonah, she could sense that he was having second thoughts. But she insisted. The people she loved were being taken from her, and she had so little power to stop it. There had to be one place to exert some control. She assured Nate that she could do it. She would go over to Jonah's apartment and show him the check; she'd let him know that as soon as he signed the agreement allowing Hailey and Maya to move, the money would be his. What would come after, she didn't know: Would Jonah tell anyone? Would she eventually have to confess to Sol? When she shared these worries with Nate, he advised her to focus only on what she was going to say to Jonah. *Don't think. Just act*, Nate said, and now she repeated that mantra to herself. Anytime she doubted herself, she reached for the check, which was in her purse. The check was a shield, it was a knife. She would be one of those mothers who, by sheer force of will, lifted cars off their trapped children, who bent bars of steel in order to rescue their loved ones.

"Is Jonah here?" Sherry whispered to Hailey as they sat in the auditorium waiting for the recital to begin.

"I'm sure he is," Hailey said.

"Do you know how his new book is coming along?" Sherry asked.

"How would I know? We don't discuss anything besides Maya."

"You don't think he would really write about us, do you?"

"He's going to write whatever he wants. He's certainly not going to worry about our feelings. He used to tell me that if I wanted to be a writer, I had to be ruthless."

"Are you worried?" Sherry asked.

"Of course I am. But what can I possibly do?"

"I don't know how you can stand to be in the same room. Don't you want to scream every time you see him?"

"Don't worry. At least we're not sitting with him," Hailey said.

Sherry looked around the room. When she didn't see Jonah, she had the unlikely hope that he wouldn't show. She took in the other parents sitting nearby and wondered if any of them would come over to talk to Hailey. She'd expected Hailey to be surrounded by friends, as she always had been, but Hailey said little to anyone—she waved to a few people, but was much quieter than she used to be.

The recital was about to start when Sherry finally saw Jonah, two rows in front of them, his head directly in her line of view. He had occupied her mind all these months, but somehow it was shocking to be in his actual presence. At the sight of him, she felt the flare of worry that it was wrong to pay him off, but quickly, she bolstered herself. It was wrong that Jonah had made Hailey move to Binghamton in the first place. It was wrong that he left her out of the blue. It was wrong for her daughter to be stuck in a city where she had no one.

"How did he get a better seat than us?" she whispered to Hailey.

The curtain rose and Sherry shifted in her seat to avoid a view of Jonah's head. Was his head always this enormous? She leaned forward, but he was present no matter where she looked. Maybe he was aware of them a few rows behind and was purposefully shifting to obstruct her view. At the very least, she hoped Jonah remembered that she was the one who suggested Maya take ballet in the first place—a bitter pill for him to swallow alongside any pleasure. When Sherry was in middle school, the only way she was going to have dance lessons was if she signed herself up, so that was what she had done. There had been a man who played piano and a barre where all the girls in their pink leotards lined up, and it was one of the few times she'd felt like she was in the presence of something beautiful. She wanted to give Maya the same feeling, but Jonah claimed she was too young. "You loved to dance when you were little, and Maya will too," she said to Hailey. For Maya's third birthday, she bought her ballet shoes and a gift card for a year of classes, which Maya was delighted by, and even Jonah had to admit, however begrudgingly, that it was the perfect gift.

Once Sherry was focused on Maya, she momentarily stopped noticing Jonah's head. Maya was beaming from a row of girls, tiny pink tutus aflutter as they paraded across the stage. Sherry glanced at Hailey, who was watching Maya, rapt. At one of Hailey's dance recitals, her jazz routine was coordinated to the song "You Are My Sunshine" and all the girls wore yellow sequined leotards. It didn't matter how many other girls there were. Sherry only saw Hailey, as if she were dancing under a spotlight made from her love.

Maya was now on the opposite side of the stage and Sherry had to shift for a better view, but Jonah's head was once again directly in front of her. She craned her neck, she changed position again, but he was still right in her line of sight. The swell of love she'd felt was driven away by a rush of anger. This was how it would always be, for years of dance recitals and school plays and birthday parties. Jonah would be a presence, not just in their lives but inside her head. Sherry reached into her purse to make sure the check was still there. She rubbed it between her fingers and felt electric with its power.

When the recital was over and the families clustered in the theater lobby, Sherry hugged Maya and gave her a bouquet of pink roses. She'd lost track of Jonah until she turned around and there he was, holding out an identical bouquet to Maya. When Maya hugged him, it felt like a betrayal. This child she loved also loved someone she hated.

"How are you, Jonah?" Sherry said, trying to sound cordial, but her body tightened. She couldn't believe that she'd once considered him handsome—his chiseled features now looked severe, and she took some pleasure in the fact that his hair had grayed at the temples and he had gained weight.

"Sherry," he greeted her. His scorn was evident, yet all these years, she had willed herself not to see it.

She cinched a smile on her face. "How have you been?" she asked.

"Wonderful," he said.

"I'm so glad."

Sherry turned back to Maya and took in her thick coating of glitter eye shadow. That morning, Maya had insisted on adding several extra layers and it had smudged so that her entire face sparkled.

"You're a beautiful dancer just like your mommy was when she was your age," she said to Maya. "And that was why I made sure you took ballet lessons. Because I had a feeling that you were going to be just like your mommy and me."

"You should get up there, Sherry," Jonah said. "I'm sure everyone would love to see you dance."

For Maya's sake, she smiled. That might have concealed the tension from the strangers milling around, but not from Maya, who was carefully surveying them.

"Grandma," Maya said, and Sherry leaned toward her, continuing to smile. "Do you hate Daddy?"

The room seemed to fall silent. Both Hailey and Jonah looked shocked. Sherry felt stunned too that Maya had detected the hatred that she'd believed to be well concealed.

Sherry gave a nervous laugh. "Don't be silly, sweetie. No one hates anyone!"

Maya looked at her questioningly, on the verge of saying more, and Sherry had the urge to gently clamp her hand over her mouth.

"We have to take pictures!" Sherry announced. "Grandpa and Uncle Nate are so sad that they couldn't come, so we have to show them how adorable you look!"

She had Hailey take pictures of her with Maya. She wanted one of her with Hailey and Maya, and though it felt like offering up an unguarded piece of herself, she handed Jonah her phone and asked him to take the picture. It used to be such a big hassle to capture these occasions. Sol always forgot the camera or they didn't have film, or even when they did, the boys were never willing to smile and pose. Now Nate teased her for wanting so many photos. "Are you ever going to look at them?" he asked. But these moments passed so quickly. If she didn't preserve them, they would be lost.

After the performance, Sherry and Hailey took Maya for ice cream, then to the playground. In the evening, Sherry helped feed her dinner and gave her a bath and read a stack of books. After Maya fell asleep, she and Hailey sat in the living room.

"I can't believe Maya said that," Hailey said, sinking into the couch.

"You can't worry about it. Kids say all sorts of things," Sherry said.

"I'm sure Jonah is going to find a way to use it against me," Hailey said.

Was that an edge to Hailey's voice? The flutter of anxiety made Sherry talk in a brighter tone and hope that her words could smooth over whatever might be wrong. She said that it was great to see Maya dance, and soon they would be coming to West Palm for her birthday party. She updated Hailey on the progress of Nate's expansion into the office next door, and said that she believed Solomon's newest medications were working; he seemed tired, but was more like himself.

"Let me cook for you," Sherry offered. "You sit back and relax. I'll take care of everything."

In the kitchen, Sherry sautéed vegetables and salmon. She made a salad and set the table. It had probably been a long time since anyone had done something nice for Hailey.

"I was thinking that when you move back home, maybe you could work for the practice. Or you could write and I could watch Maya for you," Sherry offered once they were at the table.

She waited for Hailey to respond, but she had a funny look on her face and was still not looking directly at her.

"What is it?" Sherry finally asked.

"Are we really not going to talk about the money?" Hailey said.

"I didn't know you wanted to talk about it."

"How can we not? I know I agreed to it, but I'm worried it's a terrible idea. I was going to ask my lawyer what she thinks, but I couldn't bring myself to tell her."

"There's no need for her to know, not yet anyway. Let's see what Jonah says, then we can take it from there."

"I highly doubt that Jonah will ever agree to something like this."

"It's easy to say that, but you don't know what people will do when they're under stress," Sherry said. She didn't share the rest of what she had come to realize—that not only could you never predict what other people would do, you couldn't always predict your own self. Never would she have envisioned that she would be on the verge of offering her soon-to-be ex-son-in-law a check for a quarter of a million dollars. Never would she have believed that one of her own children wouldn't speak to her.

"Sometimes you have to take a chance," Sherry said. "And what do we have to lose? If Jonah says no, we'll be in the same position we are now."

"You do realize that the second you offer Jonah the money, he's going to text me that this proves you're bankrolling the divorce and how you're trying to use your money to control him," Hailey said.

"You don't think he would do the same thing if he could?" Sherry said. "Come on, Hailey, you've told me yourself how he never backs down from a fight. If he had this kind of money or if he had people willing to do anything for him—what do you think he would do?"

"I have no idea, but I can't stand the fighting anymore. I'm afraid that if we keep going, this is really going to spiral out of control," Hailey said.

Sherry took Hailey's hand, which was as soft as it was when she was a girl. She wished that they hadn't told her about the money. Jonah suddenly allowing her to move would seem to her like a miracle.

"My sweet Sunshine," Sherry murmured.

"Don't call me that," Hailey said.

"Why not?"

"It's hardly true."

"It used to be. You were the happiest little girl ever."

"Maybe, but it's not true anymore. The divorce has taken over my life. It's the only thing I can think about."

"Why do you think I'm doing this?" Sherry said. "I want you to have your life back. I want you to be able to start planning for what comes next. You're still so young. You have everything ahead of you."

"If this doesn't work, then I'm going to give in and try to make the best of living here."

"But, Hailey," Sherry protested.

"Stop, Mom. I need you to understand that," Hailey said.

"I really think this is going to work, but if it doesn't, then yes, we'll back down," Sherry said. "But it's not going to come to that. I know it."

• • •

On Sunday morning, Sherry told Hailey she was going to buy ingredients for the sugar cookies she wanted to bake with Maya. She was probably talking too much about how this was the same recipe they'd used when Hailey was little, but she needed to fill the silence in case Hailey decided to again broach the subject of their plan. She needed to get out of the house before Hailey changed her mind and tried to stop it.

On my way, Sherry texted Nate once she was in the car.

After the store, she mapped her way to Jonah's house. At the sight of his car in the driveway, her hands began to shake and she kept driving. So many times, she'd proclaimed that she would do anything for her children, but she hadn't realized how terrifying it would feel to follow through on that promise. She felt the impulse to turn back. She still couldn't believe she was about to do this—it felt like one part of herself was shearing away from the rest.

After one more loop around the block, Sherry steadied herself. She summoned her anger. She gripped the check. Surely she wasn't the only parent who, for the sake of her child, found herself on the brink of doing something she never would have imagined.

If this didn't work—no, she wasn't going to think that way. It was going to work.

Nate had warned her that the less she said, the better, to which she told him not to worry: Jonah was the last person with whom she wanted to have a prolonged conversation. She would be at his house for five minutes, maybe less. She would recite a few well-planned sentences—*This has to end. We are willing to pay*—and that would be it. If he said no, she would leave and this would be the end.

She walked up the front walk and knocked on Jonah's door. When he answered, he startled at the sight of her. He had the disoriented bleariness of someone who'd just woken up. He was unshaven, his hair unbrushed, and he was wearing sweat shorts and an old T-shirt.

"To what do I owe the pleasure?" he asked.

Face-to-face, Sherry grew flustered. She was unable to remember the words she had planned.

"We're willing to pay," she finally said. "You have to let her go. Two hundred fifty thousand dollars."

Jonah's face turned red. "Are you serious?"

"I have a check right here if you agree to let Hailey move to West Palm," she said.

He put his hand on the door like he was about to close it in her face. "Let me make this very clear, Sherry. I am not going to let you move Maya away from me."

"You can't keep Hailey a prisoner here. You know she never wanted to live in Binghamton."

"Hailey is free to move whenever she wants, and she can visit Maya every other weekend.

"Maya needs her mother."

"Guess what, Sherry? Maya needs her father too. I'm not going to be separated from my daughter so that you can live close to yours."

"Is that what this is about? To deprive us of our family?" Sherry asked. She stepped closer to him, and still standing in the doorway, Jonah shifted as if he expected her to force her way inside.

"Do you know that Hailey used to complain about how often you called? Do you know that we used to laugh about how intrusive you were?" he said.

"That's not true," she said.

"It is true, Sherry. We used to talk about how you tried to control her. Hailey couldn't see it at first, but eventually she did. Ask her. See if she'll tell you the truth."

Sherry had held back for so long, but now her tongue felt forked and furious.

"You're a liar."

"Are you surprised? Even your own son doesn't want to have anything to do with you," he said.

"Don't you dare talk about Adam," she shouted, her hands fluttering in front of her like two small birds.

"Do you think you can control me? I can say whatever I want. You don't think Hailey told me everything? Do you think all those times when we didn't come, it was only because of me? Hailey didn't want to either. You can blame me if it makes you feel better, but it doesn't change the fact that she only puts up with you because she has no choice."

"You're the one who left her, for no reason. You're the one who broke up your family," she screamed. "Do you have any idea how much we all hate you?"

"Do you have any idea, Sherry, how little that matters?" he said.

"This is not the end," she mustered.

She spun around and started to walk down the driveway. He followed her, as if ensuring that she was really going to leave. She got back in the car, but couldn't drive away so long as Jonah was standing there, watching her. She felt a surge through her body, a jolt in her mind—all she had to do was put the car into drive instead of reverse. And then what? A shift of her hand, a press of her foot, was all it would take. The car would do the rest. Even after Jonah went inside his house and she drove away, she felt the shadow of something dark, almost monstrous, inside her.

MAINE, 2019

Every day, Daisy grows larger and slower. She spends most of the day lying in the nest of blankets and pillows that Adam has set up for her. He enlisted Maya to help get it ready, and she has added one of the blankets from our bed to the pile they've amassed. When Daisy isn't lying in her nest, she has taken to sitting in my lap, or curling up on the floor next to me, positioning herself so that some part of her body always makes contact with mine.

"When are the puppies coming?" Maya asks Adam when the three of us are in the kitchen making dinner. Patiently, Adam responds, as he does each time she asks, that it could be any day. For weeks, Maya has been fixated on the birth, wanting Adam to describe how exactly the puppies will emerge, if there will be blood, if Daisy will cry. I would have expected Maya to be afraid, but she has a look of fascination as she extracts every detail.

Today is Maya's sixth birthday, and Adam is baking her a cake, while I prepare the batter for the chocolate chip pancakes that she requested for her birthday dinner. Except for Maya's occasional question, it is mostly silent as we cook, but rather than feeling uncomfortable, I take solace in the fact that Adam and I can be together for long stretches, yet say little. Maya is still quieter than she used to be, though she has started to devise imaginary games, talking to herself and creating fantastical stories. If I address her while she's playing, I feel like I'm rousing her from an elaborate world to which I have no means of entry. The three of us have fallen into a routine. Every day, Maya and I read together, and she practices her letters, which are now neat and well-formed. I've started to teach her math and she takes particular pleasure in adding up numbers, as if everything inexplicable might somehow be solved. When she's had enough and wants to play on her own, I take out my notebook and continue to write. By now, my notebook is creased with use. My once neat handwriting now has a frenzied feel, the letters skittering into one another. I persist by hand, though, because it increases my sense that no separation exists between my mind and the page. As distant as I feel from my family, I spend every day trying to re-create them with my words. At night, I still search compulsively, both hoping and dreading that I will discover something new. Once Adam comes home, he sits with Maya and they flip through Adam's oversized volume about animals, which I recognize from when we were kids, and which I'm surprised he's saved—I would have expected him to purge any relic from the past. Now that it's the end of March, there are occasionally warmer days and the first wary buds of green are visible on the trees. Sometimes Maya and I venture into the woods together, and I no longer worry that we will take a wrong turn and end up hopelessly lost.

"Pet me," Maya says, sidling up to my leg. She has been crawling on the floor while we cook, pretending to be a dog.

As I pour the pancake batter into the pan and dot each circle with chocolate chips, I steal glances at Adam and wonder if he remembers our mother's birthday tradition. Does he recall, as I do now, waking up on a birthday, knowing that at any minute, our mother would come into our rooms singing, that the special pancakes would be on the breakfast table, that at night, there would be a cake that she baked—the green frosted tennis court for Nate, the ballerina with a pink tutu for me, the jungle of animals for Adam, whatever we loved replicated in icing?

Suddenly I am overcome by a longing to return home. I imagine my mother and Nate alone by the pool, a small birthday cake created for Maya in absentia. I think of my father, and it's hard not to cry. It's an impossible wish, but my mind creates it anyway—a knock at the door, a forgiving embrace as we find a way to be together.

When dinner is ready, I present the plate of pancakes to Maya with a flourish. Before Maya takes a bite, she squints as if trying to remember something, and two creases appear on the bridge of her nose. Even before she speaks, I know what she's thinking.

"I miss Grandma," she says.

Her words are a small explosion in the room. I glance at Adam, who looks stunned, as if until now, he'd forgotten our mother's existence, or hoped that we had.

"I know, Maya. I do too," I say and wrap my arms around her.

"Can we see her?" Maya asks.

Adam surveys me suspiciously, awaiting my response. My impulse is to fill Maya's mind with images of joyful reunions and happy endings, but it's too late for any such fantasies. Though it guts me, I recognize that she, at this young age, probably knows this as well. I remember the promise I made to myself. All I can offer her is the truth.

"I don't know if we can do that, honey. There are still some things I need to figure out."

Under the table, I scratch another line on my skin, wishing I could scrape away my outer shell and arrive at a layer that is soft and new.

Maya's face clouds. Instead of seeking consolation from either Adam or me, she bends down to whisper something to Daisy. Then, without looking at either of us, she turns her attention back to the pancakes and eats them vehemently. When she's consumed all of them, Adam brings out the cake, which he's iced with vanilla frosting and decorated with strawberries. One white candle stands in the center and the two of us sing Maya "Happy Birthday." With barely a smile, she makes a wish and blows out the candles. After the final wisps of smoke, Adam clears his throat as if he's about to make a presentation.

"Do you think you'd like to have one of the puppies?" he asks Maya. "You can choose whichever one you want."

She looks at him in joy, in disbelief. When I nod my agreement, she fires off questions—how many puppies will there be and will they all look the same and how should she make her choice? Trying to mirror her shift in mood, I feign cheerfulness as I slice the cake, but I can't shake the feeling that my entire family is somehow here, wedged around the table. I feel newly aware of how small and tenuous the celebration feels. I sense not only the shadow of my family but of Jonah as well. It's Maya's first birthday without him. My mind races forward to all the birthdays she will have without him, and backward to her last one; we had fought over who would get to spend the day with her and would have sliced her in two if we could have. Then further back too, to her first birthday, when I baked a chocolate cake that resulted in a mess of icing smeared on Maya's face and in her hair. And further back still, to the day she was born and was lying on my chest, my love for her instantaneous and fierce. In the hospital bed, Jonah lay beside me and we curled up together, marveling at this child we had made.

How else, I wonder again, might this have turned out? Could we have softly, sadly, said goodbye? Even in the midst of the pain, could we have found a way to forgive?

After dinner, as Maya follows Daisy into the other room and Adam and I clear the table, I try to catch his eye.

"Do you ever miss being home?" I ask.

Adam recoils, as if I've struck him.

"There are things you don't know," he says.

"Tell me," I beg. "Please. I want to understand."

"Why weren't you bothered by how it was? Do you remember? 'We are such a special family . . .'" he says.

"'We are such a close family,'" I say, finishing the sentence for him.

"Is that really how you saw it?" he asks.

"At the time, I thought it was true. I didn't want to see it any other way," I admit. All I can do now is hold my memories up to the light for inspection. What was once true, what is still true, I no longer know.

"I used to think that you would eventually see it the way I did. But you were the perfect daughter. You did whatever Mom said."

"Not anymore," I say.

He opens his mouth to say something, then changes his mind.

"It's true," I insist, but he doesn't seem to believe me. In his eyes, I am still the dutiful daughter doing what my mother wanted. I am the sister who adopted my mother's version of the family, who could not abide any other.

"You have no idea what it was like for me at home," he says, clutching the back of the chair. His voice is louder than I've heard the whole time we've been here and higher pitched. He is blinking rapidly as he did as a child, when Nate upset him and he was on the verge of running from the room. I'm afraid to move. We are not in this cabin, not in the middle of Maine. We are in West Palm, we are around the dinner table, in the swimming pool. We are all children again—Maya not-yet existent, a figment from the future.

I see in his eyes not only fury but pain, and I'm afraid he is about to cry or flee.

"Why are you even here? I would have thought that Mom would do whatever she could to keep you at home, especially now," he says.

I shake my head. I search for my voice. "I couldn't stay anymore," I say.

"What changed?"

"Everything."

Another sentence thrums constantly in my head. I want to speak it, but I can't.

"I still miss them," I admit, my voice a gravelly whisper. "I don't understand how you just cut yourself off."

"Maybe there was a time I could have forgiven them, but not anymore," Adam says.

He leaves the kitchen and goes to his room, where he stays, his door closed, for the rest of the night.

Sherry's sixty-fifth birthday party was outside by the pool, which she had filled with floating candles. She draped high-top tables in gauzy white cloth, and strung small lights overhead, to create the effect of twinkling stars. On every table, she arranged small stone pots of white orchids. Sherry brushed her hand against one—though they appeared delicate, they were nearly indestructible.

An hour before the guests arrived, Sherry went into her bedroom to get ready. She had decided to dress all in white and asked Hailey and Maya to do the same. In the mirror, she began to apply her small militia of serums, creams, and concealers, each one tasked with a different mission. Before she put on the rest of her makeup, she studied her face for any hint of the malevolence she'd sensed inside her—a gray cast, a dark growing spot. But though she felt its presence, she could see no trace. On the outside, she appeared the same as always.

Back outside, Sherry was adjusting the centerpieces and giving last-minute directions to the caterer when Hailey came outside with Maya. Already Maya seemed so much older. It was the beginning of August and in another month, she would be starting kindergarten. This, like every milestone Sherry would miss, made her feel the loss anew. If she had gotten what she wanted, she would see Maya every day. She would pick

Maya up from school, drive her to ballet class, then bring her home and feed her a snack.

"Aren't you the most beautiful girls I've ever seen," Sherry exclaimed to Hailey and Maya, so glad to have them home, even if just for a few days. She felt a renewed urgency: every moment had to be seized.

"Why do you look like that?" Sherry asked when Hailey's phone buzzed and she grimaced.

"It's nothing," Hailey claimed.

"Please don't tell me that Jonah is bothering you today of all days," Sherry said.

The divorce wasn't yet finalized—they had spent the summer fighting and were no closer to an agreement than they were months before. Just to get Hailey and Maya to West Palm for the weekend had been an ordeal—Sherry's birthday fell on Jonah's weekend with Maya, and because he was unwilling to trade, it had required rounds of fighting, then lawyers' deliberations, then new clauses added to the still-unfinished agreement about what family events would require a mandatory swap and how such swaps would be initiated and how they would be reciprocated.

"Jonah told his lawyer that he's no longer willing to give me the extra vacation time in the summer to come here that we had once discussed. Apparently it's 'off the table,'" Hailey said.

"I would think that he'd be more eager than anyone to finalize the divorce," Sherry said.

"We all want it to end," Hailey said.

"So why is he doing this, then?" Sherry asked. She too wanted the divorce proceedings to be over, but she also knew that once it was, there would be no chance that Hailey would be allowed to move. As long as the agreement wasn't yet finalized, Sherry still allowed herself to hope.

"Because he's furious that we tried to pay him," Hailey said. "He's claiming that we're trying to take Maya from him, and now, even though

I'm willing to settle, he's using it as a justification to ask for more."

"He would have done this no matter what," Sherry said.

"I still can't believe we did that," Hailey said. "I finally had to tell my lawyer and she was shocked."

"All we did was make him an offer."

"Mom. It was completely insane. I can't believe you don't see that."

Sherry drew back at the vehemence in Hailey's voice. "We all agreed to it. You, me, and Nate."

In the days after she'd offered Jonah the money, she was too upset to tell Hailey or Nate how badly it had gone. Even now, more than two months later, she couldn't bear to repeat any of the awful things Jonah had said. All she conveyed was that Jonah had made it very clear that he wasn't interested in their offer. She would never tell either of them how she felt herself changing in his driveway, her foot resting so tenuously on the brake, almost, almost, capable of lifting off. She was afraid that if they knew what she had contemplated, she would become unrecognizable in their eyes.

Hailey was waiting for her to say more, but Sherry didn't want to have this conversation now, not when a hundred people were about to descend on the backyard, expecting a celebration.

"Has anyone heard from Nate?" Sherry asked.

"I talked to him a little while ago. He was on his way," Hailey said.

Impatient, Sherry took out her phone and called him, trying to stifle the fear that he'd decided not to come. As close as she felt to Nate, it had occurred to her recently that she knew so little of his actual life. Despite any proximity, a child could always find ways to shut you out.

"I'm five minutes from the house," Nate claimed when he answered her call, but she knew it was possible that he hadn't yet left his condo.

"Are you bringing anyone?" she asked.

"Is that a requirement?" he said.

"I was under the impression that you were seeing someone," she said.

"What gave you that idea?"

"Why do you sound so angry?" she asked.

"I'm not angry. I just don't need an interrogation."

"We're almost ready," Sherry announced to the photographer, and beckoned to Solomon, who was sitting in a chair by the pool. He had been unusually exhausted that morning and had napped all afternoon, like a child earning the right to stay up late. At Sol's insistence, they'd told no one besides Tara and the kids about his illness, but she didn't know how much longer the secret could be kept. He didn't look well, even when he was nicely dressed in tan pants, a white shirt, and the sea-green tie she'd bought for the occasion. She had a matching one for Nate, which she would give him once he arrived.

"Is Dad okay?" Hailey asked.

"The party is more than he's used to, that's all. I'm more worried about Nate. I asked if he was bringing anyone and he acted like I'd committed a crime."

"You know he doesn't like to discuss that," she said.

"I think he's seeing someone." Sherry studied Hailey's face. "I assume you know who it is," she probed, but Hailey wouldn't oblige. Sherry had loved the fact that Hailey and Nate were close, but now she worried what they said about her when she wasn't there. How unfair it was that Hailey was angry at her but not at Nate, who'd come up with the idea to pay Jonah in the first place. It confirmed what she knew to be true. It was easier to be mad at your mother than at anyone else.

"Here he is," Sherry sang out as Nate walked into the backyard. He was wearing khakis and a white shirt as she'd requested, but she could sense how on edge he was, his jaw clenched, his demeanor stiff and unyielding.

"I was starting to think you got a better offer," she said and gave him a kiss, pretending that their earlier conversation hadn't taken place.

"I didn't realize this was your wedding," Nate joked when he saw that she, Hailey, and Maya were all dressed in white.

"This is for you," she said, handing him the tie, then called the photographer over.

"Why am I even here? Mom could have just photoshopped me in," Nate murmured to Hailey.

"Why are you in such a bad mood?" Sherry asked Nate.

"I'm fine. Never better," he said.

Sherry took a breath. She forced a smile. It was going to be fine. As her friends began to arrive, Sherry kissed them and accepted their birthday wishes. In their presence, she tried to remind herself that she had people who cared about her. For this one night, she wasn't going to worry about Jonah or Adam or Nate. She wasn't going to think about Solomon's illness or the sadness on Hailey's face.

"Look who's here!" Sherry exclaimed and rushed over. Tara had come and brought Kevin and Caleb. When Tara first told her that Kevin was returning from Winter Haven, she hadn't believed it. But if Tara was willing to give him another chance, she would try to help them however she could. She had been asking around to see if she could find Kevin a job—she was always happy to do someone a favor and everyone deserved a second chance, and maybe this would lessen Kevin's reliance on his brother, which was what Tara wanted.

Sherry gave them all hugs. "Look at this darling little boy," she said. Caleb was chubby, with curly blond hair, and was dressed up in light blue linen shorts and a striped polo shirt that she'd given him as a birthday gift earlier that year. Tara was holding his hand, but he was struggling against her, and his face was red, like he'd recently been crying.

Sherry turned to Kevin. "For years, I've told Tara that I wanted to meet you, but she was determined to hide you away."

"Maybe she's ashamed of me," he joked.

"Don't be silly," Sherry said. She glanced around to locate Nate, who would want to meet Kevin as well. He acted like he didn't care when she talked about Tara, but she knew that he was more curious than he let on. When she told Nate that Tara was bringing Kevin to the party, he said that he'd bet her a million dollars that he would never show. A few days earlier, when she confirmed to Nate that Kevin was coming, Nate snapped that she should stay out of Tara's personal life.

"Who knows where Nate went. Maybe he got bored of us!" Sherry said to Tara.

"Don't worry, we're here to see you, not Nate," Tara said, but her voice was strained.

"Are you kidding me? Nate has to meet Caleb! And Kevin! He's been as excited as the rest of us. To tell you the truth, Kevin, when I told him you were coming, he didn't believe it, so I know Tara will enjoy the chance to prove him wrong." Sherry looked around again and wondered if Nate had gone inside the house or was hiding out somewhere on his phone, endlessly texting and talking in his hushed, secretive way.

"But at least you can meet Hailey and Maya." Sherry called them over. "Come say hello!" Maya was holding a plate full of strawberries, her face stained red. She kissed Maya on top of her head. "Are you having a good time at Grandma's party?"

She expected a resounding yes, but Maya only gave a disinterested shrug. Was it her imagination that Maya seemed a little standoffish? Sherry couldn't bear the possibility that Jonah was turning Maya against her too.

No. Not tonight. She pushed Jonah from her mind and tried to focus on Tara, who was glancing at the pool. "When are you going to come over to swim? Do you know how many times I've invited her, Kevin? Caleb would love it. Maya, you could teach Caleb how to swim!

"And I haven't forgotten," she said, turning back to Kevin. "I'm working on finding you the right job."

While Hailey chatted with Tara and Kevin, Sherry brought Sol a plate of food, then looked in vain for Nate, concerned that he was in some kind of trouble. But no. She wasn't going to worry about anyone. She greeted her guests, she sampled the food, she swallowed the rest of her Merlot and asked for another glass.

A little while later, she caught sight of Nate next to Kevin, Tara, and Caleb.

"It must be nice to take off whenever you feel like it," she overheard Nate saying to Kevin.

She couldn't hear Kevin's response, but she noticed Tara's anxious expression.

"Nate," Sherry called. He didn't turn around, so she went over to them. "It's almost time for dessert. Caleb, you are going to love the delicious cakes we have."

She took Nate's arm and beckoned for Hailey as well. "If anyone is giving a toast or prepared something, now is the time," she said.

"I thought we weren't making a big fuss about speeches and songs," Nate said.

"Who said we weren't?" Sherry asked.

"Nate's giving a toast," Hailey said.

"I am?" he said.

"Of course you are," Hailey said.

"Why do you look so unhappy?" Sherry asked Nate. "If you're mad at me, then tell me."

"Did it ever occur to you that what I'm upset about has nothing to do with you?" he said.

She should have felt relief, but her unease only increased. Worried that Nate had too much to drink, Sherry was about to tell him not to make the toast, but he was already quieting everyone down. She thought about summoning Solomon to come stand next to her, but he was sitting at a table and looked more like someone who had been placed there than someone who could move about freely on his own.

"Some of you might not realize that my mother has been planning this party for years," Nate began. "And those of you who know my mother well are probably aware that she likes to say that she'll do anything for her kids. We'd like to say that we too would do anything for her, but as you might suspect, that can be a tall order . . ."

Other years, she might have laughed at Nate's words. She would have heard the love embedded inside the jokes. Tonight, she was scorched by shame. All night, she managed to preserve her smile. She carried on about how darling Maya was and how lucky she was to have her here for the weekend. She claimed to anyone who asked that Hailey was so much happier now that she was separated from Jonah. She said Sol was working hard, as usual. But she didn't know if anyone believed her. One look, and anyone could see that Hailey was not okay. Even during the toast, she was texting furiously. And she'd noticed how carefully their friends approached Solomon. They may not have known the specifics, but they could tell that something was wrong. So many times, she'd wanted to confide in her friends about Solomon or Hailey or Jonah and be bolstered by their sympathy. But increasingly, it seemed impossible that anyone would understand.

Nate was still talking, saying things that were supposed to be nice, but his words were disconnected and rearranged, emerging now in Jonah's voice.

They only put up with you because they have no choice.

We used to laugh about you all the time.

Hailey felt the same way I did.

She heard Jonah's laughter inside her. She could never keep him out.

"To Sherry," Nate concluded, and her guests all lifted their glasses. She lifted hers too but her hands shook and a few drops of red wine spilled on her white dress. But she didn't care about the dress or the party. How was it possible to feel so desolate and not one person here could see it?

Sherry walked away from the pool area, away from the sound of people talking, away from the white orchids and the floating candles and the strings of lights. She followed the illuminated stone pathway deeper into the garden. A few times she wobbled and had to be careful not to trip. Was she drunk? No, but it was a feeling of being unanchored from herself, a boat slowly drifting out to sea. Away from the citronella lanterns she would get eaten alive by the mosquitoes that were out in droves, but she kept walking. The garden was the only place she could still derive solace—it was like a child she'd nurtured into being and would never leave. She wished she had allowed it to grow wilder, the saw grass growing taller than she was, the birds-of-paradise never cut back but free to proliferate throughout the yard. She could lie down among them, let the green stems grow from her body, let their orange flowers sprout from her hair.

If she stayed in the garden, how long before anyone noticed she was gone—before anyone ventured in to find her?

Sherry heard a rustle, then someone talking softly, and she startled: Jonah. He had come, uninvited. He had been lurking in the garden all along. In fear, she stepped back, off the stone path. The ground was wet and her shoes sunk into the marshy soil.

"Kevin! What are you doing out here?" she exclaimed once she realized who it was.

He quickly got off the phone. "Sorry, I was just taking a break," he said.

With her fingers, Sherry dabbed her eyes, hoping that her mascara wasn't streaking down her face. She looked at Kevin more closely. When Tara talked about him, she'd envisioned a grown man, but he looked like an anxious kid. He was shifting uncomfortably, his foot tapping the ground. His hair was light brown and needed to be trimmed, and he was the kind of skinny that made her want to feed him a thick, nourishing soup.

"I'm so glad you came," she said.

"Tara made it pretty clear I didn't have a choice," he said, trying to make it sound like a joke, but she could hear his discomfort.

"I wanted to meet you. Tara's like a member of the family," Sherry said. "I tell her that all the time."

Now that she was closer, she noticed that the tattoo on his arm was a picture of Caleb. Beneath it, in curlicue letters, were all their names, Tara, Caleb, Kevin. When he saw her looking, he pulled up his sleeve to show it off.

"I love them. Maybe you won't believe me, but I would do anything for them," he said.

"I know you love them, but they need you at home," she said. "I know it's not my place to say that, but I care about Tara and want the best for her and Caleb."

"I know," he said. "There were some things I needed to take care of, but from now on, I'm planning to be here."

"Good. I just want Tara to be happy. That's what we all want. And I hope Nate didn't say anything to upset you. He can get carried away," she said.

"It was no big deal," he said.

"You would think I would know what's going on with him, but I have no idea why he's so upset," she said.

Maybe she was actually drunk, but what did it matter anymore? She was done holding in her anger, done trying to pretend that anything was fine.

"I know this all must look very nice, but no one has any idea what it's really like," Sherry said. "Not one person here has any idea of what I'm feeling."

"I don't know, you seem pretty angry to me," he said.

It was a relief to hear him say it. Somehow, he alone could sense her dark shadow. He could detect the presence of the other self coiled inside her.

"It's almost funny, isn't it? I dedicated my entire life to my kids, but apparently I have no idea what any of them need," she said. "Hailey is good at putting on a brave face, but she's a wreck. Jonah is the one who left her, so you would think he'd be eager for the divorce to be over. But no, he's going to fight with her about every single issue. He's going to keep going until he drives her crazy. Do you want to know what I think? He loves the fighting."

Kevin was listening intently. She was aware that she probably shouldn't be speaking so freely, but she disregarded that thought.

"Do you know we even offered to pay him to let Hailey and Maya move here? I offered him two hundred fifty thousand dollars and he laughed at me. Now he's using that as an excuse to make endless demands."

"For that kind of money, a lot of people could have done a whole lot more for you," Kevin said.

"Who could have possibly done anything else?" Sherry asked.

He gave her a funny look, and she had a sudden desire to run from the garden, back to her party, back to Sol.

"My brother, for one thing," he said.

"Maybe I shouldn't say anything, but . . ." She hesitated. "Let's just say that Tara worries about you when you're with him. I don't know any of the details, but she thinks it's a bad idea for you to be there so much."

"People can say whatever they want, but they have no idea what we went through growing up. Sam is the only one who's ever taken care of me. And he knows better than anyone that if someone hurts the people you love, there are things that can't be forgiven."

"I understand that more than you think," she said.

"I thought you might," he said.

"I'm supposed to move on, but how can I when I know that Jonah is going to fight with Hailey for the rest of her life? He's going to try to make her miserable, just because he can. No matter what we do, it's never going to end," she said.

"There's always a way. Sooner or later, everything ends," he said.

"How can this possibly end?" she asked.

"It's going to end only when you make it end."

"If I knew how to do that, I would."

"I don't know what you'll think about this, but Sam knows how to take care of these things. If you're interested, I could talk to him."

She laughed. The feeling that he could see into her evaporated. Even so, when he took out his phone, she gave him her number and he texted her so that she would have his number. Obviously she would never take him up on whatever crazy idea he was proposing, but it was soothing to know that at least one person understood.

Together, they walked back through the garden, to the patio where the party had carried on in her absence. It was time for the birthday cake, which Nate, Hailey, and Maya all carried out. On its surface, sixty-five tiny white candles were aflame.

Sherry blew out the candles and made a wish.

Hailey had been back in Binghamton for a week when her lawyer forwarded her an email she had been dreading. After weeks of threatening, Jonah had filed a motion accusing her of trying to bribe him into relinquishing custody. He claimed she was trying to alienate Maya from him. He accused her and her family of bad-mouthing him in front of Maya. He claimed that her family had tried to enlist Maya in their efforts to move Hailey and Maya to Florida and claimed to have specific examples, as well as evidence, of things her mother had said. There would be a hearing in a month, at which they would need to present a response and a countermotion.

Hailey called her lawyer, and on a scrap of paper, she scribbled down all the details, though the slew of words accumulating made little sense. Yes, they had offered the money, which she regretted, but it had hurt no one in the end. And it wasn't true that she or anyone in her family had bad-mouthed him or exposed Maya to any of the acrimony between them. On the contrary. In front of Maya, she scrubbed away any word that would reveal her true feelings. When she was with Maya and Jonah, she acted like everything was fine, a recurring performance for which Maya was the only audience member who mattered. She forced a smile when Maya told her of the activities she did with Jonah and didn't let her see the terrible fear that somehow she would lose her to him. But it didn't seem to matter. She and Jonah inhabited separate realities, not just now but in the past as well. She had done everything for Maya, and they had split the work equally. She had not wanted to give up her job to move here, and they had both agreed that this was best for their family. She was eager to come to an agreement, and she was intent on dragging this out. She had no idea anymore which version was true.

"Did you say anything to Maya about Jonah?" Hailey asked her mother over the phone once she got off the call with her lawyer. "Whatever it was, apparently she repeated it to Jonah and it's part of his latest motion."

"I didn't say anything about him," Sherry insisted.

"Are you sure you didn't talk about a house you and Maya are going to move into? Apparently, Maya drew a picture of it and showed it to him," she said.

"I might have said something about how much I missed her and that I wished I could see her more, but that's it. And we had a game about building a house in the garden, but that was ages ago and it had nothing to do with him," Sherry said.

Her mother's tone was defiant, and her voice grew more impassioned as she went on, as if she were also convincing herself. So many times Hailey had taken what her mother said as absolute fact, but not anymore. She regretted having involved her family in the divorce in the first place. She should have found a way to do this on her own.

"Why can't you admit that you said something?" Hailey said.

"I didn't say a word."

"I don't believe you."

"How can you say that? You wanted to move to West Palm. It was your idea in the first place, remember? All I've ever tried to do is help you—"

"You haven't done this just for me. I would have backed down a long time ago. How many times did you try to convince me to keep going? Sometimes I think you hate him more than I do," Hailey said.

She waited for her mother's response, expecting an eruption of pain, a thundering of anger, but Sherry spoke in a voice that was strangely ice-cold and calm.

"If someone hurt Maya, you would hate that person the way I hate Jonah."

Hailey hung up before her mother said more. Her body was shaking. She'd never spoken to her mother like that. She went into the bathroom so Maya wouldn't see her in this state. In the mirror, she looked wild, her face flushed with heat, her hair loose. Furious, and also free. It was the same tangle of feelings she had after a fight with Jonah, when the rush of adrenaline made her believe that nothing existed beyond this anger.

"Mommy?" she heard from the other side of the door.

Hailey called out that she was coming and pressed a cold washcloth to her face. She practiced a smile in the mirror, ready to recite the lines she had perfected: *It's all fine* and *Mommy is just tired* and *Mommy just has a little cold.*

"It's time to go to Daddy's house," Hailey announced when she left the bathroom—she sounded like one of the maniacally happy characters on the shows Maya watched.

In the car, at least, Maya couldn't get a good look at her face. Maybe when Maya was an adult, she would tell her the truth. How getting divorced felt like being cast out of your own life and being dropped in the middle of an always shifting wilderness. That to be around Jonah made her want to escape her own body, how in every conversation with him, she marveled at how love could turn into a dark oozing hate.

When Hailey pulled into Jonah's driveway, she texted him that they were outside and waited in the car until he came to the front door. Not once had she gone inside to witness the alternate reality of a separate bedroom in which Maya slept, separate toys with which she played. Sometimes it seemed like there were two Mayas; as soon as she walked through Jonah's front door, she became the other. A week earlier, Hailey dreamt that she'd forced her way into Jonah's house, but couldn't find Maya in a maze of rooms. She frantically searched until she came upon a little girl in an enormous room—not Maya, but someone who looked like her, wearing her clothes, sitting on a bed, brushing a doll's hair.

When Jonah came to the door, she helped Maya out of the car and they walked up the front steps. It was better to have no moment in which she and Jonah were together without Maya's presence to enforce the peace, but Maya ran inside quickly, leaving her alone with Jonah.

Do not say a word. Get back into the car and drive away. She knew this, but Jonah was lingering in the doorway, watching her with a look of satisfaction.

"I can't believe you actually filed that motion," Hailey said.

Jonah took a step closer to her. "We both know every word of it is true," he said.

"Why does it have to be this way? Why are you doing this?"

"Did you really think you were going to try to bribe me and it was just going to blow over?"

"It wasn't a bribe."

He laughed. "Please, enlighten me. I would love to hear how the Marcus family is pretending that they didn't do something that we all know they did."

"I'm sorry, okay? It was a bad idea to offer the money, but it wasn't a bribe and no one is trying to take Maya from you," she said.

"This is so like your mother. It's so like all of you. You're not going to stop until Maya is all yours. I'm just surprised they told you about the bribe. You know that's the real issue, don't you? Poor Hailey can't take care of herself. They have to come to your rescue."

She wanted to throw something at him. She wanted to hit him.

"You left me. You just decided it. You decided everything for us."

And here they were again. She was wrong to think that the wounds were starting to heal. They were still locked in battle, different words perhaps, but the same fury.

"I couldn't do it anymore. I'm sorry. What did you want me to do? Pretend for the rest of my life?" he said.

What did she want? To travel back in time and never have married him? To return to the moment when she had doubted their relationship and this time choose to run? Faced with the impossibility, she felt only the prospect of a dead end. From inside the house, Maya was calling to Jonah and he went back inside. The one who had Maya was the winner, and she wanted to break down his door, grab her, and never return.

Hailey ran from the porch, back down the driveway. Was it even Jonah she was most furious at? The strands of her anger were all knotted together, and she couldn't pick them apart. As she tried to catch her breath, she noticed Jonah's gray CR-V parked in front of her car. She looked down at her hands and at the set of keys she was holding—both her hands and the keys seemed not to belong to her anymore. She grasped the keys more vigorously, until her fingers felt their painful imprint on her skin. She walked closer to the car and stared with a kind of puzzlement. She wasn't doing this, yet a hand was reaching out and keys were scratching the driver's-side door until two long silvery lines appeared.

At the sight of them, she released her grip on the keys and gaped in a kind of wonder. For an instant, she imagined the car might bleed.

She looked up and there was Jonah's neighbor in his own driveway, watching her. For a moment, they locked eyes. For a moment, she had the impulse to show him the marks on her hand, to point to the scratches on the car. But no, that was a terrible idea. She looked again at the scratches and had the impossible thought that she could run her hands over them and erase what she'd done.

It came over her. She wished Jonah were dead. If that were to somehow happen, she wouldn't feel a thing.

She ran back to her car—she started to drive away, but her hands were shaking too hard. A block away, she pulled over on the side of the road. If Jonah were dead, she wouldn't feel so besieged. It was a terrible thought, but if he were dead, every day would be suffused with an unflappable calm. She leaned against the car window. She couldn't return home in this state and she couldn't break into Jonah's house and grab Maya. All she could do was call Nate.

"I lost it. I really did. I couldn't stand it anymore. I really feel like I could kill him," she said and told Nate what she'd done to Jonah's car.

"Rest assured, I'm fully prepared to bail you out of jail," he said.

"I can't take it anymore. I mean it, Nate. I hate him. I really hate him."

"How serious is he about this latest motion?" Nate asked.

"Completely serious. He's convinced that we're trying to estrange Maya from him, and there's nothing I can say to make him believe me that it's not true. He keeps accusing me of all kinds of terrible things—maybe at this point I should do everything he's accusing me of."

"I'm sorry," Nate said. "I never should have suggested that we pay him, obviously. It was stupid and clearly it made everything worse. But I think that, right now, we have to figure out how to get control of the situation. I know everyone is angry, but I want to be sure you understand how easy it is for things to escalate past the point of no return."

"You always said I would erupt. I guess you were right," she said.

"For now, however possible, you have to lower the temperature. If you want to scream, call me. If you want to scratch something or hit someone, I'll find you a good target to practice on. And if you can't do that, then go for a run. You'd be surprised how much anger running can get out."

As she listened to him, her body was no longer lit with a hundred small fires. "Do you ever get the feeling that you don't know what you're capable of?" she asked.

"I'm not sure, but I do think we all discover times when we can become someone else," he said.

Hailey took Nate's advice. She drove back to her house and changed into running clothes. She left her phone at home and ran up the street. At first, her body resisted, but as she kept going, the heaviness gave way, as if she'd come to a gate whose latch she could newly lift. The weather was already cooling off, though it was still August. Soon it would be cold, then dark at this time of day. It became clear to Hailey as she ran. It was time for a change. She didn't want to live with a fist of anger wedged in her chest. She was out of breath, but didn't stop. So long as she ran, she could be free.

Surely she would regret it later and surely Hailey would be furious if she knew, but that wasn't enough to stop Sherry from calling Jonah the following morning. In a distant realm of her mind, she felt an awareness that she needed to stop, but the fury was too thick.

Sherry still had Jonah listed in her cell phone. As his phone rang, she envisioned Jonah's angry reaction upon seeing her name.

"You need to stop. Hailey gave in. She's stuck in Binghamton, so what else can you possibly want?" Sherry said when he answered.

Jonah made some kind of exclamatory cackle, but didn't say anything.

"I mean it. You are going to withdraw that motion and move on, because this is over. Do you understand me? It's over."

Jonah still didn't speak. She thought that he'd hung up until she heard the sound of his breathing.

"'Little house,' Sherry? In your magical garden? Is that what you talk to Maya about?" he finally said. "Would you like to see the drawing Maya made? I'm more than happy to send you a copy. And that's the least of it. Do you know what else she told me?"

Even without seeing him, she could envision the smirk.

"Why are you doing this? What can you possibly hope to gain?" she asked.

"Are you really so delusional that you think I'm the one causing this?" he said.

"All I wanted was for us to be close. I tried, but you never wanted to come visit. You refused to be part of our family," she said, unsure if she was accusing or begging, attacking or surrendering.

"I was never, ever going to be one of you. And I'm not going to let Maya be like you either. Maya might not know now what you're really like, but she will one day. One day, I promise you, everyone will know."

It wasn't true. None of what he said was true. He could throw out accusations, he could manufacture lies, but she had to hold on to her certainty. He was the one who had left Hailey. No matter what else he might claim, he was the one who had broken apart his family.

"You act like you're so innocent, Jonah, but I know why you're doing this. You still want to control her," she said.

She was about to say more—every word aimed at the red center of his heart—but she stopped. A slow summoning came over her and her anger compressed inside her, creating a nub of calm.

"You're the reason, Sherry, that this is never going to end," Jonah said, but she was already hanging up the phone.

The calm was preternatural. It was the feeling of being spent after a prolonged cry. Sherry sat alone in the living room. In the stillness, she could think. An hour passed and she remained in the same spot. Calmly, she reached for her phone to call Hailey, not to tell her what she'd done, but to be reassured by the sound of her voice.

I love you, Sherry texted Hailey when she didn't answer. Call me when you have a chance, she wrote, but resisted the impulse to call again. For all these years, Sherry believed that she'd been spared Hailey's anger, but apparently it had been gathering offshore, gaining strength and speed.

Sherry remained on the couch, so still that were anyone to enter the room, her presence might go undetected. For a moment, she thought she heard the sounds of the kids playing in the pool, but her mind was playing tricks.

"Sol," she called as she got up and walked into the lanai, where he had been sititng all morning. He was holding a book, but his head was bent over, his mouth open, one side lower than the other.

Sherry screamed and ran toward him, sure that he was dead.

Dazed, Sol opened his eyes and looked at her in confusion. "What's going on?" he asked.

She forced a smile. "Everything is fine," she said, and there it was again, that eerie calm.

Sherry went back inside to the kitchen and returned with coffee and omelets on a tray for an early lunch. It was blazing hot outside but they sat there anyway. Once, years ago, Adam had read that you could start a fire with a magnifying glass. He talked about it incessantly, but Nate didn't believe him and demanded that he prove it. So Adam held a magnifying glass while he and Nate crouched over a piece of cardboard. It was one of the few times she saw Nate look at Adam with admiration as the harnessed heat burnt a small hole.

All day, she thought about her conversation with Jonah. All day, her mind churned. She waited for Hailey to call her back, but her phone was silent. She hoped Nate might stop by after work, but she didn't hear from him.

That night, she and Solomon watched television in the family room, where the kids once fought endlessly over the remote control. Now the house felt desiccated. The quiet was overpowering.

When the show was over, she helped Solomon up the stairs. It was only a matter of time before he would stop going into the office altogether, before he would no longer be able to drive. One by one, so many doors would close for him. She would be alone in what remained. In the bathroom, he carefully made his way to the sink and brushed his teeth. He didn't want her help, but she stood guard in case he needed her. She applied her lotions and serums, which were lined up on the vanity next to his array of amber-colored pill bottles, very much a bathroom in a house of the old.

In the bedroom, Sol was struggling to remove his pants. His legs were increasingly stiff, and getting undressed was a difficult feat.

"Here," she offered. He sat down on the bed and she helped him. Then they got into bed and she pulled the covers over both of them.

Once Sol fell asleep, Sherry slipped out of the bedroom. The night was a vast plain to cross alone. Jonah's voice infiltrated her head. She replayed everything he'd said. One day Maya would know some fabricated truth. One day everyone would. So he *was* writing about her. On the page, she was his to shape and sculpt. One day, everyone would see her as he did. In Jonah's hands, she would be twisted and dissected, then stitched back into an unrecognizable form. It wouldn't matter what she knew to be true about herself. She would never escape the version he would create.

She ended up in Hailey's room, where she curled on the bed. She went online to try to console herself, but all that did was make her feel worse. She read an article about a boy who was barred from seeing his grandmother by an angry daughter-in-law. The grandmother resorted to sending letters, though she doubted the child ever saw them. She read about parents who had done the best they could, who were left to die unloved and alone. She went to the dining room, where she sat at the table, staring at the family photo. At first, she'd sensed Jonah's ghostly shadow hovering behind the hibiscus plant. But with time, she'd stopped seeing what was no longer there and had even grown accustomed to the idea that he'd never been present in the first place.

Even though it was late, Sherry decided to swim. She slipped into the bedroom to change, then went into the backyard. She swam back and forth. There had to be a way. She'd read all those stories about mothers who lifted cars off their trapped children, who plunged into icy waters to pull their children to safety. She couldn't bear to think about the stories less told, the powerless mothers who watched as their children were crushed before their eyes, who couldn't reach them before they were swept away.

Her strokes grew faster. She was an arrow. She was a bullet. Out of breath, she kept going.

The next morning, Sherry took out her phone and went into the garden, where there was no chance she'd be overheard. Earlier, she'd received an email from a friend about a job opportunity for Kevin—it was nothing definite, but at least it was an excuse to call.

"It's Sherry Marcus," she said when Kevin answered. The background noise—a TV or some kind of video game—quickly went silent.

"I have a lead for you," she said. "A friend of mine owns a restaurant and I told him about you and he thought it could be a good possibility."

She gave him her friend's number, and after he thanked her, there was an awkward pause.

"One more thing," she said. "Something you said made an impression on me. You told me that when someone hurts a person you love, it's not always possible to forgive them."

"It's true," he said. "Maybe some people don't see it that way, but I do. There are things that can never be forgiven."

"I think you might be the only one who understands why I hate Jonah so much," Sherry said.

"You have to decide how much you're willing to put up with," he said.

"You said you could help me. I'm curious to hear what you meant."

"Let's just say that Sam knows how to take care of problems like this. He doesn't let people get away with bad things. He finds a way to make them pay."

"What did you have in mind?" she asked.

"I think you know," he said. "So if you ever want to talk about it . . ."

She let his sentence dangle. She had no idea what to say. If she hung up the phone, would Kevin not have said these words? Would her mind not be filling in what he meant?

"I don't think so," she stammered. "And even if I could do something like this, I have no idea how I'd even go about this."

"You have the two hundred and fifty thousand dollars, so we could start with that," he said. "It just depends on what you want."

"I can't believe I'm talking about this," she said.

"The way I see it, the guy gave you no choice."

She would never do something like this, yet somehow she was telling Kevin that she would think about it. She would never, yet somehow she was agreeing to call him in a few days if she was interested in discussing it further.

Once Sherry was off the phone, she went back inside and vigorously scrubbed the kitchen. There might be people who would entertain such possibilities, but an unbreachable line divided her from them. She went into the garden and snipped off the dead, dried flowers to make room for new growth. While making dinner for Sol, her hand slipped and she cut her finger with a knife, carving a thin red line on her skin. She rinsed it in cold water and the blood washed down the sink. She would never do this, yet she let herself conjure what it would be like if Jonah were simply gone—if he had never existed at all. She would never do this, yet people did all sorts of unfathomable things and still found ways to live their days, to sleep at night. She called Sol into the dining room, where the two of them sat at the long table and ate the roasted chicken she had prepared. She would never do this, yet as she cleared the table and scraped chicken bones into the trash and scrubbed clean the dishes, she had the feeling that she was finally coming face-to-face with that malignant other self.

I signed the charts . . .

Technically, Nate wasn't supposed to text Tara more than once, in case Kevin was around, but ever since his mother's party, he had trouble adhering to their plan. He was at the office, working late, as he was most nights now, overwhelmed by how much harder it was to run a practice than he'd realized. But instead of focusing on what he needed to do, he was unable to get the image of Kevin out of his mind. As far as Nate knew, he and Tara were still together, but the strain of hiding their relationship kept him on edge. He checked his phone every few minutes. Each time Tara wrote to him, he was increasingly afraid she was going to end it.

I think you might want to look at them

His phone beeped finally, and he jumped at the sound of it. But instead of Tara, it was his mother.

Can we talk?

He tried to ignore her text. He needed a break from his mother's incessant focus on the divorce, but also from the feeling that once again he had done something wrong. How could he have been so stupid as to devise the plan to pay Jonah? What was wrong with him that he managed to make everything worse? After Jonah filed the motion asking for a hearing, Hailey's lawyer advised her to counter with a claim of harassment. In response, his lawyer sent a letter accusing her of scratching his car, which she denied. Nate was the only person she'd confided in, and while he had no problem keeping her secret, he was increasingly convinced that this was not going to end well. He knew, better than anyone, how easily things could get out of control—you thought you were taking one small step, then one more, and all of a sudden, you were careening down a steep hill, with no way to stop.

Please?

Is Dad okay?

He's fine. It's not about that.

Is it about the motion? I know we have to deal with that, but I have more work here than I can handle and I just can't talk about Jonah right now.

It's urgent

Okay, okay. I'll be there in an hour.

He could only avoid his mother for so long. Even if he were to turn the phone off, even if he were to smash it against the wall, he would still feel its magnetic tug. It was futile to think he could escape. Maybe in some twisted, tangled way, the one who most needed to leave was the one who was never able to go.

• • •

"Let's talk outside," Sherry said when Nate arrived at the house an hour later. Her voice was calm, eerily so, but the house betrayed her actual state. Several nights' worth of dinner plates were piled on the coffee table. Towels and stray articles of clothing lay by the door to the pool, and piles of mail were heaped on the floor. Sherry had been coming in to the office, but keeping the same sporadic hours that Sol now did.

"I have to tell you something and I don't want you to say anything until I'm done," Sherry said once they were sitting in the chaise lounges by the pool. The last time he was outside with her like this, he had hatched his delusional plan to pay Jonah off. He hoped that this conversation would turn out better.

"This should be interesting," Nate said, and he leaned back in the chair. Maybe it was his imagination, but her jungle, as he'd dubbed it, seemed to be encroaching closer to the pool. The palmettos were so long they dipped close to the water and the elephant ear plants looked unnervingly large, like they were planning to overtake the neighborhood.

"I had a conversation with Kevin at the party. I told him what was going on with Hailey and . . ." She paused, trying to gauge his reaction before she said more.

He sat up. "Why are you talking to Kevin?"

"Why shouldn't I talk to him? Tara and I are extremely close, and like it or not, the two of them are practically married."

Nate leaned in. "Listen to me. You do not want to have anything to do with Kevin."

"When it comes to Tara, I'm already involved," she said.

"I assume you know how awful he's been to Tara. He's completely unreliable."

"Since when do you care about Tara?" she said.

He didn't say a word, and then he could see the understanding dawn on her face. Actually, he was surprised it had taken her this long to realize it.

"Are you and Tara . . . ?" she asked.

"What we are is none of your business," he said.

"Nate—" she said.

He cut her off. This was the last thing he wanted to discuss with anyone, certainly not his mother, who would ask a battery of questions he didn't have answers for and make him feel worse than he already did. "We're not getting sidetracked. I don't want you talking to Kevin. Trust me, he's not someone you want to be involved with."

"Can you please listen to me?" Sherry asked.

"Fine," he said and gave an exaggerated sigh. "Tell me what great wisdom your new best friend Kevin imparted."

"I told Kevin what's going on with Hailey, and he really understood how terrible it's been for her, and he said that he could help us take care of the problem. He said there's a way to get things to end and that sometimes you have to take action on behalf of the people you love and his brother has done this kind of thing before and—"

Nate covered his face with his hands, wishing he could stay like that until this, whatever it was, ended.

"Mom. Do you have any idea what Kevin is talking about?" he asked.

"Of course I do," she said.

"Then please tell me you're not serious," he said.

"I'm completely serious," she said.

"Are you out of your mind?" he asked.

"We wouldn't be the ones doing anything. We would pay the money that you saved for Hailey, and Kevin and his brother would take care of the situation."

"I can't believe that we're having this conversation."

"You're the one who talked about hiring a hit man," she said.

"That was a joke."

"If there was any other way for this to end, believe me, I would do that. But Hailey is going to spend the rest of her life fighting with Jonah.

She's going to be trapped in a city where she never wanted to live, where she has no one at all, and even then it's not going to be enough for him. He's going to do everything he can to make her miserable."

Nate made a noise that sounded like a laugh, but wasn't. "Okay, but—"

"I would think that you of all people would understand that sometimes you have to do whatever it takes. And when else would we ever have an opportunity like this? I didn't go looking for this, but when Kevin heard what we were going through with Jonah, he offered to help."

This time, he did laugh. "Is that what you're calling this—an *opportunity*?"

"No, I just mean . . . It's not something I would ever have considered on my own. When Kevin first suggested it, I thought obviously we would never do anything like that. But I kept thinking about it and once the idea was in my head, I realized that maybe this is the only way it will ever end."

Nate let out a long exhale. "Even if I were insane enough to agree to this, do you think Hailey would ever go along with anything even remotely like this?"

"No. She wouldn't. I know that. Which is why we would never tell her that we did this for her. As far as she knows, it would have nothing to do with her. It would just be this terrible thing that somehow happened."

"And you actually believe this is the best thing for her? I know you hate Jonah—but do you really think that?"

"I know how it sounds, but it's for her. For all of us."

"We do anything for each other, right?" he quipped.

"Nathaniel," she began.

"Don't call me that."

"Why not? I've always thought it was the most beautiful name. I remember how, when you were born, you had such an angelic face and these enormous blue eyes . . ."

"Please, spare me," he said.

"I love you. I love all of you very, very much."

Was he having a bad dream? Maybe in a few hours, his fever would break and none of this would be anything more than the distorted creation of a delirious mind. He stripped down to his boxers and dove into the pool. The water was cooler than he'd expected, and he had a momentary sensation of freedom; so long as he stayed submerged, this conversation couldn't continue. He swam the length without coming up once, the same as he'd done as a child, staying under just long enough to scare everyone. Then, it was fun to make people worry, but now the water felt like his only means of escape.

Sherry was standing by the side of the pool, silently watching him. Every time he came up for air, he saw her looming over him. Nate did a few more laps, but he was never going to extricate himself. He climbed out, his hair slicked back and dripping, and she handed him a towel.

"You realize that if we do this, the rest of our lives will be defined by it," he said.

"It's awful, yes, and it will be terrible for a while, but it doesn't have to take over our lives," Sherry promised. "We'll find a way to live with it. And one day it will finally be over."

Nate got into his car and sped away. Was he going crazy, or was she? He couldn't think clearly, not until he got away from the house.

As he drove in the direction of Tara's apartment, he texted her, but got no response, so he texted again. He'd stopped caring if they got caught. Actually, it would be a relief.

While waiting for Tara to respond, he decided to call Hailey, to at least remind himself that he had one normal relative. He would never tell her what Sherry had proposed—even if he wanted to, how exactly would he say it? Mom is planning to bump Jonah off? Surely Hailey would assume that Sherry couldn't possibly be serious, but that was only because she hadn't seen the focus blazing in her eyes. She hadn't heard the eerie calm in Sherry's voice.

"Am I waking you?" he asked when Hailey answered.

"I wish I was sleeping, but I'm in the middle of a text war with Jonah."

"I thought we agreed you weren't going to text him anymore."

"I can't help myself. He makes me so angry. He gives me orders about what I need to do for Maya and then adds a list of accusations."

"What is it this time?"

"I scheduled Maya's annual physical with the pediatrician at a time when Jonah can't make it and even though I agreed to change it, he's claiming this is one more example of me trying to shut him out," she said, sounding angrier than he'd ever heard her. "Not that he came to her doctor appointments before, or was ever this involved in every single aspect of her life. He was fine having me do everything while he wrote."

"You don't have to respond to every text he sends you," he said.

"I can't stand sitting at these appointments with him. He talks the whole time as if he's the one doing everything for Maya. Next week, I'm going to have to be with him for Maya's first day of kindergarten. Do you have any idea what that's like? He puts on this show for everyone. If I didn't know better, I would think he was the greatest person ever. I'm sure that's what everyone else thinks."

"People see through things. They know you're there for Maya."

"No, they don't. They believe every word he says, and it makes me wonder if I'm the crazy one to be so angry all the time. But he takes everything I say and twists it. He provokes me and I get upset, and then he uses that against me."

"You can't let him rile you up like this. No matter what you say, the two of you are never going to see any of this the same way. You're never going to be able to prove him wrong or get him to agree with you, so if you could just stop trying, I really think that—"

She cut him off. "Did I tell you he's trying to require me to inform him in writing a month in advance if I want to take Maya out of the state, even for a weekend? If I want to go anywhere, I have to deal with him. Every time my phone beeps, I'm terrified that it's him. Even when I'm alone with Maya, I feel like he's there, telling me what to do."

She started to cry, and he realized that any impulse to tell her to calm down was futile. They were well past the point when the anger could be reigned in. Maybe he just had to watch as it burned.

"You may not realize this, but a lot of people are willing to do just about anything to help you," Nate said.

"What can anyone do? It's never going to end," she said.

"What if I could make it go away? Would you want me to do whatever I could?" he asked.

When she hesitated, he wondered if she could sense what—apparently—he was now contemplating.

"Nate Marcus, fairy godmother?" she said.

"Something like that," he said.

Tara, I really need to talk to you

Nate was getting close to her apartment. If he didn't hear from her soon, he would circle the block until she emerged. He would park out front and knock on her door. He wouldn't tell Tara what Sherry had said, but seeing her was the only way he could calm down.

Please. It's Kevin's birthday

He tossed his phone onto the seat next to him. He didn't want to think about what she'd been doing. But he couldn't leave it at that. As he drove, he reached again for his phone.

Great. Happy Birthday. I'm a few blocks away

This is not a good idea. Kevin is already suspicious.

Ever since the party he's been acting weird.

It's important. Just say that you're going for a walk

Again, there was no response. He gripped the steering wheel. In front of her building, he parked and was about to text her again when his phone buzzed.

Fine. Give me ten minutes

He waited, but the street remained empty, and he wondered if she was really going to come out. If she didn't, would he knock on the door? That made little sense, he knew, but he wasn't thinking clearly and wasn't actually sure why he'd come in the first place. If he wasn't planning to tell Tara what his mother suggested, how would he explain the state he was in?

Finally, he saw Tara walking toward him. She was wearing jean shorts and a sweatshirt and had the hood pulled over her head.

"Let's just get away from my apartment," she said, once she was in the car. Only when she pulled down her hood did he see how exhausted she looked.

He started to drive away, with no real destination in mind, just as far as he could get from her apartment.

"What if we took off for real?" he suggested, reaching for her.

"How in the world could I possibly do that? I have a kid, remember?" she said and pulled away.

"It doesn't have to be this way. You could tell him you're done, and then you and Caleb can come live with me," he said.

"That's easy for you to say. You're not the one who has to worry about your entire life falling apart."

"I promise you. Nothing is going to fall apart. We'll be together and everything will be fine," he said.

"I'm not like you. I don't have the luxury of doing whatever I want," she said.

He held his hands up in a pose of surrender, even though he felt more determined than ever. "So how was the birthday party? Did you bake Kevin a cake? Did you wear party hats? Did you play party games?"

"Stop, okay? We just had a little celebration with me and him and Caleb. It was nice."

He cut her off. Especially right now, he couldn't stand to hear this ridiculous fantasy of domestic bliss.

"Do you know that my mother and Kevin are in touch?" he said.

"She's helping him find a new job. Why is that a big deal?" she asked.

Did she believe that? He studied her face. He considered himself a good judge of character and was fairly certain that she didn't have the guile to lie to him. If anything, she always took what people said at face value. He used to feel comforted by this quality of hers, but that, he realized, was why she was with Kevin in the first place. She wouldn't believe anything bad about Kevin. She was unwilling to face who he really was.

"She might be trying to help him find a job, but did Kevin also happen to mention that he offered to help my mother 'take care' of Jonah? Apparently, my mother took that to heart, because tonight she informed me that our hero Kevin and his trusty brother are going to 'take care of' Jonah for her."

Tara looked stunned. "That's not possible."

"I know, and yet it's true."

"How do I know you're not making this up so that Kevin looks bad?" she asked.

"I hardly need to lie to make Kevin look bad. Did you know that apparently this is what he and his brother do?"

"Okay, first of all, this is not what Kevin does, and second, there's no way he meant it like that. Sam can do what he wants, but Kevin has nothing to do with it. Ever since Caleb was born, he promised me he wouldn't be involved in anything bad."

"Why are we pretending like Kevin is such a great person?"

"You have no idea what he's been through. Do you think he had parents who did everything for him? Do you think he's ever had anything just handed to him?"

"Please, spare me the sob story," he said.

"I'm just saying that there's no way this is true. Kevin probably just said that because of how badly we need the money. He couldn't believe it when he heard how much you were willing to pay Jonah."

"I'm not sure that was something he needed to know," he said.

"I'm not the one who told him. And maybe your mom misunderstood what Kevin was saying, or maybe she took it out of context. He was probably just saying he wished he could help her because he's grateful that she offered to find him another job and she took that to mean something he totally didn't intend."

"I'm pretty sure I have the right context. But if you have some other explanation for what he meant by 'take care of Jonah,' I'd love to hear it," Nate said. "And just so I know—do Sam and Kevin kill people on a regular basis? Is this a hobby or something they do professionally?"

"Oh my god, stop," she said. "There's no way Kevin suggested that. I know him, okay? And even if for some reason he did make an offer that he would never actually go through with, do you think your mother would ever do that? I know she hates Jonah, but do you really see her as a murderer?"

"She sounded pretty serious to me."

"I know, but how many times have you seen her get really upset about something and then it blows over?" she said.

For the first time all night, he took a deep breath and considered what Tara had said. He didn't know Kevin, but he did know his mother. It was one thing to talk about killing someone, but to actually do it? The gap between those two possibilities was miles wide. People said all sorts of crazy things, and in the heat of the moment, his mother might have gotten carried away and believed herself to be capable of such an act. But Tara was right. Sooner or later, her anger would recede and she would realize that there was no way she would ever do anything like this. She would call him to say that she had a brief moment of insanity, but of course she didn't mean it. One day they would laugh that she'd proposed such an absurd plan and even more so that he'd taken her seriously.

He leaned closer to Tara. Just being next to her made him feel like everything might still be okay. "Come home with me," he said. "We don't have to talk about my mother or about Kevin, I promise. I just want to be with you."

He expected her to be as relieved as he was, but she still had the same tense expression.

"This is really not a good idea," she said. "I can't keep sneaking out like this."

"I thought you were going to make a decision," he said.

"I'm trying to, but I can't just leave him like this."

"Why not? You see what kind of person he is," he said.

She eyed him suspiciously. "What did you think? That you were going to tell me some terrible story about Kevin and all of a sudden I was going to walk out on him?"

"You know that's not why I'm telling you. But did I think this might affect whether you want to be with him? Call me crazy, but yes I did."

"Caleb and Kevin and I are a family—you have no idea what that's like," she said.

What was he supposed to say to that—promise her that they would be just as much of a family? As he started to drive in the direction of her apartment, she stared out the window, gripping the side of the car like he was holding her prisoner. It was becoming clear to him how blind she was. There was no way he could convince her to seize control of her life. In his experience, weak people preferred to cling to the unhappiness they knew rather than take a chance at something better. But he was never going to be that way. It was always better to be in motion than to be stuck where you were.

When Tara got out of the car, he realized that he was as deluded as she was. Did he really think he could be with her long term? Of course not, which was why he allowed himself to love her, or to feel the illusion of love, or whatever it was that had consumed him. It was funny, or it would be in a few days, that he'd believed that he was going to run away with his father's secretary. In the end, most things soured anyway. So what was the point? He had forgotten that he was better off alone.

In the morning, Nate bought a plane ticket and texted Tara to reschedule his patients for the rest of the week. He didn't care that the practice couldn't run without him. Nor did he care about the pile of tasks that his father had once taken care of and that now fell to him. He shut his phone as the plane took off for Las Vegas. Once he landed, he drove five hours to the Paria Canyon wilderness area and left his rental car at the trailhead for Coyote Buttes. He didn't bother trying to get a permit, which was technically required to hike there. The whole point of coming was to extricate himself from restrictions and live for a few days under the illusion that he could mount an escape.

The trail started out easily—a gentle uphill climb among red rock, with cairns marking the way. Nate walked toward what appeared to be twin buttes, using the jagged edge of a distant rock formation as his guide. He'd told no one of his plans. If he got lost, no one would save him. He didn't need to be consoled with false promises. There was no next world, no afterlife, no magical being sitting in judgment. What did he believe was awaiting him? Just a bleak endless plain. Just the arrival at oblivion.

In the end, you had to live with who you were. Surely that was punishment enough.

Nate climbed the waves of sandstone. Other people who came upon these vistas might see a placid world, but he knew better. The world was raw, rough, uncontained. He would rather confront that fact directly than pretend. An image of Jonah's face floated into his mind. He should have recoiled in revulsion at the prospect of what his mother wanted to do, but apparently he had the ability to consider it unflinchingly. It was the discovery of something new and unsettling about himself, but there it was. He climbed up one of the buttes, higher, and closer to the edge. His mind was sharpened, his body never more alive than when on the precipice of danger. If this were the end, what would he have to show for himself? He had made so many mistakes, but maybe agreeing to his mother's plan could serve as a convoluted form of penance. If nothing else, at least he could do something for his family. In the end, his love for them was all that he had.

Tara looked for Nate's car every time she pulled into the office parking lot. For the week that he was away, it took all her willpower not to text him, but even if she succumbed, she had no idea what she would say.

"Did Nate tell you where he was going?" Tara asked Sherry as she sat beside her in the office. Throughout the morning, Sherry looked jittery, constantly checking her phone, startling at the sound of the office door opening, tapping her nails against the desk in a way that made Tara feel like she was going to lose her mind.

"All he said was that he needed to get away. I assumed that you knew more than I did," Sherry said.

"He didn't tell me anything." Tara tried to act innocent, but she was sure Sherry could see through every word she said. Even the ones that were technically true felt like a lie.

Sherry gave her a suspicious, surveying look. "I know about you and Nate."

"He told you?" Tara asked. All along, she had managed to convince herself that Sherry would be happy about her and Nate, but she was starting to realize that she had no idea what Sherry might think about anything.

"He didn't tell me. I figured it out," Sherry said.

"Does Solomon know?"

"I'm not telling him anything."

"It doesn't matter because, at this point, I don't know what we are," Tara said.

"Is that why Nate left?" Sherry asked.

"Actually, I think there were a lot of reasons," Tara said.

Sherry's eyes widened, but her voice remained calm. "What do you mean?"

Tara looked around to be sure no one could hear her. "Nate told me about your conversation with Kevin."

Sherry inhaled sharply. The look of surprise should have been enough, but Tara still didn't want to believe it.

"Please tell me it's not true," Tara said.

Sherry stared at her. "I'm not sure what you're talking about."

"I know. Nate was really upset and he told me everything."

Sherry took another deep breath. She lowered her voice. "I know how it sounds, but this is the only way it's ever going to end. Maybe you're too young to realize this, but you never want to look back at a situation and feel you didn't do enough."

"I don't understand how you can even think about doing something like this," Tara said.

"My daughter is trapped. If someone was trying to trap Caleb, wouldn't you do anything you could?"

Tara was so used to believing whatever Sherry said that it was hard to find the words to argue with her. If she were a different, stronger person, maybe she would threaten Sherry that she was going to warn Jonah or call the police. She would hand over all of them, Sherry and Nate, Kevin and Sam too—but in the process, her whole life would be washed away. She didn't know how she could ever go along with this, but to stop it felt like an equally impossible feat.

Feeling helpless, she looked at Sherry, whose face had hardened.

"If we decide to do this for Hailey, I will make sure Caleb is always taken care of," Sherry said.

How would she feel knowing she had taken part in killing a man? Every day, Tara tried to imagine it. Would she be haunted by guilt? Or would she be able to put it out of her mind and carry on with her life? She couldn't sit still, she couldn't eat, she couldn't work. She felt a constant whirling inside her body, everything being shaken loose.

Every time Tara sat at her desk, Sherry gave her imploring looks, but she had no idea what to say. It was easier to be quiet. Solomon too seemed more withdrawn than usual, barely speaking to anyone. They all seemed so far from each other that it made her wonder if anything was the way she'd imagined. Maybe none of them were who she'd believed them to be. At home, she avoided Kevin so she didn't have to discover that he was one more person she didn't know as well as she'd believed. It was better to remain in a state of uncertainty. At least that way she could pretend that none of this was real. At night, she sat on the floor of Caleb's room and watched him sleep and wished she could enter whatever dream he was having. She wanted to wake him and take him far from there. She wanted to climb into her bed and believe that in the morning she would know what to do.

One night, while she was sitting in Caleb's room, Kevin came in. In the dark, she studied his face, still hoping that if she asked him, he would say that of course he wasn't going to do this. He would take her in his arms and say never—never ever, ever.

"I know about your conversation with Sherry," she said.

His body tensed. "What conversation?"

"You know what I'm talking about."

"Why don't you tell me what you heard," he said.

"Nate told me that you and Sam are—" she began, but couldn't say the words.

"I wasn't going to tell you yet. But yes, there have been a few conversations," he admitted.

"Are you out of your mind? Is this what Sam does?" she whispered, hoping Caleb would stay asleep, oblivious.

"It's not like Sam does this all the time, but it's a lot of money, so in the right situation, yes, he's willing to consider something like this."

At least he wasn't lying to her. That had to count for something, didn't it?

"I can't believe you would ever be part of this. If you get caught, then what?" she asked.

"We won't get caught. And even if this does go forward, it's not going to be me who does it. All I would do is go with Sam and be there in case anything goes wrong."

"You do realize this is a person we're talking about. Like an actual human being," she said.

"Obviously I know that, but Sam doesn't know the guy or any of the people involved, so to him, it would just be a job. And that's all it's going to be for me too. You always say how grateful you are for everything that Sherry and Solomon have done for you. And you seem pretty involved with their family right now." He gave her a probing look that made her worry he knew about Nate, or at the very least, suspected.

"What do you mean?" she asked.

"All I'm saying is you obviously care a lot about them, so here's your chance to repay them."

"Oh my god, I have no idea what I'm supposed to do," she said and lay on the floor and curled into a ball. She had been pretty sure that sooner or later it would all fall apart, yet now that it was, she felt incapable of doing anything.

Kevin crouched beside her. "You don't have to do anything. If this ends up happening, you don't ever have to think about it."

"How can I possibly not think about it?" she asked.

"This has nothing to do with you. If certain decisions are made and certain actions are taken, you're not part of it. You can just tell yourself that you don't know anything about it," he said. He was holding her tightly and she wished she could wriggle free, but she didn't have the strength. How could she muster the force to stop this when all she wanted to do was make her body go limp—let herself bob around like a piece of driftwood in the ocean?

"And then, after this, everything is going to be different," he said. "We can both forget about anything that happened while I was gone, and we can start over again. You and Caleb will have whatever you need. I won't have to rely on Sam for anything." He was talking into her ear, but his words were circling her body, they were floating out the window and into the sky.

"It's going to be you and me and Caleb, I promise."

The next night, Tara stayed late at work. She knew that Nate had a full load of patients booked for the following day, and she hoped he might come in the night before to get caught up.

When Nate walked into the office, he jumped when he saw her. "Were you trying to give me a heart attack?" he asked. He hadn't shaved and had the bedraggled look of someone who hadn't showered in a week.

"You were right," she admitted. "I asked Kevin and he told me the truth."

"Who ever said he wasn't an honest guy," Nate said.

"I need to know what to do. I really don't think I can be part of this."

"Don't you think that's something for you to tell Kevin, not me?" he said.

"Please tell me you're not really going to let this happen," she asked.

He shrugged. "What do you want me to do? If you feel so strongly, why don't you do something about it?"

"What can *I* do?" she asked.

"Oh come on, Tara. You know exactly what you can do. Call the police. Tell them what Sam and Kevin and my mother are planning and get everyone arrested."

"How could I possibly do that?" she asked.

"Why not? If you believe this is a terrible idea, then—"

"I thought for sure you would try to stop it," she said.

"Maybe you don't know me as well as you think," he said.

"Stop it, Nate. This isn't you. This isn't any of us."

"Look, I highly doubt that my mother will go through with this, but if she does, I'm not going to prevent it. It's a terrible thing, but people do terrible things all the time."

"But how can you live with it?" she asked. "How are you not going to feel horrified every single second?"

"Who told me that sometimes we do things we ordinarily wouldn't for the people we love?" he said.

"Who tried to tell me what a terrible person Kevin must be if he was willing to do this?" she said.

"I thought you'd be happy that I'm considering helping my mother do what your *fiancé* wants."

She had never heard so much scorn inside a single word.

"Are we done here?" he asked.

She stared at him as he took the mail she'd stacked on his desk, grabbed a few charts and put them in his bag. Their relationship, or whatever it had been, was already starting to feel like it had never existed, just something she'd conjured up to protect herself against the pain of Kevin being away.

"You're no different than he is," she said.

After Nate left, Tara stayed in the office because it felt hard to move. Behind her, she heard footsteps. She hadn't realized Solomon was still in his office, and he came out to the front holding a box that looked too heavy for him.

"I'm clearing out my desk," he said.

Tara jumped up to help him with the box.

"Can I talk to you?" she asked.

In the office, Sherry tried to catch Nate's eye. While he was away, she had been agitated, constantly checking her phone to see if he'd tried to reach her. Now he was back, but it still felt like he was gone. Nate was friendly to the patients, but barely said a word to anyone else. Usually upon his return from a trip, he'd tell everyone about his adventures and show them pictures of the exotic places he'd visited. Now he just shrugged and said that it had been fine.

On his third day back, Nate finally approached her.

"When can we talk?" he asked.

"Anytime you want," she said.

"How about tomorrow after work? Let's go to the Mounts," he suggested, the botanical garden where Hailey got married.

"Are you serious?"

"Can you think of anywhere more fitting?" he asked.

The next day, at the entrance, Sherry waited for Nate, wearing oversized dark sunglasses.

"Is this your new getup?" Nate teased.

"I'm glad you find this so amusing," she said.

She hadn't been to the Mounts since the wedding; as much as she'd once loved it, she had felt compelled to stay away. They followed the winding path, under an arbor encircled with vines, past stubby palm trees with latticed trunks, past pots of orchids and orange hibiscus plants that looked to her like gaping mouths. Nate was walking too quickly, and she wanted to slow him so that he could appreciate, as she did, the wonder of a world so perfectly sculpted, so outrageously in bloom.

They stopped walking when they reached a bench that was situated under a canopy of palm trees. Sitting there, it didn't feel as blazing hot as it did in the direct sun.

"I need to know what you think," she said.

"Think about what?" he asked.

"Nate, please."

"If you want me to go along with this, then you have to be willing to say it," he said.

"Why?" she asked.

"Say it," he insisted.

"But why?"

"I want to hear you say the actual words."

"Nate, please," she protested again, but his face was resolute. Next to him a tiny gecko slithered up the wood of the bench. She watched its progress, then looked again at Nate who was waiting for her.

She took a deep breath. "I want to kill him," she said.

They got up from the bench and started walking. They crossed a white metal bridge over a koi pond, where the fish were like streaks of orange paint on an otherwise green canvas. They walked past a row of strangler fig trees, their vines wrapped around the trunk of another tree until it was entirely surrounded. They passed a mother walking with two small children, who ran ahead, but came scurrying back as soon as she called. They passed a sawtooth cactus, and Nate reached out to touch one of its prickly spikes.

"Do you still think it's a crazy idea?" she asked as they came to a larger pond, where an egret patrolled the shoreline and a blue heron swooped down into the water, flaunting its monumental wingspan.

Nate stopped walking. "Of course I think it's crazy. It's very, very crazy, but I'm not going to stop you, if this is what you want to do. I'll put up the money, but I'm not going to get my hands dirty in any way."

"We're not going to have anything to do with the actual . . . with Jonah himself. All we have to do is pay and they'll take care of it," Sherry said.

"I want to be sure that you know what you're getting yourself into. I'm hardly an expert, but there's a lot to get right," he said.

"Kevin says that his brother knows what he's doing."

"Do you actually think this is something they've done before? I highly doubt that they're professionals. And there can't be any mistakes. You can't talk about it, not to Hailey, not to Dad. There's no way that either of them would go along with this," he said.

"We're not going to say anything to anyone," she agreed.

"And I assume you know that you can't have anything to do with Kevin, ever. It's bad enough that you've already talked to him on the phone. From now on, you should just talk to Tara in person if there's anything that needs to be arranged."

"Is Tara on board?" she asked.

"She doesn't sound happy, but you know how passive she is. She'll do whatever Kevin says. And if she doesn't want to, that isn't my problem."

She gave him a sharp look. "What do you mean?" she asked.

"It's over," he said.

"What happened?" she asked. She was relieved, though she didn't want him to see that. In a different situation, she would have been glad to see Nate with Tara—she would have wanted him to be happy, however it came about. But now it was best to have as few complications as possible. Once this was over, they would have to return to as close an approximation of normal as possible. They would have to find a way to pretend that nothing had happened.

"It's fine," he said. "It's not like it was ever going to work out."

She knew him well enough to recognize his hurt beneath the bravado. "Maybe, as soon as all of this is over, you can have a fresh start and meet the right person."

He cut her off. "We have more important things to worry about than my social life. At this point, my goal is to make sure your plan doesn't land us all in jail for the rest of our lives."

"Please, don't even say something like that."

"You're going to have to be able to hear much worse than that. If we go through with this, a lot of people including the police are going to wonder what role we played. It's going to be the first thing anyone thinks of. It's hardly a secret that we didn't get along with Jonah. How many of your friends know how much you dislike him? How many of his friends know how contentious the divorce has been?"

"But no one would ever think that we did it," she said.

"Are you kidding me? Everyone is going to think that. You need to understand that. If we're careful, and everything goes according to plan, they won't be able to prove it, but that doesn't mean a lot of people won't wonder. So if you're not willing to live with that kind of suspicion for a very long time, then you need to ask yourself if you really have it in you to go through with this."

With the sun beating down, she was soaked in sweat. "Do you have any idea how much I hate him?" she asked. "I think about him all the time. I feel like he's taken over my body. At night, I dream about him, and when I wake up, he's still here."

"I really think you're going to regret this," he warned.

She gripped Nate's arm. "If something goes wrong, I'll take sole responsibility. I promise you, Nate. I'll be the only one. You never have to worry about that. And don't think I don't know how loyal you are. Sometimes I think that the two of us are the most alike. We both understand that sometimes you have to do whatever it takes."

The ball was set in motion. All on its own, it would roll down a ramp, which would activate a lever, which would open a gate, which would turn a switch.

"We're good to go," Sherry said to Tara the next morning.

"I'll let Kevin know," Tara said, but wouldn't look her in the eye.

Sherry wished that she didn't have to involve Tara at all—she wished this could happen without ever having to talk about it. But Nate had made it clear that she shouldn't be in touch directly with Kevin. Though Nate intended to be minimally involved, he kept coming up with precautions to ensure that nothing could be traced back to them. He told her that they should do it as soon as possible; the more they talked about it, the more likely someone would discover their plan. He said that they needed to pay Kevin without leaving a paper trail, and he suggested that they hire Tara as a consultant for the new practice and pay her three large sums of money. They would double the salary that Solomon paid her and attribute it to her new role as manager. This way, the money would be untraceable.

Sherry glanced again at Tara who looked pale and was sitting eerily still at her desk, not doing any work. Sherry wished she had some way to console her—or to confide that she had the constant sensation of watching herself from above. But it was probably better if she projected an air of calm, if she gave the illusion that this was an ordinary day.

"I was thinking that we might want to have a grand-opening event when the new space is ready," Sherry said a little while later when she could no longer stand the silence. "I'll bet Nate would like the idea and it would be a good way to get some publicity for the new practice."

"That's fine with me," Tara said, but her voice sounded shaky.

"We might want to start designing the brochures now so we're all ready to go as soon as the construction is done."

"Whatever you think," Tara said.

"Okay, good, because it's going to be ready before we know it . . ." Sherry trailed off. She may as well have been talking to herself. One day, though, it would not be like this. They would find a way to seal off what they had done. All she had to do was get past the moment she was in now. Somehow, the days would pass, then the weeks and months. Once it was safely in the past, she and Tara would hardly remember what they had done. They would talk freely as if this had never taken place.

"I'm heading out," Sherry said as she packed her bag and forced herself to smile.

Tara gave her a half wave, but looked like she was afraid of her. Sherry rushed out, suddenly eager to be as far from her as possible. Even if they managed to be close again in the future, Sherry couldn't stand to sit beside her now, struggling to think of what to say.

On the way home, she decided to stop at the mall, where she bought Maya a navy and white dress, a pair of rhinestone-studded jeans, and a lavender sweatshirt printed with a pink ballerina. In the parking lot, she saw her friends Judy and Eleanor from a distance. Since her party, she'd barely spoken to them. She was flooded with a longing for the closeness they'd once had. If she were to run to them and confess what she was about to do, would they talk her out of it? They would never contemplate anything even half this awful, she was sure of that. They would be horrified if they knew she would even consider such a thing. Before their eyes, her monstrousness would be revealed.

She didn't call their names. It was already too late. There were parts of herself she couldn't dare let anyone see.

• • •

"They want to fly to Binghamton for a trial run as soon as possible, to get a sense of where he lives," Tara whispered a few days later, barely looking up from her screen.

"Tell them to do whatever they need," Sherry said.

Tara stared at her, and Sherry saw the look of betrayal in her eyes. All these years, she had only wanted to help Tara, and now she was the cause of this distress. But she couldn't let the thought settle inside her. It was going to be okay. Yes, it would be awful, but then, it would be over. She had to turn herself to stone. Her heart had to be clenched. Her mind had to contract. She had to remember all the terrible things Jonah had said to her. She had to steel herself against her doubts. She had to believe that it would be like the ball rolling down the ramp. A tree falling in a forest. A bird falling from the sky. In a world that she was not part of, two men would board a plane, they would peer out the window as they made their descent over what appeared to be a city of tiny cars and miniature houses. She would remain safely in her own house, far from them, while in this other world, they would follow a man they didn't know and carefully devise a plan.

"I know it feels terrifying right now, but it won't always be this way," Sherry tried to reassure Tara.

"How do you know that?" she asked.

"Because it's finally going to end," Sherry said. All she could do was offer those words, however slight they were starting to feel, and hope that they were true.

On her drive home, Sherry called Hailey, but never knew when she was going to answer. Even when she did, she said little, making Sherry feel like she had to extricate sentences from her.

"Call me later if you're free," Sherry said, remembering how, as a little girl, Hailey had wanted her to lay down with her at bedtime and, instead of going to sleep, had a seemingly endless number of things to talk about.

Sherry had known on some level that it wouldn't always be this way, but she allowed herself to hope. She believed that, of her three children, Hailey was the one who would never feel like a stranger.

Once Hailey was living in West Palm, they would return to their earlier closeness. It would be almost like nothing had happened, like no time had passed.

Tuesday night was the start of Yom Kippur, and for the first time, Sherry was tempted not to go to synagogue. How could she sit there, given what she was about to do? Services were at sundown, and an hour before, she was still undecided. What would it mean to miss this year of all years? It would be one more reminder that she had already lost so many parts of herself.

She had left in just enough time. The sanctuary was filled when she arrived. They had seats purchased and assigned for the High Holidays, but Sherry found an empty spot in the back, where she sat alone. Was it her imagination that people avoided looking at her, as if they could feel her secret radiating from her?

She looked into the prayer book, wanting the words to hold her aloft. For so many years prior the prayers had risen inside her, casings that held her sorrows, her hopes. Could she somehow draw a line from who she had been then to who she had become? Could the prayers cleanse her and return her to those earlier days—the hatred cast out and in its place, a blanketing white peace?

She tried, but in the prayer book, all she could see was Jonah's name, inscribed on every page. The thought felt nearly unbearable. He had no idea what was about to befall him.

Squeezing her fingers into fists, she beat her chest along with everyone else as she recited the confessional prayers: for the sin of gossip, for the sin of slander, for the sin of disrespect. But how could she confess the kind of transgression she was about to commit? Surely the prayers had no room for one of this magnitude. Even if people here had deeds hidden in the chambers of their hearts, none could possibly be as grave as hers. She remembered something she'd learned as a child in a synagogue class long ago: for certain sins, your soul was cut off; untethered, it would endlessly wander, never finding respite. At the time, she'd wondered what deeds were so bad you could never come home, but now she understood. You could be cut off not just from those around you but from your own self.

When the congregation rose again, Sherry slipped out. There was no place for her here.

"They're ready. It can be whenever you want," Tara said a week later. She looked a little better now, less pale, less afraid, and Sherry hoped that this meant she'd found a way to live with what they were about to do.

"Tell them to do it as soon as possible," Sherry said.

Unable to sleep that night, Sherry wandered through the house. She stood at the window, looking out at the pool. It had started to rain with a ferocity that felt like rage, and a bolt of lightning cut across the sky. The palm trees swayed precipitously, and she marveled at how, even in storms that caused immense damage, they didn't snap from the force because their trunks were able to bend.

She ended up in Sol's study, a room she rarely entered. In front of the bookshelves, she surveyed the medical texts, as if Sol's intact mind was catalogued here. She saw something in a far corner and reached for it—Jonah's novel, which she must have stashed there at some point. She wished she'd thrown it away, but now she studied the photo at the back of the book. There was the stylized pose, the look of self-satisfaction, but it didn't match the version of him in her mind in which his sneer opened so wide that he could have swallowed her. She lay down on the small couch in the room, and still holding the book, she dozed. In her dreams, Jonah was now fanged and clawed, howling and chasing her, trying to trap her, to tear her apart.

With a shudder, she awoke. She shoved the book behind the couch. Jonah could write whatever he wanted about her, but no one would ever read it. Even as he wrote them, his words would be erased.

She went back to her bed, and when she finally fell asleep, she dreamt that all three kids were young and running through the yard. One by one, they cannonballed into the pool. The water splashed Solomon, standing nearby, but instead of getting angry, he jumped into the pool too, while she did a swan dive off a high board that had magically appeared, and landed in the water beside them.

The next day, Sherry wrote Tara the first of the checks, a down payment that they'd agreed upon, and left it in an envelope on her desk chair at the end of the day, after Tara had gone home. She was glad not to hand it to Tara in person—one more way to believe that this was almost, almost happening on its own. Even so, Sherry knew that she had moved one step closer. Now any pretense that she might turn back was gone. It was like standing on the deck of a departing cruise ship about to traverse a vast ocean, while everyone on a rapidly receding shoreline waved goodbye.

That night, unable to sleep again, Sherry called Nate. She had promised to involve him as little as possible, but he was the only one with whom she could talk freely.

"How terrible are we?" she asked.

"What can I possibly say to that?" he said.

"I'm afraid," she admitted.

"I think that's a pretty reasonable way to feel."

"Are you?" she asked.

"We're about to kill a man. How do you think I feel?"

Through the window, she saw that she'd made it through the darkest part of night. Ever so slightly, the sky was starting to lighten. All she wanted was for the hours to pass, the days to hurtle forward and to emerge on some other side where she would not think about this every moment of every day

"Even if we get away with it, do you believe that we're somehow going to be punished?" she asked.

"I really don't want to talk about this."

She grew quiet. She could call this off, but what would be left? A leaden weight inside her. The knowledge that her daughter was trapped.

After getting off the phone with Nate, she still couldn't sleep. She hadn't been able to ask him what, if anything, he believed in. Did he increasingly have the sense that he was being watched? Did he believe that being a bad person was a fixed category, like a prison, in which she would forever be confined? Did he believe in another world in which they would have to give an accounting of their deeds? Did he believe they would be cut off for eternity for what they were about to do? If they were to regret it, would there ever be the possibility of repentance?

When Sherry came into the office a few days later, Tara was checking a patient in for her appointment. Once the patient went into the exam room, Tara leaned toward her, but looked just off to the side.

"They can leave next Tuesday and drive straight through. It can happen first thing next Thursday morning," Tara whispered.

All Sherry could do was nod. Her mouth was too dry to form words. Her skin felt too tight around her face. She was watching herself fall, but was unable to catch herself—a body in motion that only belatedly she realized was hers.

Sherry left the office early. In their neighborhood, she and Sol took a walk, she holding on to him tightly, aware of how easily he could take a wrong step and tumble forward. Normally, she would have tried to keep a conversation going, but one secret spawned so many others, and in Sol's presence, she said little. Had he noticed, she wondered, or was he so far away that he no longer could?

She stopped walking. He looked at her blankly. She kept her face blank as well.

The next night, Sherry had a quick dinner with Nate in the backyard. She had begged him to come over and he reluctantly agreed. They'd considered meeting at a restaurant, but she was afraid of inadvertently speaking too loudly and giving themselves away. In the distance, she heard a barking sound, but as far as she knew none of their neighbors had a dog. She lowered her voice. She couldn't shake the feeling that someone was skulking in the garden. Everything they said was being recorded.

"Do we need to do anything special next Thursday, in case?" Sherry asked, unsettled by the barking, which was growing louder, though Nate seemed oblivious to it.

Nate closed his eyes and it struck her how awful he looked, his eyes vacant, his face ashen. "We have to act like it's a normal day," he said.

"But what about Hailey? Shouldn't we at least know what she's doing next Thursday?"

"I'll take care of it," he said.

That night, she dreamt that Nate was a teenager again, holding a gun. The pool wasn't filled with water, but with blood.

When Sherry spoke to Hailey the next day, they talked about how Maya was loving kindergarten, and how Solomon was doing better, and how Nate's plans for the office were taking shape. Hailey sounded less distant—for the first time in weeks, she felt like her daughter might be restored to her.

"I don't want to get into a long conversation about this, but I wanted you to know that the hearing about Jonah's motion was postponed," Hailey said at the end of their conversation. While Sherry once would have cared about every detail, now Hailey may as well have been talking about a fantastical problem. Jonah could file motions all day, but it was one more thing that he was writing in the air.

"That's fine. Whenever it is, we'll deal with it," Sherry said.

"I thought you would be more upset," Hailey said.

"I'm completely fine," she assured her. "It's all going to be fine."

"Nate booked me a spa day for next Thursday," Hailey said. "He's been saying he was going to buy me a present when the divorce was finalized, but I think he gave up and decided to give it to me now."

For Hailey, there would be vistas of guilt-free sleep. Hailey would never wrestle as she did every night, wondering what kind of monster she had become.

"Enjoy every minute," Sherry said.

Friday night, Solomon slept the sleep of the dead, not waking no matter how many times Sherry got out of bed. Her exhaustion was overwhelming, but rest was impossible. Out the window, she now heard a multitude of dogs howling. She pulled her pillow over her head, but the sound was now coming not from the yard but from inside her body. She thought about Kevin, and how he seemed meek, almost sweet—in a strange way he reminded her of Adam, who could be both so soft and so hard at once. She wondered what Kevin was doing now. Was he too lying awake, contemplating what he was about to do? She was glad she'd never met Sam. It made it easier to believe that he would feel no rustle of doubt, no scrap of remorse.

On Sunday, Sherry awoke in the middle of the night to a patch of small welts on her arm. She tried to go back to sleep, but Jonah was all she could see. She thought about Jonah's mother, wondering if they might have been close and how all of this might have been different were she still alive. She tried to imagine Jonah as a child, but couldn't block out an image of Maya, the two of them now interchangeable.

When Sherry finally fell asleep, she dreamt that she was standing in front of the family photograph, but now Jonah was returned to the picture. As she drew closer, she realized that it wasn't a red tie he was wearing but a gash in his chest. Sherry reached for it, and the painting bled on her hands.

Driving to work on Monday morning, Sherry was sure she was being followed. She pulled over on the side of the road and turned on her emergency flashers.

"You're okay. Everything is okay," she repeated out loud like it was a lullaby and she was both mother and child.

When Sherry got to work, she ducked into the bathroom. Her face was pale, her eyes puffy. She applied concealer, but her face was no longer made of skin but of stone. She added a layer of lipstick, but that created a slash of red where her mouth was supposed to be.

She went into Nate's office and closed the door. He was sitting at his desk, staring off.

"I don't know if I can go through with it," she said.

"I would be more than happy—ecstatic really—if you want to back out," he said. "But given that Kevin and his lovely brother are supposed to start driving to Binghamton tomorrow night, you're going to have to decide very soon."

"I'm afraid," she admitted.

"So am I," he said.

If she changed her mind, could their lives return to the way they had once been? Or had she already walked herself out too far onto this gangplank and was now suspended over a dark vastness with no way back?

Later in the day, Nate motioned for her to come to his office. "I talked to Tara and she had a good idea," he said. "She's going to call you at midnight tomorrow, right before they leave for Binghamton. If you want them to do it, you need to answer the phone and say yes. After that, it's a done deed and will be too late to turn back. But if you don't pick up the phone, that means you don't want to go through with it. And if that's the case, then this is the end. We're going to pretend like this never happened and we're never going to talk about it again."

Nate's voice was steady and strong. It may have been a strange moment to feel pride in her child, but she had birthed someone who could take care of what needed to be done. Sherry felt better. She still had time. Each day was an eternity, with so many minutes to endure. By tomorrow night, she would have figured out what to do.

The next night, Nate came over, but Solomon stayed in their bedroom. Sherry grilled steaks, but neither she nor Nate were hungry, and she had the urge to push the meat through the grates in the grill and let it burn into ash.

"I just want this to be over," Sherry said.

"I really hope this turns out the way you want," he said. "Remember, Tara is calling at midnight."

"Please don't go," she said when he pushed away his plate.

"I have to get out of here," he said.

She laced her fingers through his, but he shook her off and started to walk away.

"Nate, please. Tell me what you're thinking," she called after him.

He whirled around. "Do you really want to know?"

"Yes. Please."

He stared wildly at her, his body so taut she thought he might uncoil and lunge at her. "Don't do it. Just don't."

She stared at him, unable to speak. It was the words she wished he would say, the words she couldn't bear to hear.

He started to leave, then turned back once more. "You're living in a fantasy if you think there's going to come a day when you don't think about this every single minute. We might learn to live with it, but it's always going to be there, for both of us. All we can hope is that Hailey might be free."

After Nate left, Sherry slid into the pool, her feet kicking, her arms propelling her forward. It was the same pool, but may as well have been an ocean roiled with treacherous currents. She held tightly to her memories of Jonah, his sneer and his hate and his threats. This had to end. Jonah had given her no choice. All she was doing was flipping the switch, releasing the lever. All she had to do was count down the hours, let the ball begin to roll, let this night come to a close, let this deed come to pass.

Five laps. It was getting closer to midnight. Sherry kept swimming, wishing she could travel back to the beginning—before Hailey was divorced, before she was married, before Adam left, before any of the kids were grown. They would be three small children, doing running jumps into the pool.

Ten laps. She stopped to catch her breath. All she needed to do was hold on a little longer. She glanced up at the living room window, where she saw Sol watching her. She swam faster, panting. The words swam before her. It had to end. The water had become murky and thick, there was seagrass and kelp brushing against her legs. It had to end. The plants alongside the pool had grown into trees, with roots that swooped into the water, ensnaring her body. She heard Nate's voice. *Don't do it.* It came over her. *Don't.*

His words carved an opening through which other words began to flow.

They would be killing him.

There would be no turning back.

She couldn't swim fast enough to escape this truth.

It came over her. Not just Jonah but a part of her own grandchild. In the water, she saw Maya's face. In Maya's face, she saw him.

It came over her, as if the water beheld the future and she could peer into it. If she went forward, it would be the end of all of them. Not just Jonah destroyed, but her family, Tara's family as well.

Her strokes intensified. She was passing through the tangle of reeds, she was kicking off the tendrils of green, she was gliding through the water. Her hair was coming loose from its clips, floating in front of her. Her limbs were enormous fins. She kept swimming until the walls of the pool gave way, the blue tiles opening to create passageways into the expanse of open waters and beyond.

At exactly midnight, by the side of the pool, the phone rang. Even though Sherry was expecting the call, she startled. All she had to do was answer. All she had to do was say yes and the ball would be set in motion. Yes and the gate would rise. Yes and soon she would be on the other side.

Instead of swimming toward the phone, she sank to the bottom of the pool and felt the urge to stay submerged, to let the water fill her, weigh her down. She resurfaced and gulped in the air. No. It wasn't yet too late. She was not yet irreparably cut off. She could still be gathered back inside. She swam to the shallow side of the pool and stood in the water and glanced toward her garden, where new buds were emerging every day. With the water dripping from her face and off her hair, she felt the warm breeze. She looked at the ever-rippling water and at the dark sky and at the swaying palms that didn't break because they were able to bend. No.

The phone stopped ringing and the night was once again quiet. Sherry plunged back under the water, swimming as if this were the only thing that might save her. She had been so certain, but when the moment came, she couldn't do it.

MAINE, 2019

A little after midnight, Adam walks into my room, waking me from a dream in which Jonah and I are paddling Maya up a shallow river in a red canoe.

"Hailey," he says. He places his arm on my shoulder and lightly shakes me. "It's time."

I'm relieved at the sight of him. This past week, since Maya's birthday dinner, he has barely spoken to me, spending all his time outside with the dogs or in his room. I've wanted to break the silence, but his reticence has been more pronounced than it was even when we first arrived. When I have seen him, he's been anxious and flustered, hurrying from any room I'm in, intent on putting as much distance between us as he can. Afraid that he no longer wants us here, I try to come up with options—the world outside the cabin feels vast and unsettled, yet contains no place we can go. Earlier that night, Adam stood in the doorway after dinner, watching me read to Maya. I was sure that he was on the verge of announcing that it was time for us to leave, but abruptly, he grabbed his coat. "I'm going out," he said. I heard his car start, then drive off, and I feared that he was stranding me here with Maya and the dogs.

After checking to make sure that Maya hasn't stirred, I follow Adam into the living room. Daisy is on her side, nestled in the blankets. When she hears us, she lifts her head, but doesn't otherwise move. Adam squats next to her, murmuring her name.

"Is it okay to touch her?" I ask.

"Just let her see you, so she'll know you're here," he says.

"Are you going to call the vet?" I ask while Daisy roots around in the blankets as if she's lost something.

"I don't need to. She knows what to do."

Occasionally Daisy paces, but mostly she lies there, panting, shivering, barking. When I was in labor with Maya, I howled, writhed, cursed, and sobbed with no restraint. Even Jonah was surprised by the sounds that emerged from me, as if by becoming a mother, a new version of me was being birthed as well.

"Should I wake Maya?" I ask. She had begged to be allowed to watch the puppies being born, but I was worried it would be too much for her. I tried to remember what I once would have thought about such a request, but so far removed from normalcy, I couldn't access the good mother I'd tried to be. "Please, please, please?" Maya repeated with near desperation, and I'd eventually agreed, aware of the futility of trying to protect her from seeing too much.

"I'd wait. It could still be a while," Adam says.

"Are you sure she's okay?" I ask when Daisy whines and groans.

"This is normal. Her body knows what to do," he assures me.

It's supposed to snow tonight, a late March storm, and Adam goes to check on the other dogs. When he comes back inside, he reports that they are fine, asleep in a huddle. We sit beside each other on the couch, our shoulders touching, and his proximity feels like one of the kindest gestures I've ever been offered. Adam adds wood to the fire. Daisy lies on the pillow, panting and shaking. While Adam feels her stomach, she nuzzles against him. It's just after one in the morning, and I go into the kitchen and prepare two mugs of tea.

"Will you tell me what it was like for you growing up?" I ask Adam when I'm beside him.

He looks startled by the question, but all week, I've been waiting for an opening through which I might slip it in.

"What can I say? I didn't fit into our family," he says, so softly I can barely hear him. I lean toward him, as if with my body I can elicit his words.

"You and Nate were so close, and I was on my own. I felt like there was something wrong with me," he says warily. "Mom never said it outright, but I could tell that she wanted me to be different than I was. She didn't love me the same way she loved you and Nate."

It's not true, I want to protest, but it doesn't matter that I had lived with a different version of our family. At least for this moment, I want to remain inside the one he'd experienced.

"I used to tell myself that I was adopted, and one day this nice quiet family would show up, and I'd have a home where I belonged. Do you have any idea what it was like to be sure that there's something wrong with you? Do you know how much I wished I could fit in?" he continues.

He is holding back tears, and though I want to reach for him, I'm afraid to do anything that will stop him from talking.

"I hated who I was when I was home. The few times I'd tried to talk to Mom about it, she acted like I was making it up. I realized that I lived in a completely different reality. It got to the point where I was sick of hating myself. It was easier to be separate."

Adam's voice breaks, and I wish for a way to go back and find the child he was and tend to his pain.

"After your wedding—after what happened with Luna—I couldn't talk to Mom at all. I loved that dog. I know it was an accident, but I couldn't forgive her. I felt like it was me that Mom ran over. Until then, I was afraid to cut off completely, but after that, I was finally able to do it."

"I'm sorry," I say. My apology feels so slight, so insufficient, but I don't know what else I can offer. "I wish I knew how you felt. I wish I had been there for you more."

"You tried, but I couldn't talk to you then. I don't know what's changed, but you seem different now. I feel like you understand."

"I do," I whisper.

Daisy is making small whimpering sounds, and I go sit beside her, hoping my presence will soothe her. As I kiss the top of her head and whisper reassurances, she licks my fingers. Adam crouches down next to Daisy and offers her water.

"Good girl," Adam says as she drinks. Outside, the dogs are barking, and I wonder if they have some innate awareness that Daisy is about to give birth and this is their way of offering compassion.

"It was easier with Dad. I could talk to him for a few minutes on the phone and let him know I was okay and that was enough," he says. "And then I found out that this property was going up for sale. It wasn't far from where I'd been living and I really wanted to create a dog shelter. I mentioned the property to Dad. I didn't want to admit it, but of course I knew why I was telling him." Adam gives a rueful laugh. "I might have left, but apparently I still couldn't make it on my own."

"Did Mom know?" I ask.

"I don't think so. I asked him not to tell anyone. I guess I needed to feel like I was still separate from everyone. But I was planning to come home when Dad got sick. I was finally ready to let go of all that anger."

"What happened?" I ask.

Adam pulls away from me and stands up. The openness between us snaps shut.

"There are things you don't know," he says.

I stand up too. "Tell me."

He shakes his head. "When you called that night and asked if you and Maya could come here, I had decided that I wasn't going to have contact with any of you ever again. But you sounded so scared and alone, I couldn't turn you away."

Outside, it has started to snow. The fire crackles. Daisy makes small whimpering sounds. The wind blows so fiercely that the snowflakes appear to be falling sideways. The lights flicker a few times, but go back on. Adam sets out candles and two flashlights, just in case.

He crouches beside Daisy. "If you want Maya to be here when they're born, we should wake her now," he says.

I still worry that Maya shouldn't see this, but remembering the beseeching look on her face, I go into the bedroom.

Gently, I caress her cheek. I smooth her hair. "The puppies are about to be born," I say, and Maya's eyes snap open. She jumps out of bed as if she'd been awake the entire time, waiting.

I wrap a blanket around her and we go into the living room. Maya sprawls on the couch between us. At first, she fidgets with excitement, asking Adam how much longer it will be, but soon sleep overtakes her. Against her will, her eyes flutter and close. Outside, the snow grows heavier, and the lights flicker again, but this time they don't come back on. It feels like the entire world, whatever is left of it, has shut off. The cabin grows even more silent. The darkness envelops us. Adam lights the candles, and with nothing else to do, we sit and wait.

Hailey took the day off from work and was at the spa in the Glen Hotel for her massage. She had arrived a little late and was frazzled as she gave them her name and got undressed. It had taken longer to get Maya to school that morning; Maya had lost a tooth and wanted to spend time gazing in the mirror at the vacant spot in her mouth. Hailey knew she should have hurried her along but, enjoying how happy Maya looked, she had allowed her to linger.

Hailey relaxed into the feeling of a hand on her back, just the right amount of pressure so that the tension slowly seeped out. It had been a long time since she'd done something nice for herself, and she was grateful to Nate for his gift. For the first time in ages, she felt optimistic. She hadn't thought it was possible, but the divorce no longer consumed her. It was an annoyance she had to deal with, not a catastrophe derailing every minute. Maybe it was because she'd started to have a weekly coffee date with another mother from Maya's class who was also getting divorced. Or because she liked her job more now that she'd been named an assistant editor of the alumni magazine and could choose what she wanted to write about. She ran most days, increasing the distance, working at getting faster, amazed that even small incremental improvements bolstered her as much as they did. When she received an unpleasant text from Jonah, she pictured herself in running clothes, her body sleek and alert. No matter what he did, she was too fast for him to catch her. Even her mother seemed to be slowly coming around. She spoke to her less frequently now—maybe this too was why she was doing so much better—but when they did talk, her mother seemed resigned. Instead of urging her to fight, she calmly reminded her that things had a way of working out in the end.

When the massage was over, Hailey put her clothes back on, her body still in a languid state. She reached for her phone. She had two missed calls from a number she didn't recognize. She was about to listen to the voicemail when she got another call from that same number.

"Is this Hailey Gelman?" a man asked.

"Who is this?"

"I'm calling from the Binghamton Police Department," he said.

"Is my daughter okay?" Hailey asked, a bolt of panic shooting through her.

"This has nothing to do with your daughter, but we'd like to see if you could come by and talk to us," he said.

"What is this about?"

"We need to ask you a few questions about your ex-husband, Jonah Gelman."

"Oh my god, what happened?" she asked, running to her car. There was no time, no way, to explain that Jonah wasn't still her husband but not yet her ex-husband, that he existed in the no-man's-land between the two. There was no way to ask any of the questions amassing in her mind.

"It would be best if we talked about that once you get here," the man said.

He gave her the address of the police station. It was a fifteen-minute drive, and Hailey sped. When she got there, a uniformed woman ushered her to a small, mostly bare room. The wait felt interminable, and her mind lurched to all the possibilities for why she might have been called there.

When, finally, a police officer came in, he gave her a strange, apprais-ing look as he sat at the table, across from her.

"We called you here," he began and paused, "because there's been a shooting. I'm sorry to tell you this, but your ex-husband, Jonah Gelman, was shot inside his home this morning. He was taken to the hospital, but unfortunately he didn't make it."

The police officer was awaiting her reaction, but she couldn't under-stand what he was saying. He was speaking from too far away, or maybe he was speaking too softly, or in the wrong language. Hailey's mouth opened, but no sound emerged. Maybe if he slowed down or if he wrote out the words, she might understand.

Jonah had been shot.

Jonah was dead.

"Oh my god," she cried out. She wasn't sure if she was making sense. She wasn't even sure the police officer was talking to her because she was no longer in this room but floating above it.

"I know this is a shock, but I'm hoping you might be able to help us understand what happened."

Hailey tried to rewind. Someone had killed Jonah. The sentence was impossible. She was still trying to comprehend it when the police officer began firing off additional questions.

When had she last seen Jonah?

What had they talked about?

What had the mood been like between them?

Two nights ago, she had brought Maya to Jonah's house. He was an-noyed because she was late, and Maya was cranky and clung to her, but other than that, it was an ordinary night. Even as she relayed this to the police officer, she felt like she was making it up. What was an ordinary night? It was hard to remember. Maybe it didn't matter what she said because the police officer was somehow aware that she'd privately wished Jonah was dead. Maybe he knew that she'd scratched his car, imagining it was his chest. Maybe he could see into the dark scab that had become her heart.

"Can you tell me where you were this morning?"

"What time did you leave your house?"

"Did you stop anywhere along the way?"

She answered, but was no longer sure. Was she really getting a massage? Did she drive directly here when he called? Did she call anyone while she was on the way?

"Did Jonah have any enemies that you know of?"

"Could you give us a list of all the people he had regular contact with?"

"Can you think of anyone who might have had a reason to do this?"

She stared at him blankly. Her thoughts raced, but her words were slow and slurred.

No, she and Jonah didn't get along.

No, she would never do something like this.

More questions. She looked around her frantically. Nowhere was safe. Even the floor had traps laid, but she couldn't see where they were. *Who did this? Why?* She had no idea. It felt like she'd been in this room for hours, for days, answering the same questions. How many times could she form these sentences? If she were the one conducting the interrogation, would she believe her own self?

There was a clock directly across from her. Hailey swam through the murkiness in her mind and remembered.

"I need to get my daughter," she said.

If she could drive to the school and see that Maya was safe in her classroom, then it wasn't possible that Jonah was dead. Hailey said it again, that she needed to get Maya, and braced herself, afraid they would restrain her, prevent her. She was surprised when the police officer said she was free to go, said he would be in touch, said to call if she remembered anything else.

Hailey staggered to her car, gasping. "You're okay," she said out loud, but it didn't help. For one moment, a bright spot of clarity came over her. She needed to call Nate.

"Hailey!" Nate exclaimed when he answered the phone, as if she'd caught him in the midst of a great day.

"Nate," she said. "Nate. Nate."

"What's the matter?" he asked.

"Jonah is dead." The words felt mangled. The sounds weren't recognizable.

Nate gasped. "No," he said. "No, no, no, no, no."

"He's dead," she said.

"Please tell me you're not serious," Nate said.

"Someone shot him. It's true. I've been at the police station all morning. They told me. He's dead."

When Nate didn't say anything, she wondered if he'd hung up on her—or if maybe by the same unknown force, he too was now dead.

"What did you tell them?" he finally asked.

"What do you think I said? That I was completely shocked, that I have no idea what happened to him."

"Where are you now?"

"In my car. I have to go get Maya."

"Don't go anywhere yet. Please, I just need a second to think."

"I can't be late," she said. It was the only thing she was sure of. If she could get Maya. If she could drive her home. The day would still be proceeding as planned. She wouldn't be at the police station, Jonah wouldn't have been shot, he wouldn't be dead.

"Fine, get Maya and go home. But don't do anything else. You have to promise me that you won't talk to anyone," he instructed. "And don't call

Mom. Let me tell her. You just focus on pulling yourself together. Go get Maya and then go home, do you understand?"

Hailey managed to start the car, back out of her spot, and drive through the parking lot. Each action felt like a complicated undertaking. She regarded Nate's words as orders. Get Maya. Go home. There were two of her now, one that could drive toward Maya's school, the other that remained in the parking lot, immobilized.

She got to the school a few minutes late. Maya was still in her classroom wearing a triangular hat made of colored paper, feathers and buttons glued to the front. She was holding a drawing she'd made of a dark-haired little girl floating above a garden overgrown with enormous curlicued stalks. Maybe she and Maya could hide out amid the art supplies, fold stacks of paper into hats indefinitely.

She hurried Maya outside. She didn't talk to anyone. A few of the mothers whom she'd become friends with waved to her. They had no idea about Jonah, not yet, but they surely would soon. She pretended not to see them. Get Maya and go home. This was all she could do.

"Why do we have to hurry?" Maya asked. She gave a wide-mouthed smile so that Hailey could see the small gap where her tooth had been.

"We just do, okay, honey?" she said.

"Today I made the garden picture and then we did letters and everyone loved my tooth and outside I played with Olivia and then we came inside and had cookies," Maya reported as they got into the car.

Hailey tried to give the impression that she was listening, that she was driving this car, ferrying them home to safety. Teeth and gardens and cookies, and Jonah had been shot and now he was dead and somehow, in a few hours, she would have to find the words to tell Maya.

Holding Maya's hand, Hailey walked inside the house and closed the blinds. She checked twice to make sure the front door was locked. Outside, Jonah was dead, and inside, she made Maya a grilled cheese and cut off the crusts. She placed the sandwich on a plate and forced a smile, but as Maya bit into it, her stomach turned at the sight of the yellow cheese oozing from the pale bread.

When Maya was done, Hailey suggested that they go to Maya's room to play. She left her phone in the kitchen and they went into the bedroom and she closed the door behind them, one more barrier that might somehow keep them safe. Maya pulled out her bin of dolls, and they played mommy and baby, where they fed and dressed and burped and rocked. Then Maya took out the cradle Sherry recently gave her, and she tucked her doll in with a small yellow blanket. In the other room, Hailey could hear the faint ringing of her phone, but she made no move to answer it. So long as she kept Maya in this room, they were safe.

Finally, when Maya asked to watch a movie, Hailey checked her phone. Calls and texts from her parents, from Nate, from numbers she didn't recognize, messages from people identifying themselves as reporters. The principal of Maya's school called, as did one of her colleagues at the alumni magazine, who, like everyone on campus, was shocked by the news. She wanted to ask someone to come over, but she remembered what Nate had said. Call no one, talk to no one.

She reviewed the day in her mind, trying to remember, but jagged chunks were cut out. Where was she, what did she do? She couldn't stop thinking about how furious she had been the day she scratched Jonah's car. She couldn't stop envisioning the bullet. Did it make a small, neat hole and keep going, or did it rip Jonah's body apart?

She called Nate again. "Should I not have talked to the police?"

"You're fine. You have nothing to hide."

"Do they think I did it?" she asked.

"They're going to explore all the possibilities, but that doesn't mean they think it was you. But right now, you have to find a way to stay calm."

"Did you tell Mom and Dad?"

"Yes. We're all coming. We're leaving for the airport in a little while. We'll be there late tonight."

When Hailey got off the phone with Nate, she called her mother back. It was an impossible wish, but she wanted to be assured that everything would be all right.

"What an absolutely terrible thing," her mother said. "We'll be there as soon as we can."

At the sound of her mother's voice, Hailey started to cry. "I can't believe this is happening. I don't know what to do."

"Just hold on until we get there," Sherry assured her, and she tried to believe that once her family came, somehow this wouldn't be as awful.

"Does Maya know?" Sherry asked.

"Not yet," Hailey said. "How am I supposed to tell her?"

"Wait until we're there. We'll figure out what to say and we'll tell her with you."

"No," Hailey said, clarity suddenly cutting through an increasingly thick fog. "I need to tell her myself."

At the airport, Nate shepherded his parents along, helping them check in and pass through the line for security.

"Nate," Sherry said as they made their way through the terminal.

Walking one step ahead of her, Nate pretended not to hear. He studied the screen to confirm their gate. All these other cities listed, all these flights ready to depart. He would have taken any of them if he could.

"Please, Nate . . ." Sherry called to him.

"This way," he said, finally forcing himself to slow his pace.

At the gate, she tried to catch his eye, but he couldn't, not yet. He texted Tara, but got no response.

"I didn't answer the phone," Sherry whispered to him. "I told you that. I thought about what you said and I couldn't go through with it."

"We are not going to talk about this right now," he said through clenched teeth. His father was seated calmly beside his mother, his face unperturbed. Every day he seemed less well, and Nate had floated the idea that he stay home, but Sherry was adamant that they all needed to be together.

"Have you heard from Tara?" Sherry whispered.

"Not a word."

The look on her face was desperate, but instead of feeling sympathy, it made Nate furious. He glanced at the people around them, hoping his panic wasn't evident. Would these strangers be interviewed one day, witnesses to their reaction?

"Do you want me to call her?" Sherry asked.

"Please, don't. For now, don't do anything."

"But I listened to what you said. I couldn't do it."

"Is that what you're planning to tell the police?" he hissed. "Yes, you plotted to kill him, but at the last minute you had a change of heart? What exactly do you think they're going to say? 'Thank you for clearing that up, Mrs. Marcus. We appreciate your honesty, you're free to go'?"

"Why are you being like this?" she pleaded with him.

Nate laughed, because it was the only way not to scream.

Awaiting Tara's text, Nate scrolled for news about Jonah—the only proof that any of this was real. Two television stations had live updates from reporters, one stationed in front of Jonah's house, the other outside the hospital where Jonah was brought. They reported that the police were interviewing a neighbor who had heard the gunshot and were just starting to comb Jonah's house for clues.

Two nights ago—was that all?—Nate went home to his condo after leaving his mother by the pool. Never had he wanted to fast-forward his life this much. Surely whatever came after wouldn't be as bad as these days spent waiting. For weeks, he'd been trying to think about nothing besides work. He had no one to talk to, no one to be with—it was a feeling he'd once been accustomed to, but now it gnawed at him relentlessly. He stayed at the office as late as he could, doing paperwork until he was falling asleep at his desk. But once he was home, he lay in bed, entombed in a kind of paralysis. Nothing had happened yet it aleady felt too late. Eventually he prescribed Ambien for himself so that he could lapse into a darkened absence.

On that final night, his phone startled him just as the heaviness of a drug-induced sleep was descending. "I couldn't do it," his mother said.

He hoped he was hearing her correctly. He hoped he wasn't dreaming only to soon wake again into the nightmare he'd helped to create.

"Say something," she said.

"What can I possibly say?"

"I know you never wanted to do this."

"I was willing to, for you, but of course I never wanted to," Nate said.

For the first time in weeks, Nate took a full breath. He felt the relief that came of disaster averted, when by the grace of a few seconds, you careened out of the way and emerged unscathed. Only after, though, did you realize how excruciatingly close you had come.

"I'm sorry. I should have listened to you sooner," she said.

To hear his mother admit that was, however briefly, a consolation.

"I love you, Nate. I hope you know that. More than you can imagine," she said.

When he got off the phone, he was shaking, hot and cold at once. The fact that they had almost killed a man never felt more real or more incomprehensible. His adrenaline surging, Nate dropped to the floor and did a dozen push-ups, but it wasn't enough. He got into his car and drove to the beach where, in the dark, he ran until his chest heaved and his legs prickled with exhaustion. Even then he didn't want to stop. Now that Hailey had taken up running, maybe they would train to run a marathon together. Or he could learn to sail—take the money they were going to use for Jonah and buy a boat. He and Hailey could sail around the world. His life suddenly had a hundred doors, all flung open.

By the time they boarded the plane, Nate's face was bathed in sweat. Two wet patches bloomed under his arms. He wouldn't have wanted to sit next to himself. At least he wasn't near his parents—a dozen rows separated them, but he wished it could be more.

He texted Tara, but she still wasn't responding. He closed his eyes. He was burning hot. He felt like he was choking. Maybe he was having a heart attack, which didn't feel like the worst possibility. He deserved it, or worse. When the plane took off, he reluctantly put away his phone and tried to take a deep breath. Maybe the plane would sink instead of lift and they would all come to a fiery end. He replayed what had happened, trying to trace back to the instant when the day had reversed itself: his phone rang, he saw that it was Hailey and was eager to talk now that he was no longer keeping a terrible secret from her. All these awful weeks, when he was afraid she might detect their plan in his voice, he made excuses to get off the phone. Now he wanted to propose that they run that marathon, or see what she thought about the possibility of a boat.

What Hailey had told him was impossible, inexplicable. *No*, he screamed inside his head. *No*. Maybe he screamed it into the phone as well. He'd crouched on the floor until the room steadied. He was pretty sure he managed to sound almost normal as he told her to get Maya and go home, though he probably repeated it too many times because it suddenly seemed like the most urgent thing in the world. Everything else was out of control, but Hailey could be safely ensconced in her car, the glass and steel a shield, until he figured out what to do. He ended the call, but the word *No* was still screaming inside his head. He wanted to flee, back to the mountains and the vistas of red rock. He made it only as far as the bathroom, where he splashed cold water on his face. He stared at his reflection. This wasn't happening. It couldn't be. Unable to stop himself, he slammed his fist into the bathroom wall. The pain throbbed, but changed nothing.

"Tara, can you please come in here?" he asked when he was back in his office, his voice too high-pitched.

"I just got off the phone with Hailey. Jonah is dead," he said when she stood before him.

She blanched and made a strange gasping sound.

"I assume that you know my mother decided not to go through with it," he said. "She didn't answer the phone."

Tara stared at him blankly.

"That was the plan. If she didn't answer, we weren't going to do it, right?"

"I don't know anything about that," Tara said.

He gripped the edges of his desk, wanting to overturn it. "Don't bullshit me, Tara. You know very well that this is what we decided. So I'm trying to understand what happened."

"I have nothing to do with this," she insisted and scurried out of his office.

Nate put his head down and tried to concentrate, but he couldn't form a clear thought. Only that this was not real, this was not happening.

A moment later, Tara was back. "You have a patient," she whispered.

"Really, Tara? Is that all you're going to say?"

"I told you. I don't know what you're talking about. This has nothing to do with me," she said.

He entered an exam room in a daze. *Act normal. A perfectly ordinary day*. He recited this to himself as he saw the patient, though once he left the room, he had no memory of anything that had transpired.

Then, because he couldn't put it off any longer, he walked to the front. He must have looked as horrified as he felt because his mother jumped up in alarm.

"What's the matter?" she asked.

Nate motioned for her to come into his office. She glanced at Tara who was staring silently at her computer screen like she couldn't see them. Sherry followed him and sat in the chair across from his desk.

"Jonah is dead," he said.

His mother blinked a few times. "That's impossible."

"Are you absolutely sure you didn't answer the phone?" he asked.

"I told you. I couldn't do it," she whispered.

"If there's something you haven't told me, now would be a very good time."

"I swear to god. I didn't answer the call."

Nate was the one to book the plane tickets. He told Tara to cancel all the patients for the next week. Together, he and Sherry went to Sol's office to tell him. Nate assumed he would be the one to break the news, but Sherry stepped forward, took Sol's hand and bowed her head.

"We have some terrible news," she said. "Jonah is dead. Someone shot him."

For a second, Solomon closed his eyes. "Are you serious?" he asked.

Though Sherry was the one who'd delivered the news, Sol was looking at Nate, in search of an explanation. Unable to bear his father's judgment, he turned away.

It was close to midnight when they landed in Binghamton. They took a cab to Hailey's house, which was the first time Nate had been there. Amid everything else to feel bad about, he still regretted that he'd never visited Hailey as he'd promised.

When they arrived, Hailey opened the door a crack and peered out. He hugged her tightly before anyone else did.

They sat in her living room, talking softly because Maya was asleep.

"How did Maya take the news?" Nate asked Hailey.

"It was awful. She looked at me like she had no idea what I was saying. I don't know what she understands."

"I don't think any of us can believe it," Sherry said, a better actor than he'd realized. She was soothing Hailey, she was bringing a cup of tea to Sol and talking about how they needed to find a way to support Maya. What was the right state of grief for someone who might or might not have murdered her daughter's soon-to-be ex-husband? He once would have made that joke, but couldn't stomach it now.

"For all we know, this was a random thing," Sherry said and pulled up an article on her phone about a series of robberies in the neighborhood.

"I can't believe he's dead," Hailey said.

"It's going to take time for this to seem real," Sherry said. "I think we're all in a state of shock."

Hailey was telling them how she had been interrogated, and Sherry was making sympathetic sounds and murmuring about how scared she must have been. Nate couldn't sit still. He paced the room and glanced out the window, aware that they might already be under surveillance.

"Who knows what Jonah was involved in. We might learn things about him that aren't pretty," Sherry said.

"There's no point speculating," Sol said. "The police will take care of whatever needs to be done."

At the sound of his father's voice, Nate startled. Sol had appeared to be dozing, but it was getting harder to tell when his father was awake and when he was lost, a dark ship sailing in the fog, about to run aground.

"That's true," Sherry agreed. "I'm sure the police will figure this out. And in the meantime, we have to focus on getting Maya through this."

It was past two, and finally they were getting ready for bed. Sherry helped Sol up from the couch, her hand securing him as he carefully planted both feet on the ground and slowly rose.

"We'll figure out what to do in the morning, all of us together," Sherry said, hugging Hailey, then forcing a hug on Nate as well.

Nate laughed. Only his mother could try to turn something this awful into an opportunity for family bonding.

Sol and Sherry were staying in the guest room, and though Hailey offered to give him her bedroom, Nate was fine sleeping on the couch. Hailey brought him a blanket and started to spread one of Maya's pale pink sheets over the cushions.

It hit him. Maya would grow up without a father. How had he given so little thought to this until now? How had this fact alone not been enough to stop him? As fraught as his own relationship was with his father, he couldn't imagine how he would have withstood his absence. He had the urge to go into the bedroom where Maya was asleep and promise that he would be there for her, but nothing would make up for what they'd done, or had almost done, or might have somehow inadvertently done. However it had happened, Maya would be irreparably shaped by Jonah's death.

Hailey was struggling to get the fitted sheet around the cushion, and when she couldn't get it to stay, she gave up and sank onto the couch.

"Hailey, it's going to be okay," he said, even though he didn't believe it.

"How will it ever be okay? Jonah is dead and the police think I killed him. Reporters have been calling my cell phone all day asking for a statement."

"Don't answer. You don't have to talk to anyone," he said.

"They're saying that his house was ransacked, but they don't know yet if anything was taken," she said and pulled up a news clip that he hadn't seen. Together they watched a video of a reporter in front of Jonah's house. "Today, neighbors on this peaceful street had their sense of safety and security shattered," she intoned. From there, the screen flashed to pictures of Jonah and to an image of his book, with the reporter speculating about a possible connection.

At the end of the segment, there was a wedding picture of Jonah and Hailey and a reference to the fact that they were in the midst of a contentious divorce.

"Who would give them our wedding photo?" she said.

"They can get anything they want off social media."

"Do you think they're going to have pictures of Maya too?"

"I hope not," he said, "but in the meantime, I don't think you should be watching this."

"I have to know what they're saying," she said.

Nate took the phone from her. "I can tell you if there's anything you need to know. But seriously, it's enough for tonight," he said and wrapped his arms around her.

"I keep having this thought that Jonah is going to text me and accuse me of killing him. When I was at the police station, I didn't really think that they suspected me, but now I realize that of course they do."

"I'm sure this is all standard stuff. Right now, they're just investigating all the options," he assured her.

"The crazy thing is, I think that maybe it was me. Maybe I somehow—" Hailey said and looked helplessly at him.

The room swayed. "Is there anything you want to tell me? Because now would be a good time to do that. I assume you know that you can still tell me anything," Nate said.

"It feels horrible to say this now, but do you know how many times I wished Jonah was dead?" she said.

"That doesn't mean anything. People think all sorts of things."

"I know, but I had this horrible realization a few weeks ago, that day when I scratched his car. As I was driving away, it hit me. The only way it would ever stop was if he were dead. It just felt like this piece of truth—as long as he was alive, it was never going to end."

Nate grasped the arm of the couch and tried to keep his voice as matter-of-fact as he possibly could. "Did you ever say that to a friend, or write it down anywhere, maybe in an email or a diary?" he asked.

She shook her head. "You're the only one I've ever said that to."

Feeling steadier, Nate took a deep breath. "Good. I know you didn't mean anything by it, but people can twist things when they have a reason to," he said.

He hoped that she was telling him the truth, but as she hugged him, he detected something hardened in her expression. Had she known about their plan all along? Was it possible that she had given the go-ahead? No. No. If somehow she'd found out what they were doing, she would have confronted him, demanded that he stop. Back to the simplest explanation. His mother made a mistake. Or Kevin had gotten confused. But how many times did he and Tara go over their plan? Nate didn't know how it went wrong, but he did know that it was dangerous to be maneuvering like this, in the dark, against a force he didn't understand.

Once Hailey went to bed, the house was quiet. As far as Nate could tell, they were all asleep, which was hard to fathom, since he was never going to be able to sleep again. He prowled around the house, looking through the mail and papers stacked in a bin in the kitchen for anything that might offer a clue. He checked his phone, but still had nothing from Tara. He scoured the news, but the same information was repeated in a relentless loop—there were no suspects, no motives, no leads. It was too early to derive any consolation, though. Inevitably, the crosshair of suspicion would find them.

Nate pulled a sweatshirt over his T-shirt and slipped outside. For now, the street was quiet, but surely it was only a matter of time before reporters were stationed outside the house. He entered Jonah's address into his phone and started to walk. It was a lot colder than he'd expected, and he didn't have a jacket, but that was fine with him because he deserved the pain. The houses he passed were close together, with only narrow driveways separating them. If you stood on the porch and had a fight, the neighbors could hear every word. One of them had heard the gunshot, and others had no doubt heard Hailey arguing with Jonah countless times.

Nate intended to walk past Jonah's house, just an innocent insomniac out for a nighttime stroll, or maybe a true crime buff wanting a firsthand glimpse of the scene. But at the sight of the house, he froze. There was yellow police tape unfurled across the porch, and a police car parked out front. Jonah's car was still in the driveway, but Nate didn't dare get close enough to look for the scratch marks. It hit him again. Jonah was dead. They had killed him. Nate squatted down on the sidewalk and tried to take a deep breath. It had grown colder out, but his body was burning up. How could he have succumbed to the delusion that any kind of disengagement was possible? It didn't matter that he had tried to keep his distance. It didn't matter that he had urged his mother to turn back, that in fact she had, at the very last minute, said no. He had made this happen. The gun may as well have been in his hands. He saw the trajectory of the bullet, as if he were the one to send it through the air at a thousand, maybe two thousand, miles an hour until the nose of the bullet struck Jonah's chest, piercing the skin, obliterating the blood vessels, dividing his rib like a tree branch in a violent storm, shearing through the pericardial cavity on its way to the left ventricle.

Nate needed to get up from his crouched pose on the sidewalk, but he couldn't move. A small sob escaped from him and he clamped his hand over his mouth to try to silence himself. If the police officer sitting in his car asked why he was so incapacitated, he might confess everything: talk and talk and hope that somehow it might ease his guilt. A second police car drove down the street, and Nate wanted to throw himself under the wheels, to press out every last bit of who he'd become. He wanted to fly home, find Kevin and his brother and demand that they shoot him too. But there would never be a reprieve. Even if they weren't caught, he would always be imprisoned. The only thing he could do was go back to Hailey and Maya and find a way to be there for them. He forced himself up. He sprinted away, but no matter how fast he ran, he would never be able to escape his own self.

It was after four in the morning when Nate got back to Hailey's house. He had still heard nothing from Tara, but he was no longer surprised. He deleted all their flirtatious texts and emails. He went through his photos and deleted the few he had of the two of them together.

He looked up from his phone when he heard a sound. Hailey was standing in the entryway to the living room. She came and sat next to him on the couch and he held her as she sobbed.

"What am I supposed to do?" she asked.

"Right now, we have to focus on making it through the next few days," he said.

"I can't believe he's dead. He's really dead."

"I know. I can't believe it, either."

"All those times I wished it, I had no idea how awful this would feel. How could I have said that?"

"You were upset, that's all," he assured her.

"I'm terrified that somehow. . ." she said, but didn't finish the thought.

"You had nothing to do with this. We all know that you would never do anything like this. People can say whatever they want, but that doesn't change the truth," he said.

She stared at him as if trying to believe him.

"You don't think that Mom—" she started to say, then stopped.

"Come on, Hailey. Of course not."

He tried to sound as normal as possible. He was glad it was dark so that she couldn't see his face.

"Then who do you think did it?" she asked.

"I have no idea," he lied.

She had said no. That was what mattered.

Sherry lay awake in Hailey's guest room, shivering. Sol had fallen asleep right away and she curled into his body, but the house was old and drafty and there was no way to get warm. Not even the extra blanket she found in a hallway closet helped.

Sol stirred and she gently nudged him awake. When they were younger, she had taken such comfort in the sturdiness of his body. Nestling into him, she'd allowed herself the illusion that, so long as he held her, nothing bad could befall her.

"What do you think happened?" she asked.

When Sol opened his eyes, he seemed surprised to find her so close. He looked so much smaller than he once had, almost delicate. If she were to hold him too tightly, he might break apart.

"I don't know, but we need to be very careful right now," he said.

"Do you think—" she began, but didn't finish the sentence. In another era of their lives, she would never have been able to keep this from him.

In the morning, Sherry was awake first, even before Maya had stirred. She came out of the bedroom to find Hailey sleeping on the couch, Nate asleep on the floor beside her. Nate would never have told Hailey the plan, but even so, a swell of distrust came over her. What if the two of them had somehow gone behind her back?

Maya padded out of her bedroom in a pair of pink pajamas. Usually when Sherry saw Maya, she marveled at how much she had grown, but she too seemed smaller than usual—everyone around her was shrinking, while she was growing to a hulking, ungainly size.

"Maya, sweetie," she said. "We came last night when you were asleep."

Maya blinked a few times. "Is there school today?" she asked.

"You're going to stay home with us, and Mommy is going to stay home from work, and we're all going to be together."

"Do you know about my daddy?" she asked.

"I do. It's very, very sad, I know, but we're going to take good care of you," she said and hugged Maya. This close to her, she smelled the berry shampoo Hailey had also used as a little girl.

She had not done this. She had said no. Like a dam in her mind, these sentences held back the waves that threatened to wash her away.

"Let's make breakfast," Sherry said.

"Can we have pancakes?" Maya asked.

"Of course!" she said.

She found a box of pancake mix, prepared the batter, and poured small circles into the pan, then dotted them with chocolate chips. She pulled a chair next to the stove for Maya to stand on. It felt good to be this close to the stove when she was still shivering from the cold.

"See the small bubbles in the batter? That's when you know they're ready," Sherry said, and with her hand on Maya's, they used the spatula to flip them. Usually Maya asked a hundred questions, but now she was quiet.

"Can we wake Uncle Nate?" Maya asked when she finished eating.

"Yes, but let's be very quiet so your mommy can sleep."

She and Maya tiptoed into the living room, and Sherry made an exaggerated show of trying to be quiet. When they got to where Nate was sleeping on the floor, Maya tickled him, and he pretended to snore loudly.

"Maya couldn't wait to see you," Sherry said to Nate.

"I couldn't wait to see her," he said and hugged Maya.

Once Nate was fully awake, Maya pulled him into her room, where he did his usual antics of pretending to bump into walls and break things. It almost felt like an ordinary day.

Sherry left them to play their games. Still freezing, she put on her jacket, even though she had no intention of going anywhere. She'd noticed that Hailey's kitchen looked a little grimy and she rifled under the sink for cleaning supplies and got to work. The grooves between the cabinets. The inside of the silverware drawer. The pot she was scrubbing had black marks and she found a steel wool under the sink, but the streaks wouldn't come off.

"What are you doing?" Hailey asked, standing in the entryway of the kitchen.

"I wanted to help," she said.

"Why are you wearing your coat?" Hailey asked.

It felt like an admission of guilt, but Sherry kept her voice light. "I'm not used to the cold."

Hailey sat at the table, wearing sweatpants and a frayed T-shirt, her eyes more swollen than when they'd arrived.

"I have no idea what I'm supposed to do now," Hailey said.

"Let me make you something to eat, and then what if you took a shower and got dressed? The next few days are going to be very hard, but eventually it's going to get easier."

Sherry tried to get Hailey to finish the pancakes, but she was too nauseated to eat. Instead, Sherry made Hailey a mug of coffee, but she only took a few sips. Sherry put back all the silverware in the now spotless drawer. She compiled a list of the ways she could help Hailey: call Maya's school and Hailey's friends and Jonah's father, who would want to see Maya. She would deal with all the details so Hailey didn't have to. She would deal with everything.

Hailey's cell phone rang as Sherry was cleaning up, and she wished she could grab it before Hailey did. It was good, she knew, for Hailey to have friends checking on her, but she was afraid that Hailey might accidentally confide something that could be misconstrued. It was better, for now, to say as little as possible.

"It's the police again," Hailey said once she'd answered and motioned for Sherry to leave the room.

Sherry wanted to stay, but at the insistent look Hailey gave her, she went into the living room, where Nate was on the couch with Maya, reading to her from a stack of books.

"Hailey's on the phone with the police," she whispered to him.

"Are you surprised? She's going to be interrogated many, many times. And I assume you realize that it's only a matter of time before we all are," Nate whispered back.

"It's not going to come to that," Sherry promised, but he gave her a withering look. She didn't want to admit it to Nate, but she was surprised. Somehow she had thought far too little about what this day would actually feel like—every minute of it that she would have to endure.

"What did they want?" Sherry asked Hailey once she was off the phone. Maya had gone into her room to play and Sherry seized the chance to speak freely.

"They asked if I remembered anything else. And they pressed me about whether Jonah had any enemies," Hailey said.

"You told them what you know. What more do they want?" Sherry said.

"You talked to them, and that's all you have to do right now," Nate agreed.

"No one really thinks you have anything to do with it. You were getting a massage. You can prove that," Sherry said.

"Didn't you used to talk about hiring a hit man? Maybe people think that's what I did," Hailey said to Nate with a strange smile that made Sherry want to cover it with her hand.

"Please, Hailey. Nate was obviously joking," Sherry said.

Though she was afraid of how Hailey might react, Sherry reached for her. At first Hailey stiffened, but her resistance gave way and her body melded into her. She had not done this. She had turned back. She had said no. This awful moment was going to pass. Somehow, it was going to be okay.

A swarm of reporters positioned themselves outside the house over the weekend. Sherry made sure the window blinds were all closed. The house phone rang incessantly, so Sherry took it upon herself to unplug it from the wall. They didn't answer the door for anyone, not even when the mother of one of Maya's friends brought over a box of cupcakes and a colleague of Hailey's left dinner at the front door. On Saturday afternoon, Maya's teacher dropped off a package of cards that the class had made for her. Her classmates were told that Maya's father had died, but were given none of the details, though surely some of them would hear more.

"Isn't this nice? You have so many friends who care about you," Sherry said as she sat with Maya and showed her the cards.

"Can we still FaceTime with Daddy?" Maya asked Sherry.

Sherry's hand flew to her mouth. "Oh, Maya," she said and rocked her as if she were a baby. If Sol had died when the children were this age—she stopped, unable to imagine the magnitude of the loss. She would take care of Maya. She would take care of everyone. Eventually Maya would be okay. One day, she would barely remember any of this. One day—the thought chilled her and she wasn't sure what to hope for—Maya might not remember Jonah at all.

Sherry heard from her own friends as well, even though she suspected that they were just eager for an inside scoop.

"Horrifying," she said to Judy and Eleanor, but she knew that it would never be possible to trust anyone. She would always have to hold herself apart.

"No leads, but it's still early," she said, hoping her voice had a semblance of normalcy. It felt like a long time since she'd talked to them—it might have only been months, but it had the permanence of years.

Sometimes, the facts bent and Sherry forgot her involvement. Sometimes she fully believed her own insistence that they would never do something like this. A few times, she succumbed and checked the news, but couldn't bear it. Outside, investigations and interrogations were taking place, while inside, she made dinner and folded laundry and played with Maya and washed the dishes, anything she could think of to maintain order.

At the end of the day, Sherry walked into the kitchen, where Nate was leaning against the counter, so immersed in a video on his phone that he wasn't aware of her presence.

"Is it bad?" she asked, and he jumped.

"There's some new surveillance footage," Nate said and held out his phone to show a video of a white car following Jonah on the morning he was killed.

"I can't," she said and put her hand in front of her eyes.

"You don't want to know about every detail of the investigation? You don't want to hear what people are saying about how acrimonious the divorce was, or know what mistakes your good friend Kevin made that are going to get us thrown into jail for the rest of our lives?"

"I said no. Why won't you believe me?"

His face was red, his eyes blazing. "We set this up. We paid a chunk of money. I don't know who made the mistake, but we're the reason he's dead."

"I did exactly what you told me." She grabbed Nate's arm, digging her fingers in too hard.

Nate shook her off and walked to the window. With one finger, he lifted a slat of the blinds and peered out at the reporters.

Sherry followed him. "Listen to me, Nate," she said and grabbed his arm again. He tried to wrest free, but she wouldn't allow it. "I know this is terrible and I know we never should have considered this in the first place. But in the end, I didn't do it. You can check my phone if you don't believe me. I have no idea what went wrong, and I wish I could take it all back, but this is where we are now. And no matter what happens, we have to be in this together."

"Just what you always wanted," he said.

They went to the funeral on Monday morning, the five of them, even though Sherry tried to convince Hailey that it was too much for Maya.

"Let's ask a friend if she can go play there or find a babysitter," Sherry suggested. "We don't want to traumatize her."

"Don't you think she's already traumatized?" Hailey said.

"She's going to be fine, eventually. We all are."

"How can you possibly know that?"

"I just mean—" Sherry started, then stopped. Hailey looked furious. Was it possible that she knew? No. There was no way. She was just upset. They all were. It was better to leave the room before Hailey said something she regretted. Maya was playing in her room, and Sherry helped her put on the navy-blue dress that she'd bought for her, with short ruffled sleeves and two pockets in the shape of red hearts.

"Do you understand where we're going?" Sherry asked Maya. She nodded solemnly.

"Do you want to talk about it?" Sherry asked, but Maya turned away and picked up Bunbun from her bed and whispered to him. The stuffed animal had a new hole along the ear, close to where Sol had once sewn it. She would have to remember to tell Sol, or maybe Nate, to repair it again.

"We don't have to talk about what's going on. We could make a list of all the fun things you like to do, or say our favorite memories," Sherry suggested.

Maya shook her head.

"It's going to be okay," she promised, but Maya looked impassively at her, old enough to realize how insufficient her words were.

Maya clutched Bunbun as they sat, grim-faced, in the back of the funeral chapel. A plain wood coffin was draped in a blue velvet covering embroidered with a silver star. In the front of the room, Jonah's father was surrounded by relatives Sherry vaguely recognized from the wedding, but that felt impossibly long ago. When he stood up to speak about what a wonderful son Jonah was, she shuddered. She had never realized how much Jonah looked like him. Though they shared a granddaughter, she barely knew him. As much as she wanted to look away, she saw the staggering pain on his face. This was what it looked like to lose a child. She tried to resist the thought, but it slammed against her. He had loved his child, as she loved hers.

No, she told herself once again. She had not done this, she had said no.

After Jonah's father was finished, a colleague spoke and said that Jonah had been extraordinarily dedicated to his students. Next, a friend from college, whom she recognized as a groomsman from the wedding, stood up. He described Jonah as funny and brilliant. He had a strong sense of right and wrong. He could be acerbic at times, but that was because he didn't let people get away with things. With Jonah, you knew where you stood. Another friend said that Jonah was the person you called when you needed a clear-eyed perspective. He would level with you. He said that if you ever skied with Jonah, you understood that he liked a challenge. He was never going to let any mountain—or any person—get the best of him.

She hadn't realized how many friends Jonah had. They were sitting together in the front rows, their arms around each other, crying. Sherry listened to every word, but there was no shred of the Jonah she had known. Had she simply missed it, or had he become someone else in her presence? Maybe only the Jonah that she'd known was dead. The other one, this nice stranger, was still alive somewhere, writing his book, joking with friends, skiing fearlessly down snow-covered slopes.

When his friend finished, a pause followed. What if she were to stand up and speak about how she'd lived in terrible fear of losing her daughter and then her granddaughter? What if she tried to explain that her rage had come over her like a fever dream, like a haunting? What if she described how, at the very last minute, she had said no and had believed, truly believed, that Jonah would be spared?

No, she could never say any of that. No matter how many times she might ask for forgiveness, it could never be granted. Even if she had ultimately said no, she had placed the ball at the top of the chute, she had set this in motion.

A loud sob erupted from her and she burst into tears. The people in front of them turned around, with looks of sympathy that morphed into curiosity as soon as they realized who she was. Nate gave her a disdainful look, as if she'd done something obscene. She sobbed again. She wanted to stop, but her body was acting on its own.

After the service, they followed the procession of cars to the cemetery. Nate drove, with Sol next to him in the front seat. Maya was buckled in her booster seat between her and Hailey. Sherry didn't have it in her to try to fill the silence. At least no one could see them. From the outside, they appeared like everyone else.

As the casket was carried and lowered into the ground, as Jonah's family and friends helped to shovel dirt into the grave, Sherry stood close to Hailey, who showed no hint of emotion. Sherry reached over to touch Hailey's arm, but she remained stone-still.

They were almost back at Hailey's house when Nate abruptly stopped the car. The crowd of reporters had grown larger—at least fifty people were milling around, holding cameras and microphones on the sidewalk outside the house. So many times Sherry saw people on the news who had done awful things, microphones thrust in their dazed faces. She had always assumed that she was entirely different from them, but now she understood that she was the same.

Nate drove past the reporters, up the driveway to Hailey's house. "We're going to get out of this car as if they're not there. We're going to look down and no one is going to say a word," he instructed.

They followed Nate's directions, all of them in a huddle, Maya protected in the middle. Once they were inside, Sherry made sure the blinds were still closed, but she had the urge to stay away from the windows altogether, afraid that if she drew near, the reporters would see not just inside the house but into her mind. While she sat on the couch with Maya, Sol went into the bedroom to lie down. Nate stayed in the living room and paced back and forth. The wood floor creaked under his feet and made her feel even more jittery than she already was, but she was too afraid of his anger to ask him to stop.

Hailey left the room, and when she came back, she was wearing workout clothes and a baseball hat.

"Where are you going?" Sherry asked.

"For a run."

Sherry glanced at Nate. "I don't know if that's a good idea," she said.

Before Nate could back her up, Hailey whirled around to face her, her cheeks suddenly flushed with anger. "A good idea to what? To ever go outside? To talk to anyone?"

Sherry looked again at Nate, hoping he would chime in, but he was as frozen as she was.

"Do you have any idea what this feels like?" Hailey said.

Before Sherry could formulate an answer, Hailey ran for the door and slammed it behind her. In her absence, Sherry paced the room. She ventured close to the window and peeked out, as if she could see past the reporters, past the houses, and protect Hailey as she ran.

"Well, here's something," Nate said, staring into his phone.

He showed her an unconfirmed report that the police had combed through Jonah's computer and found an angry email exchange with a writer whose book he panned in a prominent review in the *New York Times*. They also learned that he was dating a recently divorced woman who had texted about a jealous ex-husband.

"Do you think that somehow . . . ?" Sherry said to Nate. She couldn't finish the sentence, but maybe this would turn out to have had nothing to do with them. Somehow, through an outrageous coincidence, a bizarre confluence of events, a different ball had rolled down a different hill, an entirely other latch had come undone.

Nate gave her a look of disdain, which she tried to ignore. She waited, hoping he would say something else, anything. She needed this awful feeling to diminish. She needed to believe that she wasn't irredeemable. She went into the kitchen and grabbed food from the fridge and lay it before her on the counter—some cheese, some wilted green vegetables, a carton of milk. She would make dinner from whatever she could assemble. She would somehow create a feast. All she could do was take care of her family as she always had—pour every bit of her energy into ensuring they were okay. Every day she would make a multitude of small offerings, even if it would never be enough.

Fifteen minutes later, Sherry was in the kitchen when the door flew open and Hailey came running inside the house.

"They asked me if I killed him," Hailey said. On the floor of the entryway, she bent over, her head between her knees, making small gasping sounds. "They were all screaming questions and filming me. I completely freaked out. I have no idea what I said."

Sherry stood over her, rubbing her back, instructing her to take deep breaths. "I'm sure it was fine. It's all going to be fine," she promised.

Surely it was a bad idea, but once Maya was asleep, the four of them sat in the living room to watch an episode on *Insider News*, a local show, that was devoted to Jonah's murder. The opening segment recounted the facts. A beloved professor, a promising writer, a devoted father gunned down in broad daylight. Targeted, but for what reason? The music was menacing as they played surveillance camera clips of Jonah being followed that morning as he went to his office on campus, then drove home. What did he need from his office? the commentator asked. Did he meet someone there or was he alone?

The next shot was of Hailey, captioned as the estranged ex-wife, anxious and cagey. Her face appeared so drawn, her skin so pallid, that for a moment Sherry thought it wasn't actually Hailey but an unknown woman trying to impersonate her.

"Did you do it? Did you kill him?" asked a reporter following after Hailey, pushing the microphone in her face.

Keep your mouth closed and keep walking, Sherry willed, even though it was too late.

At the question, Hailey froze. "I don't know," she said, her eyes darting. "I don't know," she repeated, like a question, like an admission. And then—Sherry wished she could reach into the screen and stop her—she ran away.

"Oh my god, I sound so guilty, don't I?" Hailey asked when the show cut to a commercial break.

Sherry glanced at Nate, wishing he would say something, but his expression was blank.

"They cornered you. What could you have done? Isn't that right, Nate?" Sherry said.

Nate didn't answer. His face was just a strange, lost smile, a pair of empty eyes. She should have turned the TV off then, but they were all immobilized as the show returned and showed an interview with one of Jonah's neighbors. "She was screaming at him, and the next thing I knew, she was standing in front of his car, doing something I couldn't see. But when she walked away, I saw it with my own eyes—two long scratches across the driver's door."

A close-up of another man now filled the screen. It took Sherry a moment to recognize him as the friend who'd spoken at the funeral.

"Were you close to Jonah Gelman?" the reporter was asking.

"We were roommates for all four years that we were at Yale and we've been good friends ever since."

"And did you get to know Hailey as well?"

"I did," he said, and paused. "I always thought that she and Jonah weren't a good match. Hailey could put on a good show, but I had the feeling that she was too good to be true."

"And did Jonah ever confide in you about his marriage?" the reporter asked.

"I knew Jonah was unhappy. Her family was very intrusive. They tried to force them to move to Florida, which Jonah wasn't going to do. He used to joke about how when you married someone, you married the whole family, but it was obvious that he didn't find it funny."

"And what about the divorce? Were you surprised by it?" the reporter asked.

"I was surprised at how contentious it was. Jonah was sorry about how things ended up, and all he wanted was for the split to be amicable. But Hailey didn't want that. And it wasn't just her. Her whole family was intent on revenge. Jonah used to talk about how they would stop at nothing. They even tried to pay him off. They offered him something like half a million dollars to let Hailey move to Florida with their daughter. Of course Jonah wouldn't consider it, but it shows what they're like."

"I know it must be extremely painful for you to contemplate, but do you think Hailey had something to do with his murder?" the reporter asked.

"I have no doubt," he said.

"Turn it off," Sherry said.

No one moved, so Sherry jumped up and grabbed the remote as Hailey ran from the room.

"We need to get out in front of this," Nate said.

"Is it true about the money?" Sol asked.

Sherry glanced at Nate, who had gone so pale that she worried he was about to pass out.

"It was my idea," Sherry said. "I know we should never have done it, but the amount wasn't even close to half a million, and it was months ago," she said. "Jonah was being so awful, and I couldn't stand to see Hailey so powerless. I thought it might convince Jonah to change his mind. Nate had some money he'd set aside for Hailey, and I begged him to let me use it."

"Why didn't you tell me?" Sol asked.

"I didn't want to upset you. And I didn't think you'd go along with it," she admitted.

"We need a lawyer," Sol said, and Sherry nodded. She would do whatever he said.

Before they could say more, Hailey came back into the room and was standing in the entryway.

"What were you talking about?" she demanded.

"We're just trying to decide how to respond," Sherry said.

"Please tell me you don't think I had anything to do with the murder," Hailey said.

"Of course not," Sherry said. "Dad thinks we need to get a lawyer just to be on the safe side. People will say anything. Look at all these lies. That friend of his is telling a completely skewed version. That wasn't how it was at all. Isn't that right, Nate?" Sherry said.

She expected that he would back her up, but instead Nate started to laugh.

"Please, Nate, stop," Sherry said, but that made Nate laugh harder. She glanced at Sol, hoping he could stop Nate, but he sat there vacantly as if Nate's reaction was normal. She looked imploringly at Hailey.

"Why are you looking at me like that?" Hailey asked and started to laugh in the same hysterical way, she and Nate clutching their stomachs, tears running down their faces.

"Please. You both need to stop," Sherry begged. As they continued to laugh, she had the crazy idea that the reporters outside would hear them and broadcast their laughter as a kind of deranged confession. She couldn't understand why they were acting this way. At the funeral, Hailey's face had been so absolutely still. She had appeared entirely unmoved. As much as Sherry had hated Jonah, she'd been one step removed. But Hailey had once loved him, and maybe that enabled her to hate him more. Sherry tried to push back against the thought, but it wouldn't budge. Did Hailey somehow know of their plan? Was she able to forge ahead when she, Sherry, had turned back? It was hard to fathom, but she, more than anyone, knew that little was impossible.

As soon as that thought entered her mind, so did another one.

If Hailey were ever accused, she would take the blame on her behalf. If Hailey were to fall, she would catch her daughter in her outstretched arms.

By the next afternoon, Sol gave Nate the name of a lawyer, and they had a conference call. Nate did most of the talking, with Sol chiming in occasionally. She and Hailey both sat silently. On the lawyer's advice, a statement would be written and given to the press, their only public response. Afterward, any inquiries would be directed to the lawyer.

They worked on the statement all night, as if it were a homework assignment upon which everything depended.

"Keep it simple and to the point," Sol instructed.

"I can read it to the reporters," Nate said.

"No, I can do it," Sherry offered.

"Are you kidding me?" he asked. "Do you really think that's a good idea?"

"I don't want you to be the one to face them," she said.

"I'm doing it," Nate said.

The local TV crews were still on the sidewalk outside Hailey's house. Nate shaved and put on khakis and a tie and his dark sunglasses, which Sherry regarded as a good idea. The circles under his eyes were so deep that she'd almost suggested he borrow some of her concealer.

Before he ventured outside, Sherry clasped his arm.

"You're going to be great," she said.

"Please, don't," he said.

From the window, Sherry watched Nate walk outside, solemn and capable as he clutched the piece of paper bearing their statement. He didn't so much as glance back at her as he made his way toward the crowd of reporters.

"We mourn the tragic loss of Jonah Gelman, father of our beloved Maya Marcus Gelman. We, like everyone, are horrified by this act of violence and hope that the perpetrators will be brought to justice." When Nate was done reading it, he turned around and came back inside. Without saying a word, he tossed the paper onto the floor and went into the other room.

Sherry picked up the sheet of paper and read over the sentences until they were seared in her mind. To everyone she encountered, she would have to uphold these words as if she believed them, but she could no longer hide from the truth about herself.

It had been two weeks since Jonah was killed, and every night, Hailey had a nightmare that she was the one who did it.

Each dream was a little different. In this one, Jonah was alive, yelling at her that his death was her fault. He screamed so loudly that she fell to the floor. Suddenly he was beside her and they were wrestling and her hand brushed against cold metal and, before she saw it, she knew what it was. She grabbed the gun and pointed it at him.

Right before she fired, she woke up.

By the end of October, the leaves had changed color, blazing yellow with the occasional burst of red. Nate and Sol had flown back to West Palm a few days after the funeral. Her mother was still with her in Binghamton, and Hailey could hear her now in the other room, getting Maya ready for school.

"I don't want to go," Maya said.

Hailey knew that she should get out of bed and help, but even if she did, her mother would claim that she could manage on her own. Sherry was intent on taking care of Maya and doing every possible chore around the house. It was the same manic efficiency with which her mother had taken care of her after Maya was born, when her body was dripping and leaking and she had wanted to cling to her mother forever.

As soon as Hailey closed her eyes, her dream returned. Jonah was screaming at her and she was once again holding the gun, which had grown to the size of a small child. She struggled to raise it, her body nearly toppling from the weight. Just as she pointed the gun, she awoke again. This time the house was quiet. Sherry and Maya had left for school. Hailey tried to get out of bed, but she had little idea what she was supposed to be doing. She had already informed her office that she needed some time before returning to work. "Take all the time you need," she was told, which should have given her relief, but instead made her suspect that no one wanted to be in her presence.

Hailey stayed in bed until she heard her mother back in the living room, on her phone. She assumed that it was Nate she was talking to. It came over her, with a small burst of surprise: her mother, who was usually surrounded by friends, seemed to talk to none of them anymore. She was only interested in taking care of Maya and her.

"We need to stick together," Hailey heard her mother saying. "It's the only way. We can't control what Tara does. We can't think about any of that."

"Any of what?" Hailey asked as she walked into the living room.

At the sight of her, Sherry jumped. "It's just some things going on in the office, nothing you need to worry about," she said.

She was smiling in a way that was meant to be reassuring, but Hailey felt the spread of unease. A question hovered, but Hailey was sure that if she inquired further, her mother wouldn't tell her the truth.

When Hailey and Sherry went to pickup that day, Maya's teacher pulled them aside and told them that Maya had collapsed in a tantrum and refused to join the class activities. The teacher wrote down the name of a child therapist for her, which Hailey was grateful for, but it was hard not to feel guarded. What if Maya's teacher accused her of doing something wrong? What if, one day, when she came to pick Maya up, the teachers formed a chain around the classroom to prevent her from entering?

They left quickly, without talking to any of the mothers gathered outside the school. For the first few days that Maya was back at school, Hailey tried to catch the eyes of her friends, but they had looked away. Whatever sympathy they'd initially had for her was now replaced with suspicion. Instead of trying to talk to anyone, it was easier to disappear inside herself. Before leaving the house, Hailey hadn't changed out of the baggy sweatpants and oversized sweatshirt that she'd been wearing for days, but now she feared that her state of disarray could be taken as some sort of proof. At least her mother still looked perfectly put together, her hair styled as usual, makeup applied, but this too, she realized, could be regarded as a different kind of proof.

Once they were back at the house, they had an hour until Maya's ballet class, and Sherry made Maya a snack of yogurt and berries and bustled around the kitchen cleaning up the few dishes she'd used.

"I'm not going," Maya said when it was time to get ready.

"But I thought you loved to dance! Don't you remember how wonderful your recital was?" Sherry tried.

"I'm not going," Maya repeated and started to cry.

"Let's just go to the park," Hailey suggested.

Maya stopped crying and Hailey packed snacks, as she'd done countless times, but her hands felt cumbersome. Her mind trudged slowly. Just to leave the house felt like an enormous feat.

"Hailey?" a woman called as they were walking out the front door.

At first, Hailey thought it was a friend, but quickly realized that it was a reporter. A few days had passed since she'd seen anyone lurking by the house, and foolishly she'd allowed herself to think that there would be no more.

Hailey clasped Maya's hand and started to walk faster.

"Please? I just have a few questions," the woman persisted, walking alongside them.

"Leave us alone," Sherry said.

"Please. I can't talk to you now," Hailey pleaded.

They continued to walk and the woman eventually stopped following them. Hailey glanced repeatedly over her shoulder. Maya didn't say a word, but clung to her, as if she expected to be ripped away.

"That woman wanted to talk to us, but . . ." Hailey tried to explain to Maya, but let the sentence dangle.

"There should be a law against that, especially in front of a child. It's harassment," Sherry said.

"It's going to be like this for a long time," Hailey said.

It was only one more block to the park. She purposefully avoided the route that would take them past Jonah's house. She'd waited for Maya to ask about her bedroom there, but didn't know if it was better for her to think that it had disappeared along with him.

Abruptly, Maya stopped walking and stood on the sidewalk, her arms raised.

"Carry me," Maya begged.

"I'll do it. I can carry her," Sherry offered, already bending over to lift her.

"I want Mommy to carry me," Maya said.

"It's fine. I can do it. We're almost there," Hailey said and hoisted her up.

At the playground, Maya ran off to play and Hailey and Sherry sat on a bench, where they could watch her.

"I'm glad we're getting out. You have to take advantage of the nice weather while you still can. I wouldn't be surprised if twenty-four hours from now, it's freezing," Sherry said. "At least this is your last winter here."

"What is that supposed to mean?" Hailey asked.

"I need to go home soon," Sherry said. "And I want you to come with me."

"How can I do that?" Hailey asked.

"You don't have to think of it as moving if you're not ready. Just come for an extended visit. Let us take care of you."

"How can I possibly go anywhere right now?" Hailey asked.

"You and Maya need your family. There's nothing here for you," Sherry said. "It's an awful thing that Jonah died, but you don't have to stay in Binghamton like some kind of sacrifice for him."

Hailey recoiled. "I get the feeling that—"

"What?" Sherry asked.

"Nothing," she said and looked away.

It was unbearable to think it, let alone say it. Her mother was glad he was dead.

Maya had come off the climbing structure and was gathering a pile of sticks.

"Do you think she should be doing that?" Sherry asked.

"She's fine. It's just one of her games," Hailey said.

"Has she asked more about what happened?" Sherry asked.

"I've tried to talk about it, but she doesn't say much. I guess I should call that therapist."

Sherry paused. "Are you worried that Maya might say things that could be misconstrued?"

"What do you think she could say?" Hailey asked, not wanting to admit to the same fear.

"Maybe there's a way to help her understand that we might never know what happened," Sherry suggested.

"How is she supposed to understand that? Do you? Do I?"

Maya put down the smaller sticks and was holding a larger one in front of her.

"You're dead," she screamed at a bird.

"Maya, come here, sweetie. Put the stick down," Sherry called.

Maya ran toward them and pointed the stick at herself. "I'm dead," she said.

"Don't do that, Maya. Please. It's not nice," Sherry said.

"You're dead," she said, pointing the stick at Sherry's face.

"You don't want to say that, sweetie," Sherry said. Her voice sounded desperate as she tried to wrest the stick from Maya.

"Mom, why are you doing that? Stop," Hailey said.

But it was too late. Maya relinquished the stick, but dropped to the ground and thrashed, her body made entirely of limbs.

Hailey crouched beside Maya. "It feels awful, I know," she whispered and wrapped her arms around her daughter. Slowly, Maya calmed down. Her face was still red, but her cries grew softer. Together they stood up. All they had to do was walk home. Hailey would shut the door to the house, hold her child close, and they would never venture out again.

On the morning Sherry was supposed to leave, Hailey watched her do a final straightening, folding Maya's clothes into perfect little stacks, making her bed, and lining up her stuffed animals in the order she liked. Both she and Sherry were tiptoeing around Maya, wary of another tantrum. Even when Maya was a toddler, her outbursts hadn't contained this degree of rage.

"I hate to leave you alone here," Sherry said and began wiping down the kitchen, which had never been so clean. "You're already coming for Thanksgiving. I know it's hard to think about this now, but what if you decided to stay?"

Hailey stared, perplexed. In a matter of weeks, how would she somehow get herself and Maya on a plane?

"It might feel impossible, but you have to get back to normal," Sherry said. "You have to get dressed and leave the house and try to resume your life, even if it's just for Maya's sake."

"How can I possibly do that?" she asked. "I can't think clearly. I can't do anything."

"I know people don't like to speak badly about the dead, but Jonah wasn't going to stop. He was never, ever going to stop."

"Mom, we tried to pay him off, remember? Are you really going to pretend that he was the only one fighting?"

"He was going to drive you crazy until he got everything he wanted. I know you can't go around saying this, but I have to think that, in some way, you recognize that this might turn out to be a good thing for you."

"Oh my god, how can you say that?" Hailey asked. "My child's father is dead."

"It's a terrible thing obviously, and no one would ever wish for this to happen, but that doesn't mean it can't create some new possibilities for you."

"This is a million times worse."

"Do you really think that?" Sherry asked.

"Are you being serious? Are you actually saying this?" Hailey said.

"All I mean is that—" Sherry began.

Hailey gripped her mother's arm. "Did you . . ." she started to say, then stopped. "Could you . . ."

Her mother waited, almost daring her to finish the sentence.

"Do you promise me that no one in our family had anything to do with Jonah's murder?" Hailey whispered.

Sherry gasped. Her hand flew to her chest. "How can you even ask me that?"

A hysterical laugh forced its way out of Hailey's mouth. Of course they hadn't. Of course they would never. She laughed again. Her mother startled, but it didn't matter. Nothing mattered except the fact that her family hadn't done this. They would never do this. She drove her mother to the airport, repeating the word *never* in her head, a song, a poem, a promise. At the airport, it was hard to say goodbye. Hailey clung to her mother, wishing she could remain cocooned inside her love.

Now Hailey was on her own with Maya. When she drove her to school, her memory felt suspect. Had she ever driven down this street before? Had she walked through these doors? When Hailey said goodbye to Maya, she hugged her tightly. If something ever happened to her—no, she couldn't finish the thought. Nothing could possibly come at the end of that sentence. In sight of the other mothers, she was excruciatingly aware of her every gesture and recited directions to herself: *Keep walking. Look straight ahead.* She told herself the same thing when, for the first time since Jonah was killed, she drove to her office. As she stood in the entryway, her colleagues grew quiet. She tried to keep her expression neutral, but somehow they saw into her, they knew more about her than she knew herself. She managed to stay until lunch, then fled to her car and understood that she was never going back.

At home, she forced herself to eat a piece of toast, but her stomach clenched. Increasingly, she had the feeling that she was falling into a pool and slowly sinking down.

In the shower, she turned the water as cold as she could stand, hoping it would wake her. She put on the oversized sweatshirt and sweatpants she wore all the time now and drove to Jonah's house, where she parked across the street. In the days immediately after his death, people had left bouquets of flowers by the driveway, and they were still there, dried and shriveled. She could scoop them up and bring them home, but do what with them? Save them for Maya or crush the petals into a powder, which she would dissolve in water and force herself to drink?

She drove away, not sure where the car would take her. Wherever it wanted, wherever she ended up. In her rearview mirror, she saw flashing blue lights. Would this be the day when the police surrounded her? She pulled over, ready to hold up her hands in surrender. When the police car passed her and kept going, she started to drive again and found that she was on the way to a hiking trail Jonah had loved. She parked in the small lot and began to walk. One fall day, the three of them came here and they each took one of Maya's hands and swung her. At least in that moment, she'd believed that despite whatever tensions there were, they were going to be okay. Now the yellow glow of leaves had given way to stark brown branches and dead leaves crunching underfoot. She passed a dog walker and thought it was Jonah. But when he grew closer, he was a stranger who stared unnervingly at her. She once would have been afraid to be alone in the woods, but now she didn't care what happened to her. She broke into a run, over tangled roots, over small inclines and muddy patches. She came to a small pond and felt a longing to wade out as far as she could into the moss-covered water.

When it was time to get Maya, Hailey walked into the school building, but avoided meeting the teacher's gaze in case she was going to ask about the therapist, whom she was still afraid to call. She took Maya home and they got into her bed and they watched *Frozen* on her laptop.

"Can we watch it again?" Maya asked at the end, and Hailey agreed. She felt like she and Maya were both small children and eventually someone would come take care of them both.

Bedtime was the worst part of the day. As soon as she told Maya it was time to get her pajamas on, she launched into a screaming fit, flailing on the floor until her fury was expended. Once Hailey managed to get Maya into bed, she sat by her side, promising to stay until she was asleep. Every time she stood up, Maya woke and started to cry.

"I want to sleep in your bed," Maya begged, and she relented.

"I miss Daddy," Maya said when the two of them were huddled together in her bed.

"I know you do, honey," Hailey said, but couldn't bring herself to tell

Maya that she missed him too, at least not in the uncomplicated way that Maya did. Her grief had too many layers, not just for his death but for what had died between them along ago.

"Do you remember the time we all went sledding and the three of us all piled into the same sled and we toppled over before we reached the bottom of the hill?" Hailey asked.

"I remember," Maya said.

Before, it had been hard to talk about the past. Every memory was tainted, She'd cringed when Maya talked about Jonah, afraid that everything he did was an attempt to wrest Maya away. Now she wanted to recount every fun thing she could think of, so that at least in Maya's mind Jonah would remain alive.

"And do you remember how, when you were very little, Daddy used to carry you on his shoulders around the house, and you would go around giving good night kisses to everything in the house?"

"I remember."

Even after Maya fell back to sleep, Hailey was still remembering, not just her anger but all the other feelings that had existed alongside it. When Jonah carried Maya around the house, offering kisses to the front door and to the fridge, he would always come find her and swoop Maya down close to her face so that Maya could give her a kiss on her nose. He would say, "A kiss for Mommy," and then he would give her a kiss too. Despite the unease taking root between them, she had believed that his exuberant, unbridled love for Maya would extend to her as well. That time they went sledding, it was so freezing out that she hadn't wanted to go, but Jonah and Maya had come running into their bedroom, Maya wearing Hailey's coat, which was enormous on her, Jonah wearing her pink pom-pommed hat, and they had begged her to come. At the look of glee on their faces, she couldn't say no. The three of them squeezed into one sled, she in the front, Jonah's arms wrapped securely around her, Maya sandwiched between them, and together they sailed down the hill.

Under the dark crust of anger, these pale pink memories were peeking out. For one moment, there he was, the man she had hated but had also loved.

How many days did she pass in this state of no sleep? The memories of Jonah flooded her and then she shut them out. She searched online for everything she could read about his murder, then hid, afraid even to pick up her phone.

One night, Nate told her that they had been contacted by the police a few days earlier. With their lawyer present, they all gave statements and were interviewed.

"Don't you think this was something you should have told me sooner?" she asked.

"It wasn't a big deal," Nate said. "Of course they're going to talk to us. They're talking to everyone."

"How can this not be a big deal?" she asked. "Are you sure Mom didn't say anything she shouldn't?"

He paused a moment too long. "What do you think she could have said?"

"Don't you ever wonder?" she said.

"No. I don't. And I hope you don't either."

"Of course not," she said, but her voice emerged thin and shaky.

Hailey tried to hold on to Nate's reassurances when, a week later, she was asked to come to the police station again, though now she had a lawyer with her. She'd once marveled at the fact that she had a divorce lawyer. Now she had a criminal lawyer, whom her parents had also hired on her behalf. He spoke in clipped tones and advised her to answer every question with the barest of facts; to offer nothing other than what information they had decided upon in advance.

In the same interrogation room that she'd occupied that first day, two detectives sat across from her and her lawyer, waiting for her to make a mistake.

Was it true that she hated living in Binghamton?

Was it true her parents tried to bribe Jonah into letting her move?

Could she describe in detail their final interaction?

She followed her lawyer's instructions. She said as little as possible. She glanced at her lawyer before speaking, trying to imitate his unflappable composure. She had a hard time moving to Binghamton, she acknowledged, but she had started to acclimate. She did know about the plan to pay Jonah, she conceded, but when it failed, her family accepted the fact that she would be staying in Binghamton. She acknowledged that she was upset that Jonah had filed a motion claiming alienation, but she wasn't overly worried because it wasn't true.

"I had nothing to do with this," she repeated. With each question, she became more practiced, an actor better at playing her part.

"And what about your family?" one of the detectives asked.

"My mother . . ." She paused and her voice cracked. "My mother means well. She would never hurt anyone."

"You and your brother sound like you're very close," the other one said.

"Nate is a good person. He loves me. He's always wanted to take care of me, but he would never do something like this. We would never. You have to believe me," she said, her voice growing more vehement, almost pleading.

She felt her lawyer bristle. She should have remained dispassionate, simply said *I have no reason to believe*, or *not as far as I know*, but the other words, *he would never, we would never,* had forced their way out. She needed to insist that, even if she wasn't sure that anyone, including herself, believed it anymore.

Hailey and Maya flew home for Thanksgiving. In the past, they had gone to Jonah's friends for the holiday because he'd wanted to and it was easier to give in, though her mother had always complained.

"Isn't it nice that we get to be together this year?" Sherry said once they were all seated at the dining room table. Hailey looked at Nate, sure he would make a sarcastic comment, but his expression remained stoic.

The quiet was a relief. Hailey carried bowls of butternut squash soup to the table, but her stomach turned at the sight. As they ate, Hailey tried not to look at her father, whose hands quivered as he spooned the thick soup into his mouth, his shirt dotted with orange. She wanted to scream, but if she did, her mother would shatter into slivers and shards. The floor would become treacherous with the pieces of her.

When they were done, Sherry and Nate cleared away the bowls. When they were gone for a prolonged period, Hailey went into the kitchen, where the two of them were huddled in an intense conversation by the sink.

"What's going on?" Hailey asked from the doorway.

"Nothing," Sherry said, too quickly.

"Why do you keep whispering like that?" Hailey asked.

"Calm down, there's no big secret," Nate said.

"I want to know what you were saying," Hailey said.

"I had a disturbing incident yesterday, that's all," Nate admitted. "A new patient scheduled an appointment, but once she was in the exam room, she started asking me questions about Jonah. Apparently she's writing something about us."

"Do we have to talk about this now?" Sherry protested.

"We do," Hailey said.

"It's not a big deal," Nate said. "There are all kinds of absurd things online about how patients shouldn't trust me with a knife and some asshole claiming that we murder people in the office."

"You need to do something before the practice is destroyed," Sherry said to Nate.

"It's a little too late for that," he said.

"What does Tara say?" Hailey asked.

"Why does it matter?" Nate said.

"Didn't I tell you? She found a new job," Sherry said to Hailey.

"What? I can't believe she left!" Hailey said.

"This was hardly unexpected," Nate said. "Let's just say it was a little uncomfortable between us."

"You never even told me why you broke up," Hailey said.

"I'm not going to discuss that right now," he said.

"Tara leaving had nothing to do with Nate," Sherry said. "Her new job is closer to home. And she hasn't been as focused as she used to be, so it's for the best."

"Why didn't you tell me?" Hailey asked.

"It's a work issue. It has nothing to do with you," Nate said.

"Do you want to know what I think? You should take Tara's place," Sherry said to Hailey. "At least until you figure out what to do next. Wouldn't that be great, for all of us to be together?"

The strain in her mother's voice was so pronounced that it took all of Hailey's effort to pretend she didn't notice. She tried to envision sitting in the office next to her mother, but the image wouldn't form in her mind. She tried to say that yes, she would love to all be together, but the words eluded her.

They went back to the table, where Sol and Maya were sitting quietly, ensconced in their separate worlds. Hailey sat down, but couldn't stop staring at the family photo in which Jonah was missing. She had the strange thought that, soon, Tara would appear where Jonah once was. It was better to study the roundness of the white plates, to focus on the prongs of each fork. But not even that was safe. Directly in her line of vision was the turkey, still uncarved, its skin oiled and crisped. What if it wasn't dead, but before their very eyes, those perfectly browned wings began to spread, and this heavy, headless bird soared around the room, crashing through the glass door and breaking free?

• • •

Once she was back in Binghamton, Hailey still tried to hide, but the news found her. On the two-month anniversary of the murder, the Binghamton paper ran an article called "Massage and Murder" with her picture on the front page. A local blogger who had seized on reports that she disliked living in Binghamton wrote an angry post in which she listed ten great things about the city. A true crime blog compiled all the "Best of . . ." articles Hailey had once written for *Allure* and altered them: "The Best Ways to Kill Your Husband." "The Best Way to Get Away with Murder."

Out in the world, a different Hailey was coming to life—a creature who might have emerged from her body, but now bore little connection to it. This new Hailey was outsized and pliable. She would take on whatever shape she was given.

"Are you investigating the possibility that Jonah Gelman's murder was connected to his divorce?" she saw on a news clip one night before she could turn the TV off.

"We're investigating every angle," the chief of police said, so confidently that Hailey was sure he'd somehow rearranged the silvery scratches from Jonah's car into letters that spelled out a confession.

Somewhere, far away from her, it was New Year's, but she was no longer part of the world of calendars and celebrations. She closed herself off as much as she could—only Maya, only her family. She was afraid to talk to anyone else, afraid to check her email. When in rash moments, she succumbed to the urge, her finger was primed to hit delete before anything could infiltrate her. Many of her old Facebook posts were public, and when she made the mistake of looking at them, she saw that they were inundated with comments from people she didn't know. *Tell the truth, Hailey*, they implored her. *We know you did it*. Maybe they were right. Maybe she had. She deleted her Facebook account and her Instagram, but there were still ways to reach her. Sometimes she got emails urging her to repent or turn herself in. She got letters from strangers who claimed to understand why she'd killed him and wanted to meet her and share their own stories. Increasingly, she had the feeling that she belonged to all these people. She could hand herself over, allow them to twist her and reshape her, see themselves in her or pretend to leave themselves behind.

"I thought you weren't going to look at any of it," Nate said when she called him one night in mid-January to tell him about an email she'd received from a man who claimed to have evidence linking her to several other murders aeround the country.

"I'm trying, but it's everywhere," she said.

"Just ignore them. Will you promise me that you'll do that?" he begged.

"Why do you sound so upset? Is something going on?" she asked.

"There's nothing going on. I work and then help Mom take care of Dad. That's all there is," he said.

"Should I move back home?" Hailey asked. "The only reason I haven't is because I'm afraid it will seem like an admission of guilt."

"I don't know how much Mom is telling you, but Dad isn't doing well. He's been weaker the past few days, and last night he fell when he was going to the bathroom and Mom couldn't lift him. I had to come over and help him up. I tried to convince him to go to the hospital to get checked out, but he refused," Nate said. "And the whole time I was there, he thought I was Adam." His voice cracked. "Apparently he and Adam had a long conversation a week ago, but he wouldn't tell Mom what they talked about."

"Do you think Adam is ready to come visit?" she said.

"I'm not sure anyone's in the best shape for a family reunion right now."

"But if Dad isn't doing well—"

"I'm going over there now and I'll get a better sense of what's going on. Mom insisted that she wants to barbecue tonight, no matter how late I get there. She's obsessed with the idea of making steak for Dad and me. She's convinced that this is the cure for his weakness."

“Nate. Is it ever going to be okay?” she asked.

He gave a strange laugh. “How can I possibly answer that?”

She got off the phone and lay down with Maya in her bed. There was nowhere safe for her thoughts to touch down. Adam and Tara and her father and Jonah, all of them shapes she couldn’t make out, in an order she couldn’t piece together. Though it was early, she fell asleep with Maya. After a short hiatus, her dreams were back. Jonah was standing over her, the gun was on the floor, and she was lifting, then firing it. But now they weren’t alone. The people emailing her were screaming at her to stop, then they changed their minds and were cheering her on.

A few hours later, the phone was ringing, and in the haze of sleep, she thought that it was Jonah.

“Hailey,” he was saying. “Hailey.”

“I’m sorry, I’m sorry,” she managed to respond.

“Hailey, are you there? I need to tell you something.”

She sat up. Not Jonah on the phone but Nate.

“It’s Dad.”

She was fully awake now. “What is it? What happened?”

“We were outside having a late dinner and Mom had made steak, and he was eating, and then he started choking and he just keeled over.”

“I don’t understand,” she said.

“I was right there. I should have been able to save him, but I couldn’t. He’s gone.”

MAINE, 2019

Daisy is on her side, panting and grunting. Rooting around in the blankets with newfound urgency, she whines and barks, then squats and pushes again. This time, there is a trickle of water. A slick, brown gelatinous shape emerges from her body and lands in the blanket beneath her. Daisy grabs hold of it with her front paws, and with her teeth, she tears at the sack. It splits open and a tiny creature emerges, its fur matted and streaked with blood. Daisy starts to lick, slowly at first, then more vigorously, and the wet creature begins to take on the shape of a dog.

In awe, in relief, I put my arms around Adam and he hugs me in return.

When Daisy is done licking, she squats down, grunts again, and the placenta and cord emerge from her body. She bends over, her face low to the ground, and chews the cord to separate it from her body. With a few quick bites, she devours it all.

In the candlelight, I watch, fascinated and repelled.

I try to wake Maya, who is still asleep on the couch, but though her eyes flutter open for a moment, she doesn't rouse.

"It's time for the next one," Adam says a few minutes later.

Daisy grunts and pushes, licks and chews. Over the next two hours, six puppies are born. The puppies' tiny pink mouths open like baby birds, then close again. Their eyes will remain shut for one to two weeks, Adam tells me. Daisy lies on her side, impassively giving herself over as the puppies wriggle toward her. They attach themselves to her, their tiny paws clambering at her body, and begin to suck.

"We shouldn't touch them for the first few weeks," Adam says as we crouch on the floor nearby. "And if for some reason we need to, we have to be very careful because Daisy might become aggressive."

It's hard to believe that this dog I have come to love could be anything but gentle, but when I glance at Maya, I better understand.

Adam and I decide to bring Maya back to our bedroom—she will meet the puppies in the morning. I take the flashlight and lead the way as Adam carries Maya over his shoulder into our room. He places her in her bed with so much tenderness that tears spring to my eyes. Amid all that is lost, this is one good thing I have given to Maya. If nothing else, she will have him.

Together, Adam and I go back to the living room, where the puppies are still nursing. For the past few weeks, Adam has been making arrangements for them. Three are promised to people he knows, and he tells me that earlier today he heard from someone else who wants one.

"Once the puppies are adopted, will Daisy miss them?" I ask, sure that she will feel a longing for something that was once hers and now no longer is.

"You can't think about it like that," he says. "This is how dogs are. By nine weeks, they're ready to stop nursing. The mothers start to push them away."

He must see the uncertainty on my face and my urge to protect Daisy from this loss.

"Obviously if we were to take them too soon, she would fight it. But it's instinct. She knows when it's time to let them go," he says.

His words strike me. They return me to what I have asked every day since I've been here. How could this have happened? This question has been sharpened until it pierced a hole through me. How could they not have recognized the awfulness? How could they not have turned back before it was too late?

One last time, I let myself grasp at the fleeting illusion that I could be wrong. One last time, I try to hold on to the hope that I might still craft some other ending.

I look at Daisy and feel a glimmer of understanding. I remember how fiercely, how desperately I was loved, how tightly I was held. No one was ever going to let me go.

As the puppies huddle together, I sit beside Adam on the couch. I grab his hand with such force that he looks at me in alarm.

"They did it," I tell Adam. "I don't know how, but somehow Mom and Nate killed Jonah."

They tore their garments just above their hearts. They recited the words blessing God the true judge. The funeral service for Sol was at the synagogue where they had their bar and bat mitzvahs, where Sherry unsuccessfully tried to get them to attend services with her. Sitting next to her mother, Hailey tried to catch Nate's eye. Every other time that they'd sat in synagogue together, he'd considered it his mission to make her laugh—she wondered if he was thinking of that now as well. He held Sherry's hand as she did, but his expression remained impenetrable.

Sherry had begged both Nate and Hailey to give eulogies, but he refused, so Hailey had stayed up late the night before to write the version of the story her mother wanted to tell. They were a close family. They were a special family. For now, she couldn't allow herself to articulate anything else.

"My father was someone you could count on. He might have stayed in the background, but he took care of what needed to be done," Hailey said from the pulpit. Her body was trembling, her voice too. She looked helplessly at Nate, wishing he would rescue her, or at least come stand beside her.

When she sat down, her mother grasped her arm. "Dad loved the three of you more than anything. He might not have been the most effusive, but family was what he cared about most," Sherry said.

They drove in a procession to the cemetery. The casket was carried out and lowered into the ground. One by one, they were given the shovel and instructed to scoop dirt into the gaping hole. Nate went first, then passed the shovel to Hailey, who added a small pile.

When Hailey was finished, Sherry grasped her arm again. "We're being punished," she said softly.

"Mom, please. He was sick, you know that," Hailey said.

"No. It's true. And Dad knew something bad was going to happen," she said. "A few weeks ago, he woke me in the middle of the night. He was agitated and kept saying that all he wanted was to take care of me so that I wouldn't be alone."

"You're not going to be alone," Hailey promised. She held her mother's hand, while Nate held her hand on the other side. If either of them let go, she would surely fall.

Afterward, as they were being greeted and consoled, Hailey saw Tara lingering awkwardly at the edge of the crowd. Just before the funeral began, she had scanned the crowd in vain, wanting to talk to her, even if she didn't know what she might say.

"Tara," she called.

At the sound of her name, Tara began to walk away. The night before, Hailey had asked Nate if he was planning to let Tara know about Sol, but he gave her a funny look. "She's the last person we need to deal with right now," he said. When she pointed out that Sol and Tara had been close, his expression hardened into irritation. "Why are you so interested in Tara?" he asked, but she didn't understand it herself. It was just an image of Tara's face she couldn't get from her mind, just a nagging feeling that there was something she was supposed to see.

"Please, wait," Hailey called to Tara now.

Tara stopped, but stood warily. It hadn't been that long since Hailey had last seen her, but she looked entirely different—her eyes appeared haunted, and her face had an exhausted tarnish. She wore a black dress and her hair looked unbrushed.

"I know how close you were to my father," Hailey managed to say.

"I'm sorry," Tara said. "Your father was very good to me. I'll always remember that."

"I was surprised to hear you left," Hailey said.

"Everything felt impossible. I didn't know what to do," Tara stammered.

"Tara, what's the matter?" she tried.

"I shouldn't have come," Tara said.

"But you were so close to him."

"I'm not supposed to talk to you."

"Please tell me what's going on," Hailey said. "Is this because of Nate?"

"No. It's because of you," Tara said and hurried away.

After the people who'd come to the house for the shiva left, Hailey put Maya to bed. Hailey had arranged a babysitter for the day because it was too much for Maya to attend a second funeral in just a few months. But nothing could protect her from the loss. She clung to Hailey, begging her to sleep in the bed with her the whole night, as she did in the days after Jonah died. When Hailey acquiesced and lay down with her, Maya's body relaxed into hers. She smoothed Maya's cheek and kissed her hair and promised her that she would stay here forever.

Maya was almost asleep when Sherry appeared in the doorway. Hailey motioned to her, and Sherry came to Maya's bed and lay down with them, the three of them huddled together. Hailey wrapped her arm around her mother. She couldn't remember the last time they'd been this physically close, though surely it once felt as natural as it did to lie there with Maya.

"Why didn't Adam come?" Sherry whispered.

"I don't know," Hailey admitted.

"Dad talked to him last week. I helped him call, but he wanted privacy," Sherry said.

"Maybe it was too much for Adam, after all this time?" Hailey asked, but she didn't understand it herself. She had started to talk to Adam more in the past few months, and he sounded warmer. But when she delivered the news to Adam that their father had died and asked him to come home, he paused in a way that made her wonder if he'd understood. "I can't," he finally said.

"He's dead, Adam. Dad is dead and we need you," she begged.

"I know you don't understand, but I can't," he repeated.

In the days after, Maya was the only reason to keep going. Get out of bed for Maya. Get dressed, make food for Maya. Now that she was in West Palm, Hailey couldn't think about the prospect of returning to Binghamton. She decided to sell her house. She began to consider where Maya could go to school here. Since they'd been in Florida, Maya had been uncannily quiet and dutiful. Hailey almost wished for one of her tantrums—then at least she knew that Maya was feeling something.

Nate saw patients all day, then came over with groceries and ran around with Maya in the garden and by the pool. Only there did they seem playful and carefree. Otherwise, Nate didn't joke around or talk about upcoming trips, as he once did. He'd aged rapidly in a matter of weeks. His face was drawn, his body thickened, and he walked with a heavier tread, as if forced to carry a too-heavy burden. For the first time, Hailey realized how much he looked like their father.

"Mom hasn't left the house in days. She won't talk to anyone but us," Hailey told Nate when he came over after work.

"Get her to go for a walk. Take her to the beach. Do anything," he said. He was skittish, his knee bouncing up and down, his fingers thrumming any surface.

"Are you okay?" Hailey asked.

He laughed. "No, I'm not okay. Do you think that this is how I want it to be? I've always wanted to get away and now I'm trapped," he said and bent over, his head in his hands, like he was trying to catch his breath.

"Nate," she pleaded. "This isn't just about Dad, is it? Please, tell me what's going on."

"I can't," he said.

The next day, and every day for weeks, Hailey sat by the pool next to Sherry. In her mother's presence, she couldn't quiet her thoughts. The same question hovered on her lips every time she was alone with Sherry, but she didn't dare ask it again. Instead, she replayed the answer her mother had given her. *How can you even ask such a thing?* But how could she not?

"Mom. You need to swim," Hailey said. "Even one lap."

Sherry gazed at the motionless surface of the pool. It had stormed the previous night and palm fronds floated in the water, along with leaves and flowers. Hailey took the net and tried to fish them out, but there were too many to easily clear. It had been weeks since her mother allowed the gardener, or anyone, to come near the house, and the garden bore an air of neglect, the shrubs overgrown, the flowers parched and turning brown.

Sherry entered the water tentatively, dipping one foot in as if this was something she'd never before done. As soon as she was under the water, though, her hesitation gave way and she glided swiftly across the pool.

When Sherry was done with her laps, she floated on her back, the sun shining so brightly that Hailey had to squint in order to see her. She had no idea what her mother was thinking. Inside the locked chamber of her heart, there was a smaller chamber, and inside that, an even smaller one.

Sherry got out and stood before Hailey, dripping wet. "I never thought it would end this way," she said.

After that, Hailey started to swim too. Her strokes felt labored and uncertain, but she had to fill the days that gaped like dangerous canyons. Her body no longer felt like her own. When she unexpectedly caught a glimpse of herself in the mirror, she did a double take. Her face was sallow, her limbs gaunt.

Under the water, her thoughts, slick, unwieldy creatures, slid from her.

It had been a month since her father died and four months since Jonah had, and in Hailey's mind, the two now intermingled, Jonah choking and her father shot, the two of them in a pool of blood. She wandered downstairs. Her mother had used duct tape to hang sheets over the sliding glass doors to prevent anyone from trying to peer in. The house had the feel of a fortress: no one could enter and no one could leave.

She took out her phone to text Nate.

Are you awake?

It's the middle of the night.

I know but I really need to talk to you.

I can't do this now. I have to sleep.

Then when?

As she waited for Nate to reply, Hailey lifted the sheet that covered the glass door and looked out at the pool, wanting to dive in. She passed the wall of photos. Staring at all these versions of herself, she wished that, after a long slumber, they would smash through their glass frames and escape.

A few nights later, Hailey left Maya with Sherry and met Nate at the Waterway Cafe, which had once been their favorite place for family celebrations. She'd needed to text him repeatedly until he had finally agreed to meet her.

They sat outside on the restaurant's dock, with a view of the intracoastal waterway and the lights of ships that were far off in the distance. It was one of the few times she'd left the house since her father died, and she was afraid that everyone around her was staring accusatorily.

"I need to know why you're so upset," Hailey said to Nate.

"Our father just dropped dead, so I don't think it's that hard to understand."

"I know there's more to it," she said.

"What is it you think you know?"

"Nate," she pleaded. "What's going on? Why do you sound like this?"

"I'm sorry, okay? The pressure at work is getting to me. And I know we're only supposed to talk about how great Dad was, but I'm starting to think about certain things and . . ." He paused, each word seeming to pain him. "Did you ever notice how Dad didn't say what he really thought? He was always keeping something back. It was like this game between us, even until the end."

"What do you think it was?"

Nate met her eye for a moment, then quickly looked away.

"I shouldn't be saying anything. Maybe it was just about Tara and me. He had to know, but he never said a word."

"Are you sorry you didn't talk to Dad about her?" she asked.

"Even if I did, what would have been the point?"

"Do you ever speak to Tara now?"

"Why are you so interested in Tara?" he asked.

"I need to understand."

"What's there to understand? Tara was in a situation she never should have been in, and I blame myself for that as much as anyone, but she made it clear where her loyalties were."

The waiter brought their steaks to the table. Hailey had ordered it medium, but it came rare. She cut into the meat and watched the red juices run onto the white plate.

"I saw her," Hailey said. "She was at the funeral, in the back, and when I tried to talk to her, she ran away."

Nate blanched. "Why didn't you tell me?"

"You made it clear that you don't want to talk about Tara."

"You have to trust me that your being connected to her is a very bad idea."

"Why can't you tell me what this is about?"

"There's nothing to tell," he said, but he smiled in the way he did when he was trying to hide something.

"You're doing that smile. I know there's something you're not telling me."

He had eaten quickly, and on his plate all that remained were the fatty bits he cut off from the meat and the white piece of bone.

"I need you to tell me what Tara has to do with Jonah," she said. Even though she was whispering, she was afraid that everyone nearby could hear.

"What could Tara possibly have to do with Jonah?" he asked.

"Tell me the truth."

Nate's smile was gone and his expression had become beseeching, terrified. Her face was scorching hot. Her stomach churned. She jumped up, but knew she couldn't make it to the bathroom in time. Beside the table, she crouched, her knees on the hard wood of the dock, and retched. Nate jumped up and stood over her. With a burning taste in her mouth, she stood up and pushed her way through the clusters of tables, out onto the long stretch of empty pier that ran alongside the restaurant. Once more, the feeling overcame her. She crouched down, her face close to the wood slats, and retched.

Nate ran after her and squatted beside her, his arm wrapped tightly around her.

"Hailey, please. You have to stay calm," he begged into her ear.

"How can I possibly stay calm?" she demanded.

"You have to. We all do. I swear to you, I never thought it would be like this," he said.

"You have to tell me."

"Please trust me that you don't want to ask me this," he said.

"I need you to tell me the truth," she said.

She wriggled from his grasp and faced him, her breath coming in heaving gasps. Was he going to grab her again, pin her down? For a moment, she was afraid he might push her into the water, but then, at the desperate look on his face, she was more afraid that he might dive in and swim out into the dark expanse.

"It's not what you think," he said, tears streaming down his face.

"I don't believe you," she said.

"I swear to god, we didn't do it. In the end, we weren't the ones—"

She couldn't bear to hear him lie. She stood up and ran, away from the pier, away from Nate. Her car was in the parking lot, and as soon as she could see it, she pressed her key fob to unlock it. The lights blinked and she bolted toward it.

Hailey drove around until she thought her mother would be asleep, then went to the house. But when she walked in, Sherry was waiting for her in the living room.

"I don't know what you've heard, but it wasn't us," Sherry said.

"You did it. You killed him," Hailey said.

"I swear, it's not what you think," Sherry said.

"Then what is it? Explain it to me!" she yelled, but her mother remained silent. For so long, she'd wanted to remain in a state of not knowing. Now she wanted to press her mother until the truth oozed from her.

"Is this what you thought I wanted? Is this who you think I am?" Hailey said.

"It wasn't like that. It's not who any of us are," Sherry insisted.

"How can you still pretend? It's who we all are now," Hailey screamed.

Hailey ran to Maya's room, afraid that in her absence, she had been harmed. Maya was under the covers, asleep and safe, at least for now. Hailey ran to her own room and slammed shut the door and locked it, something she hadn't done since she was a child. Nate was texting her, but she turned off her phone. She heard Sherry's phone ringing and the murmur of conversation. A few times, she felt her mother's presence on the other side of the door, but she wasn't going to speak to her.

Hailey lay in her bed and thought about how many times, in anger, she wished that Jonah was dead.

She thought about how Nate told her about the plan to pay Jonah. Though she knew it was wrong, she was willing to put her reservations aside and hope it might work.

She thought about the night Nate floated the possibility of making this all go away. Though she didn't ask him what he meant, she felt, for one moment, the rise of hope followed by the prick of terror.

She thought about the constant texts her mother sent, urging her to fight. But in the weeks before Jonah was killed, her mother sent gentle messages assuring her that everything was going to work out. The week he was killed, her only texts were missives of love.

Close to morning, Hailey heard her mother moving around the house. From the window, she saw the backyard lights switch on. Her mother was in the pool swimming laps, and Hailey had the urge to go out there, but do what? Hold her mother down until her body sank? Or be appeased again by her mother's promises and continue to live in this haze of denial?

Hailey dozed and she woke. In the morning, she packed a small bag for herself. She tiptoed into Maya's room and gathered up her clothes and the stuffed animals and books that they'd brought with them. She took scissors from the art set her mother had given Maya and went into the bathroom where she grabbed a handful of her hair and cut off the long strands. She stared at herself in the mirror. On one side, her hair remained long, untouched. She cut again, wishing that the strands would bleed, wishing that she would feel pain each time she snipped.

She wouldn't stop until she cut away all the deadened parts of her body, until she excised her own self.

When she was done, piles of hair lay helplessly on her shoulders and clung to her back. She brushed them off and they fell onto the white tiled floor, where they lay like a sacrifice.

Hailey left the hair on the floor and went downstairs. The living room was empty, but the sliding glass door to the backyard was open. She walked outside. Maybe her mother was still in the pool. Maybe she had already fled.

The pool was empty, and at first glance, so was the garden. It was about to rain and the wind had started to howl as it did before a storm. Hailey walked along the stone pathway, deeper in. And there she was, her mother crouched amid the overgrown birds-of-paradise that had turned to brown husks, which she was desperately trying to uproot with her bare hands, either to pull them out or somehow bring them back to life.

Sherry stood up. Her face was smeared with tears, her hands with dirt. Her mouth fell open at the sight of her, as if Hailey had used the scissors to slash her skin.

"What did you do to yourself?" Sherry asked.

"How could you? How? How?" Hailey screamed at her.

"I said no. I swear to you. At the last minute," Sherry said.

"How?" she screamed again.

"I'm sorry," Sherry said. "I'm so sorry."

"I can't stay here," Hailey said.

"Please, forgive me."

"Never," Hailey said.

"Please—"

Hailey went back inside the house. She couldn't listen to her pleas.

In Maya's room, Hailey gently shook her awake. When Maya opened her eyes, she surveyed her carefully.

"What happened to your hair?" Maya asked.

"I needed a change," Hailey said.

"Why?" Maya asked.

"Maya, honey, listen. We're going to have a long drive. We're taking a trip," Hailey said.

This was the only way she could save her.

MAINE, 2019

In the candlelight, the expression on Adam's face is inscrutable, but his hand remains clenched in mine.

I tell him how, for a few months, it had been possible to hide from what I should have known right away.

I tell him how I'd believed that I was infinitely different from them, that if asked, I would have said no, absolutely no, always no.

I tell him how I have wrestled with the fear that I might have said yes.

I tell him how, every day since I've been here, I've tried to understand how this could have happened. I tell him how I've tried to write my way into their minds and into my own. I tell him I worry that, in my rendering, I have been too kind—even now, is my version clouded by love?

I tell Adam how I still hope that some other explanation might emerge. I still want to believe there are other ways that Jonah might have been killed. I still harbor the fantasy that I can travel back in time and stop them. I still wish that, with my words, I could exonerate us all.

I tell him that, despite all this, my love for them is still there. Of all things, this is what I'm most afraid to admit.

Adam's jaw is clenched, and I worry he's about to bolt from the couch, back to his room, where he can escape from me and what I've confessed. But he doesn't move. Despite his fear, he remains beside me.

"That's not what happened," he finally says.

"What are you talking about?" I whisper.

"I told you. There are things you don't know," Adam says. He stands up and walks to the window and looks out. In the flickering candlelight, I can faintly make out his form.

"Tell me," I say.

"Are you sure? Because once you know . . ." His voice is barely above a whisper, but in the silence, I grasp every word.

"Tell me, please."

"If I tell you, then you're going to be part of this too."

"I already am," I say.

He returns to the couch and sits beside me.

"I promised I wouldn't say anything," he says.

"Who did you promise?" I ask.

Next to me, his body trembles alongside my own.

"Who?" I ask again.

"Dad."

The word detonates inside me.

"I don't understand."

"I talked to Dad a week before he died," he says. "He made me swear to keep it a secret, and then he told me that Mom and Nate had it all planned out. They hired Tara's boyfriend to kill Jonah. Dad wasn't supposed to know about it, but Tara and Nate had a big fight and Tara told Dad everything."

His words swirl in the air, and I have the sensation that I am made of tiny flakes, falling alongside them.

"Dad didn't tell anyone that he knew. He said he wanted to take care of it himself. The whole time, Dad didn't believe that Mom would actually go through with it. So he decided that if she backed down, he would make sure it happened anyway," Adam says. "He came up with a plan to have Tara's boyfriend call Mom the night before, to be sure she wanted to do it. He wanted to give her a chance to decide on her own. But it didn't matter, because even if Mom decided not to do it, Dad was going to tell them to go ahead."

Nothing makes sense yet somehow a lens is sharpening into focus.

"But why would Dad do that?" I manage to ask.

"He said he didn't have anything to lose. He said, 'I had to take care of Mom. I didn't want her to be alone. I didn't want to be absent when she needed me most.'"

"Why did he tell you?" I ask.

"He said that someone needed to know the truth."

Finally, Adam meets my eye. His gaze slices through me. "I couldn't believe that this was my family—that I could be connected to any of this. When you called to tell me that Dad died, I'd already decided that even if I could get over everything else, I could never forgive this. I could never come home again," he says. His eyes are fixed on Daisy and the sleeping puppies.

"Every day since then, I've woken up panicked. I have no idea what I'm supposed to do. Should I protect my family or turn them in?" he says. He is slowly rocking back and forth. His shadow is cast against the wall and looms over us.

"Last night, when I went out for a few hours, I drove to the police station," he says.

I brace myself. Do I want him to turn them in, turn me in alongside them? Do I want him to swear that he will tell no one, ever—that we will carry this terrible truth with us and somehow try to live with it?

"I couldn't do it. I sat outside in the car, then came home," he continues.

I'm nodding, though to move my head feels like I'm swimming through water. I take Adam's hand again. No matter what he decides, I cannot save or protect them. I cannot save or protect myself.

We sit. Eventually Adam dozes next to me on the couch, but I remain awake, writing, rewriting this confession.

With my words, I return again and again to the scene. But as close as I might come, I still arrive at a chasm of unfathomability.

Even now, as I write this, I am still trying to understand.

It's just past six in the morning. The wind has died down and the sun is rising, almost blinding against the snow. The lights come back on and the hum of sound returns. Maya pads out of the bedroom. The puppies are awake too, squirming against one another and angling to secure the spots closest to Daisy.

At the sight of them, Maya's mouth falls open in amazement.

"They're alive," she exclaims, and the three of us huddle on the floor, as close to the puppies as possible, marveling at how tiny they are, how helpless.

ACKNOWLEDGMENTS

I am thrilled to be represented by the fabulous Julie Barer who encouraged me to revise and revise, and whose enthusiasm, insight, and vision shine with brilliance. I want to thank Nicole Cunningham and Brooke Nagler and everyone at the Book Group for all that they have done in support of this book. Lauren Wein is an extraordinary reader and deep thinker, and I could not dream of a better or more beloved editor. I am so grateful to Amy Guay, Alex Primiani, Caroline McGregor, Meredith Vilarello, Eva Kerins, Katya Wiegmann, Alicia Brancato, Jessica Chin, Allison Green, Ruth Lee-Mui, Cait Lamborne, and everyone at Avid Reader Press and Simon & Schuster for all the work they do to bring a book into the world. I am also so appreciative of Hilary Zaitz Michael at WME for her enthusiasm and belief in this book.

I feel fortunate to be a part of the Boston writing community and to have the opportunity to be in the company of so many fellow writers and readers. Living in walking distance of Newtonville Books is a regular source of pleasure. Mary Cotton and Jaime Clark have created a gem of a bookstore, and I am so grateful to them and all the wonderful booksellers there, especially Nick Petrulakis, for creating a warm and vibrant communal space for readers and writers (and for dogs!).

Joanna Rakoff read early drafts and offered insightful notes and encouragement that helped set me on the right path. Rachel Mesch has been a close friend for more than twenty-five years and I am so grateful for her insights about books, writing, and life.

Elizabeth Graver was one of the first people I talked to about the idea for this book, and I so appreciate the many clarifying conversations we had as she generously read multiple drafts. Rachel Kadish, a bonded-for-life, it's-all-deep-in-the-vault kind of friend, is a spot-on reader of my work, and I am so grateful that we share our drafts and our lives. Miranda Beverly-Whittemore, Claire Dederer, and Kristi Coulter have been there for every vicissitude of writing this book, and I cannot imagine having finished it without their excellent notes, advice, friendship, and encouragement.

My parents Lynnie and David Mirvis have believed in me as a writer from the very beginning and have given me so much love, understanding, and unflinching support. They are the kind of parents every writer should be so lucky to have. I am so grateful for my beloved siblings Shoni Mirvis and Larry Hartstein, and Simmy Mirvis and Elisheva Kagan, and to my nieces and nephews far and wide.

To Sunny, my much-loved muse for all matters dog-related in this book.

To my children Eitan and Shana, Daniel and Liana (art designer and Instagram advisor), who have listened to me talk about this book for years and have filled my life with humor, enthusiasm, and joy. I love you so much and am so proud of who you all are.

I am so grateful for my wonderful stepchildren Amanda and Derek, (and to Amanda for being my expert consultant on all the family law questions I had while writing the book), Austin and Irina, and April and Pat, and the adorable duo of Sabine and Poppy. And I am so appreciative of Elaine Cohen, my mother-in-law, for her wisdom and warmth.

And to my husband, Bruce, who recognized the potential when I first had the idea for this book and rightly asked me how I could resist it. Ever since that first conversation, Bruce has enthusiastically inhabited this book with me, and I am immeasurably grateful to him for listening to every idea and worry; and for challenging me and loving me and supplying me with essential plot twists, both in this book and in my life every day.

ABOUT THE AUTHOR

TOVA MIRVIS is the author of the memoir, *The Book of Separation*, as well as *Visible City*, *The Outside World*, and *The Ladies Auxiliary*, which was a national bestseller. Her essays have appeared in publications including the *New York Times, the Boston Globe Magazine*, and *Real Simple*, and her fiction has been broadcast on National Public Radio. She lives in Newton, Massachusetts, with her family. You can connect with her on her website, TovaMirvis.com.

Avid Reader Press, an imprint of Simon & Schuster, is built on the idea that the most rewarding publishing has three common denominators: great books, published with intense focus, in true partnership. Thank you to the Avid Reader Press colleagues who collaborated on *We Would Never*, as well as to the hundreds of professionals in the Simon & Schuster advertising, audio, communications, design, ebook, finance, human resources, legal, marketing, operations, production, sales, supply chain, subsidiary rights, and warehouse departments whose invaluable support and expertise benefit every one of our titles.

Editorial
Lauren Wein, *VP and Editorial Director*
Amy Guay, *Assistant Editor*

Jacket Design
Alison Forner, *Senior Art Director*
Clay Smith, *Senior Designer*
Sydney Newman, *Art Associate*

Marketing
Meredith Vilarello, *VP and Associate Publisher*
Caroline McGregor, *Senior Marketing Manager*
Kayla Dee, *Associate Marketing Manager*
Katya Wiegmann, *Marketing and Publishing Assistant*

Production
Allison Green, *Managing Editor*
Jessica Chin, *Senior Manager of Copyediting*
Alicia Brancato, *Production Manager*
Ruth Lee-Mui, *Interior Text Designer*
Lexy East, *Desktop Compositor*
Cait Lamborne, *Ebook Developer*

Publicity
Alexandra Primiani, *Director of Publicity*
Eva Kerins, *Publicity Assistant*

Subsidiary Rights
Paul O'Halloran, *VP and Director of Subsidiary Rights*
Fiona Sharp, *Subsidiary Rights Coordinator*